EVIDENCE OF DEATH

Like a sleepwalker Sarah got out of bed and pulled on a robe and left the room, went down the hallway to her father's bedroom, where she turned on the light and went to the closet to take down her father's wide-brimmed old straw hat that Carlos had returned to her. She carried the hat back to her own room.

It was badly stained with sweat, and the brim was floppy on one side, and at the back inside edge there were other stains.

"No," she whispered. "Dear God, no!"

She thought suddenly of the shadows left on the walls by the victims of Hiroshima, instant snapshots. In her mind was such a snapshot of last Monday morning when she had run down to the veranda. She examined the pieces of the picture. Rosa standing with her hands covering her face, her body convulsing with sobs. Carlos and another man pulling her father from the pool. He was face down in the water; Carlos handled him so gently pulling him out, cradling his head. Carlos's face tear-streaked. And off to one side, at the edge of the pool coping, unremarked until this minute, there was her father's straw hat. . . .

JUSTICE
FOR SOME

Kate Wilhelm

FAWCETT CREST • NEW YORK

A Fawcett Crest Book
Published by Ballantine Books
Copyright © 1993 by Kate Wilhelm

ISBN 0-449-22247-0

This edition published by arrangement with St. Martin's Press, Inc.

Manufactured in the United States of America

First Ballantine Books Edition: June 1994

10 9 8 7 6 5 4 3 2

*For Jennifer McKay
with much love.*

ONE

THE TROUBLE WAS that Sarah Drexler did not look like a judge. She knew it, and suspected that so did everyone who came before her in court. She was forty-six and still had frizzy red hair, not as red as it used to be, but unmistakably red, and she had freckles that she had long since stopped fighting, and she was sturdy. Not fat, not even overweight, but sturdy, built for endurance, Blaine used to say. She stood at her window overlooking the parking lot at the courthouse, and held the blind back to watch heat patterns rise and rise and rise. It was May, but Pendleton, Oregon, could be an inferno in May, or it could snow. This year, hell was winning. If it were snowing she would be even more dissatisfied; what she really wanted was idyllic May weather, storybook, poetry May weather.

She let the Venetian blind close again when she heard the door opening behind her. Her fingers felt dirty. The building was air-conditioned, but the blinds were always gritty, there was always pale grit on the desk, on every flat surface, on her fingers now. She couldn't understand how it got inside, not just here in the courthouse, but in her house, in the car, everywhere.

"They're ready," her secretary, Beatrice Wordley, said.

1

When Sarah turned to face her, she caught the gleam of delight in Beatrice's eyes. "Tape it all," she said, going to her desk for a tissue. Beatrice nodded. She had been with Blaine and Sarah when they were in private practice, then with Blaine here in the courthouse, and now with Sarah, altogether for nearly twenty years. Her expression of glee said clearly that she knew as well as Sarah that Homer Wickham was not willing to give any woman the authority to tell him the time of day, and that Homer Wickham was due for a surprise. Sarah wiped her hands, tossed the tissue into the waste can, and stepped into the hall outside her door.

She entered the conference room next to her office, and nodded pleasantly to the small group already there, two attorneys, and Mr. and Mrs. Wickham, who wanted to kill each other. The conference room was opulent compared to the office. Blaine had kept his surroundings nearly barren, nothing that wasn't absolutely essential had been allowed, and she had done little to change that. But the conference room had old-fashioned furniture, overstuffed chairs and sofas, a long scarred table with ladderback chairs, ferns in pots. The ferns kept dying because the humidity was too low, but when they looked terminal, new ones appeared; the old brown plants vanished as if by magic.

Everyone in the little group awaiting her had been sitting upright, stiffly uncomfortable in the comfortable chairs. The two attorneys had risen with Sarah's entrance, and belatedly Johnny Weber hauled Mr. Wickham to his feet. Mrs. Wickham glared at her husband and then nodded to Sarah. Sarah sat in her own chair and said, "Thank you for coming. I wanted this informal conference before the hearing in order to make a suggestion. Mr. Weber, Mr. Howell, please understand that this is an informal proceeding."

The attorneys nodded.

"It is agreed that Mr. and Mrs. Wickham are exemplary parents, and the custody of the four children is the major difficulty to be resolved."

Mr. Wickham shook himself and muttered, "And the house."

"Yes, the house," Sarah said, nodding. "You have both stated that one parent should be allowed to remain in the house where the children have lived all their lives, so they can continue to attend the schools they are familiar with, enjoy the friendships they have made, and suffer the least amount of trauma. This arrangement, of course, would mean that one parent would have primary custody; however, you have both requested and agreed to joint and equal custody, and this issue must be resolved. The court appreciates that you both recognize," she went on smoothly, "that divorce is always traumatic, and that probably the children suffer even more than the parents in these cases. In studying your financial statements, I came to the conclusion that the parent who must move out will suffer a severe economic hardship in trying to maintain a second house large enough to accommodate the four children during their visits. Therefore, that cost must be borne equally between you, since you are being awarded joint custody, and it is the stated purpose of this hearing today to assure that your children are not plunged into poverty along with one of the parents."

Mr. Wickham glowered, but almost instantly he crossed his arms and then nodded. Mrs. Wickham began to shake her head; her eyes filled with tears. "I don't have enough money for another house," she whispered.

"I know you don't," Sarah said. "And neither does Mr. Wickham, not really, although he may think at this moment that he could manage it."

"What I said all along is that we gotta sell the house," Mr. Wickham said.

"No," Sarah said firmly. "You have very little equity in the property, although the payments are quite manageable, but payments on two houses, or even two apartments large enough for four children, would be a burden. Everyone would be impoverished very quickly."

She paused a moment, then said, "What this court is prepared to order is that the children remain in the house, and that you take turns living in it with them. Their trauma will be lessened considerably, and you could joint rent an apartment, or rent separate affordable apartments, as you prefer." The silence in the room was profound for several seconds as they all stared at her. Mr. Wickham began to change color, his ruddy face growing darker and darker red, and Mrs. Wickham was shaking her head again, harder this time.

"You can't do that!" Mr. Wickham cried. He turned to his lawyer. "She can't do that!"

"Yes, Mr. Wickham, I can," Sarah said, and stood up. "You both asked for custody of the children, and this court will grant joint custody on those conditions. Now, what I suggest is that all of you discuss this, either here, or perhaps across the street in the coffee shop. Let us meet again this afternoon at four. Thank you."

She walked to the door, and glanced back at them. Johnny Weber had moved to stand behind Mr.

Wickham's chair, and had his hands firmly on the larger man's shoulders, holding him down. Johnny Weber met her glance and winked.

Carol Betts was the prosecutor for the state against Steven Mancero that afternoon. It was a simple matter: the restaurant where Mancero worked had come up two hundred dollars short and the manager had accused him of stealing from the cash drawer. Sarah listened, but without a lot of attention. She was more interested in watching Howard Bartles, the defense attorney, who seemed to be in an endless whispered conference with a man seated behind him. He appeared unaware when Carol Betts concluded and sat down.

"Mr. Bartles," Sarah said, and he hurriedly faced her and half rose.

"Sorry, Your Honor. Mr. Mason wishes to plead guilty."

She glanced at the sheet before her. Steven Mancero. She was well aware that in large cities, New York, Philadelphia, and sometimes in not-such-big cities where the attorneys were overworked, they often spelled out their clients' names in big block letters for easy reference during a hurried trial, but here in Pendleton, Oregon? No one had rushed in Pendleton since the Oregon Trail was first blazed. Now she looked more closely at the young man, too thin, very dark, dressed in jeans and a sport shirt. He looked young enough for juvenile court.

Bartles nudged the young man. "Stand up, Mason."

He stood up and clasped his hands before him, watching her with big frightened eyes.

"Mr. Mancero, are you ready to plead?" she asked.

He looked quickly toward Bartles, who nodded. "Yes, ma'am."

"Have you ever been in court before, Mr. Mancero?" He shook his head.

"You have to answer," she said, "so the court recorder can hear your words and get them in the record." She added to the recorder, "Indicate the answer was no," and then turned to the young man again. "How old are you, Mr. Mancero?"

"Twenty-one."

"And how long have you worked for the restaurant?"

"Three years."

"Mr. Mancero, do you understand that you have the right to a trial by jury? Has that been explained to you?"

He shook his head, then quickly said, "I didn't know that. No, ma'am."

"Did anyone explain what reasonable doubt means? Or preponderance of evidence?"

He glanced at his lawyer, who was staring off into space. "No. Nobody told me anything, except to stand up and say guilty."

"Did anyone promise you anything?"

"No, ma'am."

"Or threaten you with anything?"

"No, ma'am."

"Did anyone tell you what the sentence could be if you're found guilty? Were you told you could be sentenced to jail?"

"No." His voice was a near-whisper. He moistened his lips.

"Mr. Mancero, did you have a conference with your attorney?"

He shook his head. "No, ma'am."

"When you went to his office, didn't you talk with him?"

"He wasn't there. His secretary said it would cost a hundred dollars, and I should be here today, and today he said I should stand up and say guilty."

"I see. Please be seated, Mr. Mancero." She waited until he was in his chair, stiff, wary and frightened. "Mr. Bartles, Ms. Betts, please," Sarah said then, and stood up. "We will be in recess for twenty minutes."

In her office she watched Bartles and Betts as they entered, and he started to sit in a chair close to her desk. "Don't bother to make yourself comfortable," she snapped. "I will file a formal complaint, Mr. Bartles, charging you with malfeasance. I am removing you from Mr. Mancero's defense and will have a continuance until he can arrange for other counsel. If he can't afford counsel, this court will appoint a defender. And you are ordered to return the hundred dollars you accepted from him."

"Good Christ," he muttered in disbelief. "Sarah, that kid's as guilty as hell and you know it!"

"I'll add contempt if you push me," she said fiercely. "I am Judge Drexler in these chambers and in that courtroom, and don't forget it!"

"Yes, ma'am, Your Honor," he said with heavy sarcasm.

"I want that check made out to Steven Mancero, that's Man-cer-o, by five. Now you may leave."

He shrugged and went to the door. Carol Betts followed him. She paused at the open door and gave Sarah a long searching look that revealed nothing, and then she left.

Sarah sank down into her chair and drew in a long breath, curiously weak now. That sarcasm, that eloquent shrug, she knew exactly what he had meant: what possible difference could it make if she filed a complaint, since she was only a fill-in judge serving out her dead husband's term? And she wondered what in the world she was doing here. She didn't look like a judge, didn't think like a judge, didn't talk like a judge. She could not think of this bare little room as a judge's chambers. Blaine, she thought then, oh, Blaine, damn you. Damn you. She trailed a finger over the desk that had been Blaine's, and would be hers for a few more months. Then she closed her eyes and took several deliberate breaths and finally stood up, ready to go on with the day.

By three on Friday afternoon of that week she had her desk as cleared as it was ever likely to be, and she was ready for her vacation. First, haircut, she was ticking off as she walked to her car. The lot was broiling, the concrete sent heat through the soles of her shoes, made her toes want to curl up. Then, dry cleaning. A little laundry . . .

"Hey, Sarah!"

She turned to see Dirk Walters hurrying toward her. He was a long thin man, with what seemed to be too many angles, although it was hard to say just where the extra ones came from. Blaine used to say Dirk was a pol's pol—a politician's politician. In his mid-sixties, he had been in politics long enough to have met everyone, and he remembered every name, knew everyone's histories, their triumphs and tragedies, never forgot a face or a vote. He never had run for any office, and it was said that no one ever won a major office in Oregon without his help. He was grinning broadly as he approached her, both hands outstretched exactly as if they were friends of long standing.

"Hi, Dirk. What are you doing out here in the wilderness?" With some amusement she submitted to having both hands held warmly for a moment.

"Just passing through," he said, as she had known he would. That was his stock answer. "Buy you a nice cold drink?"

She shook her head. "Sorry. Things to do, vacation coming up, you know."

"Yeah. Down to good old C.A. How's the old man? What's he now, eighty, eighty-one? You're going for his birthday party?"

"How do you know all that?" she asked, laughing. "You're just showing off." Actually he was wrong. Her father's birthday had come and gone back in April; now the family was having a reunion. She did not correct Dirk; she felt that catching him in even a simple little mistake like this gave her a certain edge.

"True," he admitted cheerfully. "Look, I really want a word with you before you take off. Later today? Lunch tomorrow? When are you leaving?"

"Dawn or even earlier tomorrow. Oh, come on. Just so I get to the beauty shop by four."

He glanced at his watch. "Plenty of time."

"Benny's?" she asked, glancing toward the coffee shop across the street.

"Too noisy. Let's go to your place. You can kick off your shoes and we'll talk. You have air-conditioning, don't you?"

When she hesitated, he patted her shoulder. "You just go on ahead and I'll be along in ten minutes. See you."

She watched him as he went back to the courthouse and entered; then she got in her car and turned on the ignition. He wanted a private talk, she understood. It was all right for him to be seen talking with anyone briefly at a party, in the parking lot, even in a restaurant with others, but this was something else. In a town like Pendleton everyone would know if they sat in a booth in Benny's and discussed anything of substance. There was nothing of substance for them to discuss, she told herself, and engaged the gears, started to drive.

When Blaine died three years earlier, it had been Dirk who came to talk to her, offered her the appointment to finish Blaine's term as county judge. She had been too numb to respond, and he had returned in a month, and this time she had said yes. She had seen him infrequently since then, and always at an official function at the side of the governor, or a senator, or a foreign dignitary, never alone.

She had been driving automatically, she realized when she started up the bluff road to her house. No doubt she had nodded to people, or waved, smiled, but she had no memory of them. What did Dirk want? Were they going to call in their chips? Try to call them in?

The narrow, twisting road demanded her attention now. The pines in the valley below did not try to climb the dry hills; instead there were dusty cottonwoods, and dustier junipers with a straggly sparse understory of sagebrush. No houses were visible from the road, but here and there lush green grass and shrubbery stood out glaringly, as out of place in this arid land as sequins on cowboy boots, and as durable. She turned into her own driveway at the summit of the bluff.

The house and the dry grass might have been painted with the same camouflage brush; the building was low and almost as unadorned as Blaine's office at the courthouse. There were native grasses and sage, contorted juniper shrubs and trees, but when she went into the house the drabness changed. Here were new colorful pottery vases, some taller than Sarah, glazed with brilliant green and copper finishes, with plumes of pink pampas grass, snow white grasses. The furniture was covered with fine glove leather, mahogany-red in the living room, and bright yellow and white and green in the dining room. The walls were stark white that showed off the Navaho rugs hanging on them, and the copper plates and shields. . . . The rear of the house overlooked the valley and from here it seemed that Pendleton huddled so close to the Columbia River it was in danger of tumbling into the water and drowning. The Columbia was so blue it looked uncanny, so still it looked painted.

When Dirk arrived minutes later, he was carrying a paper bag with a bottle of wine; condensation had turned the bag into a pulpy mess. "Oh well," he said, laughing as he peeled bits of sodden paper away from the bottle. "Not the suave entrance I was planning, but what the hell." He opened the bottle and poured, and they took their glasses to the living room where they sat near the wide windows. "Real nice," he said. "Very nice indeed."

Sarah sipped her wine and waited. It didn't take long.

With a decisive motion, Dirk set his glass down on a low table and said, "You don't need the beauty shop.

You look just fine. We're all impressed very much, Sarah. That's the word."

"We who?"

He shrugged. "Look, I know you said in the beginning that this was temporary, you accepted the responsibility of finishing Blaine's term. We all understood that this was an interim appointment, and everyone was grateful. But it's gone way beyond gratitude, Sarah, way beyond that. You're one hell of a judge."

In spite of herself, she felt a warmth on her cheeks. She looked down at the glass in her hand. "Thank you, Dirk."

"Sarah, we want you to run in November."

She looked up in surprise then. "I'm not a politician, Dirk. I told you that. I hate the whole idea of campaigning, of trying to sell myself. Shaking hands with everyone, smiling at everyone, saying the right things all the time, being circumspect every second of my life. It's . . . it's not for me. I hated it when Blaine did it and I had to go along sometimes. I despised it all. And I'm very bad at it. I don't remember names, and I say the wrong things." Helplessly she shook her head.

"Sarah, hear me out," Dirk said. "We chose Blaine, you know. Every step of his career was planned after a certain point. He had everything going for him. Yale Law School, private practice, prosecuting attorney experience, and then district attorney, and finally county judge. Like a neat ladder without a missing rung. The next step was to run for state judge in November, and then after another year or so be appointed to the Ninth District federal judiciary. That was the plan, Sarah."

"What do you mean, plan? Whose plan? Blaine made

those choices, he decided to run for the judgeship. . . ." State judge? He had not mentioned that at any time.

"He had guidance and advice every step of the way," Dirk said flatly. "Believe me, he had help. And then he died in that accident. And one day we realized that whatever Blaine had, you have double in spades. Except for the prosecuting experience, but you handled a private practice that included a lot of plaintiffs, as well as defendants. Your grades were higher than his. Your win record was better than his. And you had two kids to look out for. If you were black and in a wheelchair, it would be heaven." He flashed a grin, then added, "But, Sarah, I kid you not, you are one hell of a judge. You've made a lot of friends; others have noticed even if you're not keeping score."

She felt as if she had wandered into a mire that threatened to drag her under. What made it even more ridiculous, she thought, was that she could recognize what he was doing, where the traps were, and yet her familiarity with the game was of no help whatever. This was how Blaine used to get his way: he would propose something, and if she protested, he would come back at it from a different angle, over and over until he won. "Why don't you listen to me?" she said. "I told you I can't campaign. I won't campaign."

"You campaign every time you open your mouth," Dirk said, and picked up his wine glass, drank. "When's the last time you turned down an invitation to talk to a school group? A college assembly, or a class? A local meeting for whatever cause comes along? How many committees are you on? How many hours a week do you put in? You're already campaigning, Sarah, whatever you call it. That's all campaigning is, you know.

It's getting out there and selling something, and for most of us all we've got is ourselves, but you've got the law, and some kind of integrity that shows, and wisdom that shows."

She realized she was staring at him fixedly. She had found herself believing him, accepting his words, and that was the real trap, she knew. She looked away.

"We don't want you to do a thing you're not already doing," he said; he drained his glass and put it down. "You just say yes, and we'll take care of the rest."

"We again. Who? Judges are supposed to be nonpartisan, I thought."

"And you will be, too. A committee, Sarah, of your peers, if we can find anyone who qualifies. We'll form a committee and take care of it, the ballot statement, the bio stuff, all of it." He laughed suddenly. "No one's going to run against you, you realize. A sitting judge is as automatic a shoo-in as you can get."

He stood up and stretched. Daddy Longlegs, she thought; he could touch the ceiling if he chose. He looked at her appraisingly, then smiled. "I'm afraid you've missed your appointment with the beauty shop, but like I said, you look fine the way you are. How long will you be at your father's place?"

"Two weeks."

"Okay. Think about this, and I'll give you a call a week from Monday, see what you've decided." He regarded her thoughtfully for another moment. "You're so suspicious of politics, aren't you? It's endemic, I'm afraid. But it isn't a dirty word, and it doesn't have to be a dirty business. If we wanted a corrupt judge, we'd go buy one. There's no shortage of candidates. If I offered Bartles two hundred, he'd agree to be a lap dog;

for three hundred he'd poop on command." He laughed. "And, Sarah, while you're thinking about all this, remember that Blaine came to us, but this time we've come to you. It makes all the difference who does the asking. All the difference in the world." He walked toward the door. "I'll call a week from Monday, in the afternoon. Say hello to the old man for me."

She stood at the wide window for a long time, no longer seeing the town or the river, thinking, three years and six weeks. Blaine had gone skiing in April with half a dozen others, and the group had been caught in an avalanche. Three of them died, and one should have been left in the snow a few hours longer. He was in a permanent vegetative stage. Someone had come to tell her, and she had never been able to remember who it had been. A shadow against the white wall, evil shadow, evil words. She had not wept then, and for weeks she had not wept, but then one day, the tears had come, unexpected, out of place. And after that she had found herself weeping again and again at inappropriate times; while doing the dishes, or backing the car out of the driveway, or reading the newspaper, suddenly she would be blinded by tears.

She had not wept in court, but twice she had called a recess and fled to Blaine's office, her office, and cradled her head in her arms on Blaine's desk, her desk, and wept like a child.

"Three years, six weeks," she said silently. The hurt kept changing; a physical hurt, her body demanding his body, aching for love, for a caress, for a touch. Then, forgetting that he was not there, and starting to speak to him, that brought a sharper pain, a life-threatening spasm of pain. And anger. She could admit anger now, and strangely, admitting it lessened it, lessened the intensity of the pain it always brought with it. The pain of guilt was as fierce as it had been from the start. They had quarreled; he had wanted her to go to the ski lodge even if she had not wanted to ski, and she had said no. Too much work, a case pending, just no. She did not like to ski, did not like snow sports, did not like sitting in the lodge with other women whose husbands were out on the slopes, and later would drink too much and play cards most of the night.

She realized with a start that lights were coming on in Pendleton, twinkling stars in the dusk below, and her legs were aching, her back hurt. She had not done this for a long time, lost herself in glimpses of the past, how he had come loping up the hill with sweat dripping, three times a week. How he had hunched over the newspaper in the evening, how he had looked up at her and smiled. His arms around her. His body and hers joined in love. She hugged her arms about herself and turned from the window. That was the hurt she could not bear, the need her body had for his body, her need for his love, his passion and hers.

She had to do some laundry, had to eat something, had to start packing. Instead, she went to the bedroom they had shared, that she had abandoned after two weeks of trying to sleep in their bed without him. She stood in the doorway; the room was spartan, the way he had liked things around him. It was almost obsessively clean; she used to leave a blouse on a chair, or panty hose on the chest of drawers, her purse on the dressing table, something that indicated she lived here, too. Now every surface was bare, the bed made with the green spread he had liked, drapes closed the way he had liked them.

The children had come home for Blaine's funeral, had stayed with her for the next two weeks, then had gone back to school. The night they left she had made up the bed in Winnie's room and had slept in it, the first night she had been able to sleep without pills. She had slept there ever since. They weren't coming back, she had realized that night. Blaine had left her, the children had left her, and none of them would ever come back.

She entered her room. She had taken out most of Winnie's things, replaced frilly curtains with lace panels and drapes, put in a blue rug, and an easy chair and reading lamp, made it her own, with the children's pictures on one wall, every stage of their childhood faithfully recorded, framed. They were both beautiful, she often told herself in wonder. Even if Winnie had inherited her frizzy red hair, she had been a beautiful girl, was a beautiful young woman now. And Virgil was so like his father, with brown hair, dark eyes that often looked black, but were actually dark blue. The same crooked grin. He was twenty-three and lost. Somehow he had become lost. And that was what the reunion was all about, she admitted to herself. She had to have a little time with the children, find out what Virgil was doing, what he wanted to do, why he had dropped out of school, if he intended to go back. Find out if he was sick, into drugs. In serious trouble. And if the children wouldn't or couldn't come to her to spend some real time, she had decided to go where they were willing to be, her father's house. She gazed at Virgil's picture, his crooked grin, and she wanted to demand: Who are you?

What are you turning into? Abruptly she swung away from the picture.

She had to pack, she reminded herself, and remembered that she still had not done the laundry. And a few minutes later, starting the laundry, she remembered that she was overdue for dinner. Some nights she forgot to eat until it was almost bedtime. She had posted a note on the refrigerator: *Seven o'clock, Eat!* She sat down at the kitchen table and drank another glass of Dirk's wine and then wrote a list of things that had to be done. First, dinner. It was after nine.

It was one-thirty when she finally dropped into bed, exhausted and restless, the way she was before a trip. She wished she had sleeping pills, anything to put her over the edge swiftly, stop the tape loop that played endlessly in her mind. Virgil, her eighty-year-old father, Winnie, Dirk and his proposition, her own future.

For a time everyone had kept asking, what are you going to do now? What are your plans, and she had had no answers. She still had none. Five-year plans, forty-year plans? One seemed as meaningless as the other. Then she remembered another night when she had been too restless to sleep; she had dressed and had gone out in the car, down to the Spurs Bar and Grill. She had walked in and been greeted by a few people there; the place was full, with people playing pool, drinking, huddling in booths whispering, and she had been shocked by the realization that she was there looking for a man. Any man. No long-term commitment, no promises for even another day, just a man for one hour. She had fled, had driven for hours, and returned home only when dawn was breaking.

She sat up and hugged her knees hard against her

chest and thought so clearly that she knew she had been thinking this for hours, and had denied the thought for hours: If she were appointed a federal judge, she would move out of Pendleton, where everyone knew everyone; she would live in a big city where she would be unknown, and where it wouldn't matter if she were known. She could see men if she chose to, date them, sleep with them. If she were appointed federal judge, it was for life. She would be free. No more impossible decisions about tomorrow, next year, no more worry about what she would live on when Blaine's term ran out, no more worry that she might not be able to get another job as a lawyer anywhere.

And if she had wings, she thought bitterly, rocking back and forth—but she could not see herself with wings flying through the air, and she could see herself at the bench. Curiously, the image of herself at the bench was sharper, more in focus than the memory of Blaine there. She pressed her face hard against her knees, rocking back and forth.

"Were you their man, Blaine?" she whispered. "Were you?"

TWO

ALL FRIDAY AFTERNOON Winnie Drexler had been overseeing the construction of a fantasy as workmen laid
sod and struggled with tubs of plants to create the illusion of a suburban yard. A fence line was being delin-
eated with potted roses and junipers. This was supposed
to be a corner of a yard, and it probably would fool
most people, who would pay little attention to the background and would not suspect that the lush grass was a
postage-stamp-size patch of new sod. Where it ended,
near-desert conditions began—brittle gray or tan
grasses, pale cracked earth.

Ringing the immediate setting, mountain peaks
reached the sky, a few of them with the sheen of snow,
but most of them bare, some close enough to make out
individual slopes, some lost in a hazy distance. Closer,
behind the potted shrubs, a hill rose steeply, brown already with clumps of dead-looking grass, a few scattered, tired pine trees, and many pale rocks. In another
direction the background was rows of greenhouses and,
finally, dusty old poplars between here and the road.
None of this would make it to the video.

"Okay," Winnie said, as the men working with the
heavy pots waited, sweating. "We'll go with that. It
looks good." After the men gathered up their equipment

and loaded everything onto heavy wagons and left, Winnie walked around the small area critically, thinking about light, about shadows, about two people filling that space and not getting in each other's way.... The sky was brilliant—too brilliant? She considered it, then forgot it. Not much to be done about the sky. Here in East Shasta, California, the sky was almost always brilliant blue, the sun almost always glaring white, the air almost always oven-dry.

She glanced around for her brother Virgil, but he had vanished back to the greenhouses or the tropical dome, or somewhere. It didn't matter, not yet. Today she was getting things ready, in the morning they would tape.

Winnie was a month short of twenty-seven, one year out of graduate school which she had not actually finished, and this was the third video for her. And the most important. The other two had been simple indoor training films, done within a few hours; this project would take a week or longer. At the moment she wasn't altogether sure she would be paid for it. Oh, she'd be paid for the materials, certainly, and the processing, but her time? Maybe, Virgil had said, and had not referred to it again, although, she thought darkly, he knew she was dead broke.

She believed she had no illusions about herself when actually she was much harder on herself than anyone else was. She was sturdily built, muscular from running every day, with a body she thought of as simply heavy and others saw as strong, well-built, even beautifully muscled. All that people saw of her, she had always believed, was her hair and her freckles; now she could feel freckles popping out all over her legs, her cheeks, her arms. She moved into the shade of the poplar trees.

What the workmen called her, she also knew, was "the
Flaming Bush." The aridity here made her frizzy red
hair more frizzy than ever, a flaming bush.

She let her gaze wander over the rest of the grounds,
two acres of water gardens and greenhouses, with
hardly enough room to park a car anymore. The pond
they would start digging in the morning was the sixth
and last of a series, no two alike: different sizes, shapes,
different plants. And she would put the catalog together
for it all, her biggest job to date, her most important
even if she never made a penny from it. A catalog and
a video.

She started to walk toward the tropical dome where
she had decided Virgil would be, at least if Maria
Florinda was still working on the tropical lilies. She
didn't actually smile, but resisted only through an effort, as she thought of the way Virgil looked at Maria,
and then she did smile because they were to be her actors in the video, playing the part of a happy yuppie
couple with a couple of grand to spend on a water garden. Poor Virgil, she thought, and followed the thought
swiftly with an admonition. She would not tease Virgil,
she told herself. She would not tease Virgil. She would
not . . .

The tropical dome was divided into two sections, the
smaller one the showroom that looked like a piece of
Eden. An irregularly shaped pool was backed up by
lava rocks and lush tropical plants. There were two wa-
terfalls, and the water was dyed black; it looked like
velvet. Lotuses rose seven feet high, eight feet, with gi-
gantic leaves that looked large enough to lie down on,
and great brilliant red, yellow, white flowers. The tropical lilies stood above the black water in every possible

color, bicolors, some that changed throughout the day from yellow to orange to red, some as blue as the sky. The air was so fragrant it was stifling, and as soon as she entered the dome, the sweat that had not collected in the arid heat outside became a clammy second skin.

The heat, the humidity, the heavily scented air suddenly became overwhelming; she felt her stomach churn, and ran through the showroom. Her footsteps signaled the fish in the pool; to them people meant feeding, and they came to the surface and milled about in abandon—reds, oranges, yellows, whites, blue and white. . . . When Virgil first told her the fish were tame, she had laughed, but he had told the truth. Some were so tame they came up to be stroked, to take food from human fingers. She looked at them and kept hurrying; the fish followed as far as the confines of the pool permitted.

The workroom was several times larger than the showroom, and in here half a dozen people were busy at long benches, at tanks of water, at tables in the center of the room. The air was as hot and humid as in the showroom, and nearly as fragrant. Virgil had taken her on a tour a year ago, had pointed out the tanks, some as much as two feet deep, some so shallow they had no more water than the absorbent lining held. He had pointed out the wicking system, which made working on some tropical bog plants much easier than if they were submerged. Under the shallow trays was a trough of water that was regulated by valves, he had gone on, so that the wicks drew up exactly enough water. . . . He had given her a mini-lecture on the systems—automatic humidity and temperature adjustments, automatic watering, draining, the vents and fans, the oxygenating system. . . . She had stopped listening, and merely observed after that. And when she realized that he intended to point out every plant, every detail of the maintenance, she had regarded him with disbelief and excused herself.

Today, people at the central table were packing plants for shipping; rolls of the green feltlike material hung over the table, rolls of heavy plastic, rolls of plastic bags, flattened plastic-lined boxes in stacks, insulation, plastic bins with labels. . . . The water gardens did a big mail-order business, and this was their busy season. She nodded to the few people who glanced up at her, and went on past to where she had spotted Virgil and Maria. They appeared to be performing surgery at the tanks of water lilies.

Most of the workers in here wore shorts, some of the women wore halters, and everyone looked very moist. Maria had on a white T-shirt and white shorts, rubber thongs on her feet. Her skin glistened. Virgil had cut-off jeans and no shirt. He was very tanned. He had missed out on the frizzy-hair genes from their mother, and had got the smooth, dark, slightly wavy hair from their father. And no freckles. So, Winnie sometimes told herself, aiming at a philosophy that was bearable, her little brother got the good looks and she got the brain. Fair enough. But it irked sometimes, like now, to see him looking so handsome, so comfortable when she felt like something just out of the dishwasher. And Maria Florinda looked like a model pretending to be a botanist. She was beautiful, with long black hair that she had pulled off her back and neck in a ponytail; she had fine high cheekbones, and the coloring of a Polynesian princess.

Maria was detaching minute new plants from the leaf joints of a mature water lily. The plantlets were no bigger than Winnie's little fingernail. Maria's fingers were long and shapely, and very sure as she wielded a scalpel to cut the new plant free from the parent, and handed it to Virgil, who was just as steady and sure as he planted it in a small pot, spread out hairlike roots with a dowel hardly thicker than a toothpick; he added soil and sand, and finally lowered the pot gently into a shallow tray with enough water to cover it. The little lancelike leaves twisted, then rose through the water to the surface, where they floated. When he finished, Maria had another one ready.

"And life goes on," Winnie murmured. They both looked up as if surprised by her presence.

"Viviparous reproduction," Maria said. "Aren't they lovely? The little ones?"

They were. Perfect Lilliputian water lilies. Neither Maria nor Virgil moved, and suddenly Winnie felt awkward, like an intruder. There had been some sort of communion here that she had interrupted. "Just wanted to say we're all ready for the break of dawn tomorrow," she said. "I'd like a word with you about it before you take off," she added to Maria.

"We'll be done in about half an hour," Virgil said. "You want to wait?"

"Not in here," Winnie said, wiping her upper lip with the back of her hand, fighting nausea again. "I'll be at the house."

She did not go back through the showroom, but headed toward the nearest door. She glanced again at her brother and Maria; their heads were bent over the work: communion reestablished.

She was facing the fish hatchery when she stepped
outside, where surprisingly the air felt cool and fresh.
She leaned against the door breathing deeply, gratefully.
Carlos Chiricos entered the building opposite, walking
around a hand truck of shipping boxes at the wide
doors; today, Friday, they would send out a shipment of
fish and plants, a busy day for everyone. Rusty Curlow
flew two shipments in his Cessna each week down to
Reno, where they were transferred to a commercial line
on their way to the customers.

"Shit," Winnie said under her breath. That meant
that her grandfather would already be in the shipping
room overseeing the packing of the fish, snails, whatever they were sending, or on his way there, or on his
way to the plants room. He always oversaw this operation. He still didn't fully believe you could send fish
by mail to anywhere in the world without heavy mortality rates, although by now experience should count
for something. She started back toward the house. She
had hoped to corner her grandfather this afternoon;
she had hoped the same thing yesterday when she arrived, and now she would have to put it off until Sunday. Tomorrow she would be too busy with the video,
and he never really talked after dinner. Besides, Virgil
would be hanging around, or someone else would
drop in. She had to see him alone. And she had to see
him before her mother arrived on Sunday.

Slowly she walked around the pond nearest the
house. This was the first one her grandfather had in-
stalled, for therapeutic reasons. When her grandmother
had a stroke, he had retired from government service,
and they had come out here, the area of his childhood,
and just for something to do, he had taken up water gar-

dening and fish breeding. At first he had said it was for his wife; he had read that watching goldfish and koi was relaxing, that it took the blood pressure down measurably just to sit and watch the fish swim. Now, twenty years later, the little hobby had become a million-dollar business, but the first pond was still his favorite, and it was the prettiest of them all.

Winnie moved into the shade of the veranda where she could still overlook the pool; she leaned against a post, trying to think of a way to get her grandfather alone for ten or fifteen minutes. Then, surprised, she heard his voice.

The house was not air-conditioned; he did not like air-conditioning, and usually there was enough of a breeze up here that no matter how hot it was in the sun, the house stayed cool and airy. But now she could hear him, apparently on the telephone in the living room, a dozen or so feet away from where Winnie was standing.

"For God's sake, make sure!" he said in a harsh, unfamiliar voice. "No innuendos, no suggestions, no suspicions. Make sure!"

There was a pause, and then he said more quietly, "When can you come out here?" Another pause. "Sunday it is, then. And bring everything you have. All of it."

There was another silence that extended so long that Winnie thought he had hung up. She wanted to leave, but now she was afraid he might see her and think she had purposely eavesdropped. She had decided to back away, approach the house again and this time go straight into the kitchen around the other side, when he spoke once more.

"I know. I know, by God! But this isn't a court of

law. Whatever it takes to convince you, that's probably enough. Sunday, late in the afternoon, then. We'll give you some supper."

The harsh note was gone; he sounded choked, as if he was fighting tears not too successfully. Winnie felt a clutch of fear at the sound of his voice. He was old, she thought suddenly, eighty, an old man. And something was desperately wrong.

She ran from the veranda to a clump of pine trees near the driveway, and sat down on a bench to think. At first she had believed it was a medical problem, something about the harshness of his voice had suggested that, but he had said a court of law. Something to do with Winnie's mother? She almost laughed at the idea of anything about Sarah causing that pain in her grandfather. Not Sarah. And almost as certainly not anything to do with Virgil; her grandfather was blind where Virgil was concerned. Winnie couldn't even imagine what it would take to make him turn against his only grandson. Not Sarah, his daughter; not Virgil, his grandson. Not his brother Peter, what could there possibly be about Uncle Peter to cause grief? Not any of Uncle Peter's family; her grandfather was not close enough to any of them to sound that upset. She came finally to the point she had been driving toward all along. It had to be about her. The clutch of fear returned, redoubled, making her stomach spasm.

A truck rumbled behind her on the driveway, heading toward the fishery and the plant room. A few minutes later Maria approached her, pushing a bicycle. Virgil was supervising the shipments, she said, and Winnie couldn't remember for a moment what she had wanted to bring up with them.

"Seven okay with you?" she asked.

"Sure. No problem."

She thought Maria was eyeing her curiously, and she remembered. "Oh, yes. No white. It makes too much glare."

Maria nodded. "Blue jeans, blue shirt. I'll even wear shoes," she added, laughing.

Winnie stood up and said, "Blue's good," she said. "See you in the morning." She knew she sounded brusque, and seemed unable to think of anything to say to soften it. She started toward the house, and Maria got on her bicycle and pedaled toward East Shasta half a mile away.

The truck left before Winnie reached the veranda, and Virgil came running from the fishery, carrying a sheaf of papers. She stopped walking to wait for him.

"Where's Maria? I thought you'd be talking."

"She went home, I guess. I told her no white clothes, that's about all I had to say." A few steps short of the veranda, she suddenly took his arm and steered him away from the house. "Virgil, what's wrong with Grandpa? What's going on?"

"What do you mean?" he demanded, but a hidden expression came over his face, and for a moment he looked so much like their father, it gave her a jolt.

"I don't know. That's what I want to find out. Something's going on with Grandpa, isn't there?"

He looked down at the papers he was carrying, copies of the orders they had filled, and then he looked past her toward the house, and at last he said, "Yeah. Something, and I don't know what it is. He hired a detective."

"For heaven's sake, why?"

"I don't know."

"Well, something must have happened. When did he, and how do you know? Did he tell you?"

"He hasn't told me shit," he said sullenly. "Back in April the insurance guy was here, renewing policies or something like that. Routine. Grandpa asked him for the name of a detective about a week after that. I heard him on the telephone. And he called her, a woman detective. Her number was on the phone bill and I called and her answering machine said it was a detective agency. I hung up. I don't know what he's doing." He looked at the papers again and shook his head. "I think he's checking up on me, and he'll boot me out," he said in a soft voice.

All trace of their father was gone; the expression had been so fleeting, she felt she might have imagined it. Now he was her little brother again, and she wanted to hold him and comfort him and tell him it would be all right, but she couldn't because she didn't know what the problem was, where the hurt was, where the danger was.

Before she could say anything, Grandpa called from the veranda, "Hey, you two fixing to get sunstroke or something out there? Want some lemonade?"

Virgil drew in a breath. "Don't ask him anything," he muttered. "You know how he is if he thinks you're prying."

She nodded, and they walked toward the house to join their grandfather. "Last-minute arrangements about the epic tomorrow," Winnie said.

Grandpa nodded and held out his hand for the papers Virgil carried. "You'd better plan to get in all the filming you can in a day or two," he said. "That grass will be deader than last year's hay if we don't get some rain, and that's as likely as snow you know where."

He was a tall man, broad in the chest and shoulders, too heavy, but he was not willing to give up a thing he liked at the table, and he liked most things. A few years earlier he had had a cancer removed from his nose, and since then he had worn a wide-brimmed straw hat whenever he walked out the door; he had one on now. They teased him, claiming that he had salted his entire property with straw hats; they turned up everywhere. He had been an outdoorsman all his life, and his skin had gone past preserved leather to old, well-seasoned wood, with deep wrinkles on his forehead, deep vertical gutters up and down his cheeks, and a permanent squint that the straw hat did not alleviate. Now he surveyed the surrounding hills with troubled eyes.

"We're going to start losing pines," he said gloomily, and turned to reenter the house. At the door he said, "Thanks, Virgil, for handling the shipments for me." His back was almost rigidly straight as he went inside.

Virgil was right, Winnie knew; she could no more ask Grandpa what he was up to than she could demand an explanation from God for the continuing drought.

"Lemonade," she said then. What she really wanted was some of the good white wine he kept stashed away for special occasions, but lemonade would do. She suspected that no one in her family would think her pregnancy was cause for a celebration. Wrong kind of special occasion.

As she and Virgil walked across the veranda, she said in a low voice, "Whatever is going on could come to a head Sunday. I think the detective is coming out here on Sunday afternoon."

THREE

THE NEXT MORNING Winnie shivered in a sweatshirt as she taped Virgil and Maria playing their parts of the young married couple. They all had pretended not to notice Virgil's blush when they began the charade. He and Maria moved a white rope around on the grass to outline a shape, stepped back, moved it again, and finally were satisfied. Virgil began to dig around the edges; he lifted out the sod as if it were actually anchored with roots, placed it aside, and Maria looked beautiful watching.

"Okay," Winnie said. "Next step."

It was all planned to the last detail; after the editing, a script had to be written, an actor hired to do a voiceover. Another man and Virgil would be shown digging, then they would bring in a small backhoe to deepen the hole, Maria and Virgil would step back into the picture from time to time to smooth out the ledges ... Winnie taped for ten minutes, waited for the next phase, taped again. Virgil was working hard; he was very muscular, very tanned. She was making her little brother a star, she thought at him, taping, watching.

They stopped for lunch, and went back to it. Now she wore one of her grandfather's straw hats under the merciless sun. By late afternoon the hole was finished and they had the plastic liner in place. She taped Maria when she brought a hose into view and started running water into the pool. Virgil moved close to her and put his arm around her shoulders, exactly right for a young married man in love with his wife, but Winnie knew that the stiffness that came over Maria would be apparent on the cassette. It could be edited out, she told herself, but she stopped taping. Maria pulled away from Virgil and walked to the opposite side of the pool. He kicked at the grass and looked at the surrounding hills.

"We'll wait until it's about full to finish up," Winnie said. She had hours and hours of material on tape, and another ten minutes or so to be added, then all of it had to be edited down to twenty minutes, and that would be the real work.

It was nearly five, and all at once she felt exhaustion hit like a landslide crushing her, exactly as if she had done all that digging personally. She sat down. It was always like this with her; she seldom realized how hungry she was until she felt weak; she seldom realized how tired she was until her legs gave way. Her interior signals were a mess, she told herself. She needed a timer to remind her of things other people took for granted.

Virgil looked miserable, and Maria, on the other side of the pool, to all appearances was entranced with the rushing water; Winnie took pity on her brother then. It might be puppy love, she thought, but it hurt like the real thing. "Maria," she said, "tonight I'm going over to Ghost Lake to take some pictures by moonlight. You want to come along?" She did not add that she had dragooned Virgil into helping with gear. When he said the real reason she wanted him to go was because she thought the lake was spooky, she had not denied that.

Maria looked doubtful. Slowly she walked around the pool and sat on the grass beside Winnie.

"Have you seen the lake?" Winnie asked.

"Yes, but in daylight, and with a lot of people around. It's a full moon tonight, isn't it?"

Winnie nodded. Last summer she had been out at night to the dry lake, and she had cursed herself for not having a camera with her, and for the intervening months the image of the lake under a full moon had come back again and again, until she had determined that this summer she would get it on film.

"All right," Maria said. "I'll go with you. It must be very different in moonlight."

Winnie liked it that Maria had not said beautiful, or exciting, or scary, none of the expected things. Different was exactly right. They had met only two days ago, and had not talked more than polite-deep, and all Winnie knew about her was that Virgil was in love with her, and she was a botanist. She was okay, Winnie thought then.

"Ghost Lake isn't even the real name," Winnie murmured, almost as if to herself. "It's really Rabbit Lake, or used to be. I think it's still on the maps that way, you know how they show a dry lake, with dotted lines."

"Mrs. Betancort says there's quicksand," Maria said. "She says the ghosts of all the people who have been taken under stir sometimes, move the sand trying to get out. She says if you listen you can hear their voices."

"Mrs. Betancort says a lot of things," Winnie said. "And sometimes she's even right. There's quicksand. The whole lake is posted. I don't intend to get out on it, believe me." And Mrs. Betancort had called Winnie by her grandmother's name, Rebecca, from the first time they had met. The only way to deal with Mrs. Betancort was not to deal with her, Winnie had decided. The woman must be pushing a hundred, and she looked as if time couldn't touch her ever again; everything it could do had been done.

It was taking the pool a long time to fill. The idea, Virgil had told her, was that they would demonstrate that a pool could be put in on day one and filled, wait two days and add plants, wait two more days and add fish, and presto you have a complete water garden in five working days. Start Monday, have a garden party on Saturday. He wanted to franchise the whole package, and it would sell, she had realized with surprise. The idea of having a lovely little water garden in the back yard was a good one if all you had to do was sign a check.

It was time to put a finishing edge around the new pond, and Maria and Virgil started that for the tape, then moved aside for the workmen to finish, and within a few minutes the water level had risen to lap against coping stones that looked as if they had been there from the beginning of time. It was done.

"Have dinner with us," Virgil said to Maria when Winnie started packing up her gear.

"Oh, no," Maria said quickly. "Rosa and Carlos will be expecting me. But thank you."

She left hurriedly on her bicycle, and now Winnie wondered if she had made a mistake in not telling her that Virgil would be their driver later that night. At first she had believed that Maria was simply not interested, was even a little embarrassed by Virgil's attention, but it could be more than that, a real aversion, maybe justified. Virgil was not her baby brother any longer, she reminded herself; he was a gorgeous young man who had lived his own life for five or six years now, a life she knew very little about actually. They were to pick Maria up at nine-thirty, and she could back out then, Winnie decided, suddenly very unhappy with a new and unpleasant thought, that she was pimping for her brother. To call it matchmaking was simply gilding the lily, she added silently; it was all the same thing.

East Shasta was a pretty town, Winnie thought, as they drove through it that night. There was a stable population of about two hundred, most of them employed by the Lister Institute, which was really a hospital/ physical therapy facility, or by the gardens, or on one of the ranches nearby. While it would never be mistaken for Palm Springs, neither was it shabby or run-down. The houses were mostly frame, well maintained, and the stores and public buildings were all in good condition. There were many trees, many gardens, one traffic light. The police force had one member; the mobile library visited once a week; there was a movie theater, and several bars, several churches, a hardware store, a drugstore with a department store attached, a K-Mart, a hobby and craft shop . . . A *Saturday Evening Post* cover sort of town.

Tonight, Saturday night, the bars, or as they insisted here, saloons, would be jammed; the Saturday night dance was the social event of the week. Virgil had protested wasting a Saturday night looking at a creepy dry lake, and she had said patiently that it was the only time. On Sunday their mother would arrive, on Monday the whole family would be together for a dinner, and by Tuesday the weather might change, and, besides, the moon wouldn't rise until near dawn, Wednesday morning. She didn't know if that was true, but she did know that Virgil wouldn't think of checking it for himself. Besides, she had added, it would take a couple of hours, and afterward he could dance until his feet fell off.

He stopped in front of the Chiricos' house and started to get out.

"I'll go," she said hastily, slipping from the passenger seat. She had to give Maria one more chance to avoid being stuck with Virgil, an awkward business with Virgil at Winnie's elbow.

At the house, she knocked on the screen door; no one was in sight in the living room on the other side of the door, but then Carlos, Rosa and Maria came into view from the rear of the house. Carlos opened the door and stepped aside for her to enter.

"We are ready," he said. He was a barrel-chested man with short legs, black hair cut so short it stood up all over his head like porcupine quills that had not yet fully developed. He was the general manager at the gardens. Rosa, his wife, was the housekeeper for Grandpa, and they were both at the gardens more than they were home. She was only five feet tall, as dark as he was, and very handsome, with features that could have been on a Mayan wall. She stood with her arms crossed, a stern expression on her face. She looked remote and unapproachable.

"We?" Winnie asked. "You all want to go?"

"No," Carlos said. "I do not want to go to Ghost Lake, but you girls can't go out there alone. So, I will go with you."

Maria said sharply, "Carlos, you're being foolish, and patronizing. We are not children!"

Equally annoyed, Winnie said, "We won't be alone. Virgil is going with us."

Carlos opened the screen door to peer out at the car at the curb, and then nodded. "That's good. Going out there at night isn't good, but taking Virgil with you is. Then we can go to the dance, Rosa." His wife relaxed and nodded, smiling.

"I'm sorry," Maria said, as they walked to the car. "He treats me like a child, as if I were his daughter or ward."

Then why don't you move out? Winnie started to ask, but held her tongue. "Forget it," she muttered instead.

She wanted a shot from the westernmost side of the lake, she told Virgil when they arrived at the ghost town and Ghost Lake. She would set up her Hasselblad first, half-hour exposure, and move on down the lake with the Leica, twenty-minute exposure, twenty-five, she was not sure yet, both cameras on tripods, of course. She would shift back and forth between the two cameras, and gradually work her way in toward the town along the road. She realized that Virgil had stopped listening, and she stopped explaining what she intended, and considered the problem of the lake. The quicksand, if there was any, was said to be out toward the center of the lake bed, nowhere near the old shore, but she was not interested in going out on it. She wanted the lake as it was, ghostly, uninviting, resisting intrusion.

Ah, she thought a few minutes later, wide-eyed in the eerie light. The lake was as white as she had remembered; the sand in daylight was pale brown, but now it was as white as the moon that had just cleared the horizon. She had a view of the expanse of lake, from a low angle that made it appear endless, with the moon bigger than a mountain ... A few jutting rocks, some boulders, some clumps of sage cast long black shadows that looked like caves. Wind-driven sand had filled in the deep spots, had created dunes whose shadows were higher, sharper than the sand hills themselves, black swords cutting through white satin. A moonscape, dreamscape, nightmarescape where the shadow, the illusion, had more reality than the original.

As the moon sailed higher, the shadows changed; she moved again and again, and then she heard the rustle of the wind in sand, like whispers. She strained to hear better.

"Winnie? Aren't you done yet?" Virgil asked, at her elbow.

She started, nearly knocking her tripod over. And fatigue hit her like a hammer. She started to take her camera off the tripod, and nearly fell down; Virgil's hand caught her arm and steadied her. Maria was at her side, her hand warm on Winnie's other arm.

"I'm just tired," Winnie said, embarrassed.

"No wonder," Virgil said. "We've been out here for hours."

The moon was nearly overhead; the shadows were gone, the sand quiet.

"Not just tired," Maria said in a low voice. "It's this place. Nothing's real. You look at one of the houses, and it looks whole, as if people are still in it, and then you see there's no floor, or no roof, or nothing behind a wall except sand. And then another one looks complete, and another, and they all are illusion. You think you see water, hear waves against a beach, and it's illusion." She stopped as abruptly as she had started; her hand fell from Winnie's arm and she turned to walk toward the car.

"Let's get out of here," Virgil said; he took the camera off the tripod, hoisted the tripod with his other hand. Winnie took a step, and felt the ground shift. "Back up," Virgil said hoarsely. "Hurry up." They both backed away from the edge of the lake.

Winnie realized that she had worked her way from the far end past the ghost town ruins, and had stopped on a low bluff, no more than eight feet above the lake bed, an area where the desert was still forming, where the edges crumbled and fell and added to the expanse of dry lake. The dry lake was devouring the land. She had been inside the posted hazard signs.

Then she and Virgil were on the roadway again, near the car. Maria was already in the back seat, a shadow among shadows. After they stowed Winnie's equipment in the trunk, she stood for a second or two at her car door, listening. The whispers were gone; the silence was profound, and under the full moon the ghost town appeared ready for the return of the inhabitants, who had stepped out for a while. Winnie blinked hard, and the derelict buildings became ruins again, tilted porches, leaning walls, roofless shells. One building looked as if it had melted down into the ground with only part of the upper walls and roof remaining, and they appeared intact. The sun- and wind-bleached wood reflected the moonlight like ghastly skeletons, as colorless as lead.

Winnie shivered and got inside the car and they started the drive back, the twenty-three miles of narrow winding road that was almost as rotten as the buildings in the ghost town. No one spoke until they reached East

Shasta, and Virgil said, "I'll take you home first, Winnie."

She had drifted into a somnolent state, and his voice jerked her wide awake. She nodded. All she wanted was a cup of hot anything to drink, a long hot bath, and a long, long sleep. "Thanks for going with me," she said to Maria, over her shoulder.

Maria looked as distant as the moon; her face was as pale as the moon, her features craters of deep shadow. "I'm glad I went," she said.

But she wasn't glad, Winnie thought then; something had happened out there, something had made Maria retreat, back so far she looked untouchable, unknowable. Illusion, Maria had said, it was all illusion, and for a moment she seemed as much an illusion as the ruined buildings, the destroyed town, she looked as eerily colorless as the bleached wood, as cold and unyielding as the moon, no more than a pale face, detached, floating among shadows.

Virgil turned onto the driveway to the house. Briefly she wondered if he and Maria had said a word to each other out at the ghost town, but she was too tired to pursue the thought as they stopped at Grandpa's house and she pulled herself from the car, shouldered her gear; they all said goodnight, and she trudged inside.

FOUR

At six on Sunday evening Sarah pulled up to her father's house, shocked, as she had been on her last visit a year earlier, at how much space the ever-expanding business was taking. A new greenhouse edged the back lawn, and there seemed to be more pools than she remembered. She should have parked under the trees, she thought, glancing at several cars already there, but she did not turn on the ignition again. Later.

She walked to the front door slowly, tired from her long drive, stiff, and too hot. The house was wide open as usual, and as soon as she stepped onto the covered porch, the air cooled by many degrees. Through the screen door she could hear Winnie's voice: "Hand me that tape, will you?"

Sarah entered a large foyer. A few feet to the right an archway framed the living room entrance. Stairs on the left led down to a hall that ran the length of the house, front to back, and ten feet straight ahead stairs went up to the second floor bedrooms. She turned to the steps going down, then stopped when she saw Winnie in the hallway taping a picture to the wall.

"Now a pin," Winnie said, and a man's arm moved into view and reached out toward her. "Damn you, Freddie, do that again and I'll pin you to the wall!"

Sarah had not seen what he had done.

From beyond them came Virgil's voice, "Big brother is watching *you*."

Sarah went down the remaining steps, and now she could see Virgil at the end of the hall, on the far side of another set of steps that matched the ones she was on. His head appeared to be stuck between two banisters.

"Mother!" Virgil yelled; he pulled back and stood up. Winnie jumped off a low stool she had been standing on and came running, and beyond her, Virgil was making his way cautiously; he was on ice skates, Sarah realized.

She hugged Winnie, kissed her, drew back to examine her again—too sunburned, and her cheek felt hot—then she hugged her some more. Virgil had covered the distance by then and they embraced awkwardly as he tottered on the skates, laughing.

"You know Dr. Wolper, don't you?" Winnie asked, when Sarah and Virgil drew apart. Winnie nodded toward the man who apparently was the Freddie who had to be warned about his hands.

"Of course," Sarah said, and shook hands, with only the vaguest memory of him. He was tall and blond, with blue eyes, in his forties probably, a touch overweight.

"Well, I'll be leaving," Dr. Wolper said. "Leave you to your reunion. See you tomorrow."

As he went out, Winnie made a face at his back, then turned to her mother. "You look tired. Bad trip? You want something to drink? Booze, wine? Water? Iced coffee?"

"Iced coffee sounds wonderful. Virgil, for heaven's sake, why are you wearing ice skates?"

He had seated himself on the steps and was unlacing the boots. "Turned my ankle last year, and one of the guys here said if I'd walk on skates half an hour a day, three days a week, I'd strengthen them. Worth trying. I keep the blade covers on," he added hurriedly.

The urge to pat him on the head was so strong she had to clench her hands, and she consciously did not sigh. No more patting, no more sighing, she and Blaine had agreed more than five years ago.

"Because he's a nut," Winnie said cheerfully. "Come on out back where there's a breeze, and I'll rustled up the coffee. Sure you wouldn't rather have wine, or a bloody mary, or something?"

"Coffee," Sarah said, and followed her daughter through the hall to the back veranda. "Where's Dad?" Virgil padded after them in bare feet, carrying the skates.

"In his office," Winnie said.

"Talking to a buyer," Virgil said at the same time.

Sarah caught the swift glance that passed between them, and shrugged. All their lives Virgil and Winnie had shared secrets; she found it oddly reassuring that they still did. She sank down into a lounge chair in the shade and surveyed the scene before her in contentment. The pool was prettier than ever, more flowers were blooming than she recalled, and the air was fresh and fragrant.

While Winnie was gone to get the drinks, Virgil began to talk about the idea he had come up with to franchise instant back yard water gardens. She watched the animation play across his face as he added detail after detail, and she knew today was not the time to bring up his plans, his future. There would be time, she told herself.

Winnie returned, and they were chatting about Ghost Lake and their visit out there, when Sarah's uncle Peter strolled around the house. Sarah stood up to kiss him. "How are you?"

He looked very much like her father, tall, broad in the chest and shoulders, and a little too heavy, but where her father was weathered from a life outdoors, Uncle Peter was pale, and appeared weak in comparison. His life had been spent in academia, where he had made a name for himself as a professor of biochemistry.

"I'm fine, fine," he said. "Sarah, you look wonderful! Michael came in yesterday and we sat up talking all night. He's looking forward to seeing you."

"Michael's getting a new job," Virgil said. "Provost."

"Uncle Peter, that's wonderful!" Sarah said. He smiled, but she knew he was as disappointed in his son Michael as Blaine had been in Virgil. Michael had no interest in science; Virgil had no interest in education, period. "Is Michael going to be around a bit? It's been ages. Is Bernice with him?"

"No, she's been over in Colorado Springs visiting her folks. She'll fly into Reno with the kids tomorrow and he'll pick them up. They'll stay a few days. I believe they'll be here for dinner tomorrow."

He wouldn't stay long, he said, but something cold to drink would be good, a vodka collins, maybe? Winnie went inside to make him a drink. "Just popped in to say hello," he went on, smiling at Sarah. "It's good that the family's getting together for a bit. We should do it more often." He laughed softly. "Sometimes when I'm alone in the old house, I find myself wishing it was like it used to be, your mom and dad, you, my kids all jammed in there together, yelling, laughing, singing. Eating. That's what I remember most, all the eating that went on around the clock. Remember?"

She laughed, too, remembering very clearly. It had been fun, and she was eager to see Michael again, her cousin who had been more like a brother, her Virgil. Winnie returned with a frosted glass and gave it to Uncle Peter.

"Thank you, my dear," he said, and took a long drink. "Ah, good. You were talking about Ghost Lake when I came around the house," he said to Winnie. "That's a pretty dangerous place to be at night. You know about the quicksand, don't you?"

"It's perfectly safe as long as you use your head," Winnie said, then added, almost too sweetly, "No place is safe for idiots, is it?"

He chuckled. "You are your mother's daughter, Winnie. No doubt about that." He drank some more, and put the glass down. "Talking about eating makes me realize I probably should be on my way and get some food instead of alcohol. Well, I'm off." He stood up, then stopped again. "But, Winnie, it really can be a dangerous place, out at Ghost Lake. Quicksand can be deceptive. Have you read anything about it? I have a book that is very good."

"Uncle, I'm not going back. And I know about the quicksand."

He was like that, Sarah thought, remembering this, also. He never could leave a topic alone until he had finished what he intended to say about it, and he could never leave the young people alone, but had to treat them all like students in a classroom. She wondered when he had let her cross the line to adulthood, and no date came, but it had been late; she had had two children, when suddenly he had started treating her like a grownup. She avoided looking at Winnie, whose face, she knew, would be flushed in anger.

Uncle Peter grinned at them and waved. "Right. Well, I'll see you all tomorrow."

The other thing about him, Sarah remembered then, was that he seemed to know that he overstepped that line again and again, but knowing it did not deter him a bit the next time. His mission in life, by God, was to instruct, and instruct he would.

He looked so much like her father, Sarah thought, watching his straight figure; he even sounded like him when he laughed. How deep the connections ran, she continued the thought, Winnie so like her, Virgil like his father, on and on, connecting links in an invisible web stronger than steel.

"Mother, I have a surprise for you," Virgil said then. "Right after we eat, I'll show you. It has to be a little later than this."

Then her father and a strange woman appeared in the doorway, and she went to greet them, shocked and alarmed by his appearance. He was as deeply tanned as ever, but he looked very tired, almost haggard. Just a year ago he had been robust and youthful, jaunty, playful, but this evening he looked stiff, as if movement gave him pain, and his eyes were clouded. He had aged terribly, she realized, and felt a deep pang of regret, guilt, fear for him, something she could not identify. Eighty, she thought almost wildly; he was eighty.

His arms were strong when he embraced her, however, and his voice was steady when he introduced the stranger. "Fran Donatio," he said. "My daughter, Sarah. And that's Winnie and Virgil." He said this as if she should know who they all were, and she nodded at them generally and did not offer to shake hands. "Did you put her car in the shade?" he asked Virgil.

"Yes sir. I left the keys in the car," Virgil added to Fran Donatio. "Is that all right?"

"Fine," she said. "Thank you." She was in her early forties, with black hair cut short in a style that was very becoming to her oval face. Her eyes were dark and beautiful, her best feature, and she used eye makeup, but none other than that. She was a bit too full in the hips for the pants suit she wore.

"Well, come on in," Grandpa said. "I told Rosa to put supper on the table."

At the start of the meal, there was a palpable tension that baffled Sarah. She was too tired to try to make small talk, and she never had been clever at small talk even at her best. But then her father began to reminisce about some of his adventures when he was with the government Department of Fish and Wildlife. "Remember that geyser we found?" he asked Sarah. "Up near Steens Mountain in Oregon. Pretty as a picture, and not on any map. I named it Rebecca Spring. It spouted every fifteen minutes, about three feet up. Hundred forty degrees," he added, and then laughed. "I usually named things and then took off the names, not my job to name them, but that one I left, and it's still there, Rebecca Spring. I was in the business of tracking streams to their sources, making maps, things like that, and up until Sarah had to stay in Portland to go to school, the three of us went. Rebecca, Sarah, me. We slept in tents, stayed in trailers, falling-down houses, whatever was available." He took a bite of salad and looked thoughtfully into the distance. "Best days of our lives, and we didn't know it. Didn't know it until I was sent to Portland to work at a desk, and then, by God, we know." He looked at Sarah with a soft, distant expression. "Those were the days," he said.

She nodded. "Remember the bears up in the Blue Mountains?"

Again he laughed, and he told the story of the bears with sound effects, enjoying himself, growing younger and more vigorous by the second. The bears had come out of hibernation to find humans on the trail, and he had slung his family inside the truck, and had backed out of the campsite as fast as the machine would go. "They come out hungry," he said. "Real hungry. They tore up our gear to hell and gone. I think they ate my shoes."

"Mother and I were more afraid of the mountain road we were racing down backward than of the bears," Sarah said emphatically.

"How did you end up here?" Fran Donatio asked when Ralph finished the bear story.

"Home," he said. "I grew up in these parts. Retired here, just like I planned from day one. Let me tell you about East Shasta. Bet your map shows it about midway between California Highway one thirty-nine and U.S. three ninety-five. Most maps show it there."

Frank Donatio looked thoughtful, started to say something, then shook her head. "I think you're right."

He laughed.

Sarah watched him with great love and amusement; he enjoyed talking about East Shasta, betting with new-comers that their maps were wrong.

"Way it happened," he said, laying down his fork, settling in for some real storytelling now, "some folks came wandering by along about eighteen thirty-six or close enough, and for no reason known to man they stayed. There was a lake, and they had just come through Nevada and passed a hell of a lot of dry lakes, and a lot of mountains. Maybe one of them said, no more mountains, no more looking for water where there wasn't any. No more. Rabbit Lake must have been a pretty sight, with rushes all around, clean, sweet water, and a lot of it, forty acres of lake that attracted game, and could be used for irrigation. So this group, no more than twelve or fourteen, accounts vary, started building houses. Maybe some of them thought they'd farm, but they'd have been fools to think so. Rockiest valley in the state. Maybe they thought they could hunt and trap, or be a trading post. The old Modoc trail, that's three ninety-five now, was just twenty-two miles to the east, and another trading road where one thirty-nine is was twenty-four miles to the west. Must have seemed a likely spot to settle."

Silently Rosa began to clear the table. He did not pay any attention. "My grandfather showed up a few years later. He was twenty-six, and said he was a doctor, and maybe he was. He could set a bone, deliver a baby, stitch up a cut, the usual things. He had his pregnant wife and a baby with him. The town folks begged him to stay, even built him a house, and he became part of the community. By then it had grown to fifty-four people. My father said my grandfather talked like an Easterner, maybe even an Englishman, but we never knew; as far as we were concerned, he was Adam, and history began with his arrival in East Shasta. But he was educated. And after a couple of years he became a regular Jeremiah, from all accounts. He began to warn everyone that the water was drying up, the lake was shrinking.

And he was right, even if the town did deny it until the water got so silted up and poisonous they had to abandon it in eighteen sixty-nine."

Rosa had brought in coffee service and placed it before Winnie; she came back a second time with a strawberry shortcake, and put it down before Sarah along with dishes and forks. She looked over the table, mouthed a goodnight, and withdrew silently. If Sarah's father noticed any of this, he gave no sign of it, but continued his narrative as Sarah served the cake and Winnie poured coffee and passed the cups around.

"My grandfather knew a thing or two about geology, I guess," Ralph was saying. "Anyway, he found this site, with half a dozen strong springs, and he said he was moving here if anyone else came with him or not. My father was the first baby born in the new East Shasta. Most of the folks followed, but they never got around to mentioning the move to anyone, not the government, no one, and the old town was left without a name, to fall to pieces by the side of Rabbit Lake that finally turned into Ghost Lake." He began to eat his cake and only then appeared surprised that it had appeared.

"Ghost Lake," Fran Donatio murmured. "Why that?"

The old man snorted, whether with indignation or laughter, or both, was hard to say. "That's old lady Betancort's doing," he said. "Silly old witch. They've been around as long as the Kellermans, she says longer, but who knows? Anyway, her father bought up the whole shebang, lake, town, everything back in the late twenties, early thirties, thereabouts. He claimed that the water would come back, and he'd have himself a resort like that one over at Eagle Lake. Makes a fortune, so they say. Anyway, he died eventually and his daughter Leona inherited, and she's kept it, waiting for the water to come back, I guess. But it won't. Back in the late sixties she tried to start a commune over there, a real back-to-the-Bible-and-no-nonsense-about-it commune. She got a handful of believers to join her and promised them water, but there wasn't any water. They took out a dowser or two, but then they began hearing strange noises all over the valley. Ghosts, they said. They abandoned the attempt to build a new city of God, but the name stuck, and Ghost Lake it's been ever since."

"Wow," Fran Donatio said softly. "I wonder how many other small towns have stories like that, or not like that, but strange."

"All of them," he said soberly. "Every last one of them."

For a few moments they were all silent until Fran Donatio glanced at her watch then and said, "I should be leaving. It's a long drive."

"And I'm about ready for bed," Ralph said.

"First you have to see the pictures I posted in the hall," Winnie said quickly. "You don't have to comment, or make any decision, but you have to look. You promised," she added, grinning like a four-year-old.

Ralph looked at Sarah with lowered eyebrows. "You taught her to do that, didn't you?" He patted Winnie's hand. "Right. No commentary, though."

Virgil had said very little during the meal; he had watched Fran Donatio with great wariness in the beginning, then had relaxed as his grandfather had gone into his entertainer role. Now, as the meal wound down, the wariness returned.

They went to the hall to examine the pictures Winnie

had put up. They were possible choices for the catalog cover, she explained. In each of them a water garden was featured in the foreground, while the background changed from one to another. There was a stylized mountain, a photograph of Mount Shasta, another aerial photograph of the mountain, line drawings of mountains . . . Ralph looked them over silently, then went back to the one of Mount Shasta from the air, with the water garden in the foreground.

"That one," he said. "I like it."

Winnie nodded soberly, but then she whooped and hugged him. "I knew you would! I knew it would be that one! Thanks, Grandpa!"

He looked bewildered.

"My turn," Virgil said. He sounded almost petulant. "Come on, Mother."

"You go ahead," Ralph said, when Virgil turned toward him. "I'll wait here." He glanced at Fran Donatio. "You might enjoy this. Why don't you go with them, won't take more than a few minutes."

Virgil ducked his head and started toward the door. "Yeah," he said, "you can come if you want. It's just some night-blooming lilies."

"I'd love to see them. I was afraid I wouldn't get a peek at all," Fran said with a wide smile. "Sort of like going to the zoo and not seeing the animals. You know?"

Winnie stayed in to clear the table, and Virgil, Sarah, and Fran Donatio walked to the tropical dome along a path lighted with low, dim lamps. The light reflected off the surface of water here and there, and glowed on the petals of the night-blooming lilies; the air was as fragrant as a bordello. Inside the dome, Virgil turned on another dim light; the effect was that of having stepped into a moonlit paradise. He took Sarah's hand and led her to the far end of the pool.

"There," he said, pointing.

It was a water lily with a flower eight inches across, cerulean blue, with bright red jagged petals in the center. It stood six inches or more above the water, and was perfectly reflected on the black velvety surface.

Sarah caught her breath. "It's beautiful," she said after a moment, puzzled about why they were here, what the rest of the surprise was.

"I'm calling it *Sarah D*," Virgil muttered. "I thought it looks like you."

"*You're* naming it? What do you mean?" Sarah asked. Then she said, "You developed it? Hybridized it? Whatever you do with lilies?"

"Yeah. We'll have enough to start selling in a couple of years."

"I'll be damned," Fran Donatio said. "You mean this is the first one of its kind?"

Virgil looked uncomfortable, shifted his weight from foot to foot, and mumbled, "Something like that."

Fran moved closer to examine the flower, but Sarah could not look away from her son until she felt tears in her eyes. She put her arms around him; he was unyielding at first, then softened until he was embracing her fiercely. "Thank you," she whispered. "I think that's a terrific honor, isn't it? To have a flower named after you, I mean."

He pulled away and shrugged. "I guess."

They lingered a few minutes longer, admiring the flower from different angles, and finally they started back to the house, Virgil walking ahead of the two women. For a second Sarah saw Blaine in the figure, then he passed into a shadow, and the illusion was gone when Virgil reappeared. The air was very cold now. The moon had risen and cast long dark shadows; it gleamed on the water in the pools, brighter than the lamps that lighted the path. A bird called faintly, and a distant chorus of coyotes welcomed the full moon with song. At Sarah's side Fran Donatio began to walk faster, touched by unease perhaps, as Sarah was, by the reversion of civilization to wilderness with the passing of daylight.

At the house, Ralph met them; Winnie had gone up already. Fran excused herself to use the bathroom before her trip, and Virgil went out to bring her car around to the front of the house. The rejuvenating magic brought on by retelling stories of the past had vanished, leaving Ralph drawn and old again; he looked very tired. Now Sarah felt her fatigue hit her in the legs, in the back, behind her eyes; as soon as Fran returned, she said goodnight and went upstairs, leaving her father and Fran talking in low voices in the foyer.

Minutes later, when she dropped into her old bed, she felt as if she plunged straight through it into a deep, dreamless sleep. No twisting, no adjusting of her body for position, just the deep fall into timelessness, into the void. Then she was jolted wide awake by a piercing scream, and another and another.

She tugged on her robe as she ran from her room, down the stairs, through the hall to the back veranda. The screams had stopped, but Rosa was standing there with both hands over her face, shaking convulsively, and beyond her Sarah saw Carlos and another man pulling her father's body from the pool.

FIVE

SARAH WALKED SLOWLY among the headstones in the cemetery overlooking East Shasta. She was alone. A cool wind whipped her hair, short as it was, plastered her nylon jacket to her body; it whistled in the dry grasses edging the cemetery, and whispered in the dry sandy dirt where the grasses had withered and given up. Among the headstones and markers, between the angels and pillars, the obelisks and statuary, the wind moaned. She reached the Kellerman plots and sat on a wooden bench. Her great-grandparents were here, Matthew and Maud; her grandparents, Ezra and Isabel; now her parents, Ralph and Rebecca.

The past week was a kaleidoscope, with everything happening together, followed by vast blanks. People had stepped in, people who seemed to know what had to be done. Carlos and the workers, Rosa in the house; her father's lawyer had appeared and said he would handle all the details, her father had given him explicit instructions. The lawyer had told her the general details of the will, and what-all had to be considered, discussed with Virgil and Winnie later. Freddie Wolper had come and talked in medical terms about her father's dizzy spell, maybe even a little blackout, a fall, unconsciousness and drowning. Painless, he had said, and Winnie had fled, tears glistening on her cheeks. She had stayed away all day. When Carlos and the others started to drain the pool, Virgil had run, also weeping, to drive away with a rattle of thrown gravel, a scream of stripped gears. "It has to be done," Carlos had said apologetically, and her stomach had churned as understanding came. Uncle Peter and Michael had wandered in and out, in and out, almost as aimless as she had been, and Michael's wife had been there briefly, then was no longer there. Sarah couldn't remember where she had gone with the children, or when. And the local people had come, all of East Shasta, people from Susanville, people from the Bay area, from Sacramento . . . All week she had been surrounded, and had never felt so alone.

"Why didn't you wait another day or two?" she said silently, addressing the raw dirt of the new grave. "I needed to talk to you, tell you things, get advice." She lowered her head, remembering how tired he had looked, how troubled, and she saw the spray of roses she was clutching; she had forgotten them. He had said no flowers, a lot of foolishness to waste money on flowers, give donations to the institute instead, or the youth program down in Susanville. Slowly she stood up and approached the grave and placed the spray of roses on it, and then she turned and started back.

She parked under the poplars, out of the sun, and regarded with resignation another car parked in the drive at the front of the house. More, she thought, and braced herself to deal with yet another grieving well-wisher. She felt her own grief could not be examined, experienced yet, not until the others all were finished and gone. Then she could grieve.

As she walked toward the house a man stepped out of the shadows on the porch. "Judge Drexler?"

Being called "judge" here was so startling that for a moment she felt confused, as if he had the wrong person, the wrong address.

"Your housekeeper said I should wait out here," he said, coming down the steps toward her. "I'm Lieutenant Arthur Fernandez, with the State Police, Special Investigations." He held out his ID for her to inspect. He wore pale chino trousers and a short-sleeved white shirt; he carried a windbreaker. Slender, no more than five feet eight, he was almost delicate-looking. His hair was thick, wavy, black, streaked with pure white; his eyes were bright blue.

After looking at his ID, Sarah said, "What can I do for you, Lieutenant?"

"I know this is a really bad time for you, ma'am, and I'm very sorry to intrude, but could we sit down for just a couple of minutes?" He motioned toward a group of chairs at the end of the porch where it turned the corner of the house and joined the wide veranda, which had been an afterthought, her father's afterthought.

When they were seated, Lieutenant Fernandez said, "This sure is a pretty place, all those pools and flowers."

Sarah had positioned herself with her back to the pools. She felt certain he had not missed that. She waited silently.

"We're trying to track the movements of a woman," he said, bringing his gaze around finally to her. "Frances Donatio. Did you know her?"

Sarah shook her head. "I don't think so. What do you mean, *did* I know her?"

"She's dead, ma'am. I think she called herself Fran, short black hair, forty-six . . ."

"Oh," Sarah said, remembering, also fighting annoyance at his use of the word "ma'am" for her. He was at least as old as she was, maybe older. "Yes, I met her. She was here on Sunday for dinner. She had some business with my father earlier."

He nodded. "Do you know what time she left?"

"About ten, I think."

"And did she mention where she might be going?"

"No. Just that she had a long drive. I arrived an hour or two before dinner, and we met so briefly. I didn't really talk with her about anything, just table talk. I understood that she was a buyer or something like that, and I was very tired, inattentive. What happened to her?"

"She was shot," he said, and gazed past her broodingly. He took a deep breath. "She was a private detective, Judge Drexler, doing some work for your father apparently. Do you know what it might have been?"

Sarah shook her head in disbelief. "I told you, I thought she was a customer. A detective? I can't imagine why he might have hired her, if he did. When was she killed?"

"Sunday night," he said, and lapsed into silence again as if deep in thought.

"Lieutenant," Sarah said sharply, "stop this game! She left here at ten Sunday. When and where was she shot? Why come here now, days later?"

"Right," he said. "Okay, here's what we've got. Sunday night she ran out of gas on the old East Shasta road, about five miles in from three ninety-five. Someone approached her car, fired several shots into her through the window, took everything loose, and then started the car rolling down into a little ravine, off the road, out of sight. Thursday, yesterday morning, some kids took dirt bikes up the old road. You know, it's pretty steep in places, and rough, good for thrill rides, and they spotted her car and investigated. And called the state police." He spread his hands. "And here I am."

"The old road? Why? Why drive over there?"

"Wish we knew. That's one of the things I'm trying to find out. We got her identification through the license plates, and we traced phone calls, quite a few back and forth between her number and this one. It's a starting place."

"You said my father hired her. Why do you think so? Did you find papers in her things to indicate that, or are you guessing?"

He nodded, and a suggestion of a grin passed over his face and vanished swiftly. "Just a guess. Her office and her apartment were both cleaned out. Whoever shot her took her keys." He shrugged. "I don't have a search warrant or anything, but could I have a look at his papers? Maybe there'll be a clue about why he needed a detective."

"If he did," Sarah snapped. "And you know you can't."

"Right. Who else was at that dinner?"

She told him, and he asked if he could speak with Virgil and Winnie. "I'll see if I can find them," she said. When she stood up, he did, too, and she understood that he would stay with her, not give her a chance to say anything to the children first. Doing his job, she told herself, and led the way into the house and the intercom unit in the office. She rang the tropical dome and passed a message for Virgil to come up to the house, and then went to the stairs to get Winnie. When the lieutenant started up with her, she hesitated, then called her daughter.

"Winnie, will you come down, please?" There was a muffled answer.

Sarah looked at the lieutenant and for a moment she thought she detected a trace of understanding, appreciation, sympathy, something that was warm and cordial; it vanished and he glanced around. "Living room a good place to talk?" he asked.

"Yes. In here." She had been afraid he would suggest going out to the veranda; none of them had been out there all week. The pool looked scorching hot in the sunlight, bare, empty, a gaping black pit. They couldn't bring themselves to fill it with water, restock it, pretend nothing had happened; neither could they bring themselves to fill it with dirt, smooth it out, and pretend nothing had happened that way.

He examined the large living room with interest while they waited silently. This was the biggest room in the house, with three outside walls and wide windows on all three sides. The fourth side had a massive fireplace flanked by bookcases that stretched from floor to ceiling, with books in untidy disarray. Twin arches at the ends of the bookcases opened to the wide hall that also was the length of the house. The furniture in this room was grouped in three separate sections; a sofa and chairs drawn in a semicircle at the fireplace were the only pieces that showed wear. The sofa was covered in deep maroon plush, the chairs, also plush, were bright green, and it should have been discordant, but it wasn't. Another group of chairs had old rose-colored damask covers and looked very uncomfortable; no one ever used them. The third arrangement of chairs was almost sun-room informal, with flowered chintz covers, very bright and gay—Sarah realized that she had been examining the room as if with new eyes, seeing it as he must be seeing it. It had been a long time since she had actually looked at the room; it simply was there. Then the children came in together.

Sarah introduced Virgil and Winnie, and then sat down and let Lieutenant Fernandez ask his questions. She had steered them all to the front end of the room with the flowered chairs. Normally it was very bright in here—the sun would be hot at this side of the house—but it was almost dim this afternoon. On Monday she had closed the drapes and they had not been opened since. Not only did they not want to go out to the veranda; they didn't want to look at it or any of the ponds.

When the lieutenant shook hands with both children, again she thought she detected sympathy, and she felt grateful for it. Winnie's eyes were red and puffy from weeping. She couldn't seem to control her tears that flowed off and on throughout the day. Virgil's eyes were reddened, and he had become withdrawn and silent.

As Fernandez questioned them, told them what he had already told Sarah, and they answered his questions, she realized that they were lying, both of them. When he told them that Fran Donatio had been a detective, something in Virgil's posture, the way Winnie opened her eyes in surprise, told Sarah more clearly than words that they already knew that.

"She came about five," Winnie said in response to his question. "I didn't pay much attention. They went into Grandpa's office and I didn't see her again until dinner."

"You thought she was here to buy fish, or plants or something?" he asked. "On Sunday?"

"Is it any stranger to have a buyer out here than to have a detective on Sunday?" Sarah asked sharply.

The lieutenant inclined his head fractionally. "Good point." Then he turned back to Winnie and waited.

Winnie shrugged. "When he had open house for dealers or the public, it was always on Sunday. I didn't give it a thought."

"Did any of you touch her car? We want to eliminate fingerprints if we can," he added, almost kindly.

Virgil stiffened, hesitated, then he said, "Yeah, I did. I parked it out of the sun and then brought it back around for her when she was ready to leave."

"Did you notice the gas gauge?"

"No."

"Was anything in the car? Suitcase? Papers, anything?"

"A map. On the passenger seat. She brought a briefcase in when she got here. I might have glanced in the back, but I didn't see anything that I remember."

Virgil said he had not paid any attention to the map. All he could say was that it was folded with roads showing.

"Did you stay here after Fran Donatio left on Sunday night?" Fernandez asked, glancing at Sarah first.

"I went straight to bed."

He nodded and turned to Winnie. "Ms. Drexler?"

"I took a walk, here, around the grounds," she said.

Virgil said, "I went out in the truck. I went downtown and hung out a while, until Dacey's closed at eleven."

"Then what?" Fernandez asked. "You don't usually drive into town, do you? It's only half a mile, I think."

"I drove around a little and then I came home and went to bed," Virgil said sullenly. "Why? You think I might have followed her and shot her?"

"Do you have a gun?"

"Everybody out here has guns," Virgil said.

"Could I see yours? Are they in there?" He nodded toward a gun cabinet across the room.

"Yeah." Virgil walked over to the cabinet and unlocked it and opened the door. There were two rifles and a shotgun. One rifle and the shotgun had been used a couple of weeks ago, Virgil said, as the lieutenant examined them. Virgil and one of the guys had gone out to try to scare off coyotes, keep them away from the pools. Sarah remembered learning to shoot with the old Winchester rifle still in the cabinet.

"Anyone else have a key to the cabinet?" Fernandez asked.

"Grandpa did."

"You have a truck, and the judge and your sister have their own cars. How about your grandfather? Did he have a car? Was he still driving?"

"Lieutenant!" Sarah snapped. "What are you getting at? My father was eighty years old!"

"Just filling in blanks," he said, his expression as bland as tapioca. "Getting a complete picture. Did he drive?"

Virgil glanced at his mother, then said, "Yeah, when he wanted to. Usually I drove him. But he could drive okay. We have a car and a truck. You think he followed her out and shot her? Man, you're loco!"

"Probably," the lieutenant said. Then, placatingly, he added, "What we think happened was that she ran out of gas and stopped to wait for daylight before walking on over to three ninety-five. Maybe she thought there was a gas station closer that way than going down one thirty-nine to Susanville. Most likely someone happened to come in from three ninety-five and found her, maybe already asleep, and saw the chance for an easy robbery, first her in the car, and then her office and her house. That's the most likely scenario, but we have to fill in as much as we can."

"That night," Sarah said slowly, "at dinner on Sunday night, we talked a little about Ghost Lake. It's on that road. Maybe she simply wanted to have a look at it."

"Maybe so," he said. "First suggestion of a reason I've heard yet." He stood up.

"Lieutenant," Sarah said then, "you didn't mention what kind of gun was used."

He nodded. "I know I didn't. We'll send someone around to get your fingerprints," he said to Virgil. "You know, to eliminate them, see what we have left. Now, if I could have a few words with your housekeeper? I'm afraid you'll have to tell her to answer some questions. She wasn't willing to tell me anything, not even that you were visiting," he said to Sarah, with a suggestion of a grin softening his face. Before following her out, though, he glanced at Virgil again, and asked, "You know what time you actually got home Sunday night? See anyone while you were driving around?"

"About twelve probably, and I didn't see anyone, not

to notice. I drove down one thirty-nine toward Eagle Lake for a while and then came back."

"Pretty night for a drive," Lieutenant Fernandez said. "Big full moon and all. Thanks."

After leaving the lieutenant in the kitchen with Rosa, who was clearly hostile, Sarah returned to the living room arch. Virgil and Winnie were by the front windows talking in low voices.

"When he's gone, I want to talk to both of you," Sarah said in an equally low voice. They both looked irredeemably guilty.

She did not pause, but turned quickly and walked to the first of the two offices. This was the one her father had used for his personal affairs; the other, larger one, that used to be a den or family room or something, he had maintained for the business of the gardens. She had not been in either on this trip, until today when she had entered this one to use the intercom. Now she closed the door and stood with her back against it for a minute, almost seeing him in the great high-backed swivel chair that he had liked for as long as she could remember. When she was very small, he had given her rides in his chair, spinning it around and around until she was dizzy.

The room was crowded with a desk, his big chair, a filing cabinet and two straight wooden chairs with a small table between them. The intercom and a telephone were on the desk, as were a few papers and a magazine. She glanced through the papers: a Bureau of Land Management bulletin, a letter asking for money for an environmental cause, a postcard from Amarillo signed with an illegible name. She looked through the desk drawers, and it was the same—nothing. There was no Donatio in the file cabinet, no Fran, no detective—nothing. She found several thick files that appeared to hold every letter she had ever sent home, every postcard, every scrap. And he had kept a file for Winnie, another for Virgil. He had been so methodical, so practical, so retentive. He would have kept everything to do with a detective. But if not here among his personal papers, it had to have been something about the business, she decided, and was taken aback by the surge of relief that passed through her.

She left the office and went down the hallway to the large business office that was cluttered with two desks, a typewriter, a computer, a television, several file cabinets, a table piled high with pamphlets, catalogs, advertisements for various pond-keeping supplies ... Again she found nothing to do with Fran Donatio, but she had to admit, her search in here had been rudimentary at best. There was too much to search through, all business.

She noted with dread the amount of correspondence that was accumulating. Carlos was opening mail every day, separating orders from checks from invoices, but beyond stacking things he was leaving it alone for someone else to deal with. And her father's attorney had said they shouldn't do anything with any of it until he sent out an accountant next week.

There had to be something about Fran Donatio, she told herself uneasily, a note, a memo, a phone number, something. She glanced at the outside door and tried it and, of course, it opened. Nothing was ever locked in this house. Anyone could have walked in, taken away papers, checks, anything.

She left the office, and returned to the wide main hall

and the stairs to the bedrooms. Slowly she went up. When she opened her father's bedroom door, she felt such a mixture of resolution and guilt for prying that for a minute she wavered. Everything was neat in here; there were two pictures of her mother, one as a young woman, his bride, one taken when she was about fifty. Even Sarah could see how strong the resemblance was between her and her mother. There were two pictures of Sarah, as a child of three or four, and when she graduated from law school, already married, already a mother. There were pictures of Winnie and Virgil. She forced herself to stop studying the pictures, and began to look through the drawers of his bedside table, his bureau, the closet. There was a television but no books in the room. A few years ago her father had complained about his eyes, cataracts forming, and he had not done anything about them. Next year, he had said whenever she asked. The television schedule had programs circled for the month of June. Sarah's eyes were burning as she backed out of the room, paused in the doorway, and then pulled the door closed softly.

Virgil was sitting on the bottom step when she went down, and Winnie was at the long hall table that held a basket of cards and letters of condolence. "He's gone out, back to the sheds," Virgil said.

"Let's go to the living room," Sarah said.

Virgil stood up and walked ahead of her, his shoulders slumped, his hands in the pockets of his cut-offs, eyes downcast. Winnie trailed behind them.

"You both knew that woman was a detective, didn't you?" Sarah demanded as soon as they were together. "Didn't you?"

Virgil glanced at his sister and Sarah snapped, "No more evasions. No signals. Just tell me!"

"Yeah, we knew," Virgil said.

"What was she doing?"

"I don't know," Virgil said quickly. "Honest to God, Mother, I don't know."

"Me neither," Winnie said. "I overheard Grandpa on the phone telling her to bring everything she had found. He didn't say any more than that."

Again, Sarah thought, watching her daughter. Wearily she said, "Just tell me what he said, all of it."

This time Winnie cast a hasty look at her brother, but then she told the rest. "He said if she had enough to convince her, it was probably enough because this isn't a court of law. He said to bring everything she had and we'd give her some supper."

Court of law? Sarah could feel a distant throbbing in her temples, a tremor of pain raced behind one eye, subsided, then raced again. This was how her infrequent headaches always started, as if something in there was revving up, testing the system. She walked to the fireplace, back to the chair where Virgil slouched, to a table where she touched a deep red water lily in a crystal bowl of water. With her back to them, she said, "I don't know what your grandfather was having investigated, and I have to believe you don't either. But I want to tell you something about investigations, about how the police operate, how the system works." Now she faced them. Winnie was listening intently, with maybe a little fear; Virgil was studying his foot in a rubber thong. "That police officer is experienced," Sarah said. "He's done a lot of interrogations, watched a lot of people answer questions, evade questions, lie. I've seen witnesses

lie in court, and when I was in practice, and you know
they're lying, just not always about what. And once you
accept that they're lying, you have to treat everything
with suspicion. Everyone lies about something, sooner
or later, but when it's a matter of the law, and you know
someone's lying, or has lied, what other course can you
follow except to be suspicious of everything?"

"I didn't lie about anything except that!" Winnie said
stiffly. "And it doesn't make any difference. I still don't
know why she was here."

Sarah nodded. "I believe you, but what the lieutenant
believes is anyone's guess." She looked at Virgil. "How
did you learn about her?"

He told about hearing his grandfather ask the insurance agent for a detective, and then the phone bill with
her number, about dialing it. He told it in a swift mon-
otone and didn't look up at his mother. Something else,
she thought. There was still something else.

"And what about papers? Did you see documents of
any kind?"

"No. I told you. She had a briefcase, closed. They
went to his office and shut the door. She had her briefcase when she left. I don't know if she gave him anything. How could I?"

"I looked in both offices and in Dad's bedroom,"
Sarah said. "There aren't any papers. No notes. Nothing. Not even her name in his memo book."

Virgil shrugged, but Winnie jumped up; she looked
very frightened. "Someone came in and stole them!"

"Maybe," Sarah said. Was it the idea of someone en-
tering, stealing that frightened Winnie so much? But the
house had swarmed with outsiders every day this past
week; they had come in groups, alone, had stood and

talked in low voices, patted her shoulder until she felt bruised, wandered about. Too many people, too many opportunities to enter either office, both of them, go upstairs. She returned to the fireplace and gazed at a scattering of ashes. "Maybe he got rid of them himself."

She turned to the archway to the hall then when she heard Uncle Peter's voice, and started to walk toward the front door.

"Sarah, are you here? I want to talk to you!"

He had come into the house, followed closely by his son Michael. They saw Sarah and came into the living room. "Sarah, my God, there are detectives here asking questions!"

"I know," she said quietly. "They were here."

"What are they after? For God's sake, what is going on?"

"Take it easy, Dad," Michael said. "Sit down." He was tall, like his father, as Sarah's father had been, but there were no visible traces in him of academia. He was muscular from regular workouts, from bicycling, from running; he was taking care of his body. His hair was sand-colored, and he had the light blue Kellerman eyes, and he was deeply tanned. Uncle Peter looked old and frail and even ill next to his son.

But there was nothing old or frail about his voice then as he yelled, "Like hell I'll take it easy! Sarah, answer me! What are they after?"

"I don't know," she said, more harshly than she had intended.

"What have these kids been up to? You, Virgil, what have you been up to?"

"Nothing," Virgil said, almost as sharply as Sarah.

"The gardens here. Some hanky-panky with the bookkeeping? Something like that?"

"Jesus!" Virgil yelled. "I said I don't know. There's nothing wrong with the books!"

"He didn't tell me anything about a detective. He always told me everything, but he didn't say a word! That means it has to do with family, or he would have told me. Not a word."

"Uncle Peter, please sit down. Apparently he didn't say a word to anyone. This has nothing to do with you. Please, calm yourself. Why are you so upset?"

He did sit down, so hard and so abruptly it was almost a collapse. "He should have told me if there was trouble. We always talked things out. He should have told me what it was."

"Why is he so bothered?" Sarah demanded of Michael then.

Michael sat down also and rubbed his eyes. "It's the name. Kellerman. You know, no scandal, no rumors, no talk."

"Yes, exactly," his father said in an acid tone. "There have been Kellermans here since there was a here. And never a word. Never needed a private detective before. And now. At this time. Michael's appointment coming up. Any scandal, and you know how that goes. We have to know what he was investigating."

"Not just my appointment," Michael said quietly. "They're naming a chair for Dad over at Hayward. Fully funded for a visiting big name in biochemistry to come lecture one semester a year. He was going to announce it last Monday at dinner. We even had champagne for a toast. That's why Bernice came, that and the reunion, I mean."

Now Sarah remembered that Bernice and the children had been around earlier in the week, Bernice pale and very helpful about food, about the endless stream of guests, of mourners, but most of all concerned that her children should not be traumatized by death. The week had taken on some weird aspects of a strange social event; Bernice had taken the children home immediately after the funeral.

"Uncle Peter, that's wonderful news!" Sarah said. "I'm so happy for you!"

He scowled. "Let's wait and see if anything changes," he muttered, and then he heaved himself upright again, and began to pace the room. "That crazy old fool," he said, "what in God's name did he think he was doing?"

Sarah and Michael exchanged a look. They had played together as children, had been around each other for vacations, for family outings all their lives. She remembered walking at his side, heading for his house, complaining that her father was in a snit, better to stay out for a while. And times when it had been his father carrying on. He raised his eyebrow now and shrugged slightly.

Uncle Peter had always seemed to think that his brother Ralph was a bit simple, that he had spent his life in the woods because he was not equipped for real business, or academia, or research, or anything in the creative arts. For as long as Sarah could remember Uncle Peter had always been around to tell her father how to do things, when to do things, what things meant. And her father had indulged him, that was the only word for it; he had indulged him and then had gone on to do exactly what he had planned from the start. He had treated his little brother as if the only family derangement existed in the one who had chosen to spend his life in musty classrooms with hordes of young people who would rather have been out throwing Frisbees, or fishing, or fucking. He had said this more than once, and each time, it had been enough to send Uncle Peter away, his lips pursed, a deep frown on his face.

While Sarah's thoughts roamed, Michael had gotten up and had gone to his father to take his arm.

"Dad, Sarah's had quite enough without this. Let's go."

."All right, all right, don't manhandle me," his father snapped. "Sarah, if you or the kids find any papers or notes or anything that tells you what he was doing, call me. You have to let me know what it was, if the family is involved. You hear me? Do you promise?"

"Of course not," Sarah said, and suddenly she felt her anger blazing. Her father had indulged him, but she would not; there was no reason for her to be patient with this imperious old man. "I'll use my discretion, if I learn anything. If he had wanted you to know, he would have told you."

"God damn it! I have a right—"

"You have no right to come here and give us orders, and you know it!"

"Dad, come on." Michael started pulling on his arm.

"I told you not to do that!" his father yelled. "God damn it! Don't do that!"

Suddenly Winnie jumped up from the chair where she had all but cowered before, and she ran out, up the stairs, weeping again.

Sarah hurried across the room and went to the front door, jerked the screen door open, and she saw Lieutenant Fernandez leaning against a post on the porch. He wiggled his fingers in greeting.

"Didn't want to interrupt a little family gathering," he said.

She slammed the door. When she glanced back at her uncle, he looked drained and ashamed. Michael strode out past her with a muttered, "Sorry, Sarah. My God, I'm sorry." Uncle Peter followed silently. He did not look at her.

Fernandez waited until Uncle Peter and Michael were crossing the driveway on their way home before he beckoned a woman to join him. She looked too young to be in a uniform. "She'll get your son's prints now, if he's around."

"You know he's around," Sarah said.

"Yes. Sergeant Boyar, Judge Drexler. You'll find the young man in the living room, I think."

He leaned against the post again, gazing after her uncle and Michael. "They always walk over?"

"Yes. It's not far."

"I know. Small towns like this are funny, aren't they? I mean, you've got all this open space, no one in sight, no building, nothing but mountains and trees, and yet it's claustrophobic. Everyone's close by all the time. For instance, I heard that your son left in the truck and stayed out all one day, Wednesday, I think it was. And your daughter took off in her car and was gone all day Tuesday. Dr. Kellerman was gone all day Monday, buying tomato plants in Susanville, he says. And his son was gone all day meeting his wife and kids in Reno." He looked at her musingly. "Everyone in your family had a chance to run over to Sacramento and go through Donatio's apartment and office."

"That's insane. It's three hundred miles!"

"Two thirty," he said mildly.

"And not everyone," Sarah snapped. "I was here every minute."

"I know," he said. "I know."

The sergeant came out and nodded to him. "We'll be on our way now," Fernandez said. But he paused and looked at her. "The old man has quite a temper, doesn't he?"

Sarah did not respond.

"You handled him, though. Bet you're good in court. Know what your voice reminded me of when you put him down?" He didn't wait for any response this time. "Ice cracking and breaking. It's a memorable thing to hear, ice breaking up on a lake. You don't forget how it sounds. Be seeing you, Judge."

SIX

When Sarah reentered the living room she yanked the drapes open. If there were going to be eavesdroppers, at least let them be visible, she told herself, and then she paused, gazing at the black hole of the empty pool. The plastic would be ruined exposed to the sunlight; it would not take long at this time of year. She left the living room, stalked through the hall, through the dining room and on to the kitchen, where she knew she would find Carlos. It was after five, quitting time. One day last week Rosa had asked if Sarah would want her to stay on.

"Rosa! Please, don't leave. Not now."

"No, no. Only if you want me to," Rosa had said. She had been weeping that day.

"Everything should stay exactly the way it was," Sarah had said. "The gardens have to continue, we need you in the house."

"Not the same," Rosa said firmly. "You and the children should be together for supper, not out here like we always did. Carlos will come in and eat with me, and you and the children in the dining room, be a family for a little while. You have things to talk about."

Sarah's father and Virgil had eaten in the kitchen with Rosa and Carlos every day unless there was company. Her father had wanted it that way. When he first introduced her to Rosa, he had simply said, "My daughter Sarah," and Rosa had called her that ever since, and she had called him Mr. Ralph.

Now Sarah found Rosa and Carlos at the big oak table in the kitchen; he was drinking a beer, she had coffee. "Carlos, if you have a minute, I'd like to talk to you," Sarah said, passing them to go to the cabinet for a glass, then to the refrigerator for ice cubes. She poured coffee over the ice and took it to the table and sat down. Rosa looked at her glass with disapproval; she thought Sarah ruined perfectly good coffee that way, and she knew her coffee was the best to be had in the whole county. She had told Sarah this the first time she fixed herself iced coffee.

In his will Ralph Kellerman had named Carlos as one of his beneficiaries, leaving him ten percent of the business, Sarah and her children thirty percent each. After a moment of thought, Sarah had understood precisely why. There wouldn't have been a business without Carlos as manager. He had known, Carlos admitted to her, the day the attorney revealed this. He had tried to talk Mr. Ralph out of it, not right to give property to people not family, he had said, but there it was. No one knew how much money there would be, or if there would be any, not until the accountant did his work, but Ralph Kellerman had shared what he had.

Sarah stirred her coffee, helping it chill faster, and watched the ice cubes racing around and around. "We have to fill the pool," she said, and looked up at Carlos.

He nodded. "Yes. He would be unhappy to see it now. I helped him dig it. Did you know? The first time I worked for him was when he hired me to help with that pool, but he dug like a prairie dog right there with me. That was when I met Mr. Ralph, when we dug that pool. From that day to this, that pool never was drained."

"I know. I think you and Virgil should fill it, restore it. Did you save the fish?"

He nodded. "They are in a holding tank, also very unhappy. That is the only home most of them have known. They want to go back home." Some of the koi had been there for twenty years.

Sarah sipped the coffee; it was delicious iced. Then she said, "I think you should be the one to talk to Virgil about it, ask him to help you restore everything."

"Yes," he said. "That is right." He reached over and patted her arm. "Virgil will be all right, Sarah. I tell you this. I know he's a good boy."

"Yes," she said. "I know it, too." She took a deep breath and stood up. "I won't keep you. Thanks, Carlos. I'll leave it in your hands."

She wandered out the back door and saw Virgil and a young woman with a long black ponytail standing together near the driveway. She was holding a bicycle; they were talking with their heads lowered, not looking at each other. The woman shook her head violently, making the long hair swish back and forth; she jerked her bicycle around and got on, almost upsetting it in her haste, and then sped off down the driveway, leaving Virgil with his hands clenched, looking after her. He took a step or two toward the house, saw Sarah, and turned and walked back to the tropical dome.

Was his problem that simple, she wondered, girl trouble? "God," she breathed, "please let it be so."

She went back inside the house and eyed the stairs,

hesitated, then started up. Winnie, she thought. Next on her list.

Upstairs, she tapped on her daughter's door, waited for the invitation to enter, and opened the door. This was Virgil's room, which he had given over to his sister for her visit; it was full of boy things—posters of sports figures in action—Sarah could not identify any of them. A large poster of rocks and minerals—feldspar, mica, chalcedony . . . Album covers taped to the wall—Pink Floyd, Prince, The Grateful Dead . . . With a start she realized these were all relics from his childhood, his preteen, teen years. Blaine had given him the sports poster; they had attended a rockhound show and purchased the rock poster when he was twelve. One shelf of a bookcase held models he had made—the *Enterprise*, a futuristic racing car, a robot . . . All gifts of his father. It was as if he was trying desperately to hold on to those years, the years before he and Blaine had stopped talking, stopped reaching for each other, before Blaine had given up on him. Blaine had tried so hard to direct him into sports, into science, engineering, law, anything. It was like pushing soap bubbles, Blaine had said finally, in defeat. Beside the bed was a stand with a CD player, and a shelf of discs, and over it another poster that proclaimed in red letters: *Mapplethorpe Forever!* Over the bed was a large poster of a serene Buddha. Sarah stopped examining the room that seemed to represent nothing more than a cry of anguish, and looked at Winnie.

She was sitting crosslegged on a window seat with a view of the back property, greenhouses, the tropical dome, and beyond them, the mountains. She had a book in her hand, her finger ostentatiously on a line of print, as if she could afford very little interruption. Sarah crossed to her and gently removed the book from her hand, placed it on the bed, and then sat on the foot of the bed within reach of her daughter.

"Virgil and Carlos are going to restore the pool," she said. "And I think you should get on with the photographs for the catalog. Can you manage that?"

Winnie nodded. "If you think I should. It will be good to get back to work. I'm not used to so much leisure." She attempted a smile that came off very badly.

"Are you going to tell me about it?" Sarah asked in the same tone as before.

"What?" Winnie asked, much too quickly. "Tell you what?"

"Whatever it is that you haven't brought up yet. If I knew what, I wouldn't be asking, would I?"

Winnie stared at her, then lowered her gaze to her hands, and finally back to the scene out the window. "I don't have anything to tell you," she muttered.

"Virgil knows whatever it is, doesn't he? And were you planning to tell your grandfather? Why not me?"

Winnie shrugged. "I was going to tell everyone. It's not the sort of thing that stays a secret, but not just now."

"You're pregnant?" Her fatigue, the pallor, her nausea, the way she looked at her food . . . Sarah didn't need an answer to her question. She got up and knelt on the floor at the side of her daughter and took her hands. "Winnie, you're my child, my only daughter, and I love you very much. Whatever you do now, please, know this, I love you very much, and I'll be there."

Winnie twisted on the window seat and abruptly launched herself into Sarah's arms, weeping violently.

Sarah held her and comforted her, and remembered the last time she and Blaine had discussed their daughter. She had voiced her suspicions, and he had raged, and denied them. "She just hasn't met the right guy yet," he had yelled that night. "Mr. Right hasn't come along, that's all. When he does, we'll hear about him, she'll bring him around. My God, Sarah, you're talking about your daughter, my daughter. An affair with a married man? Good God, what next? Ask her. If that's what you think, why don't you ask her?" She would have asked that spring, but he had gone skiing in April, and it hadn't seemed to matter any longer if Winnie was happy, not happy, having an affair ... None of it had mattered.

She stroked Winnie's frizzy hair that looked wiry but was as soft as baby hair; she stroked her back and held her close until her sobs eased, her body stopped its convulsive shuddering.

"Want to talk about it now?" Sarah asked finally.

Winnie drew away and went to the adjoining bathroom and washed her face. She came back holding a washcloth to her eyes. "Back in March Virgil called and said he and Grandpa had this scheme for franchising pools, and did I want the job putting the catalog and video together. Did I? Jeez, I was down to nickels and pennies and wondering if I could afford a cup of coffee. Business is really slow, you know?" Sarah nodded, waiting; they both knew this wasn't what Winnie should be talking about, but Winnie pressed on, not really asking for comment. "So I came over and we talked it out, and I took some pictures. That's when I got the stuff I used for the cover proposal. And I made up cost estimates, and looked at other catalogs, researched everything I could think of. Grandpa was as enthusiastic about it all as Virgil was then. But when I came back everything was different. Grandpa was ... funny. He didn't have time to talk to me, or want to talk to me, and I felt it was only fair to tell him that he could fire me and get someone else if he thought I might hurt his business."

Sarah felt that somehow they had suddenly jumped tracks. She held up her hand. "Back up. What might hurt his business, how?"

Winnie kept moving around the room, holding the washcloth first on one eye then the other, forcing Sarah to twist and turn to keep her in view. In exasperation Sarah reached out for her wrist and pulled her back to the window seat. She took the washcloth from Winnie's hand. "Tell me the rest," she said, "and please sit down before my head falls off."

Winnie perched and let her hands drop between her knees. "I probably will be arrested, and my name will be in the papers, and you know how they like to find family connections. Kellerman is sure to come up. I thought it was only fair to warn him."

"Arrested for what?" Sarah demanded.

Winnie looked up in surprise, as if she thought she had already explained this part. "The demonstration. For the summer solstice. You know Andi, that's short for Andrea, she's gay, and most of our friends are, and it's hell on them, and we're demonstrating. There's sure to be some arrests. Civil disobedience, or something."

"Oh my God," Sarah whispered. Suddenly she thought of Uncle Peter, and she made a wry face. "You, I suppose, feel you have to be part of it," she said, not a question, not questioning at all that Winnie would feel that.

"Sure," Winnie said. "You would, too, in my place."

Sarah wasn't that certain. She was grateful that there had been no need to test her in such a way. She stood up, and studied her daughter for a moment. "You were going to tell Dad, but not me?"

"I was going to tell you," Winnie cried. "First him, though, because of the job, and . . ."

"Who is the father, Winnie? Does he know?"

"He knows," she muttered, and sat down on the bed. "He wants it aborted, but it's getting too late already, and I wouldn't anyway. I want the baby. I really want the baby, Mother."

Sarah nodded. "Who is he?"

Winnie jumped up and began to pace in quick furious strides. "Jackson Wilkes," she whispered, after another minute.

Sarah stared at her. "The football player?"

"Yes."

"But I thought he was in jail."

"He is, but he wasn't three months ago."

"You've been seeing him for the past three years?"

Winnie looked surprised. "Yes. At first he was going to get divorced, you know that story. But I believed him. Then, he was in trouble, and his wife walked out, and it seemed as if no one was going to stand by him, so . . . Anyway, here we are."

"Yes, here we are. He's a racketeer, Winnie. You do know that, don't you?"

"I do now. That's another one of those things I didn't believe. But none of that has anything to do with me, or the baby."

Sarah started to walk to the door, dazed and numbed, and Winnie rushed after her.

"Mother, I'm sorry. I didn't know how you'd take it. I was afraid you'd be hurt, and angry, and give me lectures, and talk about a counselor or something. Maybe even abortion. I just didn't know. When I thought of you and Dad, how you were with him, I just didn't know how you'd take it."

"What do you mean? How was I with your father?"

"Nothing. You were such a perfect wife, you know. Super wife, super mom," she said with a crooked grin that faded rapidly. "Not just that. You never got mad at him, or told him to buzz off, or crossed him in any way. And then, after Dad died, and I came home for a few days, I really wanted to talk about things, you know, but you were like a ghost, only half here, half gone. It was too spooky. Like he died and took part of you with him. I don't know," she cried helplessly. "Anyway, now it's out and I'm glad. No more pretending anything."

Sarah had reached for the doorknob, but now she drew back and faced her daughter. "Not yet, Winnie. As long as the police are still coming around and asking questions, not a word of this to anyone."

"What's that got to do with me?"

"Nothing, and I want to keep it that way. I'll have to tell Uncle Peter, prepare him, and I'll tell him to keep away from you altogether. He won't say anything about this, of course, to anyone else. But he has to be told, just in case it gets spread in the papers at a crucial time for him. It's quite a story, isn't it? Pregnant by racketeer, in a gay rights demonstration, arrested for civil disobedience. The papers will love it."

"They won't make the connection to him," Winnie protested. "He's hardly even a relative, a great uncle?

And a different name even. I'm a Drexler, even if he does seem to overlook that."

"I'll point that out to him," Sarah said dryly. She was still holding the washcloth; she put it into her daughter's hand and left her.

She went to her room, the same room she had used on her visits home through the years, but a room never really lived in, as devoid of individuality as a motel room. It was comfortable, with twin beds, enough furniture, a good closet, and an adjoining bath; that was all she could say about it, and after leaving it, she would have had difficulty describing the contents.

Now she pondered: Would the news of Winnie's child, her arrest, if she managed to get arrested, and she probably would, reach Pendleton, Oregon? Fifty-fifty, she thought, but Dirk Walters would know. Dirk had sent a telegram of condolence; he would call the week after next, it had also said, and she had put him out of mind, put his proposal out of mind. Now it came swimming back to the surface and she regarded it for a moment and said, "Not yet," as if the thought were an entity in its own right, and, obedient for the time being, it would slink back into some dim recess and try again later.

What she had to think about now was the mystery of what her father had hired a detective to do. According to Virgil he had got her name from his insurance agent, and had called her in April. But he wouldn't have hired anyone by phone, not for a confidential investigation. They must have met. Not at the house, or Rosa, Virgil, someone would have mentioned it. She would ask Rosa if he had gone to Susanville back in April. It could be, she continued, that there really weren't any papers, that her report had been verbal only; she shook her head. Her father would have insisted on some documentation of whatever he was after. If Fran Donatio had shown him reports, anything, it could be that she had taken them away again, and there never had been any papers in the house. But if there were reports, papers, someone had those papers now.

Sarah had been pacing the nondescript room abstractedly as she thought, and finally she sat down in an uncomfortable chair. Suppose, she told herself, Lieutenant Fernandez's scenario was right, and someone had driven in from 395 and killed Fran Donatio and robbed her, had burglarized her office and home. Whoever that was now knew what Fran Donatio had been working on.

Her experience as a trial attorney, following Blaine's cases first as a prosecuting attorney and then as a judge, as well as her own court cases, all convinced her that innocent people seldom were found guilty and sentenced to prison. Also, she knew that nearly everyone lied about something during interrogations; they all had things they did not want found out, and they worked hard at concealing them. Usually, if caught in the lies, they excused themselves with the explanation that whatever it was had nothing to do with the case at hand. And, usually, they were right.

She had to abandon her thoughts then because dinner was ready. She went down to join her children in the dining room. Virgil had lost some of his sullenness, and Winnie actually ate her food. Rosa nodded at Sarah with approval, evidently satisfied that she had worked this minor miracle.

Late that night Sarah came back to the line of thought she had been pursuing. Someone had Fran's papers; that person either had tossed everything not immediately negotiable, or else now had damaging information about a family member. She was certain her father would not have hired a detective for anything except the family, or the gardens. If it was the gardens then it had to involve Virgil or Carlos—family, or near enough. And it had to be bad, or he would have asked directly what someone had been up to. She could imagine him confronting Virgil: Did you at sixteen steal a car and go joy-riding? And Virgil would have said yes. Or saying to Carlos: Did you borrow money from the cash box, and Carlos would have said yes or no, end of matter. Would he have asked Winnie if she had been having an affair with someone like Jackson Wilkes? Sarah could not answer that. She didn't know.

She began eliminating family: not his two sisters who lived in Florida. Neither had come home for the funeral; one was too arthritic, and the other didn't travel. She had made the trip from East Shasta to Florida and had never made another trip. Uncle Peter had three children: Michael, Daisy, and Liza. Not Daisy, she thought; they called her the Domestic Cat, three children at hand, plumping up with the fourth, Uncle Peter had said. Liza had three ex-husbands, all wanting back in her bed, from all accounts. Sarah did not strike her name, neither did she believe her father would have been concerned with her affairs. And Michael? Maybe, she decided. Her father had been very fond of Michael, often treating him like the son he never had. Michael's wife Bernice? She shook her head, not believing for a second that her father would have cared about anything that Bernice had done in the past or might do in the future. Unless Michael was also affected by it. But Michael was fond of his wife. Sarah remembered clearly the shock she had felt when Michael confessed to her six years earlier that he and Bernice were not exactly lovers any longer, but that he was quite fond of her. When she asked if they planned to divorce, he had been shocked. "What for?" he had asked. "She likes her life; we're comfortable; and the children need a stable home. Neither of us had that, Bernice nor I, and we both think it's important." Bernice was tall, a good physical match for Michael, good genetic material for the children, who were all tall and fair and very handsome. Did Bernice have a lover? Did Michael? If so, any affair was very discreet, and outwardly the younger Kellermans were the ideal couple, the all-American family. Sarah put their domestic arrangements out of mind again, and thought of the list she was trying to compose.

Too short, she thought with dismay. Her own two children, Uncle Peter, Michael, maybe his wife. Carlos and Rosa?

She kept her own name on the list. He would have cared desperately if anything had come up concerning her, and, she reminded herself, innocent people seldom were convicted, but they were frequently accused.

And finally, Blaine. A few weeks ago she would have stricken his name instantly, but Dirk's words ran through her head: "He had help all the way." And she knew the Blaine he had talked about was a stranger to her; the Blaine she had known had done it the hard way, alone.

She had to find out what her father had hired the detective to do, find out what she had reported, what her father had meant when he said this wasn't a court of law. There had to be a way to find out.

SEVEN

ON SATURDAY MORNING Carlos and Virgil brought the cart with the rocks down from behind the greenhouses where Carlos had taken them to be scrubbed, sanitized, and preserved. Sarah stood on the veranda watching. No one spoke; Carlos and Virgil worked well together, not needing any instructions or suggestions. Virgil left again and headed back toward the sheds for a hose. Carlos pulled a tarp off the rocks and then stood still looking at the rocks, the cart, something; finally he cast a glance toward her of misery and indecision, and then reached down and picked up a big straw hat, one of her father's hats. He handled it almost reverently.

Silently he approached her and handed the hat to her. For a moment she felt only bewilderment, but then understood; when he cleaned up the pool, hauled away the rocks and plants, he had taken the hat, too. She remembered seeing it that morning, on the edge of the pool. She cleared her throat and then thanked him, and went back into the house, up the stairs, and to her father's room, where she put the hat away on a closet shelf. There was another one up there just like it. She would have to go through the closet, sort the clothes, give away usable items. . . . Later, she said to herself, and went back to the veranda.

Carlos knew where every rock belonged in the pool; some of them had supported shelves for plants that did not like deep water; some had held individual heavy tubs to keep the plants at exactly the right depth. The pump had to be repositioned, the hose reconnected to the waterfall. She watched him and Virgil for another minute or two, and then saw the burning bush of Winnie's hair, as she leaned over, adjusting her camera on a tripod at a more distant pool. Sarah nodded, and went back through the house, out the front door, and started to walk toward Uncle Peter's house.

It was a little more than a hundred feet to the road along the driveway that curved in such a way that the house was not visible to any passerby. Her father had redone the original drive to provide a little privacy. At the blacktop road, the town of East Shasta was off to her right, half a mile away, and the drive to her uncle's house was about a hundred feet to the left, across the road. She turned toward it, not hurrying, not at all eager for the scene she expected.

The old Kellerman drive went in for twenty or thirty feet, and then turned to parallel the road into town. At an early date this had been the road, but the county had come along and straightened out a crook here, a rise and fall there, and when they were done, the road was thirty feet farther north, and this section was a private driveway that went only to this one house, past it, and to the far east end of the town. She walked slowly. Before she reached the house, Michael appeared, carrying pruning shears.

"Scrub sage everywhere," he complained. "This place is a mess."

There were pines on both sides, and an understory of

sage and rabbit grass. The air smelled astringent. This was the land the first Kellerman had bought, where he had built his house more than a hundred years ago. It was easy to imagine a horse-drawn wagon wending its way home, a tired doctor nodding at the reins.

Some years ago Michael had said that if it were not for his father, he would never come back to East Shasta; it was nothing to him, a place to which he had been dragged repeatedly on summer vacations, a place that he viewed as no more than a semi-wasteland. He was staying now because he believed his father needed someone, a bit of family, for a week or so. Sarah understood exactly; they were the homeless ones, she and Michael, with no sense of place always calling them back, no sense of belonging among the ancestors in the hillside cemetery, where, she felt certain, she would be treated as an intruder.

"Is Uncle Peter here?" she asked as Michael fell into step beside her. "I have to talk to him."

"Yes. He's out back doing something in the garden, probably trying to revivify his tomatoes."

It was a family joke that every year Uncle Peter planted tomatoes and every year they died before they produced a single fruit. He always used to go back and forth so much, here, then over to Hayward, back here for a weekend. Once he had called from Hayward to ask/order her father to water the tomatoes for him, and her father had forgotten, had been too busy, or just not interested in tending them. Actually he rarely had done any of the things Uncle Peter ordered done. He had never argued about them, but had simply listened with a distant look, and then had forgotten the whole thing, over and over. Uncle Peter had blamed him for his lack of success with tomatoes that year. He always found something or someone to blame. Sarah remembered the skepticism in Lieutenant Fernandez's voice when he commented that Uncle Peter had spent the day buying tomatoes, but she could believe that. Not just tomatoes, but fertilizer, pots, supports, anything innovative that had come along during the past year, whatever he thought it would take to make them produce. And he would have shopped every garden store in town, picking out the healthiest plants, the biggest.

They had drawn near the house, a tall, two-story frame house with big rooms and several fireplaces, and not quite enough windows. Sarah's grandfather, who had died before she was born, had left this property equally to his four children. The two sisters had chosen to sell their shares to Ralph and Peter without delay, but for years, twenty or twenty-five, Ralph and Peter had jointly owned the property, although no one had actually lived here. Throughout her childhood this was where Sarah's family had come for vacation, for time out, for family gatherings; she had played all over this property, had hidden in every nook, had climbed many of the trees. It had been the same with Uncle Peter's family; this had been their vacation house also. Then, when her father decided to retire out here, he had sold his share to Peter, but only after months of negotiating; Ralph had wanted the old homestead and land, and Peter had said no, not willing to give up his retreat, an attitude her father grudgingly had admitted he understood. With the proceeds of the sale to Peter, Ralph had bought the gardens site and house there. This was still more like home than the new house, Sarah thought, gazing at the ungainly structure that was too high and narrow, with windows too narrow. They had repainted it tan some years ago, but in her mind it was white, and as soon as she turned her back on it, it reverted to white again.

She had come to a stop under a pine tree near a brush pile, Michael's trimmings, which he would not dare burn. "I have to tell you, too," she said reluctantly. "Maybe it's better to tell you first."

Michael was wearing old scruffy jeans, a tattered shirt with both elbows out, and boots; he looked nothing like a soon-to-be provost, no more than she looked like a judge, she thought. She looked away from him, not willing to witness his reaction.

"Winnie is pregnant. The father is Jackson Wilkes, and, of course, he's in jail." She drew in a breath and said in a rush, "But there's more. She's going to take part in a gay rights demonstration next month, which she thinks may result in some arrests, probably including hers. If she's arrested, she'll probably name the father for a bit of added publicity." There was a long silence.

"Boy, oh boy, oh boy," Michael said finally. "Is she gay?"

"No. But many of her friends are, including her business partner. Jackson Wilkes certainly isn't." Wilkes was serving time for throwing games and illegal betting on the outcome, and other charges all stemming from association with gangsters. A few years earlier he had been indicted for rape and assault; the woman had decided not to testify and the case had been dropped finally. And Winnie must have found him exciting, Sarah thought bitterly. When she faced Michael, he was gazing at his father's house with a deep frown line on his forehead. The Kellerman frown line, she thought distantly. Her father had had it, Uncle Peter had it. Maybe it went with the light blue eyes, the wide shoulders, broad chest, all in the same little gene package. Her own eyes were more green than blue, her mother's eyes.

"He'll blow," Michael said then.

She nodded. "He's not to say a word to her, no orders, no reproaches, no suggestions. Nothing."

"Right. I'll see to it. And tell the wind not to blow, and the sun not to shine while I'm at it."

"I won't have him harassing her now. She's got enough on her mind. Even if I have to order him to keep off our property. I'm quite serious, Michael, try to make him understand that." He shrugged. "Will this have any effect on you, your appointment?" she asked then.

He looked blank for a moment. "Why would it? She has nothing to do with me, nor I with her. She's a distant relative, that's all. I just feel sorry for the kid. Illegitimate child, single parent, I think the fun ends with the first earache, or cutting the first tooth."

Sarah started to walk slowly toward the house. "Well, he isn't likely to show any pity, is he?" she murmured.

Michael was walking with her. "It's funny, but he always had infinite patience with his students, maybe he used it all up with them. He's guided more brilliant young scientists to successful careers than anyone I know, has more big prizes among his students, even the Nobel, than anyone. Some of them have been gay, pairing up, whatever, and he ignored it all, but with his own family . . . No, he isn't likely to show much pity or understanding."

"Well, I'll go wander around back. See you later, Michael."

Uncle Peter had already watered his tomatoes and was tying one to a four-foot stake, a cruel joke because the plant obviously was dying. The leaves looked lifeless, curling at the edges. There was a big garden patch, gone to weeds, with only one small section in use, planted to squash, beans, and tomatoes. The squash and beans were fine; they always did well with neglect. He was wearing a visor cap pulled low on his forehead, hiding his eyes in deep shadows. She called out good morning, and he finished the plant he was working on before he turned to her.

She stopped a few feet away, and used almost exactly the same words she had used with Michael, but Uncle Peter's reaction was instantaneous.

"Get her to a psychiatrist! She's sick!"

"She isn't sick, she's pregnant. And she doesn't need a psychiatrist any more than most of us do."

"You'd see her ruin her whole life rather than admit you've got a sick daughter? Are you that ashamed of her that you can't help her when she needs it? Who's going to support her child? A felon? All right, let her have a bastard! She doesn't have to broadcast it! Jesus God, is she proud of herself, is that it? Is it asking too much for her to show a little discretion?"

"Uncle Peter, I had to tell you because it may be in the news. I simply wanted to prepare you for that. I'm not looking for advice."

He began to walk toward the house. "I'll get Wolper. He'll know a good discreet man, someplace where she can stay a while. Therapy, that's what she needs. Maybe it isn't too late to abort. Wolper will know."

"Stop that! You'll do no such thing!" Sarah ran to block his way. "You won't interfere in her life in any way! Do you understand? I won't have you trying to manage her life! She's not a child. And it's none of your business!"

"It's family business," he snapped. "That makes it my business."

"Uncle Peter, I'm warning you. Stay away from her. And you're not to discuss her with anyone, doctor or otherwise."

"You think I'll just stand by and let that snit of a girl ruin my son's life? Sarah, you're out of your senses as much as she is."

"Michael said it won't make any difference to his career."

"Then he lied, or he's stupid, and he's not stupid. Maybe with some people respectability doesn't matter, not to *politicians* maybe." The word was gall in his mouth, his face contorted as if it hurt even to say it. "But in some circles it counts, Sarah. And we've always been respectable. Always. Now, why don't you run along and let me get on with what I know is important."

"Uncle Peter, don't you do anything until you've had time to think about this. You're talking about protecting a name, an abstract, but I'm talking about protecting my child. Don't interfere!"

"For God's sake," he muttered and brushed past her, started up the steps.

She turned to watch him and caught a glimpse of Michael behind the screen; his expression was murderous. He vanished back into the shadows of the house.

Sarah paused long enough to say, "Uncle Peter, if

you harass my daughter, I'll advise her to file a complaint, and that, by God, will be public knowledge." She did not wait for his response, but walked away rigid with fury, at him, at herself for losing her temper, at Michael, at Winnie for starting all this. She echoed Uncle Peter's furious words: would it be asking too much for her to show a little discretion?

She walked briskly, and entered the town proper where the old gas station, which had not been in service in her memory, hugged one corner and opposite was Dacey's Tavern, with a parking lot out of proportion to the small building. On weekend nights the lot was always filled. She turned left and passed the Betancort house, one of the oldest in town, built at the same time the Kellerman house had been built. The Betancort yard was meticulous, with shrubs so precisely pruned they looked like statues, and grass that looked painted on; the house was just as rigorously maintained. It was green with yellow shutters. To Sarah's eye it looked like the first daffodils from a distance, showing color, but not yet open all the way. People said that Mrs. Betancort had married a young man back in the twenties, they had gone off together, but within a few months she had returned home, had taken up her maiden name, and never mentioned him again.

This was the nice part of town. Mrs. Betancort had fought against Dacey's and the gas station strenuously, and, some said, had cursed the gas station into bankruptcy. If asked why she hadn't got rid of Dacey's the same way, they cast furtive glances around and muttered something indecipherable. Sarah's father had said it was because the old witch owned the land Dacey's was situated on and she made a tidy little sum on rent.

Sarah crossed the old Shasta Road, which they called Main Street in town, and turned down the next side street; there were only half a dozen side streets altogether, and the houses on them were modest, one story for the most part, with human-sized lawns and gardens. At Rosa and Carlos's house, she hesitated only a second to make certain her fury had dissipated, and then strolled to the front door as if she paid a call on Rosa routinely.

Rosa was clearly surprised to see her. She opened the screen door wide and stepped aside. "Are you all right? Is anything wrong?"

"Nothing, Rosa. I just began to wonder about something while I was taking a walk, and decided to come ask you."

Rosa put her finger to her lips and shook her head slightly, but it was too late. From the kitchen came Mrs. Betancort's gravelly voice: "A talebearer revealeth secrets; but he that is of a faithful spirit concealeth the matter."

Sarah rolled her eyes in exasperation, and Rosa smiled slightly and shrugged. Mrs. Betancort came into the living room, leaning on a cane. She was a shriveled woman the color of dry ocher clay, with yellowish-streaked hair pulled back in a bun. Her hands were so gnarly it seemed incredible she had enough function in them to grasp the cane, much less rely on it for balance or support.

She hobbled slowly into the living room, peering at Sarah through slitted eyes.

"I told him. I told him. The Lord would cast him

down in the waters like the soldiers of the Pharaoh. It was my water. The Lord told me to lead my people there and He said, Behold, I will stand before thee there upon the rock of Horeb; and thou shalt smite the rock, and there shall come water out of it, that the people may drink. But he called and taketh with himself seven other spirits more wicked than himself, and they enter in and dwell there; and the last state of that man is worse than the first. Even so shall it be also until this wicked generation. And I saw three unclean spirits like frogs come out of the mouth of the dragon, and out of the mouth of the beast, and out of the mouth of the false prophet."

Sarah had taken only a few steps into the room; now she began to back up again. "Rosa, I won't stay. I'll see you up at the house."

"Whose daughter art thou? Tell me, I pray thee: is there room in thy father's house for us to lodge in?"

Sarah was shaking her head. "Mrs. Betancort, I don't understand what you're saying, what you mean. I'm sorry I interrupted your visit."

"He brought you back and you cast eyes on him and made him to do your bidding, buy me a fine house, take up the water. But I tell you yet through the scent of water it will bud, and bring forth boughs like a plant. But man dieth, and wasteth away: yea, man giveth up the Ghost, and where is he? As the waters fail from the sea, and the flood decayeth and drieth up: so man lieth down, and riseth not: till the heavens be no more, they shall not awake, nor be raised out of their sleep."

Suddenly Mrs. Betancort waved her cane before her, as if clearing the air for her passage, and she began to cross the room, moving much faster than Sarah would have thought possible. Rosa moved aside out of her way, and Sarah stepped away from the door to let her pass.

"You're not Rebecca," the old woman mumbled. "I say to you this, how long wilt thou go about, O thou backsliding daughter? for the Lord hath created a new thing in the earth, a woman shall compass a man. A woman in pants is cursed in the eyes of the Lord."

She had reached the door and Sarah had drawn back against the wall in order not to touch her as she passed. The old woman laughed. "And I say to you this, now the waters will dry up and I shall smite the rock with the rod and the waters will come forth that my people shall drink, and no more wilt he call up the spirits to moan and bewail their fate, for they shall be swept away in the floods." She went out onto the small porch and started down the first step, muttering, "And I say to you this, Behold, every one that useth proverbs shall use this proverb against thee, saying, As is the mother, so is her daughter."

Neither Sarah nor Rosa moved yet. Mrs. Betancort's voice drifted back: "Tittle tattle, tittle tattle, but know that he who gossips . . ."

She was out of hearing. Sarah drew in a long breath.

"You're shaking," Rosa said. "Come on, let's have a cup of coffee. No ice. Just coffee. Come on."

"She's crazy," Sarah said, following Rosa through the living room to the kitchen. The house looked as if Rosa had opened a Sears catalog to *Furniture* and selected an arrangement she found there: a dark blue sofa with random red stripes, a chair that matched exactly the red, and drapes that picked up the blue, a red and blue rug . . . It was very neat and clean.

"Sit down, Sarah," Rosa said in the kitchen. "I'll put on coffee. She's crazy enough." She waited until Sarah was seated at a small Formica-topped table that looked like pale wood, and then she began to assemble the coffee pot, coffee, filters . . . "Back in El Salvador when I was a little girl we had an old man who was like her. They said he was lost in time, all time was like now for him, yesterday, fifty years ago, even things that might happen tomorrow were like now. Everyone was very kind to him, poor old lost soul."

"She thought I was my mother, and Winnie said she called her Rebecca . . ."

"So it was with this old man I'm telling you about. It must have confused him to see more than one generation of the same family, so he kept joining them together, just like she was doing."

Rosa chatted as she prepared the coffee, and by the time she brought it to the table, Sarah was no longer shaking, no longer disturbed by crazy Mrs. Betancort. The coffee was steaming, and delicious, as always.

"Rosa," she said finally, knowing very well that Rosa would never ask why she had come, "I'm trying to find out why my father hired that woman, the detective. No one seems to know. Back in April did anything happen to him, anything out of the ordinary that upset him, or seemed to make him angry, anything like that?" She knew that approaching this so directly could make Rosa become as silent as a tree, or it might work the other way. She waited.

Rosa looked out the back screen door, considering. At last she slowly shook her head. "Not angry. Not that. Troubled. Very, very troubled. After Winnie left, something happened. She came in March, and they were like three children playing, laughing all the time. He loved them so much, the grandchildren, he was so happy then." Her voice became husky and she sipped the hot coffee before she went on. "Then a week, maybe two weeks, something happened. I don't know what. He told me he would go to Susanville with me when I did the shopping. That's always on Wednesday, every week, so I can get fresh fish. He knew. He told me to drop him at the hotel, and pick him up again at two. I did, and we came home, but he never said a word, not a word all the way home. Very troubled."

Sarah remembered that Winnie had said she left on March twenty-ninth, a Friday, and the insurance agent had come out on Monday, April first. Her father had still been all right then, she reasoned, or he would have asked in person about a detective. So, she continued the thoughts, something came up in the next few days and he got the detective's name, called her, made an appointment for the following Wednesday. Why meet her in the hotel at Susanville? Why not have her come to the house? If he hadn't been sure yet that he wanted to hire her, it might make sense; or if he didn't want any questions about her, what he was up to, that might make sense. Or another reason that she hadn't thought of, she added irritably. But why ask an insurance agent instead of his own attorney for the name of a reputable detective? No answer she could come up with satisfied her.

She became aware of Rosa, who had not moved while she examined these thoughts. Rosa could be as still and as unfathomable as a rock, as patient as a rock. Sarah lifted her coffee. "I can't make any sense of it," she said. "Something happened in the first week of April—a newspaper story, a bit of gossip disturbed him,

a phone call, a letter, something." She drank the rest of
the coffee and put her cup down.

"We think, Carlos and me, it must have been the telephone," Rosa said calmly. "He stopped reading the papers four, five years ago when his eyes began to bother
him. Sometimes he asked Virgil, or Carlos, or even me
what was happening in the world, but he didn't really
want to know. He had his own world. And not a letter
because Carlos or I brought in the mail every day about
ten, and what happened was late in the afternoon. I
don't know what day, but it was afternoon, not lunch or
before. Not gossip in town, because when he walked to
town it was before lunch, then he ate and took a nap every day. And one day at supper I thought something
was on his mind, something bad was on his mind. Not
at lunch, but at supper I thought that."

Sarah looked at her in wonder, and agreed with her
totally. "A phone call," she said. "That's it." For a second she wanted to ask Rosa how much of this she had
mentioned to Lieutenant Fernandez, but she held the
question back; she did not want to know. It might be
improper for her to know, because she suspected that
Rosa had not said a word beyond yes or no to any of
his direct questions, and had looked dumb at his indi-
rect ones.

Sarah stood up then. "I have to get back. Thanks,
Rosa. I'm glad I came by."

As she started to leave the kitchen, a strikingly pretty
young woman entered, carrying a vinyl suitcase. Belatedly Sarah remembered that she was Maria . . . The last
name was gone. Today she was dressed in a pale blue
dress with a matching jacket, hose and high heels;
Sarah would not have recognized her if they had passed

on the street. This was the young woman she had seen
Virgil with, she realized.

"Mrs. Drexler, I have to go home," Maria said.
"There is illness in my family. Please tell Virgil good-
bye for me."

"I'm so sorry," Sarah said. "You will come back,
won't you?"

Maria shrugged. "If I can." She moved her suitcase
out of the way. "My ride will be here in a minute, I just
wanted to tell you good-bye." She turned and went back
through the hall, out of sight.

When Sarah glanced again at Rosa, for an instant the
expression she saw was of grim satisfaction; it passed
quickly, and Rosa said, "It is sad. But she will come
back."

Sarah hesitated a moment; there was something, she
felt, that she should understand, she should know, but
she had met Maria only one time for just a minute, and
she knew nothing about her, only that Virgil was interested. She started to walk toward the front door.

Rosa went with her; she was so small she barely
reached Sarah's shoulder. At the door she said, "Last
night when we came home, I told Carlos not to worry
himself so much because you will find out what troubled Mr. Ralph, what hurt him like that. Not the police,
I told him; they don't understand things, but Sarah will
find out."

They regarded one another for a moment; Rosa
looked as calm as a Buddha, and as certain. "I'm going
to try," Sarah said.

Rosa nodded. "Yes. You will find out."

EIGHT

SARAH DID NOT have a chance to tell Virgil about Maria until dinner. When she did, he jumped up from the table, and with a low anguished cry he ran to the kitchen. Sarah half rose, then sat down again.

Winnie stared after her brother. "What's happening?"

"Don't you know?" Sarah asked, not quite scathingly. They always knew each other's secrets, she thought, why not this time?

She could hear Virgil's voice raised, then Rosa's quiet murmur, and Carlos's deeper sonorous voice, then Virgil again. She could not make out the words. She turned her fork this way and that, no longer interested in the very good food Rosa had served. Neither she nor Winnie spoke again until Virgil came back into the room, his face set in hard, angry lines, the Kellerman lines, she thought in wonder. She never had seen any Kellerman in him before.

"She's an illegal alien?" she asked softly.

Virgil shrugged, then nodded almost in defiance. "So what?"

"So nothing," Sarah said. "They don't let single young women in very often, do they? With an investigation going on, I think she was wise to leave for a time. Don't you?"

He regarded her for a long moment, then sat down again; the little-boy hurt look was back, the Kellerman look gone.

"Do you know where she's from, where her family is?" Sarah asked.

He shook his head.

"Does Rosa? Or Carlos?"

"I don't know. They wouldn't say if they did."

Of course, she thought, they wouldn't. And they would deny any irregularity, as she would in their case. As she might have to do, she added, if anyone asked her. Obstruction of justice, she mocked herself, and then she thought, some justice. She had said they don't let single young women in often, but in fact, it was so rare as to be newsworthy when they did. Talented, educated, intelligent, it didn't matter, those women of color simply wanted to come north to land rich white American husbands, and that could not be tolerated. Damn uppity women, let them stay home in the fields where they belonged— She cut her thoughts off sharply.

"Just try to be patient," she said, toying with her fork; the food now was taking on a repugnant look. She put her fork down and pushed her plate back a little. "When the investigation is over, she'll come back."

His look was bitter. He stood up. "I'm going for a ride."

"Me too," Winnie cried. "Let me come, too. I have to get out of here for a while."

He shrugged and stalked out, with Winnie close at his heels. Sarah watched them leave together, grateful for Winnie, knowing she would talk to him, get him to talk now that the secret was out. She left the table with three perfectly good dinners hardly rearranged on the plates.

* * *

After Carlos and Rosa left, the house felt desolate, and eerily quiet. She turned on the stereo, but then turned it off again. If anyone came, she might not hear them, she thought, and knew the momentary fear was irrational, but she did not turn the music back on. She wandered to her father's office and after hesitating, she sat at his desk, and searched through his checkbook until she found the first check to Fran Donatio, dated April seventeenth. A Wednesday. The second check had been written on the day Sarah arrived, just a week ago. She marveled that it was only a week; it seemed a lifetime, and yesterday. She remembered what Rosa had said about the madman from her village: he was lost in time. She shuddered, and turned back with determination to the checks. The first was for five hundred, the second for two thousand five hundred. Three thousand dollars! What had been worth that much to him?

The phone bill, she thought then, and looked for it. She found it in the utilities folder in the file cabinet in the other office. She found the insurance office number among the many calls: the eighth, a Monday, one week after the agent's visit. The call to Fran Donatio was on Friday of the same week, the twelfth.

She returned to the private office and found a sheet of paper and wrote down the dates. Something happened, she told herself, after the first of April, and before or on the eighth. His birthday had been on the sixth. She remembered a newspaper article Virgil had sent her from the Sacramento paper; a Saturday feature in the home and garden section, it had focused on the second career at his age, and the success of the water gardens.

Slowly she added the date April sixth to her paper.
Had someone seen the article and called as a result?

On Monday he had gotten the name of Fran Donatio,
but had not called her until Friday. Sarah nodded
slightly; he had been mulling it over, she decided. He
would have. She put herself in his place: first an upsetting phone call, his reaction of anger, disbelief, whatever it had been that made him find the name of the
detective, and then reflection: did he really want to follow up on this? Would it be better to leave it alone, not
expose anything that must have been very bad, too bad
to ask anyone about outright? And his final decision
that he had to find out, had to prove or disprove whatever it was.

She turned off the office light and went out to the living room, where she closed the drapes. It had become
very dark; she felt almost spotlighted, as if an invisible
viewer was watching her every motion. "So I'm Fran Donatio," she said under her breath, pacing, "a private detective, and I agree to meet this man in Susanville. I take on
the job." She paused in her pacing. He would have mentioned a name, or an event, she thought then. So and so
called and said this, or there was an anonymous call about
some particular thing. Why hadn't the person called back?
she asked herself suddenly. What had he wanted? A
threat? Blackmail? Just to stir up trouble?

But maybe he had called back, she went on, and realized how futile this was. She couldn't learn anything when
the only two people who knew about it were dead.

Presently she found herself pacing again. It didn't
matter if the caller had called repeatedly; her father had
hired Donatio, who had investigated and had brought
her findings to him. And she could not have worked in

a void; she had to have had a name to work on, an event, a date, something concrete.

No one existed in a void: there were always tax records, property taxes, credit reports, automobile registrations, police records, FBI records, a multitude of reference works from *Who's Who* to alumni association magazines, newspaper morgue indexes . . . And anyone who searched this maze left a paper trail, she added to herself. Fran must have left a trail of her own.

Her telephone bill, her credit card charges, things she might have checked out of the library, or accessed by a computer and read on the spot.

Briefly Sarah considered hiring her own detective, and discarded the idea emphatically. Already there was someone out there who knew what Fran had learned, and who might try to use that information at some future time. And it had to be bad; she felt certain of so little, she had to admit, but that was certain: whatever it was, it was bad. Not merely harboring an illegal alien, or having an illegitimate child. And, she reminded herself, Winnie had planned to tell him. She had known it would be all right to tell her grandfather, even as she dreaded telling her mother.

Wearily Sarah let herself sink down into a deep chair, one of the worn ones near the fireplace, and she thought of Uncle Peter and the honor of having a chair named for him. And Michael's appointment as provost.

And her own future, she added bleakly. Federal judge! She shook her head. She felt as if someone stood ready to pour water into sand before the eyes of a person dying of thirst, and she was that person. She rubbed her eyes, thinking clearly that someone out there had information that possibly could ruin any one of them, all of them, none of them. Not Winnie, she thought with relief; this certainly wasn't the first time; people forgot illegitimate births, single parents became acceptable. Uncle Peter had overreacted, as she had known he would. But without knowing what information it was out there, she did not dare tell Dirk yes. Not with a possible sword swinging invisibly over her.

And, she thought even more bleakly, if she were a federal judge already she wouldn't give a damn what anyone knew about her, her dead husband, her living family.

She remembered what Winnie had said about her and Blaine, called her the "super wife." Super wife, malleable, docile even. Never crossed her husband, trailed after him when he changed jobs, two steps behind him all the way, as was proper, and did the best she could with her own career. Super wife. Her lips tightened as she recalled what Dirk had said: if she were black and in a wheelchair it would be heaven.

She started when she heard the front door open and slam shut. Winnie and Virgil came into the living room; she was as stiff as a righteous Joan of Arc, and he looked pale and defeated.

"Tell her," Winnie ordered sharply. She nudged him and they came to the fireplace furniture where Winnie plopped down on the sofa and crossed her arms, glaring at her brother.

"Oh God," Sarah breathed. "Virgil, sit down and tell me. What now?"

Virgil sat opposite her on the edge of a chair. "It's pretty bad," he mumbled. "I think Grandpa was investigating me and found out things." He looked down at his hands.

Sarah felt as if all the air rushed out of her and nothing came in to fill the void. "Just tell me what it is," she said, her words sounding faint to her own ears.

"Down at UCLA," he started, "when I just got there, the first year— You know I didn't want to go to college there, or anywhere, but Dad . . ." He glanced at her, then at Winnie, who had not softened a bit. "I got in some trouble. Me and a lot of others. We used to go down to Mexico, you know, just fooling around, and this guy said we could make a little money and still have fun, nothing to it. What we did was load up a car or a station wagon or van with a bunch of kids and go down, and we'd switch people and bring home other people."

Sarah stared at him. "You smuggled in aliens. Is that it?"

"Yeah."

"What about the people you left there? How did they get back?"

"They had their passports, or driver's licenses, you know, the right papers, and they just went to another crossing and came over, and got picked up and taken back to campus. That part was easy."

"And the aliens you brought in had false papers?"

"Sort of. They were real, just for other people. No one paid much attention to students."

"Then what happened?" she asked, when he paused too long.

"One of the guys didn't want to do that anymore," he said in a low voice, keeping his gaze on his hands; they looked as lifeless as fish dangling on a line. "He said some of the aliens we brought in were doing drugs, we were bringing drugs in, and he got scared. They took him out and beat him pretty bad and told us to show up Friday as usual, or we'd get the same thing but worse."

Sarah could almost smell his fear, his shame. "You showed up on Friday?" she asked quietly. "You continued?"

"Two more times," he said. "I . . . I didn't know what to do. I thought they'd come get me, too, and they probably would have. Then I ran away." He became silent, motionless.

"Is there more?" Sarah asked.

He shook his head.

"What about Maria? Did you bring her in?"

He looked up quickly. "Yeah. Then I saw her again a few weeks later, waiting tables," he said bitterly. "We talked a little, and she told me she was in college down there, in El Salvador, studying botany, and here she was waiting tables, and that's all she'd ever be able to do. I told her about the gardens, that maybe she could get a job here, and gave her the address, but she laughed at me. She thought I was kidding, and she told me to get out of all that stuff, to leave, because they'd kill me sooner or later."

"So you came here," Sarah said finally. "Do those people know where you are? Have they been in touch?"

"They couldn't know," he said, sounding desperate. "They knew the name Drexler, not Kellerman. I never dreamed anyone would make the connection and cause trouble." He was close to tears.

But Maria knew, Sarah thought, and abruptly she stood up and started pacing the room again. From the front window she said to him, "You think that's what someone told Dad, that's what he was having investigated?"

"What else?" Virgil muttered.

What else? she echoed silently, tracing her finger on a tabletop. But this was an opening, she thought then, something that could be looked for, an event, a series of events, a bust down at UCLA; something might have appeared in print.

When she turned back to the room, she saw that Winnie had moved, all her righteous anger gone, and she was now holding Virgil's hand protectively. Another scene superimposed itself: they had started a fire in the back yard when Virgil was no more than six, Winnie nine, and when the fire department had come and gone, the excitement ebbed, Sarah and Blaine had gone looking for the two children and had found them exactly like this, Virgil looking terrified and miserable beyond words, and Winnie, equally terrified, holding his hand. There was no follow-up memory of the incident, no memory of their punishment, lectures, nothing except this one glimpse into the past. It had brought her to tears then, and it threatened to do the same now.

Briskly she said, "Virgil, I want the names of everyone who ever was connected with that scheme, everyone. And dates."

He looked at her blankly. "Why?"

She sat down then and regarded her two children. "I have to try to find out what was being investigated. We have to know. Tomorrow afternoon I'm going over to Sacramento, and I'll stay a day or two and see if I can turn up anything. What I want you both to do is stay here and do exactly what you've been doing, your work, the photos, everything you're supposed to be doing. And if anyone wants to know where I am or why or anything else, you just say I'm taking care of some business. No more than that."

"I know what she was investigating," Virgil said morosely.

"We don't know. Not for certain. Now fill in the gaps, after you left UCLA were you still in touch with Maria?"

"No. I went back to the restaurant once, but she was gone, no forwarding number, nothing. I didn't see her again until she showed up here last year and asked for a job."

Sarah did not press him about Maria. "All right, you left UCLA, and then what did you do, where did you go?"

He told it haltingly with omissions that he backed up to explain, then leaped forward again. It was hard to follow, but when he was done, Sarah felt a great relief; there had not been time for him to become involved with alien smuggling or drug smuggling during the past two years. He had come here, worked through the summer, and in the fall had enrolled at Chico State. She knew that already; she had written the check for his tuition. What she hadn't known was how he attended classes, only those few that seemed relevant to him: some botany classes, some business classes, some marine biology. He audited most of them, he said in a low voice, no grades, no credits because they hadn't allowed him to enroll without a number of prerequisites that he skipped.

He had lived here, he added, had driven over to Chico in the morning, had classes, and had come home again to work or study.

No credits, no transcript, no records, Sarah thought near despair, her relief of only a minute ago forgotten; there was no proof of where he had gone all those days he had left early and returned late. She rubbed her eyes; for days a headache had threatened, receded, threatened again, and now it had arrived with a throbbing intensity.

When Virgil finished, Winnie jumped up. "What we

all need is something to eat," she said. "Come on, I'll make pancakes. Maybe Rosa has some huckleberry syrup stashed away."

They trailed out to the kitchen, where Virgil offered to help, and Winnie pointed to the table. "You sit and start dredging up names out of that murky mire you call a mind." She flashed her quick and crooked grin at Sarah. "And you sit and egg him on."

Later that night, unable to sleep, waiting for aspirins to take effect, Sarah made a list of things to do; she always made lists, and most often left them on the table, or forgotten in a pocket, or in her purse. Sometimes she came across a list from months past, and marveled at the things she found on it, usually the same things on any current list: buy wine, dry cleaning, buy gas ...

She stopped her flow of thoughts, and added, *Buy gas.* First stop, Susanville for gas, then on to Sacramento, say five hours; she wanted to arrive before too late in order to find a motel or hotel early enough to have dinner and then get a decent night's sleep.

If only Fran Donatio had mentioned being low on gas, she thought with regret. East Shasta's single gas station had been closed for decades, and everyone had grown used to the idea of keeping extra gas on hand. Here at the gardens there was a large tank kept filled to run a generator in case the electricity failed, but not only here; everyone had gas cans. She remembered Virgil's comment about guns, and added to herself: *All god's chillun got gas and guns. Amen.*

Then she thought, if only Fran Donatio had gone out the usual way, by 139, she still would have run out of gas, but not on such an isolated stretch of bad road.

And now are we going to play blame the victim? she asked herself mockingly, and went back to her list, but her mind kept wandering, and she gave it up and went to bed.

When she finally slept, she dreamed. She and Blaine were walking hand in hand among easy rolling hills, like the Palouse country. The children had gone ahead, out of sight; they were small, the way they always were in her dreams. A wind came up and swept Blaine's hat off and it went rolling away from them, and laughing, holding hands, they started to chase it. The hat was a brown fedora that rolled like a ball before the wind. The country changed, became sand dunes that she struggled through, and now she was alone and the hat was still out of reach; although she could no longer see it, she knew it was in front of her, moving away from her farther and farther. She stopped pursuing it and looked for Blaine, for the children, for anyone. The wind whistled through the dunes and she was alone in a desert that stretched on all sides to the horizon. She began to struggle harder than ever in the sand, and then was struggling with the sheet and the blanket, and then was on the side of the bed sitting up, shivering.

"The hat," she whispered.

Like a sleepwalker she got out of bed and pulled on a robe and left the room, went down the hallway to her father's bedroom, where she turned on the light and went to the closet to take down the wide-brimmed old straw hat that Carlos had returned to her. She carried the hat back to her own room, closed her door softly, turned on a lamp and sat down to examine the hat.

It was badly stained with sweat, and the brim was

floppy on one side, and at the back inside edge there were other stains.

"No," she whispered. "Dear God, no!"

She thought suddenly of the shadows left on the walls by the victims of Hiroshima, instant snapshots. In her mind was such a snapshot of last Monday morning when she had run down to the veranda. Uninvited, it had returned over and over. She called it up now and examined the pieces of the picture. Rosa standing with her hands covering her face, her body convulsing with sobs. Carlos and another man pulling her father from the pool. He was face down in the water; Carlos handled him so gently pulling him out, cradling his head. Carlos's face tear-streaked. And off to one side, at the edge of the pool coping, unremarked until this minute, there was her father's straw hat.

When she blinked the images away, the hat seemed to re-form in her hands; she looked at it with horror. Slowly she put it down on the table and stared at her hands as if they might have become bloodstained also. She had no doubt that the stains at the back of the hat were blood, that there was hair matted in the blood, that the straw fibers were broken, crushed.

Carlos had not noticed, she thought then, but he had had no reason to examine the hat closely, not the way she had done, the way a lab would do. She bit her lip. She had to call Fernandez, tell him, start a whole new investigation. She was almost surprised then to find herself pulling on jeans. She dressed hurriedly, slipped on her sandals, and went downstairs, out the back, and toward the tropical dome. The low dim lights were spectral, the path of bark mulch eerily white, and in the distance a coyote yelped, and then a dog barked. The tropical dome was not locked; nothing here was ever locked. She went in by the back entrance, to the long work table in the center of the packing station, where she picked up a large plastic bag and a tie for it; then she retraced her steps to the house, back up to her room, hardly thinking of anything now. It was as if her mind had divided completely into halves, one part logically following the steps she must take: call Fernandez, describe the scene, state her fears; and the other part directing her actions that seemed to require no thought at all.

She carefully placed the hat in the plastic bag, tied it, found her car keys and went down one more time, out the front door, and to her car parked under the poplar trees. She opened the trunk, placed the plastic bag inside, and gently closed it again, checked to make sure the lock had caught, and then went back inside and up to her room.

After she was in bed again, shivering violently, her toes and her fingers icy, she considered what she had done, what she had been thinking, and she knew once more that she had to tell Fernandez, had to, had to . . . Dr. Wolper lied, she thought then very clearly. He had talked about a faint, a dizzy spell, and he had lied. Hadn't he seen a wound on the back of her father's head? How had he not? That other, more rational and separate, part of her brain answered: Wolper had not known her father was found facedown. Fernandez would order an autopsy, that part of her brain then said, and she turned her face to her pillow and cried like a small lost child.

NINE

Late Monday afternoon Sarah admitted to herself that she needed help. The Sacramento newspaper had given her the name of Fran Donatio's next of kin, a sister, Patricia Lagorno, and the phone book had supplied the telephone number and address, but no one answered the many calls she had tried to place. Of course, she told herself; the family was grieving, arranging for a funeral, maybe out of town altogether. Her eyes burned from hours of scanning microfiche copies of the *Los Angeles Times*, with no success; she had found no story that mentioned Virgil, any of the names he had given her, any mention of an alien/drug smuggling ring. Nothing. She had driven past the building where Fran's office was located, and again, nothing. A three-story frame structure a few blocks away from the Capitol Building and the courthouse, convenient for those most likely to use the services of a private detective. Anyone with a key could have walked in, gone up the steps to the second floor, entered Fran's office and searched it. No security, no one paying any attention. She had driven past Fran's apartment building also, and it was much the same: anyone could have entered that, too. A complex of apartments with offsets of entrances, and shrubs to afford a little privacy to those coming and going.

Now, at five on Monday afternoon, her eyes hot and stinging, the sun scorching white-hot outside, she sat in a coffee shop near the library and tried to think of the plans she had formed, the steps she had thought she might take, and she recognized the futility of her endeavor.

What had she expected, she asked mockingly, to go knocking on Fran's neighbors' doors and demand they tell her what Fran had been investigating? One look at the apartment complex had stifled any such idea. It was raw-looking in its newness, the sort of place where no one knew anyone else, she suspected, and the tenants preferred it that way. And an experienced detective wouldn't tell neighbors anything, she knew and had denied the knowledge. The library did not keep records of who used the microfiche, who read old papers, who read reference works within the building. It did keep records of who checked out what books, and the librarian had told her haughtily that it was policy never to divulge that information to anyone—police, FBI, CIA, IRS . . .

Sarah had ordered iced coffee, which turned out to be cold and undrinkable. After toying with it until the ice melted, she reluctantly gathered her purse, the map she had bought, the check, and headed for the cashier, and then outdoors again, where the heat was a physical assault. Now what? Not the library. She felt she would go blind if she tried to read any more microfiches or computer printouts. She walked toward her car slowly, dreading opening the door; it had been parked in the sun. As she neared a telephone booth, she paused, then stepped inside and tried the Patricia Lagorno number once again. This time a man answered on the third ring.

"May I speak with Mrs. Lagorno, please?" Sarah was surprised to hear her other voice, the judge's voice; it was different from Sarah's voice, she thought, sure of itself, very cool, a no-nonsense sort of voice. An impostor's voice.

"What for? More questions? Hasn't she had enough of that?"

"Just another point to clear up," Sarah said. "It won't take long."

"Jesus Christ! You want to talk to her, go over to the apartment and talk to her, and stop calling!" The phone banged down.

The apartment! Sarah fairly ran to her car and opened the door; the heat wave was like a bomb blast in her face. Gingerly she slid in and turned the key, turned on the air conditioner, and started driving back to the apartment complex. He had meant this one, she thought; he had to have meant this apartment.

Traffic was heavy, the stop lights interminable, and a trip that had taken only twenty minutes last night now took forty-five minutes. She parked at the complex in a space marked *Reserved*, and hurried to the front of the building. The main door was unlocked; it opened to a small foyer with four mailboxes, stairs going up, and two doors to the first-floor apartments. Fran's was upstairs. Sarah climbed the stairs and at the landing turned to the door marked *2B*, and drew in a deep breath to steady herself, wishing her heart were not pounding so hard, wishing she were not sweaty all over. She knocked, and when the door opened, she gasped because for a moment she thought it was Fran Donatio standing there.

The woman looking at her warily said, "Well?"

The differences became apparent: she was thinner, and a little younger, her hair a little longer . . . "Mrs. Lagorno? May I speak with you? I'm Sarah Drexler."

"I'm sorry . . ." Mrs. Lagorno said, starting to pull the door shut. Her eyes were swollen and bloodshot, with deep shadows.

"It's about your sister," Sarah said quickly. "I'm sorry to intrude now, but please."

"What about my sister?"

"I met her last Sunday night, at my father's house. She was working for him. If I could only come in a minute or two."

Patricia Lagorno studied her for another second, then pulled the door wider and stepped aside. "You saw her on Sunday night?"

"Yes. We had dinner, your sister, my father, my two children. Mrs. Lagorno, I'm so sorry." The woman's face tightened, became masklike. "Your sister died on Sunday night, and my father died the next morning, Mrs. Lagorno," Sarah said in a low voice. "I am truly sorry, for both of us."

Patricia Lagorno's face twisted and she looked away from Sarah before she said, "Yeah. What can I do for you? I'm sorry, I didn't hear your name."

"Sarah. Sarah Drexler. My father's name was Ralph Kellerman."

"Yeah, she mentioned that. She said he was old."

"Eighty."

"Look at this place! Why'd anyone have to tear it apart like that?" She indicated the apartment with a sweeping gesture, as she walked into the living room with Sarah close behind her. Cushions and pillows had been pulled off the sofa, books and magazines were all over the floor; across the room a desk had been emptied, the drawers thrown down to the floor. A chair was on its side. There was a CD player, a television, a computer on the desk. Papers were everywhere, bills, receipts, letters, envelopes, cards ... "It's worse in the office," Patricia Lagorno said tiredly. "They won't let me in there yet—padlocked, like this place was until a while ago. I looked in, it's like a paper blizzard hit."

She picked up a piece of paper from the floor, held it a moment, let it drop again. "They said after I straightened this place up again, maybe I'll be able to say if anything's missing. I don't even know where to start," she cried huskily, her face wrinkling again as if she was fighting back tears.

"I'll help you," Sarah said. "Let's start with the sofa."

Together they got the cushions back on it, and the pillows, and then they moved around the room picking up papers, stacking them on the desk, putting desk drawers in place, straightening things that had been knocked over. Now that she was busy, Patricia Lagorno was businesslike and moved with purpose, until she came to a broken vase. This time the tears streamed. She ran from the room, saying in a strangled voice, "I'll pick up in the bedroom."

As soon as she was out of sight, Sarah ran to the desk and snatched up several bills she had already separated from the rest; one was the phone bill from April seventh to May seventh, and the other was a credit card bill through May tenth. She jammed both into her purse, and then went out to find a broom and dust pan, and proceeded to sweep up the broken crystal vase.

In the kitchen a few minutes later she picked up the

flatware that had been dumped on the floor and shoved it all into the dishwasher. A few boxes of crackers and one of cereal had been pulled out of a cabinet; some pans had been thrown around. She spotted a coffee maker and filters under a mass of dishtowels, sorted them out, and made a pot of coffee.

A few minutes later, the kitchen more or less usable with things stashed wherever they would fit in, she went down the hall to the bedroom door and said, "Let's take a break. I made some coffee. I hope you don't mind. I'll just wash my hands."

Patricia Lagorno was sitting on the side of the bed, holding a lavender garment crushed in her hands, rocking back and forth. Sarah continued to the bathroom, closed and locked the door, and then pulled out the two bills and hurriedly copied into a notebook everything listed after April eighth. There was a lot.

When she returned to the kitchen Patricia Lagorno was stirring coffee in a cup. "We don't have any cream," she said.

"Black is fine."

Sarah poured her own coffee and they went to the living room to sit on the sofa and the one chair.

"I still don't know why you're here," Patricia Lagorno said. "You know, when I got here today, I just stood in the room, like Lot's wife, a pillar of salt or something. I couldn't seem to move. Thanks for helping."

Sarah nodded. "I don't know why I came, either," she said after a moment. "To talk to someone about it maybe. To ask some questions."

"Yeah, questions," Patricia said bitterly. "They're going to write it off as a random killing and robbery, like a freeway shooting or something." She sipped the coffee. "Fran was worried about your old ma—your father. She said he was too old for this kind of hassle."

Sarah caught in her breath and asked, "Did she say more than that? What kind of hassle? Anything else?"

Patricia shook her head, but now when she looked at Sarah there was sympathy in the expression; before she had been too wrapped in her own grief to express anything else. "You don't know what she was doing for him?"

Sarah explained her visit, her bad timing, her father's death. "We would have talked on Monday, but it was too late that night after dinner. I was tired, he was tired, your sister had a long trip. . . . It's driving me crazy trying to imagine what he could have been doing," she added truthfully, her gaze on the cup in her hands.

"I guess it would," Patricia said after a moment. "I don't know what she was trying to find out. She never talked about her work. I didn't want her to go into that kind of work and she knew it, but sometimes she'd say something, like this time she didn't want to take the case at first because he lived too far away, but she went out and talked to him, and said he needed someone, and there wasn't anyone out there in the boonies. So she took it. She went down to LA once, looking into something about it," she added almost absently.

She was a nurse, she said, worked nights, but on Sunday after mass she always had brunch for her two kids, her husband, and usually Fran. Fran brought nice things: good danish rolls, or fresh strawberries, papayas or mangoes, stuff that Patricia couldn't see buying. That Sunday Fran had come to brunch, she said.

"She got over to the house about eleven, same as

usual, but she stank of gas. She'd filled the car to over-flowing and she was mad because she had gas on her nice shoes. Anyway, she said she had to leave by twelve because it was a long drive, four or five hours, and I said something like for God's sake you're working on Sunday? Even I don't work on Sunday anymore. That's when she said she felt sorry for the old man because he was too old for this kind of hassle."

"If she left here at twelve she must have gone straight over to my father's house," Sarah said, per-plexed. "She drove a small car, didn't she? I saw a small car parked when I got there."

"A Mazda. Small," Patricia said, frowning. "Why?"

"They said she ran out of gas on that old road. But a full tank of gas, and only two hundred thirty miles or a little more. Maybe she didn't fill the tank."

"She always filled it to overflowing," Patricia said flatly. "She hated to pump gas, just like me. She had gas on her hands, and on her new shoes. That's why she was going on about it, they were new."

The phone rang then and they both started in sur-prise. Patricia became pale, and moistened her lips when her sister's voice floated through the room with the taped message from the answering machine. Then a man's voice came through: "Pat, you still there? For Christ's sake, come on home. Dinner's ready."

Sarah looked at her watch, after seven. "I'm sorry if I've kept you," she said. "I'll go now."

"Yeah, me too. He made dinner," she said, so softly it was hard to catch. "I've got to go, too."

Sarah ripped out a piece of notebook paper and wrote her name, her father's number on it and handed it to

Patricia. "If you think of anything . . . You know. Please give me a call."

"Yeah, I will. And Mrs. Drex—Sarah, thanks for helping. I mean it really helped me. I might have stood there until tomorrow."

Sarah walked out of the building into the sunshine, which was still glaring, still blistering hot, and stopped at the edge of the parking lot when she saw the slight figure of Lieutenant Fernandez strolling toward her, coming from the shade of an oleander bush. He was in his chinos as before, and a short-sleeved shirt. From a distance he could have passed for a college boy.

For a moment they regarded each other, his expression friendly, until she said, "If you're looking for Mrs. Lagorno, she's still inside. You may still catch her."

"I'm not," he said. "Her husband called the department a little while ago, sore as hell because we were pestering her again, and when I got the message, I thought maybe I'd better have a look, see exactly who is impersonating an officer."

"I didn't impersonate anyone," Sarah said sharply. "I asked if I could talk to her, that's all."

"And somehow he got the impression you were with the department," he said musingly. "Funny. Anyway, we came over and when I saw your car, I sent the others on their way. Told them I thought I could handle it alone," he added, not quite mockingly.

She shrugged and started to walk again.

"I told my driver maybe I could get a ride back downtown with you," he said, falling into step beside her.

"Why don't you call a cab?"

They had reached her car and when she unlocked it

and opened the door, she stepped back quickly to let the hot air out, and then glanced at him.

"I guess I could get a ride with Mrs. Lagorno," he said thoughtfully. "Maybe she'd even tell me what you asked her."

"For heaven's sake! Leave that poor woman alone. Get in." She slid behind the wheel and reached over to unlock the passenger door. He walked around the car and got in.

When she started driving he told her to turn left on the street. She looked at him questioningly.

"Short cut," he said. "You probably came by the main streets, fighting traffic all the way. This is better."

She made the turn and then another at his direction, but then, after several minutes of silence, she pulled over to the curb and stopped under a tree. "Where are you directing me? This isn't the way back to town."

"Good," he said approvingly. "I was betting it would be another five or six blocks, and two more turns before you'd notice. Just up ahead, and turn left again," he said. "And actually it's really not much out of your way."

Since she had no idea now where they were, she drove straight ahead and made the next turn, and before them stretched a park, with inviting deep green shade. She looked at him quickly, but he seemed absorbed in the scenery.

"There's a nice spot to park a few minutes on," he said, not looking at her. "Around another curve or two."

She drove to the area, parking spaces under trees, with a guard rail and then a dropoff to the river below. She turned off the ignition.

"You don't really want to get in the water," he said, "but it's nice to look at from a distance, isn't it?"

"Is this where you always bring people to interrogate them?"

He laughed. "I wish. You're trying to find out what Fran Donatio was poking into?"

"Yes, of course."

"And did you?"

"No."

"Okay. End of interrogation. Look, there's an awfully good Italian restaurant near here. Not too fancy, but good. Good selection of Italian wines. You're alone in a strange town, and you've been too hot all day and it's dinner time, and I'm alone, and I've been too hot all day, and I'm hungry. And before you say no, tell yourself why not."

She gazed at him searchingly and could not think of a reason to follow why not. Because suspects didn't get involved with the police investigating them? She wasn't a suspect, and having dinner was hardly getting involved. And he was not investigating anything to do with her anyway.

"I hate chianti," she murmured.

"Me too. You back out and go back the way we came. I'll tell you when to turn again."

"I think candles in chianti bottles are tacky."

He laughed, and she turned on the ignition and backed out.

The restaurant was not far, and it was not very large, but quite busy. A plump waiter greeted Lieutenant Fernandez by name and appeared happy to see him, and very quickly they were seated with menus before them.

Before he opened his menu, Lieutenant Fernandez said in a rush, "I'm divorced, two teen-age daughters, very beautiful, both of them, although the fifteen-year-old won't smile. Braces. They live with their mother, who is also very beautiful and who has a new man who is much richer than I am, and much better-looking, and is not a cop. I'm always broke. My daughters are named Ramona and Serena; they have raven hair down to their fannies, olive complexions, almond eyes, meltingly lovely. Ramona taught me to say that."

Sarah burst out laughing, and he looked hurt. "Why are you telling me all that?" she asked finally.

"To clear the air, show my hand. Now you know all about me."

"Oh, I doubt that very much," she said gravely, but she could feel the laughter in her throat. It felt good. And now she could see mirth behind his hangdog look. "What's especially good here?"

"Everything."

They discussed the menu, he discussed wine with the plump waiter, they nibbled on a platter of antipasto and sipped a very good dry wine that looked like honey.

"If I tell my mother I had dinner with a judge she will be pleased," he said. "She always said I could do better than I do. She thinks I hang out with lowlife. You know the saying, if you want to jug the devil you have to go to hell for the witnesses. She knows that one and uses it a lot."

"Of course," Sarah said, "if she presses you with questions and you admit the judge was female, and middle-aged, and with red hair, her pleasure might evaporate."

"I won't tell her any of that," he said firmly.

"Middle-age, what a thought. Both of us, middle-aged. Somehow I never put myself in this place before. Don't eat too much of that or you won't be able to enjoy your real food," he added, and sounded very like a father advising a child.

She grinned and picked up one more mildly hot pepper.

"Tell me the funniest thing that's happened to you in court since you've been a judge," he said a few minutes later.

"And then you'll tell me a story?"

"Sure. Them's the rules."

She thought about it, nodded, and said, "It was quite early, my first week or so. I was terribly uncertain about myself, you understand, never having been a judge before. I was watching my every move, practicing every word before I uttered it, making notes of everything anyone said, and using a tape recorder to boot, the whole insecurity bit to an extreme. So this case came up, plaintiff sued the defendant for damages caused by negligence, resulting in injury to the plaintiff. This happened on a working ranch where they also had a mountainside with veins of jasper, picture jasper, blue quartz, other valuable semiprecious rocks that they exploit as a profitable sideline. They blast the mountain from time to time to expose more of the rocks and people go in and pick through the rubble, buy tons of the material from all accounts, to make jewelry, knickknacks, clocks, you know the sort of stuff. Anyway, the plaintiff was injured following a blasting operation that he claimed was not done properly, causing boulders to fall later. One of them hit him. It all seemed pretty clear-cut at first."

She was watching the lieutenant to see if he was getting bored, but he appeared interested. The waiter brought their dinners, and they both took a bite or two before she continued. "So the plaintiff stated his case, a few rockhounds testified about the value of the rocks, the procedures they followed, a doctor testified. All the usual sort of thing. I was scribbling away with my notes, and then the last witness for the plaintiff was on the stand, saying something like he was thinking how . . . But I didn't catch what he was saying. He was mumbling, uneasy about being a witness, hurrying through his lines. So I stopped him and asked him to please back up and repeat what he had said. He looked at me and said, 'Huh?' Very nervous, more nervous than I was, if that was possible." She paused, remembering, then said, "Well, what I said to him was: 'You were thinking what?' And he said, 'When?' 'Just now. What were you thinking?' "

Sarah laughed softly. "And he told the court what he had just been thinking: that if anyone found out that the plaintiff was going in there at night and loading his truck and setting off the blasting powder when no one was around, they'd both be in for it."

Fernandez began to chuckle, and then he threw back his head and laughed loud and long. "I bet everyone was hopping," he said when his laughter died down.

"Oh my, yes! And that poor man never took his eyes off me. He truly believed I knew what he had been thinking. The defense attorney got the whole story, of course. The witness and the plaintiff had gone in the night before the injury and blasted a bit, loaded a truck, and left, and the next day sure enough rocks tumbled down and hurt our hero."

They both ate for a while. The food was delicious, as promised. Then Sarah said, "Your turn, you know."

He put another bite of pasta in his mouth, and said, "I can't top you."

"Don't talk with your mouth full," she said.

He grinned, chewed, and swallowed. "Right. We were doing undercover once, down around LA, trying to nab a gang of kids who were hitting women, grabbing their purses and pulling a disappearing act. They had it down to a real art, making the grabs in the parking lot most of the time, but sometimes at one of the entrances. So I was in jeans, you know, kid stuff, and I was near one of the entrances, keeping my eyes open, and from out of nowhere this broad—this woman slugs me. She's big, five eleven, two hundred plus, and she hits me hard enough to knock me off my feet. And she plops herself down on top of me. I mean, she could have killed me! I open my mouth to tell her I'm a cop and she slaps me, and all the time she's yelling her head off, screaming like Fay Wray." He nodded thoughtfully. "A good screamer. And I'm passing out, can't breathe, can't move. So now a security cop comes tearing up and he yells at her that she's sitting on a cop. She cuts off a screech in midstream and gets on her knees and starts to shake me like a rag doll, yelling, 'You're all right. I didn't hurt you. You're all right.' And I'm so woozy I can't even tell her I'm dying. Next thing, this broad picks me up and slings me over her shoulder and runs out of the mall, to her station wagon, and shoves me inside. Only now I'm starting to come awake and all I can think of is that I have to kill her. It's her or me, that was in my head, and she's driving like a maniac, and I'm thinking as soon as she stops I'll kill her. Only

I don't know how I'll do it. I mean, no gun, no rock, no brick, no rope, just my hands, and they wouldn't even reach around her throat. Then we're there, wherever that is, and she gets out and opens my door, and before I can even think of grabbing her by the throat, she's carrying me, for Christ's sake. She carries me into a house and puts me down on the couch and begins to make noises about Band-Aids, or chicken soup, or a hot soak in the tub, she's going on about vitamin E, for Christ's sake, and she's blubbering like a baby, a big fat overgrown baby who's scared to death she's killed a cop."

Sarah was staring at him in horror. "That's not funny," she whispered.

"Maybe not so far. I didn't think it was either, far as that goes. By then every squad car that had inflated tires must have drawn up to her house, and an army came busting in, and they found me sitting on the floor by her, patting her hand, telling her it was okay." His eyes seemed to unfocus as he gazed past her. "And then," he said slowly, "when I got to the station the next day, there were pictures. God, were there pictures. We'd been doing surveillance, remember, and there were guys with hidden cameras all over that mall, and between them they had caught every second of the action from the time she swung at me until they busted into her house. Every bit of it, dozens of pictures lining the walls, and I looked like an idiot in every single one. There I was on the floor with her on top of me, my tongue sticking out. There I was rolling with a slap, cross-eyed. In one it looks like I'm groping her, and I am, trying to find a place to get hold to move her off me. And over her shoulder as limp as a suit of clothes.

And finally one where we're sitting on the floor playing pattycake. That station sounded like we were on laughing gas for the next month. Someone new would wander in and just sort of glance at them, and then start to really look, and next thing it's rolling on the floor time."

Sarah's lips were twitching. "Why didn't you take them down?"

"I did. Three times, and like magic, back they came the next day."

Sarah was laughing now. "But that's so awful," she said, laughing harder.

"Yeah, awful." He laughed with her.

Later, he drove her back to the motel. "You've had too much wine," he said when she protested. "Wouldn't do to have a visiting judge cited for driving under the influence."

When he parked at the motel, she asked, "How will you get to where you're going?"

"I'll call a cab." He continued to hold the steering wheel with both hands, and looked at them, not her. "Like I said before, you're probably one hell of a judge, but probably a lousy detective. You assume, of course, that if someone has Donatio's results of her investigation, that person could go in for a spot of blackmail. Someone in your family might be targeted, and, naturally, if that happens we'd like to know."

She stirred but did not respond.

"The blackmailer in that event would be a killer," he said soberly. "That makes it my business." He faced her, and his own face was deadly serious. "And if that's the case, the killer might be perfectly willing to kill again."

Now she should tell him about the hat, she thought, tell him her suspicions, tell him everything. Now. She bit her lip. When he continued to watch her silently, she said, "What other case is there? An opportunistic passerby took the chance, and then he probably threw away everything except money and credit cards."

"We have a problem with that," Fernandez said. "Everywhere he went he left smudges, not prints, just smudges, the sort that rubber gloves make. Not your typical hyped-up killer or burglar." He regarded her for another long pause and added, "And he left smudges on the gas cap. We're thinking our original scenario might have been a bit simplified."

"I'd better go in," she said in a low voice.

"Without asking what I meant by the smudges on the gas cap?" His face changed subtly; the new look was not threatening, not mocking, but neither was it the friendly expression he had maintained all evening. He looked sad, she realized. "If you're jumping through the same hoops we are," he said, "you've already considered how unlikely it was for her to run out of gas, and you've considered the implications."

"Why are you telling me these things?" Sarah asked. "I was a trial lawyer for many years, you know, and I don't think any of my clients mentioned discussions like this." Her tone was sharp; she did nothing to soften it.

"I know. I know. Back when I was a rookie, life was simple. Someone committed a crime, we went out and got him and turned him over to others who would take care of things, so we could go out for the next one.

Simple. Like digging worms to feed the fish; after you toss it in, it becomes the fish's business." He shifted, placed one arm over the back of the seat, and looked totally relaxed, except for his face, and it was not relaxed at all, but looked carved. "Then things got more complicated," he said. "Much more complicated every year. The district attorney keeps a score card, so many wins, so many losses. The defense lawyers keeps theirs, wins, losses. At my end, it's the same; how many arrests, how many convictions, how much of a raise does that warrant, how fast up the ladder does it get you. Like the kids' game, *Chutes and Ladders*, remember that? Aim for the ladder, avoid the pits, and keep climbing, keep playing the game. And then, one day you're reminded it's not a game. Not to those whose heads get blown off, or the parents watching their kids taken away in manacles, or . . . You get the picture."

She nodded slightly.

"I never had the chance to ask a judge this," he said then. "Is it like that with judges? A big game complete with score card? Not wins and losses as such for judges, but what? What's the plus side, the minus?"

"Reversals," she said in a low voice. "You don't want to get the reputation of having a lot of reversals. And sometimes you might make case law, be in the textbooks, be cited in other cases."

"Ah. Fame. That's the biggie for judges? Within a narrow circle, granted, but a big frog in a small pond must feel pretty good."

"That's too simple," she said hotly then. "Some judges also try to put things right. And my God, in this country in this time, someone had better try to do it!"

He nodded, and now he removed the key from the ignition. "My starting point," he said easily. "Try to put things right. We all know that the prosecutors and the defense attorneys are biased as hell; they have to be. At my end, and yours, the rule is to be impartial. A good rule. For one thing, it gets harder when you're biased, doesn't it?"

"Now what do you mean?" she demanded, and opened her door.

"Oh, I admit to bias. Fran was a friend. At one time more than that maybe, but a good friend. I'm going to put things right for her. And I'd like to do it before you meddle too much. I'd hate to think you're finding out anything that's getting deep sixed, making life harder for us. And before someone gets the idea that your meddling could be dangerous and puts a few bullets through your head. Come on, I'll walk you to your room."

At her door he handed her the car keys. "Thanks for a nice dinner," he said, when she opened her motel door. "Goodnight, Judge."

TEN

SARAH TOOK A long tepid shower, and then, dressed in a thin cotton gown, barefoot, she found that she was too restless to consider trying sleep yet. The phrase *try to put things right* kept playing in her head, over and over until it acquired a metronomic rhythm of its own.

She thought of the things he had said, what she had said, what she should have said, and through it all the phrase *put things right* kept up a contrapuntal beat. All right, she taunted herself, so lurking under that practical exterior is a full-blown Joan of Arc complex, a need to fix the world. She nodded. Yes. A need, a real need. Egotistical, she thought, then; sanctimonious, and again she nodded. It was. But she knew she was good, better than some—better than most, she said to herself almost savagely. "God damn it, admit it, you're better than most!"

Curiously, the image of her mother flashed in her mind, how she had wept when Sarah told her she was getting married. She had wept even more when Sarah announced her pregnancy later the same year, but that encounter was not as sharply etched in her memory as the first one. Sarah had been furious with her mother; her own happiness had been overwhelming, the tears had seemed a deliberate attempt to destroy everything.

"You know what you'll be, don't you?" her mother had cried. "A tag-along wife, just like me. I wanted more for you. You're better than that."

Tag-along wife. Sarah could hear her mother's voice uttering the words in despair. What had her mother wanted to do? Sarah never found out. When she asked, her mother had shrugged and said it didn't matter. Later, Sarah asked her father and he had simply looked blank.

She had been padding around the room in her bare feet as the thoughts raced, always against the background music of the phrase *put things right*. Stop! she ordered herself. Abruptly she sat down and pulled her notebook from her purse and looked over the list of numbers she had copied from Fran Donatio's phone bill. Twenty calls, thirty, or more. Area codes widely scattered. Well, she would turn that chore over to her secretary in the morning, let her run them down, link names and addresses to the telephone numbers. Beatrice Wordley had done similar chores in the past for Blaine.

And then she was thinking of Blaine, when he first became a prosecutor, the long talk they had had about how awkward it would be to oppose one another in court. He had not asked, or even suggested, that she stop taking criminal cases, she told herself sharply; they had joked about it that night, laughed about it. But she had stopped handling criminal cases. A game, Fernandez had called it, the game of cops and robbers and lawyers, and she had been a good player, better than Blaine. She hurriedly got up and started pacing again.

But she had been better, she repeated sharply, and they had both known it; she had stopped taking criminal cases because if she had opposed Blaine, she would have beaten him, and their marriage would not have survived that.

Everyone had been surprised when she first announced that she was going into law; no one in the family had done that before. Doctors, scientists, a preacher or two, but no lawyers. Then, in the beginning, corporate law, contractual law, tax law, estate planning all had seemed as dull as accounting; what she had wanted from the start was to become a trial attorney. The excitement of dealing with real people in serious trouble, of helping them battle an inhuman system, of securing their rights when the system would scuttle them, of winning, she admitted, the excitement of winning had been a powerful stimulus, more powerful than drugs or alcohol or even sex.

But something happened; something always happens, she added bleakly. Too many lies, too many prostitutes with too many diseases, too many bruises, missing teeth, broken noses, broken arms; too many drug deals; too many beatings and knifings; too many threats and too many deals; too many corrupt police officers; too many lazy or corrupt trial attorneys; too many lazy or indifferent judges; too many juveniles in jeopardy; too many assaults, robberies, crazies, swindlers, cheats of every variety.

At first they all had been exciting, worthwhile, but the time came when only one of three seemed worthwhile, then one of ten, one of twenty, until in the end, she knew she had lost sight of the people altogether, and there was only the courtroom drama, a new opening night over and over in a production ever-changing, ever the same, and always starring her, Sarah Drexler. By then the win was all that was worthwhile. She remembered again how excited Blaine had been when he started as a district attorney; so keen on law and order, she had teased him gently, and he had said very seriously, *Absolutely*. He had been keen then, and later as a judge. He had carried his prosecutorial attitude to court undiminished and had earned a reputation as a tough judge who had little sympathy for the crooks and loved to send them away.

She had been very surprised at the difference in her attitude and Blaine's about the role of judge. He had started with the presumption of guilt every time: "They wouldn't be here, you know, if there wasn't a good case against them." And, yes, she had to admit, that was true, and most of those accused were indeed guilty, but still ... Anyway, she told herself, she knew all the tricks Blaine had used as a prosecutor, and she certainly knew all the tricks she had used as a defense attorney, and on the bench she could see others using the same tricks again and again, as if they personally had invented them. She marveled that some prosecutors didn't seem to realize that she might notice that a key question had not been asked, that she might ask it. Or that a defense attorney had failed to follow up a key line of questioning, and that she would. The jurors were not allowed to ask questions, she reasoned, and how could they do their job with inadequate information?

It made her uneasy at times to realize how disapproving Blaine would have been to observe her courtroom manner. He had believed the law was as rigid as a steel bar; if one law didn't get the desired outcome, there was a large library to peruse, another law to be found that would. She thought of law as a flexible tool to serve people and seldom bothered citing cases. Her uneasiness turned to dull helpless anger when she thought of all the political appointees, the legal hacks, the lazy judges, the inept ones, the toadies serving unnamed masters, sitting on the bench with agendas they never divulged, perusing the libraries, or, more likely, ordering their clerks to find the laws to fit the desired ends.

She suddenly had a flash of memory from the past. She had come home tired, defeated in court that day, and complained that the judge had openly sided with the prosecution. "It's not right," she had cried. "Judges shouldn't come out of the prosecutor's office."

"Like me?" he had asked coldly.

"I wasn't thinking of you," she said. "You try to be fair."

"What do you mean, try? I am fair."

But he wasn't, she had known, and had held her tongue. He assumed guilt every time until it was proved otherwise. He had earned the reputation of being a strict judge, a hard judge, but fair enough, as fair as could be expected. She bit her lip and consciously changed her line of thought.

What had truly surprised her, more than anything else, when she took the bench to serve out Blaine's term was that she was dealing with people again, the defense attorneys, the prosecutors, the plaintiffs and defendants, all had become people again. And the second surprise had been the knowledge that calling it a win/lose game was wrong, totally wrong. It was a lose/lose situation, not a game at all. They were people and most of them were hurting, and their resorting to the process of law meant that they already had lost a great deal.

If she had been honest with Fernandez she would have said that she didn't give a damn about reversals, or being in textbooks, or being cited in other cases. That was meaningless where she was concerned because she so obviously didn't think, act, or talk like a judge. No win or lose, she continued the thought, no scorecards, just people in trouble and a system that was out of control, and she was better on that bench than a lot of people would be, and she was better than Blaine had been.

The suddenness of this thought, the vehemence, stopped her in the middle of the room. "But I am," she whispered, almost as if to still the denial that already was forming.

She went to the bathroom for a drink of water. If Blaine hadn't died in that stupid accident, she asked herself, would anything have changed? She looked at her image in the mirror and slowly shook her head. She would not have changed her life, she knew, she would have continued with her eyes half open, her brain on slow forward, pretending, always pretending. If she had had questions, they had been so deeply buried she never had been aware of them, no questions, no denials, no resentment. *Super wife*, she mocked her reflection, then turned off the light and went back to the bedroom, pulled off the bedspread and stood another moment looking at the great expanse of king-sized bed.

In her mind's eye was a tiny, barren cell with a hard narrow cot, a hard wooden chair, nothing else, and it was her cell. "Get thee to a nunnery," she whispered under her breath, and then sharply, "Forget it." She got into the enormous bed.

At ten the next morning she was shown into the office of Harry Manderlay, the agent who handled insurance for the water gardens. He was almost obscenely obese, with a florid complexion, white hair. He ushered her to a soft chair, almost begged her to accept coffee, tea, something cold to drink. She felt he would have patted her hand if she had allowed it. The office was dimly lighted; he had turned down the lamps, closed the blinds in deference to her. He sat very close in a second soft comfortable chair, his knees wide apart, and his little feet pointing toward each other. His shoes were so highly polished they gleamed and reflected light with every suggestion of movement. He smelled of cinnamon and grease, as if he had only a moment ago eaten a cinnamon doughnut. The desk across the room was completely bare, without even a picture or telephone; it could have been delivered only moments earlier.

Mr. Manderlay wiped his neck with a handkerchief, wiped both hands, returned it to his pocket, and said, "Mrs. Drexler, I begged him not to cash in his life insurance. I really did, but to no avail. He was adamant. He said one way or another it would go to his beneficiaries, either as a cash payment, or as a better business, and he preferred the better business."

"I know," she said, trying to hide impatience. "We talked about it. I agreed entirely. What I want to know is what he said the day he called you for the name of an investigator. Why did he call you for it?"

His face seemed to close; the obsequious manner vanished, leaving behind, she thought, the real Harry Manderlay, a shrewd and cautious businessman.

"I don't know," he said. "I was surprised. But since this office has used the services of Ms. Donatio in the past and found her efficient and reliable, I didn't hesitate to recommend her." He wiped his neck again, then his hands. "I assumed there was petty pilferage going on, nothing more than that."

"At some point you must have mentioned to him that you sometimes used a private detective."

He shrugged. "I really don't recall, Mrs. Drexler. Perhaps he assumed that."

She regarded him for another moment, then said slowly, "We'll be reviewing all the insurance, naturally. I'm sorry to bother you now. We'll be in touch at a later date."

"Ah, Mrs. Drexler, you know we, your father and I, spent an entire afternoon going over the property, the new additions, all of it. I believe you'll find everything in perfect order. The old policy, of course, doesn't come up for renewal until the end of June, but the sooner the matter is concluded, the better. Always the best way, do it, be done with it. One more thing not to have to worry about."

"I wonder," she said. "We may want to trim expenses, do a little comparison shopping. You understand, I'm sure."

"You won't find a better deal than I gave him," he said, nearly whining. "I go out of the way for old clients, go the extra mile and then some. You won't do better."

She stood up, regarding him coldly, without comment.

"All right," he said with a motion that might have been a wave for her to resume her chair. She refused to acknowledge the signal, and stood waiting. "I told him about Fran when I was out there. We chatted a little, you know, just chatting. I mentioned a case of fraud that Fran worked on for us. That's all."

"Did you tell him she specialized, anything like that?"

"No. No. That never came up. And anyway, she didn't. She handled pretty much anything that came along."

"And when he called you, what did he say?"

He got to his feet awkwardly, but once upright, he moved around the office easily, almost gracefully for a man as fat as he was. "It was a strange call," he said, not looking at her. "At first I thought it was sticky fingers in the till, like I said, but he went on about needing someone who could be counted on to be discreet. He asked me . . ." He gave her a sidelong glance, and then went to the window and opened the blind. "He asked me if she would feel it was her duty to report a crime if she came across one." He stared out the window as if fascinated by the parking lot beyond it.

"What else?" Sarah whispered.

He shrugged and turned to face her. "That's about it. He asked if she had done things for us that were really serious, if she had been discreet. I remember he kept saying discreet. I reassured him that if she worked for him, she'd report to him and no one else, and that was it." He spread his hands. "I didn't hear anything more about it. I wasn't even sure he had called her until I read about her death in the paper, where it happened, I mean, and I assumed she had been over to the gardens."

Sarah asked him another question or two, but he added nothing else, although he repeated himself at length. Finally she left him and went out to the broiling parking lot. The weather report had said a change was due later in the day or early evening, a system moving in from the Pacific Ocean would bring cooler temperatures, maybe rain, maybe even a thunderstorm. She hoped it brought in a crashing, brilliant storm.

By the time she got back to the motel, it would be time to call her office in Pendleton, she thought. Beatrice Wordley was working half days while Sarah was gone, unavailable until after eleven. And after putting Beatrice to work, then what? She had no answer.

Had she learned anything from the insurance agent that she had not already known or guessed? she wondered, driving again. Only that her father had known he was looking into some sort of criminal activity. Virgil? She bit her lip and blinked hard.

Had her father gone to the agent instead of his attorney because he was not certain an attorney would not report a criminal act if he learned of it? Was it that easy?

In her motel room she called Beatrice, who voiced her sympathy and went on to gossip a minute or two about things in court. Sarah listened absently, and then asked her to take down the numbers, and read them off slowly. "I'll call you from the gardens tomorrow," she said. "There's a fax machine, but I don't know the number. Think you'll have names and all that by tomorrow?"

Beatrice assured her that she would, and she would have the fax message ready to send as soon as Sarah called, and they hung up.

She realized her phone light was blinking, and squinted to see why: A message at the front desk. The desk clerk read it to her when she pushed that button: *Call F about gas.* There was a number. She thanked the clerk and asked him to prepare her bill, she would be checking out in about five minutes. There was little packing to do, little to take up the five minutes she had given herself, and then, ready, she sat down and dialed the number.

She was passed through three different people before Fernandez came on the line. "You left a message," she said.

"Yes. Are you at the motel now? I'll come over."

"I'm sorry, Lieutenant, I'm on my way out. I'll be going back to the gardens."

"Hm. Judge, there are a couple of things we need to clear up, and with you here it seems now's the best time. You know. Save me a long drive tomorrow or the next day. Why don't you get a cup of coffee in the coffee shop and I'll pop in, ask my two or three questions, tell you about the gas, and then you can be on your way?"

If she said no, what would he do, send a squad car after her with sirens blaring, lights flashing? She wanted to demand he tell her about the gas, but she knew perfectly well that the carrot served no purpose unless it dangled out of reach.

"All right," she said. "I'll be in the coffee shop." And she had to get her suitcase into the trunk before he got there, she knew, or he might insist on going with her, watch her open the trunk, see the plastic bag with her father's hat ... She shook her head almost violently. Not yet!

She was eating a sandwich when Fernandez appeared. How many identical sets of clothes did the man have? she wondered. Always the same trousers, the same shirt, the same how-could-this-man-possibly-be-a-cop look.

"Ah, Judge. Mind if I order something? Haven't had lunch yet, or breakfast either, I think." He waved to the waitress.

"Busy day?" Sarah asked noncommittally.

"Yep." The waitress came, pencil poised over order pad. "Roast beef, whole wheat, milk." The waitress left and Fernandez leaned back. "You leaving town?"

"As soon as I'm done here."

"Coming up some weather," he said. "We won't get rain, most likely, but it could whip up a dust storm. You read about the mess we had with dust few weeks back?"

She nodded. "Lieutenant Fernandez, we really don't need small talk, do we? You have some questions, you said, and you said you have some information. I gather the questions will be first."

He grinned. "Tell me something about the Lister Institute."

"The institute?" she said in surprise. "I don't know more than you'll find in the newspapers, your own files."

"You know more than I do. How was your father involved?"

"He wasn't. His father was. My grandfather and a man named Oskar Zugman, or something like that, started it back around the turn of the century. My grandfather was a doctor, and Zugman . . . I don't know what he was. Anyway, it was started as mineral baths and hot springs for the treatment of polio and other crippling diseases. And they named it the Lister Institute because, the story goes, Zugman, or whatever his name was, said it would be a draw using Lister, and a handicap using Zugman. And my grandfather agreed." She shrugged. "Dossier stuff, as I said."

His eyes were narrowed as he thought about it. "But your father was on the board of directors, wasn't he?"

"Oh, that. I guess so, and so is Uncle Peter." She sighed deeply. "I'd be willing to bet Dr. Jarlstadt has me pegged for the board now."

"Who's he?"

"He bought controlling stock sometime back in the fifties, I think, another doctor, retired now or just about completely retired, but he's still on the board, still lives on the institute grounds in his own house, and oversees things generally, I suppose. I think it was his inspiration that turned the institute into a general therapy treatment center, not just a polio treatment hospital. He bought it cheap, or so the story goes, because it was nearly bankrupt. He's old, in his eighties. Anyway, my grandfather didn't stay in the business very long, a few years at the most; he didn't like being a tame doctor with his time locked up at the facility there. I think he sold his shares to Zugman, or my father sold them later. I'm not sure about this part. But my father didn't have any real interest in the place within my memory. His name was on the board, and even that was a joke since he lived out of state and never came to meetings or did anything."

"But your uncle might be more active there?"

"I just don't know. I suppose he could be. Why? Where is this leading?"

"A minute," he said. The waitress brought his sandwich and he began to eat. Sarah had finished, and nodded at the offer of more coffee. "Okay," Fernandez said after several very large bites. He would get ulcers or something, she thought. "Like you, we're really curious about why your old man, your father, hired a detective. First place you look is where there's money, real money. The gardens make money, some, not enough to get all that excited about, if you want to be honest. But the institute is in the big bucks category. So we go poking around there. And your father's name does seem to be linked to it."

She never had thought about it one way or the other; the institute was just there, the way Ghost Lake was there, the ghost town was there, part of the landscape. After the Salk vaccine came along and the number of polio cases started to dwindle, there had been a crisis at the institute, she remembered, although she did not know the details, just the general story. Reacting to the danger of bankruptcy, they had switched their focus onto patients with disabling diseases and injuries—stroke patients, burn patients, congenital deformities—and these patients or their families were mostly wealthy enough to afford very expensive treatments, sometimes for prolonged periods. There was a large staff, she knew, and several very good doctors, therapists, nurses. Some of the staff lived in East Shasta; more, she believed, lived in housing on the grounds. The institute had an impeccable reputation. She told Fernandez what she remembered about it, adding details when she thought of them, as he ate his lunch; at length he held up his hand for coffee.

"Is that it?" she asked, when she could think of nothing else connected with the institute.

"I suppose. See, you knew more than I did. Your name is on the board. Non-paying position?"

"No doubt. And apparently they think they don't need anyone's permission to include them. Next topic?"

"A minor point," he said almost apologetically.

"How'd your father get Fran's name? Who recommended her? Not his lawyer, I asked him."

Trick question? she wondered. Manderlay had not got in touch with the police, and there really had been no reason for him to do so, he surely would argue, but now, after her visit, not knowing what she might do, it seemed inevitable that he would call the police. He would worry first, sweat a lot, start to call, back off, but he would make the call to protect himself in the event that Sarah divulged his name. Let him sweat, she said to herself, and told the lieutenant about him. She doubted that the insurance agent would be as open with the police as he finally had been with her. What did they have to threaten him with?

"Get anything useful from him?" Fernandez asked.

She shook her head. "He doesn't know what the problem was."

"Okay. About the gas tank. We got the report this morning. Tank's intact, in perfect shape, cap fits perfectly. No leaks. And the car's equipped with an idiot light that comes on when the gas gets below two gallons. It works just exactly the way it should."

"Two gallons," she said frowning. "That should have been enough for fifty miles at least. She should have made it out to three ninety-five unless it was already blinking when she arrived. But that doesn't make any sense, either. Wouldn't she have mentioned that she needed gas?"

"Would you start off on a strange road late at night with an idiot light blinking at you?" Fernandez asked.

"No, of course not."

"Neither would Fran," he said softly.

Sarah considered it. After leaving the house Sunday

night Fran could have driven for a few miles before the light came on and then she would have had to decide, keep going to 395 where there might be a gas station within her range, say fifty miles; from East Shasta to 395 was about forty-six, forty-eight miles. Close, but she must already have covered part of the distance before the light came on. It would have been Sarah's choice to keep going. The alternative had been to return to East Shasta, head down 139 and run out of gas on that stretch. By 139, it was seventy miles to Susanville and a gas station. And Fran had known that; she had driven in that way. Would it have occurred to her to ask if anyone had extra gas at the house? Probably not. When had she noticed how low it was? How far had she gone? It seemed terribly irresponsible not to know how much gas was in the tank, especially driving in a near-wilderness area at night.

"The light must have malfunctioned," Sarah said finally. "Obviously she didn't have as much gas when it came on as she thought she did, or else she sat with her engine idling until it ran dry, and that's insane."

"We think so," Fernandez said. "System checked out okay. Well, back to work. Oh, by the way, how long did it take you to drive over from the gardens?"

"I didn't notice," she said; he grinned. It had taken her four hours and five minutes. And she could have trimmed that if she had wanted to.

"I made it in three hours, twenty minutes," he said. "Be seeing you, Judge."

Fran must have taken nearly five hours on a Sunday afternoon, but late at night, before dawn, any weekday it would be faster. Fernandez was still thinking someone from East Shasta had driven over to search Fran's office and house. Timing it. He would be back over there asking questions again, she thought, and she still had the straw hat in her trunk, and still couldn't think of anything else to do with it, any other place to keep it safe.

She remembered what he had said last night: he didn't want a visiting judge cited for driving under the influence. How about obstruction of justice? she asked herself bitterly. And swiftly followed the question with another: whose justice? She had been a debater once, taking the position that justice not only could not be achieved, but also that few people really desired it. We pay lip service, she thought. But it was a good question: whose justice? The Ku Klux Klan's; the Ayatollah's in condemning Rushdie; the interrogators' of Central and South America with their torture instruments ... the justice Anita Hill found before the senatorial inquisitors? The justice Rodney King found in Simi Valley? In each and every case the dispensers of justice could rationalize their position, justify, explain; each was seeking justice. She had concluded her argument that day in her debate: we make laws and claim to enforce them with impartiality, but even then we know that those who are weak are not permitted to legislate power to themselves, away from those who are strong. So how can those laws reflect a true justice that serves everyone impartially? In fact, there is no true justice, only an ideal.

So, if she was obstructing justice, what exactly was she guilty of? It would not be justice if she pointed a finger at Virgil. He was so guilt-possessed, so ashamed, so filled with self-loathing, he would be judged guilty before he said a word; an accusation of murder or anything else would be all that was required. Protecting the innocent could not be equated with obstruction of justice, she told herself, and knew she was rationalizing.

Not much longer, she promised herself then. Tomorrow she would get the list of names and try to make sense of them. If they were unknown to Virgil, had nothing to do with his past crimes—she winced at the word, and repeated it—crimes, then she would look up those people, try to learn what their connection had been with her father. And she would tell Fernandez about the hat. Eventually she would tell him that she was reasonably certain that her own father had been murdered also. And if the names were connected to Virgil in any way? She knew she could not decide. Her father, her son. She knew, she reminded herself, that Virgil would never have harmed his grandfather. She was as certain of that as of her own innocence, but Fernandez, his officers, the system couldn't know that, and Virgil could be arrested, could be tried, could be found guilty, all because he had done such stupid things in the past. She knew very well the tenor of the times, the crusade to get the drug dealers, especially at his level and below. If you could not get them for drugs, you got them for something else, Blaine had said positively. She knew he had voiced a position that few in the system would argue with. And she knew that if handing over the hat meant she was handing over her son, she would keep the hat until hell froze.

She was back in the car, driving away from Sacramento; the wind had started to blow fitfully, stirring clouds of pale dust, making the air thick and visible. It entered her car freely in spite of the closed windows, the air conditioner. The dust was as fine as talc and stung her eyes.

Why didn't he go ahead and ask that one question that must be uppermost on his mind? Playing with her, pretending an openness that was really a bait to entrap her? He would ask it sooner or later, she understood quite well: why would anyone have killed Fran Donatio and burglarized her house for the information she already had passed on to Ralph Kellerman? Unless that person knew Ralph Kellerman would conceal or even deny the information, or else that person knew that Ralph would not live long enough to do anything about it.

Her hands were so tight on the wheel that it was hard to keep from oversteering. She relaxed, and slowed down; the dust churned up dust devils in a field to her left. Traffic got crazy as people raced to beat the rain, raced to beat blinding dust storms, raced to beat the slurry that would form if only a skim of rain fell. Sarah raced along with everyone else, and when she reached Susanville, the dust and the winds were far behind her on the other side of the mountain; she had been driving for two and a half hours, with another hour to go to the gardens.

Anyone could have driven over and back in a day, an overnight trip. Any one of them.

ELEVEN

She bought gas in Susanville, but instead of heading north on 139, she continued east and then north on 395. The highway followed the lowlands in the shadow of the mountains all the way into Oregon. Her knowledge of the road was based entirely on her map; she had never driven it, and was not certain where the turn was to East Shasta, or if the road was even marked. It was about fifty-five miles according to her map, which was admittedly not reliable; it showed East Shasta where the ghost town was today. A farm truck came from nowhere and passed her, dropping potatoes that hit the road and spattered. She slowed down until the truck vanished in the distance. She strained to see a turn-off ahead.

It was marked with a county road number, not a name; she passed it, stopped after another few hundred yards to consult her map, and then turned around to approach the intersecting road again, and this time made the turn. Five miles from 395, Fernandez had said. She made a note of the odometer reading: 38542. 43: the land began to rise as soon as she left the highway; it seemed to twist and turn its way as straight up the mountain as a road could manage, hairpin curves, steep climbs, switch backs. 44: there was sparse, desertlike growth here; dusty, scattered, stunted trees, gray-green

159

understory sage, brown grass, cactus ... The steepness of the dropoff increased, a sheer fall down fifty feet, a hundred feet, two hundred feet, and no guard rail ... Finally, five miles in, she slowed, stopped the car, pulled on the hand brake, and then got out to stand in the road. That was where Fran's Mazda had gone over the side, she thought, noting a line of broken and twisted weedy growth, sage, grasses, destroyed by the car rolling over them. Not destroyed, she realized, moving closer; it would recover. The human had been destroyed, the wildlife would come back.

She looked at the place where Fran must have rolled to a stop on a fairly steep section with a sharp curve several feet ahead. Fran must not have known how close she was to the highway. She remembered the look of apprehension that had crossed Fran's face when they heard the coyote on Sunday night. Out here, she must have felt she was at the end of the world, and even though the moon had been full and brilliant, she would have been reluctant to leave the safety of the car.

Anyone coming in from 395 would have been startled, coming around that sharp curve, suddenly to be confronted with another car dead ahead. The other driver might have pulled over too fast, grazed a rock or a tree ... She did not move to examine the rocks and the few trees that could have been at risk. She felt almost certain that the car had not come from that direction.

Back the other direction then, from East Shasta, someone could have come down the hill carefully, knowing very well that Fran's car was ahead, out of gas, not precisely where it was, only that it was stopped, waiting. She realized that she was making the assumption that the killer had done something to Fran's gas tank, siphoned out gas, something. She shook her head irritably. And Fran didn't notice the idiot light blinking? Either it had been in working order and she should have reached the highway, or it had malfunctioned, and cured itself before the police could test it. It did not matter, she told herself sharply; he did not have to know where she would be stopped, only that she would be on the road out of gas somewhere. Let Fernandez worry about the idiot light.

There was no good place to turn around, Sarah realized, standing in the center of the narrow road, looking first one way, then the other. With a lot of backing and filling, a U-turn was possible, but he would have marked his car, brushed the hillside, scarred the paint on a rock. Had Fernandez considered that? Or else he must have stopped up there somewhere, come the rest of the way on foot.

She started driving again, going very slowly now, upward, toward East Shasta, watching for a place to stop and survey the scene below. She found it very soon, a wide enough stretch to park in, high enough to give a good view of the road below where Fran's car must have been waiting in the cold indifferent moonlight. Less than half a mile. She could imagine Fernandez and his men spreading out over the sides of the road, above it, down the steep bank, searching for rubber gloves, for an emptied purse, a gun, anything to lead to a killer.

There would have been shattered glass, she thought, glass fragments on Fran's purse, her briefcase, embedded in the killer's clothes. Bloodstains on his clothes? She thought of the plastic bag in her trunk, and another picture came to mind: the killer could have dressed in a throw-away garment of some sort, a cheap plastic raincoat, or even just a sheet draped over him, and, of course, the gloves; he would have carried a plastic bag, a garment bag, something to put things in. If he was clever enough to arrange for Fran to run out of gas, wouldn't he have thought of that? A leaf bag, a yard trash bag, something of that sort; they all used them. No one dared burn anything for fear of wildfire. A packing bag like the one in her trunk. She bit her lip.

She drove again, up the tortuous road that climbed, climbed, twisted, often crumbled near the edges, sometimes so rotten it seemed no road had ever existed here, only a narrow clearing through the rocks and scrub growth; other times the blacktop appeared nearly intact. The sun was getting low; when she straightened out of a curve and found herself heading west, the sun was cruel against her eyes.

Then she reached the old ghost town, and stopped again but did not leave the car, or even turn off the motor. Pale Ghost Lake with its whispering sand at her left, edged with a cliff on the far side; the ruins of the town on her right, and then the other barrier cliff with a fringe of fallen rocks at its base. Her father had said that at one time this entire valley had been a lake, a mile wide, three miles long, back when the glaciers started melting. There must have been a dam, he had said, ice dam maybe, or rocks, or maybe just an earthen dam, and when it gave way, a flood poured from the valley like water running out of a bathtub, leaving behind the shallow lake. On the far side, lapping the opposite cliff, the lake had lingered for thousands of years, shrinking year after year, century after century. He had shown her the ravages still visible from swiftly moving water wielding rocks and trees that had scoured and gouged the land in passing, leaving their marks.

The lake had been formed by runoff water, a product of the melting of the last ice age, he had said; it had not been spring-fed. Drying up had been a foregone conclusion, a necessity. Mrs. Betancort, he had said, had hired a hydrologist to find water for her commune, and when he failed, she had fired him and brought in a water dowser. If the ghosts hadn't run them all off, she would have had to fire him, too. Mrs. Betancort claimed that Moses had been a dowser, he had said, laughing, but not even Moses could find water where there wasn't any.

Driving again, Sarah tried to remember just what Mrs. Betancort had said in Rosa's house. She had been talking about the ghost town, Sarah realized, about her dowser who would smite the rock and bring forth water. If you knew what she was talking about it didn't sound quite so crazy, but that was going about communicating backwards. First you know, then you listen to confirm what you know? Crazy or not, she found herself wishing she had paid more attention to Mrs. Betancort's words; she had an uneasy suspicion that there had been other sense-making bits mixed in with the madness.

As she drove through East Shasta on her way home, she knew that those who didn't see her at the moment would hear from those who did that she had driven in by way of 395 and Old Shasta Road. She muttered crossly, "To hell with it," and kept going.

At the house there was left-over chicken stew, which was delicious, and strawberries with cream. And there was a message from Dr. Jarlstadt: would she please give him a call at her convenience?

"Anything else?" she asked Winnie, who kept her company as she ate. Virgil was still working in the tropical dome, doing his work and Maria's, apparently.

"Nope. What did you find out?"

"Not a thing yet. Maybe tomorrow." She gave Winnie an abbreviated account of her days in Sacramento.

"I've been thinking," Winnie said. "You know, what Grandpa was having investigated doesn't have to be something real, or about any of us. It could be a rumor about Grandpa, or Grandma from years ago. Or you, when you were still a kid. You know what I mean?"

Sarah nodded. "I know exactly. And we may never find out."

Winnie looked stricken. "And we'll have to live with that," she said in a low voice. "Not knowing, not knowing what he was told, what he believed, how unhappy it was making him." She had poured herself a cup of coffee and stirred it around and around blindly. "Virgil and I were talking last night. What if whatever Grandpa learned was something that made him have a heart attack? What if it killed him? Something about me, about Virgil? Even if it was a lie, what if it was something about me that did that to Grandpa? Or Virgil?" She lifted her face to regard her mother. "This is so shitty!"

Sarah put her fork down and Winnie cried, "I'm sorry! Jesus, this is so awful, nothing we do is right, nothing we say works the way we meant it to. I'm sorry."

Winnie insisted on cleaning things up in the kitchen, and remembered that the accountant had come and gone, and would give his report to the attorney who had been named executor of the estate. Sarah was at the table while Winnie moved back and forth putting things away.

Suddenly Winnie paused. "If nothing was taken from

Fran Donatio's apartment, I mean, not the television or CD player, pawnable stuff like that, it must mean the person was searching for information, papers, reports."

Sarah was unbreathing then as Winnie went on, "Why? I could see someone maybe going through her office stuff, but her house, too? That doesn't sound like a guy looking for dope money."

"I know," Sarah said quietly. "Honey, I think we should not talk about any of this to anyone. You, Virgil, and I can discuss it, but no one else at all. Okay?"

Winnie's eyes widened, then narrowed. She nodded. "Jesus," she whispered. "When you get those names, what then?"

"I don't know yet. First we'll see if we recognize any of them, and go on from there."

The next day when Sarah studied the names on the fax printout, she felt only bafflement; Virgil looked mystified and Winnie shook her head.

"Virgil, are you certain? None of these people could have been mixed up in that trouble in Los Angeles?"

"I don't know any of those people," he said.

There were twenty-two calls, seven to the surname Leszno in the Chicago area, a Herman, Stanley, Wanda . . . There were four calls to people named Bookman in the Ogden, Utah, area. Three calls to Barcleighs in Los Angeles, and the rest scattered with no two to any one name. Those three names were the significant ones, Sarah thought with certainty; they all followed calls to directory assistance in the three locations, and they were grouped within days of the day Fran started working for Ralph Kellerman. First she had found the names, the numbers, and then she had started calling. Her sister had said Fran even went down to Los Angeles once on this case. One of the Barcleighs?

Sarah had called Dr. Jarlstadt, and agreed to visit him at eleven. She folded the fax report and slipped it into her pocket. No word from Maria, Virgil had said glumly when she asked; he looked years older than he had on the Sunday afternoon when Sarah arrived here. She wanted to pat him, to hold and comfort him, to soothe him in some way, but he was keeping himself aloof and distant, and so terribly busy back in the tropical dome, in the various pools ... She could envy his ability to work almost as many hours as he was awake; he was young enough that he could still do that. And Winnie had taken over one of the second-floor bathrooms and turned it into a darkroom, where she was developing and printing pictures for hours at a time. The video was just about done, she said; if Maria were here, she could have finished it completely by now, but without her ... Maybe they'd edit her out from the start, instead of having her vanish midway ...

Sarah left them both to their worries, and walked slowly to the institute for her meeting with Dr. Jarlstadt. The three names kept playing over in her head, almost as if she knew them and simply had forgotten for a moment, like forgetting an ingredient in a recipe, a haunting lack of something that she couldn't quite name.

The institute could be reached by the road, or by the route she chose, through the grounds here, along a stony path through a bit of woods, and then onto the grounds of the institute, like wandering into the land of Oz, where everything suddenly became technicolor. There was no brown grass, no dying bushes, no dusty trees here; everything that should be green was green; grass was clipped short and looked like an immense golf course; flowering bushes were abloom, and hedges were neatly trimmed to the point of looking like magazine illustrations. The paths on the grounds were wide and level and very smooth; nothing to impede a wheelchair, or someone on crutches out for exercise. Her father had put in a large pond here, and a branch of the path led around the circumference, with many seating arrangements spotted along the way. Very good, very handsome sculptures appeared almost randomly around the entire parklike grounds. Everything was expensive, handsome, beautifully landscaped, beautifully maintained.

Look where there's money, Fernandez had said, and this beyond a doubt represented great wealth. Sarah never had thought of this before; the institute was just there, the way a hospital was in a city; she never had questioned why such a rich-looking hospital was out here so far from any city.

As she drew nearer the main building, patients and personnel from the institute began to appear: a few people in wheelchairs, a few with walkers; several people strolling with elaborate care, accompanied by staff members who did not seem to wear uniforms here but still managed to look like nurses and therapists. Something in the way they watched the patients, the way a hand seemed always ready to reach out and provide support, to steady a faltering step.

Sarah entered the main building and paused at a desk where a young woman was keying something into a computer. He was expecting her, the young woman said, and pointed down a corridor. The fourth door on the left, she said smiling, and went back to her computer.

Sarah had known Dr. Jarlstadt most of her life; he had been a frequent dinner guest when her uncle and her parents still shared the Kellerman house, and then had been a guest in her parents' house; and they had come over here regularly, with her if she was visiting.

He was in his eighties, and looked very frail. He was in a wheelchair with an afghan over his legs. The room she had entered was a conference room, not an office; she doubted he had a real office anymore. The room was discreet in pale green and rich brown furnishings, a thick pale green carpet on the floor.

"My dear Sarah, I am so glad to see you. I must apologize for my not attending your father's funeral, my dear. Some days I don't leave the house, I'm afraid."

She bent over to kiss his cheek, and then sat near him in a soft comfortable chair. "I understand, Dr. Jarlstadt. Please, don't concern yourself. I'm sorry you're not well."

"It's the legs," he said with a shrug. "They simply stopped working. Knees folding backward, hip joints frozen . . . Getting old is not a pretty business, my dear."

"I don't want to keep you," she said gently. "You left a message for me?"

"Yes, yes. I'm afraid I told that policeman you were a director here, and I've been worried about it ever since. I mean, I would like very much for you to assume your father's position, but I quite understand if you prefer not to do so." He covered his mouth for a raspy little cough, a biscuit cough. His hand was milk white with midnight-blue veins. "Honorary position, of course. Dollar-a-year sort of thing. There's always been a Kellerman or two on the board."

"But I'm not a Kellerman," she said. "Uncle Peter is on the board, isn't he? Is Michael eligible?"

"Peter, of course, but not Michael; we prefer not to have father and son, you see. Smacks of nepotism or something equally ridiculous, but it's in the bylaws."

"Well, it should be someone available to attend meetings, I think," Sarah said. "Have you considered Virgil?"

"But he's hardly more than a child!"

"Almost twenty-four. In any event, whatever you told the police can't be a problem, I'm sure. I just don't see how it matters one way or the other to them." She stood up.

"Well, I'll straighten it out when that lieutenant comes back. Today or tomorrow, he said. I don't like leaving the wrong impression, and I did speak hastily. Think about it, my dear. You may find that a periodic visit here has some appeal."

"The lieutenant is coming back here? Did he say that?"

Dr. Jarlstadt looked at her curiously. "Yes. He called yesterday and said he would have a few more questions. About one of our former patients. I just don't understand what the connection can possibly be between him and that poor woman."

"A patient?" Sarah repeated. "Connected to Fran Donatio?"

"No, no. That's what I'm saying, there can't be a connection. It was years and years ago. Wesley Leszno. He vanished nearly thirty years ago, presumably he died in a tragic accident on the coast, and why the lieutenant has brought up his name now is a mystery to me."

Abruptly Sarah sat down again. Leszno. One of the

names on her fax list. Dead? "I remember something about that," she said. "Several young men disappeared, didn't they? That young man, and some others, all students, vanished? Isn't that the same name? They came here, didn't they?" The memory was coming back in bits and pieces, not making any sense at all yet.

"Yes. Wesley had been a polio victim, and he was here for treatment for several years off and on. That night he showed up with two other young men and said they were celebrating, and he wanted me to be the first to know. But I had dinner guests and I asked the boys to come back later. If only I had asked them to wait in the house, or to join us at dinner, or anything else. But they left and no one saw them alive or dead again. They vanished." He shook his head, his face troubled. "Why the police want to ask about that is more than I can guess."

She stood up, kissed him on the cheek again, and went to the door. He said it would be a pleasure to have lunch with her before she left the area, and she said she would let him know, but her mind was on the long-forgotten story about the three students who had vanished after a trip to East Shasta.

She knew the story, everyone in the family knew it, as did everyone in East Shasta, everyone who had read the daily papers back in the sixties. Dr. Jarlstadt's words had brought it back intact. The three students had been Uncle Peter's students; he had been a youngish professor of biochemistry. He had met the youngest of the three at the institute, she recalled, walking home, seeing nothing now of the lavish grounds. Leszno had been a brilliant prodigy, stricken with polio at an early age, undergoing treatment at the institute. Peter Kellerman had testified that he met the boy, they talked, and he told him that when he was ready to go to graduate school, to give Peter a call. Several years later the boy had called, and he had become one of the stars in Peter's class.

The disappearance had been devastating to Uncle Peter, she remembered. She and her parents had been at the house here when he came out, shaken, nearly incoherent, and crying. She remembered that in particular; he was the first adult male she had ever seen weeping.

She didn't know the details of the work the boys had been doing, only that it was brilliant, and incomplete when they vanished. According to the reports that she could remember, they had come out here to visit Dr. Jarlstadt, to tell him something, and he had sent them away until later that night. They never returned. Their car had been found the next day down the coast somewhere; not a trace of the boys had been found then or ever. Drinking, the papers had said; they had been drinking beer all evening. It was conjectured that they had gone out onto rocks with a high surf running, and had lost their footing, had been swept out to sea.

It was all public knowledge, she told herself. Nothing new could have turned up after all these years. There had been a complete investigation, of course. And Uncle Peter's devastation, she now remembered, was partly due to the fact that by vanishing at that particular time, they might have lost him the Nobel Prize. The work they had been doing—his project—was leading them inevitably toward it, but then everything had come to a standstill with their disappearance; and Watson and Crick had made the breakthrough first with the discovery of the structure of the DNA molecule, the double helix. Uncle Peter's one really big chance had vanished as completely as his students. She remembered with a flush of embarrassment saying to Michael about his father, always the bridesmaid. Too close to the truth to be funny, she knew. But she hadn't thought about all that miserable past for more than twenty-five years.

And that was the problem, she thought, walking more and more slowly. It was a story from the early sixties, public knowledge, nothing to make her father start his own investigation. Unless, she added, Uncle Peter had lied about his part in it, and had gotten away with the lie until now. But who from nearly thirty years ago would know anything to make her father open that particular door? Dr. Jarlstadt? He had had witnesses who had confirmed the story he had told; his dinner guests had all overheard the whole conversation with Wesley Leszno. They had looked out and had seen the three boys. And several of the dinner guests were also house guests who had sat up with Dr. Jarlstadt until after two in the morning.

If anyone had found new evidence of any sort, why hadn't he gone to the police, or Uncle Peter? The three students had been his; her father had had nothing to do with them. Why call her father? What had that been for? She was not even certain the three students had died; who had Fran Donatio been calling? Looking for one of the students? A surviving family member? Why? She remembered what the insurance agent had said about her father insisting on confidentiality, even if Fran uncovered a crime. But what the crime could have been was as elusive as ever.

And now Sarah tried to rethink the conclusions she had drawn about her father's death. She could not believe anyone would have had a reason to kill him over that incident from so many years ago, an incident that had been public knowledge, and that never had involved him. He could have fallen, she told herself, hit his head, twisted in such a way that his hat fell off to one side. It was not what anyone might expect, but she had seen a lot of cases where the truth was the least likely of the many theories and even lies that surrounded them.

All right, she told herself, feeling as if she had shrugged off the weight of a mountain from her shoulders. He had Fran investigate something to do with the students: maybe they had stolen money, or cheated on test results, or fudged their work, something, but whatever it was, it had nothing to do with her father, nothing to do with Virgil or Winnie, or Sarah or Blaine. Fran had found whatever she was looking for and reported back. It sounded to Sarah as if at least one of the students must be alive; who else would know anything about the past? And then Fran had decided, for whatever reason, to drive the old Shasta Road to 395. She had run out of gas, someone had come in from 395 and killed her.

If that someone now had information about the students and that incident, she thought, so what? Maybe one of the students, now a middle-aged man, had done something to turn the spotlight onto himself, had drawn attention, and that had inspired the call to her father. But it didn't matter. None of it mattered now. If there was a killer/blackmailer out there, he would be after the one with something to hide, the student who had vanished, whose death had been assumed, and now maybe was alive and well.

She considered and dismissed the idea that the student, a middle-aged man now, had made the call. It made no sense for him to have called her father instead of his former teacher, who was still listed at the university, still had his apartment, and was easy enough to track down.

Before, she had been driven by a terrible need to move, to try to find out what the investigation had been about, driven to take action, any action; now, she felt relaxation ease the tension that had tightened her shoulders and neck. She found herself thinking about Dirk Walters and his phone call that would come on Monday or Tuesday. She thought about calling a meeting with Winnie, Virgil, and Carlos to decide the future of the gardens. She thought about calling the attorney to find out the state of the finances of the gardens. She had planned originally to go to the coast for a week before starting her drive north again, back to Pendleton. She began to think of the coast, of the waves washing the shore, the crashing of storm waves, of walking for miles on hard-packed sand, of eating steamer clams and drinking fine white wine, and reading a book with the music of the surf in her ears.

She felt as if she had put the whole world on hold, and now she released the button and the spin resumed, her future was still there waiting, tomorrow was still there, her decision was still to be made, although she felt that was a lie, that it had been made when Dirk told her what they wanted. What they wanted was what she wanted. What decision?

And suddenly she was thinking of love, of being loved, of being held and kissed and caressed, of opening her legs, and the fiery pain and pleasure of the first thrust ... She gasped and closed her eyes hard and caught a tree trunk for support.

TWELVE

SARAH'S MIND KEPT drifting during the business meeting they held that afternoon. Carlos and Virgil would continue the business as usual; Winnie would take over the publicity/advertising department, complete the catalog, complete the video, take charge of the mail-order department. Sarah's thoughts were far away ... Monday or Tuesday Dirk would call, she would pack up her things here and leave for the coast, and then back to Pendleton, where she would have a conference or two with Dirk, and plan her campaign strategy ... Let him plan it, she corrected herself, and did not even question the stiffening of her hands, the tightening of her neck muscles.

"Mother?" Winnie said impatiently.

"Sorry. What?"

"Do you intend to be an active partner? We've skirted all around that question for the last fifteen minutes."

"Of course not. In fact, as soon as everything is settled here, I intend to sign my shares over to you and Virgil."

There were no false protestations, merely acceptance, an understanding that her decision was the only sensible one. There was very little money, there would be financial problems for a long time; she simply hoped Virgil would make enough money to live on, to maintain the house, keep a decent staff in the gardens so that he didn't have to work too many hours a day. Her father never had made real money, she thought then, listening absently to Virgil, who was outlining his plans for the next six months, all meaningless to her. Had her father ever developed a new lily? She thought not, and smiled to herself. He must have been pleased. She imagined the grandfather, grandson together, talking, talking; Virgil never had spent more than a minute at a time talking with Blaine, she felt certain. All she could remember between them was a certain kind of uncomfortable silence, the kind there was between Virgil and Uncle Peter.

"We could save the delivery costs," Carlos said, "if one of us could drive over to Las Vegas and pick up the liners ourselves. Twenty percent."

"I'll do that," Virgil said. "I'll go in the afternoon, sleep in the truck, pick up the stuff the next morning, and head home. No big deal."

"It will get old after a trip or two, but it's a big savings," Carlos said. "We could take turns."

There never had been real money in the family as far as Sarah knew. Her father had had a substantial pension, and a little bit extra stashed away against retirement. That money would vanish fast. If the gardens didn't make it on their own, the business would fold. It was that simple, but at the moment, listening to her son, whom she had always considered a failure, exactly as Blaine had done, she realized that he had every intention of keeping the gardens alive, making the business succeed. And he would, she thought, almost surprised but not quite. Blaine's father had been an attorney, and his grandfather, and he had had every expectation that his son would carry on the tradition, and Virgil was almost exactly like his maternal grandfather.

Her drifting thoughts were taking her further and further afield, as she considered how snobbish Blaine had been, and she also, she added, and on her part it had been an act of deception because she was as practical and down-to-earth as her father had been, as Virgil was, with little time left for flights of intellectual speculation—

"Mother!" Winnie again.

"Sorry."

"What I said was that if you don't have anything to add, this meeting is going to adjourn. Rosa's home with a car full of stuff and I told her I'd help unpack and put things away."

Winnie's eyes were gleaming the way they did when she was angry, and she was being excessively polite at the moment. Sarah smiled at her. "I have absolutely nothing to add."

Late that night Sarah walked outside, all around the house, making certain Virgil's lights were off, and Winnie's, and then she went to her car and retrieved the plastic bag with her father's hat, and took it inside to return it to his closet. She could not think now of the chain of reasoning she had followed to the conclusion that her father had been murdered. The missing information about Fran Donatio? Not enough. He could have destroyed it himself, or maybe there never had been anything tangible. The thought that Fran's killer had struck him down to keep him silenced about the investigation results? Not enough. All that had been hashed out many years ago. Public knowledge. The hat? Not enough.

Inside her father's room, she blinked hard several times, and then went purposefully to the closet, unfastening the tie around the bag as she walked, and then she came to a stop again. The other hat was gone.

There had been another one exactly like the one she was holding; there were several others scattered around the house and grounds, in the outbuildings. But one had remained in the closet when she took away this one.

She backed away from the closet and sat down on a wooden chair, and began to retie the bag, not thinking what she was doing, not giving herself a reason, simply refastening it, to keep the hat safe.

Who could have taken it? Anyone. The family here, Rosa or Carlos, a visitor, Uncle Peter, Michael . . . They had gone back to the Bay area on Monday, she knew. Either of them could have walked over Sunday night, early Monday morning. One of the workers, a stranger, anyone.

"Why don't they lock the goddamn doors?" she muttered, and finally stood up, turned off the lights again, and left the room. She stood undecided for only a moment, then went back downstairs, back to her car, and replaced the bag with the hat in the trunk.

When she reentered the house, she made a circuit of the ground floor, checking the doors, locking everything. Three doors were not locked; when she came to the sliding patio door, she realized the futility of her actions. There was no lock on this one, only a simple latch, operable from either side. Tomorrow, she thought, she would get a bar to put in the runner.

In her room she got ready for bed, and then stood at

the windows looking out for a long time. Anyone could have taken the hat, she told herself, for an altogether innocent reason. Rosa or Carlos, someone could have wanted a sun hat, that simple. Or maybe she had been mistaken and there had not been a second hat on the shelf when she looked before. That was possible. She had been upset, had not slept enough for nights, she could well have made a mistake. She bit her lip.

Tomorrow she would talk to Lieutenant Fernandez, she said to herself, and was finally able to move away from the window, let herself sink down into the bed. Where would they start? An autopsy, she answered her question, staring dry-eyed into the darkness. She wanted to tell her father she was sorry, and she did not know if she meant sorry because she had delayed this, or sorry to disturb his rest. She wanted desperately to tell him, but there was only the darkness, the silence, the void.

Finally, drifting into sleep, she glimpsed scenes of her mother working on her notebooks. She had not called them diaries, or even journals, but simply notebooks. And she had kept records of everything. Her entries had consisted of a few lines of script, not on a daily basis, but when something happened that she had found interesting. She had included line drawings or photographs, or a scrap of fabric, a letter, a card, a pressed flower or two, newspaper clippings, whatever had been available and necessary.

Sarah sat up, wide awake, and thought, of course, there would be a notebook filled with clippings of the disappearance of those three students. The notebooks were here in the house somewhere; her father never had thrown anything away, and her mother's notebooks spanned her entire life; there was a big box of them somewhere.

It was after two in the morning when she swung her legs out of bed; she hesitated, and then stretched out again. Tomorrow, she told herself. Tomorrow.

The next morning she was sorting out the notebooks by date when she heard Lieutenant Fernandez's voice at the front door. Rosa's voice was too soft to carry up the stairs.

Sarah went to the head of the stairs, started to go down, but then heard Lieutenant Fernandez again, "I'll finish up out here, first, ma'am. It's going to be a while."

She went down slowly, giving him time to leave the porch; at the front door she watched as he walked to the parking spaces under the poplar trees and began to talk to two men there. Then she went to the kitchen.

"What are they doing?" she asked Rosa, who was cleaning a cabinet.

"I don't know," Rosa said. "Where is Maria? Where is Carlos, where is Virgil? Is that where people always park? What do we do with our trash?" She glared at Sarah. "Loco! That man is loco!"

"Trash? What on earth . . . ?"

"Don't ask me. I don't know. I say he's nuts. What does that have to do with that lady detective's death, I want to know. Crazy police."

Sarah walked again to the front of the house but did not go outside, rather she watched from a window; one of the men was lifting dirt samples carefully, putting them in a plastic bag, moving, doing it again, each sample in its own little bag, which he then labeled. The other technician was walking back and forth in the driveway studying the ground, moving forward inch by inch, apparently intending to scan the length of it from the parking area to the road. In exasperation Sarah turned from the window and went back to her room, back to the box of mementos, the legacy of her dead mother.

There were only fourteen notebooks; Sarah had thought there would be more. As far as her memory extended, she remembered her mother jotting down notes, making drawings, pasting things in one of them. The early ones were loose-leaf binders, but later she had gone to spiral notebooks. Sarah opened one at random and read about a frog trapped in a pail. She remembered the incident. They had turned the pail over eventually when it became apparent that the frog did not know enough to leap straight up, or else was not able to leap high enough. And her mother had recorded the incident.

Again and again as Sarah scanned one of the notebooks after another, the past came alive for her; many of the incidents she also had seen, some she had been told about. Now and then she found something previously unknown. And someone had torn out pages, she realized at one point where a story was not continued, but something altogether different was at the top of the following page. Nothing significant, it seemed to her; a party they had gone to in Portland, a list of attendees, and then they were digging for clams on the beach, months later.

Now and then she came across what could only be labeled an aphorism:

Babies always know when a trip is scheduled and become ill accordingly.

Newspaper recipes fail in one of three ways: they leave out a major ingredient and fail, they foul up the measurements and fail, or they are very bad variations of classic dishes, and fail. Sometimes they fail in all three, and even invent new ways.

Men understand women quite well; they pretend not to because they are cowards.

Sarah read that last one several times; it was tucked in between Christmas stories, shopping expeditions, a description of a store's decorations. Sarah put down that notebook and picked up a different one, and this time found one of her high-school report cards taped to a page, and a few lines about how precocious she had been. And then: *Widowhood signifies freedom for women.*

Carefully Sarah closed the notebook and placed it back with the others, and then closed the box. Another time, she told herself. She would read them all word for word, but not now, not today, not soon. She felt that she was trespassing in the private affairs of a total stranger.

She went outside a minute or two later, and stood on the porch watching the lieutenant and his two men examine the ground at the edge of the stand of poplars. Lieutenant Fernandez looked up and waved, spoke to the two men, and came toward her.

"What are you doing?" she asked, staying in the shade of the porch. It was pleasantly cool in the shade, but still very hot in the sun.

"Good morning, Judge," he said. "I was going to

come looking for you. Would you do us a favor?" He didn't wait for a response. "What we need is for someone to walk us over to your uncle's house, show us the path you would normally take, that all of you would normally use. Would you do that?"

"You're kidding," she said. "What's there to show? Out the driveway, cross the road to his driveway, and up to the house."

"I know it sounds easy," he said, "and until we got here, I thought it was exactly like you just said, but it gets a little complicated in reality. Which driveway, for instance?"

He pointed to the old driveway that went straight out through the young trees her father had planted, and was unusable by automobiles, but still passable on foot, and then to the newer drive that he had put in.

"Okay," Sarah said. "Now?"

He nodded. "Yeah, now's fine."

"This is the way I've always gone," she said, "and I suppose most of the others go this way, too. But I couldn't testify to that."

"Fair enough."

They walked toward the trees, then followed the new drive around them. Lieutenant Fernandez motioned to his men to follow along, and they all walked silently to the road.

"See, here's another one of those points of confusion," Fernandez said at the road. "You cut right across, or stay on this side?"

"Stay on this side for a little, then diagonally across and end up at the edge of his driveway. What is this all about, Lieutenant?"

"Curious, that's all. This was the old road? Too wide for a regular driveway."

"Yes."

He stopped again a few feet farther in. "Someone's been cutting stuff."

"Michael was pruning last week."

"Uh huh. What's that?"

He was pointing to a small path through underbrush that had grown so much the path was nearly invisible now. A tangle of sage, rabbit grass, poison oak always had made it a challenge; when they were children, they had kept it open. She realized that Michael must have been working on it that day she found him with the pruning shears. She could not imagine why he would have been working on this path now.

"It goes to the house," she said. "Or, I should say it used to. I doubt that it's passable any longer."

He nodded. "Hold it a sec," he said, and stepped back to speak with the two men who trailed them, and then rejoined her.

They finished the walk to the house. Sarah wondered if all the tomatoes had died yet, and suspected they had. The house was looking lonely, she thought, uncared-for; Michael's sporadic trimming and clipping were not enough, and Uncle Peter never really had done much maintenance. There used to be a man who came around once a week or so and did the routine things, but apparently he had not been employed with any regularity for quite some time. She wondered again why Uncle Peter even bothered with the property here; he was really a city person, enjoyed restaurants, movies, museums, events at school.

"Okay," Lieutenant Fernandez said then. "We'll leave

them to it. That way goes to the other side of town, doesn't it?"

"You know it does," she said.

"Yes. So you can use this old road and bypass the town altogether. No one the wiser about your coming and going."

She laughed. "Don't believe it. They know, all right. Mrs. Betancort lives at the east end of this road, and she knows every time a mouse crosses it, I think. Nothing happens around here that isn't known within minutes, it seems to me."

"That's about what I thought," he said. "But no one seems to know what became of Maria Florinda. Do you?"

"No. She said there was illness in her family and she had to go home. That's all I know."

"That's what I heard. Your son kind of likes her, doesn't he?"

"Why don't you ask him?"

"I will. When we get back to the house, I'll want to see her personnel records, you know, social security number, education, references, stuff like that." He grinned in a friendly way, and added, "I got a search warrant for all that."

"When? Why are you looking for Maria?"

"Yesterday, and because she's gone. We got a tip that she took off in a real hurry right after we found Fran's body. That's all. I got the search warrant just to ease things a little, you being such a stickler for due process and such. Rightly so, I might add. But if anyone gives you any static, you have an out, see?"

"Why on earth do you think anyone would give me a hard time over Maria?"

"Oh, well. You never know."

A high breeze rustled the branches above them, the old pines creaked and groaned; a bluejay squawked and something stirred in the withered grass at the side of the road. Any motion set off puffs of dust: birds taking off, landing, the small creatures of the underbrush, the footsteps of the people walking on the old road all created varying eddies of dust. The sunlight shafting down through the tree limbs caught the swirling clouds and magnified them, turned them silver.

"Something else," Lieutenant Fernandez said after a few minutes of silence. "I have a few things to do at your place, you know, the employment records, a couple of questions for your son and for Carlos, little things, and then I wonder if you'd do me another favor."

"Lieutenant," she said dryly, "I hardly think in a murder investigation favor is the appropriate word."

"Sure it is. I figure you and I have a lot in common, more than either of us has with anyone else within miles. You've seen it all, and so have I. You know? We make up sort of parentheses, with most of life and death inside; you're at one end, I'm at the other, but there we are, you don't find one without the other. See, what I have to do is time how long it took Fran to drive to where she finally came to a stop. I'd like you to come along. We can exchange information."

She looked at him sharply. "I wonder why that sounds like an inducement instead of a statement of fact."

"Well, it's an inducement," he admitted with a grin. "I also have a cooler with some sandwiches, and some beers for lunch later on. Now that's a real inducement."

"Exchange information about what? What do I know that you want?"

"Oh, family stuff. Like your Uncle Peter and the affair of the missing students from back in the sixties. Little things like that."

She drew in a quick breath. "You probably know more about that than I do."

"Maybe, but mine is from news accounts, not from family. Makes a difference, don't you agree?"

They had reached the gardens, and he went straight to the house. "First, employment stuff."

Virgil met them in the front hallway. He was dressed in his cutoffs, and thongs, with a sweatshirt draped over his shoulders. "They said you were here again," he said sullenly to the lieutenant. "What do you want now?"

"I'm really looking for Maria Florinda. You know where I can find her?"

"No. What do you want her for?"

"Just some questions. We got a tip that she took off right after we found the body of Fran Donatio, and there's a possibility that whatever Donatio was looking into might have concerned Maria Florinda. Maybe someone has those papers and called Maria, threatened her. Maybe she just believes she might be at risk. We don't know."

Virgil's look was hostile and unbelieving; he said nothing.

"I want to see the personnel records," the lieutenant said easily. "Where she came from, where she worked before, her references, you know."

Virgil glanced at Sarah, who shrugged. "He has a search warrant," she said. "We have to show him the files." What else did Fernandez suspect, or know? she wondered. He knew that Virgil would be the one to cause static over Maria. She did not look at the lieutenant; she thought there might be a smug expression on his face.

Wordlessly Virgil led the way into the business office and opened one of the file drawers, began to rummage about in it. His motions were hurried and clumsy, then he stopped and turned toward the lieutenant. "I can't find them." He began to go through folders more methodically, more efficiently. He finally drew back, shaking his head. "I can't find anything about her."

"May I?" Fernandez asked, already at the file, starting at the beginning. Virgil withdrew only enough to give him room to maneuver, near enough to watch closely.

Finally the lieutenant stepped away from the cabinet and let his gaze roam the office: three other big file cabinets, two half-sized file cabinets, various desks and tables with papers strewn about, papers on shelves. He sighed. "What we'll have to do, I'm afraid," he said, almost mournfully, "is seal off the room and have a couple of my people go through it all. What a nuisance for you guys."

"Jesus!" Virgil snapped. "A nuisance! You'll shut down the whole business!"

"Who had access to the files?"

"Everyone here. Me. Carlos, his wife, my sister, my mother, my uncle and cousin, a dozen workers here, your people, you. Everyone who's been in the house in the past. The files aren't kept locked."

"And your grandfather," Fernandez added sadly. "Too many. Okay, I'll just give my guys a buzz and get them started. Shouldn't take them too long."

Virgil glowered at him, then turned and started to walk out of the office.

"Mr. Drexler, if you don't mind, while my guys are going at it in here, there are a few things I'd like to clear up with you. Maybe on the patio round back?"

Virgil had stopped at his words; he shrugged. "Whatever you say," he muttered, and went out to the hall.

Fernandez spoke into a cordless phone, and then motioned Sarah to precede him from the office. "You're welcome to sit in on this if you want," he said. "Just routine stuff."

She hesitated, then nodded slightly.

"Is that how the pool was before?" Fernandez asked on the terrace a moment later, regarding the pool with appreciation. "That's really pretty, isn't it?"

The plants had been returned, and the fish. Nothing hinted of the tragedy that had taken place here.

"That's how it was," Virgil said.

"Tell me about him, your grandfather," Fernandez said softly. "He liked to get up early and walk around the grounds here?"

Virgil nodded.

"He fed the fish every morning?"

"No, it was usually too early, they'd be sluggish until the day warmed up some. He just liked to walk around and look at things."

"A long-time habit of his?"

"As long as I've been around."

"He did the hiring here?"

"Yes."

"Okay, tell me about Maria, when she came, how she was hired, you know. Fill in the gaps."

Virgil looked at his hands and opened them, closed

his fists, opened them again. "She just turned up one day. I don't know if she called him first. I never asked. He talked to her, and then brought her around back where we were working, and introduced her. And she gradually took over all the plant supervision. She's a botanist."

"Where'd she go to school?"

Virgil shrugged.

"Okay, where'd she live before she came here?"

He shrugged more theatrically.

"Virgil, come on. Loosen up. Have you considered that she might be in danger? She might have heard or might have seen something that puts her in danger."

Virgil's fists tightened visibly. "I didn't cross-examine her about her past."

Fernandez nodded. "Okay. I'll see you later on." He left the terrace to meet his two men, who had come into view from the Kellerman house. They conferred at length, then all three came to the terrace, and Fernandez escorted his two assistants inside.

Virgil watched them through narrowed eyes; he looked terribly young, Sarah thought, and very frightened. He caught her fixed gaze on him, flushed angrily, and stamped away. "I'm going back to work," he muttered.

Sarah watched him out of sight, then turned to see Fernandez at the doorway, also watching. "Ready?" he asked.

"Ready?" She had forgotten, he wanted her to go along for the ride, for sandwiches and beer, a picnic at Ghost Lake. She wanted to laugh and to cry. "Yes," she said. "Just a second."

She told Rosa that she would be out for several

hours, that she would have lunch out. Rosa looked at her with disapproval and made no comment.

"All right," Fernandez said when they were both in the car, seat belts fastened, ready. He made a note of the miles and engaged the gears. "It's ten at night, and you don't know the area. Sunday night, not much going on in town, I guess, is there?"

"Not really. But someone must have seen her drive past. They don't miss much."

"We're checking on that today," he said. "Door-to-door stuff, a real drag." They had passed the entrance to the institute, and were going through town at a sedate pace; they stopped at the solitary traffic light and waited for it to turn green. No other car was at the intersection. Sarah was very aware of the people they passed, several in the hardware store, more at the grocery store, three women at the discount store entrance . . . Everyone stopped whatever they were doing to watch the policeman and Sarah.

"See what I meant?" she asked, trying to keep it light. "They know if a mouse sneezes."

Some kids on bikes passed them, waving, and then they were passing Mrs. Betancort's house, passing the abandoned gas station, Dacey's Tavern, leaving town. The road began to curve instantly.

"It wasn't terribly dark that night," Fernandez said, "but on the other hand this road doesn't have a mark on it, no center stripe, no shoulder stripes, nothing. She would have been cautious." He held it to twenty-five miles an hour, now edging up to thirty, back down to twenty-five. When it became hillier and curvier, he shifted down and held it to twenty, to fifteen at a series of hairpin curves.

"And this is the good section," he said cheerfully, twisting the steering wheel hard. "I guess the locals take it a bit faster than this."

"Right. It's about half an hour to Ghost Lake, twenty-three miles. That's in daylight."

"Tell me something," Fernandez said after another switchback yielded to a straighter section of road. "What do you look for when you're working, as a judge, I mean? The way people answer questions? If they get shifty eyes? The facts presented by the opposing sides? What?"

"That's too simple," she said, thinking about it. "You can't simply decide this witness is lying, that one isn't. Some judges use a philosophical approach, weigh the logical symmetry, the logical necessities of the evidence; some look for historical precedents, anachronistic discrepancies, even tradition and customs. Some decide almost entirely on the weight of the customs of the particular trade or business as it is practiced today. And for some judges the social implications count most, the social politics behind the rules or the laws. It can become extremely political, and those judges are generally considered to be the activists, as opposed to the strict constructionists, who, although they deny it through their teeth, are even more political in reality than they can ever admit."

Fernandez was watching the road closely; there were deep potholes in this section, and a crumbling shoulder. "Where do you fit into that scheme?" he asked, keeping his gaze on the road ahead.

"Here and there," she said, laughing. "I'm afraid I don't have a clear-cut agenda of my own. I like what Learned Hand said, something like, a judge is the declarer of the common will of the people, as expressed in law. He was a great believer in common law, of course. You know, what has been will be, what goes around comes around, however you want to put it."

"You put more faith in facts, or rules?" he asked, glancing at her.

"Back and forth," she said after another brief pause. "Facts, I think. Rules can be pretty inhuman."

"Yeah, me too. At my end facts are all we've got."

"Actually," Sarah said slowly, "you know, don't you, that almost everyone in the business, from your end all the way through the system, behaves in almost exactly the same way? We all work backward. First there is the notion of what the truth is, and then the facts are discovered to back it, and the legal principles are applied to enforce the police work. Backward. Just like in Alice. Except we all pretend otherwise."

"Tell me about Alice," he said. He had let the car edge up past thirty, and braked again, back to twenty.

"Give me a minute. I used to know it pretty well." She gazed out the widow at the dry trees, the rocky hillside, the crumbling road. A hawk flew overhead, circled back into view, studying them, no doubt, and vanished. She quoted the White Queen:

"He's in prison now, being punished: and the trial doesn't even begin till next Wednesday: and of course the crime comes last of all."

"Suppose he never commits the crime?" said Alice.

"That would be all the better, wouldn't it?" the Queen said.

Fernandez nodded gravely. "That makes perfect sense to me."

"Oh, me too," Sarah said. "Of course."

They both laughed.

"You said we would exchange information," Sarah said after another minute or so of silent driving. The road demanded attention, but not total concentration, she had decided. At least, she could drive and talk at the same time, and she suspected that he could also.

"Right. We traced the numbers Fran called. As you did?" He didn't wait for confirmation. "And came up with a nearly thirty-year-old mystery. I hate that a lot. When you ask questions, you should get answers, not just deeper questions." He was scowling at the road, at the world now. "You were here at East Shasta when it happened? When those kids disappeared?"

"Yes. You tell me your version and I'll tell you if it's like the one I know."

He nodded. "Right. My version is from police files and news accounts. The three boys worked under the supervision of your uncle at Hayward, and were on the verge of a monumental discovery. Since they were graduate students, it didn't mean much to them when the term ended, but they decided to celebrate it anyway, and came out to East Shasta to share their good news with Dr. Jarlstadt. The doctor was too busy to see them instantly, and they drove away and were never seen again. Their car was found the next day south of Hayward on the coast in a particularly bad stretch of road. It was assumed that they horsed around on the rocks and were swept to sea. Period. Case closed."

"That's about what I remember," Sarah said after a moment. "I had forgotten that it was at the end of the term, but that explains why I flew in to Sacramento. I was going to UCLA then. My father met me and we drove on out to East Shasta the next day, Saturday. Mother was already at the house, straightening up generally. She hated it when Uncle Peter and his crew left things a mess, and they always did. Anyway, he came in that Saturday night, really upset, crying, and that's when we learned about the students."

"Why'd he come out here?" Fernandez asked. "He had a family back on the coast, didn't he?"

"Oh, something else I had forgotten," Sarah said. "His divorce was happening at that time. A nasty one, bitter recriminations on both sides. Anyway, their kids were with her, and he was spending most of his time at school. He had an apartment nearby and a cot or something in the science department lounge. I don't know the details, only that he spent more time at school than at home. No one thought it strange for him to come out to East Shasta when there was trouble. He had nowhere else to go. My father was his real family, I guess."

"But the point is that you, your folks, everyone knew about his students, how his work was delayed, all that?"

"Of course. That's why it doesn't make any sense for Fran Donatio to have been investigating any of that."

"Right," he said.

The car bumped over the bumpy road, skirted the potholes, and edged lower and lower down the mountainside. They had long since passed Ghost Lake, without stopping, and were approaching the spot where Fran had been killed. They both became silent as he pulled to the side of the road where the view overlooked the stretch where her car had rolled to a stop.

He made a note of the time; it had taken them an

hour and forty minutes. But someone familiar with the road could have driven it in less than an hour, another five minutes to walk down to the other car, five minutes, ten at the most, to kill Fran, gather the papers, her belongings, and return to this spot, and then turn around . . . The whole thing could have been done in two hours.

Sarah was startled when Fernandez said, "I'm just a little surprised that she got this far before she ran out of gas."

"What do you mean?"

"Later," he said. "Still thinking it through. Let's go."

He drove back much, much faster than he had driven coming this way. And this time when they drew up to Ghost Lake, he stopped and parked. "Lunch time," he said.

They got out of the car, but he made no motion to open the trunk yet. He stood looking over the ruins of the town where at one time a hundred people had lived, loved, worked, slept. Then the water had left, and they had, too.

"Let's stretch our legs a bit," Fernandez said. They walked together toward the largest of the standing buildings, a general store, from all appearances, with a porch long since sunken into the ground, a high step up and over the doorjamb, and an interior where the air was yellow with dust and age. The floor was unsafe, rotted through in places, gone in places, revealing a crawl space five feet deep, and then a basement that seemed to be under only part of the building. Sarah did not move into the building more than a step or two, but Fernandez cautiously made his way farther, and then stopped, and listened with his head tilted, a frown on his face. He nodded.

"Gives me the creeps," he said. "You ever visit any of the big ruins, the tourist attraction sort of thing?"

"No." She retreated, and stepped over the high door-jamb, out into the air and light, where she took in a deep breath as if she had been breathing far too shallowly.

He followed her outside. "I've seen some of them. Spooky, Machu Picchu, Chichén Itzá, they're spooky. For one thing they're too quiet. Oh, there are ghosts, I have no doubt, but they don't make a peep, not a sigh, or moan, nothing, and that makes them scary. What are they waiting for?" He was looking about the ruins with interest. "Saloon, barbershop maybe, hotel, restaurant, homes. No school. Guess they held school in one of the homes. Church. You think that's the church?" He pointed to a building. It was the remains of two upright walls now, and a tumble of timbers and sand piles inside the walls. He had come to a stop again, this time in the middle of the road, Main Street of old East Shasta, no doubt.

"Fernandez, what are you doing?" Sarah asked finally. They had not entered any of the other buildings, but approached one or another, stopped to listen, moved on.

"Food," he said then decisively, and turned to go back to the car. Long black shadows were filling the valley, striping it. The contrast of the dark shadows and the sun-silvered wood was so intense that the buildings looked like polished silver and jet, and the shadows of the ruins were grotesque, nightmare buildings.

"You know anything about the commune that was

started in here, back in the sixties?" Fernandez asked, opening the trunk now. He pulled out a cooler, looked around, then shrugged and set it in the shade of the car.

"Mrs. Betancort started a commune," Sarah said. "She's dotty, of course, and I suppose always has been. Anyway, she gathered a bunch of people, convinced them that the world was going to end, or that Jesus was on his way, or something, and that salvation lay in establishing the commune here. They came out and set up tents, did whatever people like that do, and eventually moved out again, back to East Shasta for her, scattered to the wind, as far as I know about the others." She watched him spread a blanket on the ground, and sat on it when he was through. "Your turn. What do you know about the commune?"

"About like that. Milton Flink, your very own local pharmacist, told me about it. He was here, a teenager. He said every day about this time, before dark, when the sun was going over the hill there, they heard ghosts. Day after day, moaning, wailing, crying, begging for help, he said. Not loud, he said you had to strain to hear the actual words, but the moans and sobs were clear enough. They started in the afternoon, sometimes continued all night. Must have been eerie."

"We've been listening for ghosts," Sarah said. "Right?"

"Yep. Didn't hear one, did you?"

"Nope. Sorry. I told you Mrs. Betancort is quite mad. Everyone except her knew there was no water here, but she insisted on the commune, and believed, or at least declared that God would reveal water for them to drink."

She gave him the brief geology lesson her father had

given her many years earlier, and they looked out over the pale dry lake examining it for signs of quicksand. If it was there, neither of them knew how to identify it. The lake bed was a dusty, tan expanse of dirt and sand, with tufts of bitter grass sticking out here and there, clumps of creosote sage tenaciously clinging to life. Rocks, boulders, sand dunes gave the lake character, she thought, but did they mean the quicksand was where boulders and rocks were not? She did not know the answer.

Fernandez handed her a sandwich and they both ate ravenously and drank the beer.

"I suppose that when the police were looking into the disappearance of those students, they did a thorough job on my uncle," she said, when she had finished her sandwich. She kept her gaze on the lake bed, her tone noncommittal.

"They did. They checked him for sand from the stretch of coast where the boys vanished. Not a trace on his clothes, or in the car." His tone was as dispassionate and remote as hers had been. They might have been talking about a historical figure. "They tried to check his alibi at the school, but that was a little harder, no one saw him and no one should have because his lab was pretty isolated. He used the science lab computer all that weekend, logged on and off properly, and that was as much of an alibi as he could come up with. But everyone also agreed that he had no motive for any hanky-panky, and if it was an accident, there was nothing to link him to them that night. The whole thing was put on hold and has been there ever since."

She exhaled softly. "There has to be a catalyst, doesn't there?" she said slowly. "Something happened that set things in motion. The phone call to my father was the result of something else, and the cause of a whole new chain of events. That's how it works. Cause, effect, more cause, more effect, but never an act in a real vacuum."

Fernandez stood up and dusted himself off, then held out his hand to help her up. She took his hand and got to her feet, and for a long moment they did not release each other's hand. Oh, God, she thought suddenly. Oh, dear God!

His face changed subtly, and then changed again to a mask. For a moment she had seen a man desperate in his hunger for a woman, not just any woman, hungry for her, and she knew she wanted him more than she ever had wanted any man. Not just a man, but this man. Carefully he withdrew his hand from hers, and just as carefully she took a step backward, and leaned over to pick up the beer cans. Without a word they cleared the blanket of the picnic and put everything away in the car trunk, and then, still in silence, they got inside.

He was looking straight ahead, not at her, when he said, "Thank you for a very nice few hours, Judge."

"It was my pleasure, Lieutenant," she said, also looking out through the windshield.

Both voices sounded fake, theatrical.

He did not start the car yet. "There's something else," he said. "What I really wanted to tell you, why I wanted you to come out here with me. I got the search warrant yesterday, and I also got an exhumation order. I've ordered an autopsy on your father's body, Sarah. I'm sorry."

THIRTEEN

FROM A HIGHER point than the valley offered, it was readily apparent that this was one insignificant valley in a series of mountains, passes, valleys, and more mountains, more passes, more valleys. But from within the small valley, it seemed the world began and ended here; no other mountains were visible except these enclosing slopes with their dying or dead grasses, their dead or dying trees; the lake was already dead, the houses dead, crumbling to pieces, silvered and spotted with rust where nails had long since vanished. The sand of the lake bed whispered as it shifted under a steady breeze. There was always a breeze here in the valley; the wind was funneled through the pass, strengthened, and while it might appear to be dead calm out there, in here the wind blew and made the sand unquiet. Had the whispering sand given rise to ghost stories? When this was still Rabbit Lake it must have been a lovely place with sparkling water, a time when the green things were truly green, when children's voices sounded, and no sand whispered, no ghosts stirred.

"You've been playing games with me," Sarah said after a long silence broken only by the restless sand.

"No. Not that. I did want to talk to you, and I did

want you to come out here with me. And, Sarah, I am really sorry."

"Why are you doing it? What does it mean?"

"A lot of reasons. All that missing paperwork, for openers. Your father's death was too coincidental. I don't buy many coincidences at my end. Do you?"

She shook her head. "Rarely."

"Right. You're not surprised."

"No." Still facing away from him, her gaze fixed on the lake that she no longer saw, she told him about the hat. "I've been back and forth with it," she said. "I don't believe he could have fallen in such a way to do that to the hat, leave blood on the back of it, and then have the hat on the ground, and him facedown in the water. I don't believe that. Today I planned to tell you, let you decide."

He was silent then, and she wondered if he believed her, that she had intended to give him the hat. She did not look at him.

"We're both running the same track," he said then, "with a high fence between us, and now and then there's an opening and we see, by God, we're still nose to nose in a dead heat."

"You said a lot of reasons. What else?"

Slowly he reached past her to the glove compartment and brought out a manila envelope. He was very careful not to touch her in passing. She found herself watching his hands now, tan, long and thin, with prominent veins, one misshapen knuckle, as if it had been broken and not set properly. "We came across this," he said, opening the envelope. He fished out a strip of green feltlike material, about eighteen inches long, an inch wide. "It's the wicking material they use in the greenhouses. This isn't the piece we found, but like it. I got this sample to-day from Carlos in the greenhouse."

She looked from the wick to him, back, and shook her head. "I don't understand."

"Suppose you wanted to make sure someone ran out of gas. You could siphon most of it out, but you wouldn't want to take out too much, or the person might not start at all, not with an idiot light blinking. So you loosen the cap, insert a wick, and let the wind and aridity do the rest. In an hour and a half a lot of gas would go up in evaporation."

"That's reaching," she said. She felt a deep chill that had nothing to do with the breeze.

"I had the wick analyzed. It had dried gas the entire length of it."

"Where did you find it? Your men were looking for traces of gas on the ground where Fran parked that night? Did they find any?" The chill had reached her vocal cords, made her voice sound hollow and distant. She turned again to gaze at the dead lake, the sand that looked quiet, but whispered when she stopped watching it.

"No, they didn't. I'm not surprised. I'd say the best thing to do with siphoned gas is put it in another car, not waste it on the ground. We found this at the landfill. Everyone in East Shasta uses the same service, the same landfill. Nasty job, digging through the junk. We recovered it yesterday. A strip like this, Fran's purse, rubber gloves, a few other things. All in a plastic bag, tossed out with the garbage."

His voice was as distant and dispassionate as a news announcer's—just doing my job, that voice said clearly in every way but words.

"Am I to assume the plastic bag came from the gardens, not just a discount-store bag?"

"Right," he said flatly.

"I see. Why are you telling me this, Lieutenant?" She looked at him, her voice as flat and cold as his. She might have been asking a defendant before the bench if he was ready to plead, if he understood his rights.

Fernandez started the engine. "Professional courtesy?"

"Bullshit!"

He laughed and began to drive. After a moment he said, "I'm telling you things because at heart you're still a trial lawyer, asking questions, making decisions about who might have done this, who might have done that. But this time, in this place, with this cast of characters, it isn't all that safe for you to be asking questions. And I'd appreciate it a lot if, when you get some answers, you let me in on them. Sooner than you did with the hat, I mean. And, I guess, just to warn you that there are more kinds of danger than most people think about. Some of the worst kinds are those you walk into with your eyes wide open, hoping just to pull it off. And that in some cases it isn't the stranger you should be scared of, but someone you might have trusted for a long time." Before she could respond to this, he said, "Tell me something, what's the burnout period for trial lawyers?"

She shrugged. "Million-dollar-a-case lawyers, never. The rest of us, five years, and we've had it with perps, prostitutes, crooked D.A.s, inefficient investigating officers, lazy judges. Most of us can't quit, burnout or not, can't afford to quit. What's the period for police lieutenants?"

"Eight years from the time you start. Same list of reasons as yours, and a few more tossed in probably; night-life on the streets loses its attraction pretty damn fast." He glanced at her. "How about doctors?"

"No idea. I suspect the specialists start to despise noses, or bad knees, or kinked bowels pretty damn fast."

"What about judges?" he asked, keeping his gaze on the road ahead.

"Eighty-five years old, burnout. Or ninety. What's the name of the game we're playing, Fernandez?"

"Just wondering how long before you'd start thinking of retiring. That's a long time," he added soberly.

This time she laughed.

"What about college teachers?" he asked after a lengthy pause.

For a time there was only silence. Then she said, "Or administrators? Can we lump them together? I've known people who never got tired of their jobs, actually."

"Yeah, me too. Some of them are burned out, but they just don't know it, and they get worse and worse, meaner and meaner, and think it's caused by lumbago or something."

She found herself nodding silently. Right.

Soon after that they pulled up alongside her car under the poplar trees back at the house again. "Thank you for coming with me, Judge," he said then. "I'll just pick up that hat now."

It was strange, she thought when she got out; she could relax with him, play games with him even, and find it pleasant, and then a word restored the proper order between them. He was investigating the murder of

her father, suspected her son, suspected she might aid
and abet her son in any way she could to keep him out
of prison. She did not look at him when she got out,
went to her car to open the trunk and remove the large
bag with her father's hat in it. He opened his trunk and
deposited the hat inside, slammed the lid closed, hesitated a moment, then nodded to her politely and got behind the wheel; she walked to the house as he started
his car once more and drove away.

Winnie was waiting for her. "Mother! Uncle Peter
said they're going to exhume Grandpa! They think he
was murdered, too!"

She was deathly pale, haunted-looking, and haggard.
She had lost weight during the past few weeks, her face
was too thin and drawn. Her freckles seemed painted on
skin that was too colorless in spite of a peeling sunburn.

"Is Uncle Peter here?"

"No. He was and he left again. Michael said he had
to drive him back over from the coast. He was raving,
and was going to come alone otherwise, and he's in no
shape to drive that far right now. Michael's worried
about him. Is it true?"

"Yes. Winnie, let's sit down a minute. I have to talk
to you. Are you feeling all right?" They entered the living room and sat down near the front windows.

"I'm okay. Just tired. And Uncle Peter was yelling a
lot. He's not easy to take."

"I know. Winnie, have you considered what tear gas
might do to the baby? If they use it at the demonstration, I mean. And they might."

"Oh God, Mother, not you, too! You're telling me to
behave, just like Uncle Peter!"

"No. Nothing like him," Sarah said harshly. "I'm telling you that from now on everything you do, everything you think, everything you say will in some way be channeled through your child. Every decision you make will be reflected in another being, another person. You're not alone any longer and you won't be alone again for many, many years. That's what I'm telling you. If you don't want a child, for God's sake, abort it now. If you do want it, you have to consider its well-being."

Winnie was staring at her, wide-eyed. "I have friends, too," she said. "Promises, obligations, duties. I can't just pretend they aren't there any more."

"Pretend be damned! It's started, Winnie, and it won't end. You'll be pulled a hundred different ways— duty, friends, family, child, principles, love, you name it, there will be conflicts from now on. It's your decision. But for God's sake, do a little reading, a little research. What does a strong dose of tear gas do to a fetus? Or a kick in the stomach to the mother? Or being dragged by the hair? Or a night in jail? What psychological trauma of yours will have an effect on the baby? When you know the answers, make up your mind."

"That's shitty," Winnie whispered. "Why are you doing this to me?"

"When I became pregnant with you," Sarah said, in a low voice now, "my mother cried. That's all. She just cried and cried. I hated it. I was happy, in love with your father, delighted to be having a baby, and she cried. She never told me why, but I came to understand. She thought my life was ending, and in a sense it was. One life ends, a different one begins. For her, it all ended with marriage, motherhood. That's all she could

see for me. Someone's wife, someone's mother, nothing
of my own. If she had talked to me, if she had told me
how hard it would be, the decisions, the tearing apart
and trying to put yourself back together again and
again, being pulled this way and that over and over, if
she had told me, it would have made a difference. So
many times I thought I was selfish and silly, maybe
even a little crazy, worrying over nothing. Blaine
laughed and told me to just be myself, do what I
wanted; he never understood that you can't just be
yourself again, not until you reinvent yourself. And no
one tells you ahead of time that you'll have to do that,
reinvent yourself over and over."

Abruptly she stood up, aghast at the things she had
been saying to her daughter, amazed at the vehemence
of her words, the passion. Winnie jumped up too and
threw her arms around Sarah, buried her face in her
shoulder and held her.

After a minute or so Winnie sniffed and said, chok-
ing, "Oh, God, I'm crying again. Mother, I love you."
She ran from the room, up the stairs.

Sarah sank down into her chair. Instead of talking
about the murders, about her father's exhumation, about
having her own son probably suspected of murder, she
finally had got around to talking to her daughter about
the facts of life. And by talking about them, discovering
them for herself.

She had decided to have a glass of wine, take an aspirin, and lie down until dinner, but her plans were scut-
tled when her uncle Peter, Michael, and Dr. Wolper
appeared together at the front door.

"Sarah, is it really true? They're going to exhume

Ralph's body?" Uncle Peter asked. His voice was tremulous, he sounded and looked very old and tired.

"Come on in. I was going to have wine. It's true, Uncle Peter. Do you want wine, booze, anything?"

"Good Lord! This is terrible! Terrible! Michael . . ."

"I was afraid of this," Dr. Wolper said. "If there's any question at all . . ."

"You did what you thought best," Uncle Peter snapped. "Michael, there must be a way to stop that man."

"I'll see what Rosa has to drink," Sarah said hurriedly. "Go on into the living room and make yourselves at home. Right back." She fled.

In a few minutes Rosa brought a tray to the living room, and Sarah let the others help themselves. She had a glass of wine finally, and she had swallowed her aspirin in the kitchen, and now waited for it to take effect.

"Sarah, what did he say? Why are they going to do an autopsy? Is that man out of his mind?" Uncle Peter gulped scotch and looked surprised when Michael took the glass from him and added a lot of water.

"Sit down, Uncle Peter. You seem to know more about it than I do. When did you find out? How did you find out?"

"Freddie called earlier today," he said, but he did sit down and glared at his glass, at his son, at Sarah, at Dr. Wolper. For a moment the strong family resemblance was obvious: he looked like his dead brother; then it was gone. He was too pale, too jumpy, too bookish, although physically he was very like her father. Nature had started them more or less alike, and then nurture had worked its way with them, and the two individuals had developed into themselves, and

although they could never have been mistaken one for
the other, now and then a trick of lighting, a fleeting
expression, something appeared in Uncle Peter that
seemed to belong to his brother. Sarah had seen it
with her father also, a momentary flash of Uncle Peter that had come and left mysteriously.

"I thought we were putting this behind us, getting on
with things," Uncle Peter said wearily, "and now ...
Why is he doing this?"

"Dr. Wolper, what did he say to you?" Sarah asked.

"Nothing. Nothing. Just a few questions, routine, I
thought, and then he sprang this."

"Dr. Wolper," Sarah said sharply, "for heaven's sake!
What did he ask?"

"You know," he said resentfully. "The usual things.
Time of death, did I see the body, how long had he been
in the water."

"And the cause of death," she said coldly. "Didn't he
ask that, also?"

Wolper glanced at Uncle Peter, and then at Michael,
and he shrugged. "That, too."

"And what did you tell him?" she demanded. "Do
you know the cause of my father's death?"

"Sarah, this isn't going to get us anywhere," Michael
said. "Freddie talked to Dad and me the day your father
died. There was no reason to suspect anything but a
heart attack. You know that. We all agreed it would be
best to just sign the death certificate without delay, get
on with the funeral, get it over with."

Sarah sipped her wine, her gaze fixed on Dr. Wolper.
"You don't know, do you? A blow to the head, heart attack, stroke, drowning accident ... You don't know."

"Mrs. Drexler, I was treating him for a heart condition, you realize—"

"No, you weren't. He had nothing at all wrong with him. No medications, no restrictions in his diet, nothing."

"I was monitoring his heart closely," he started, and she shook her head at him. "Your father was eighty years old!"

"What do you want from me, Dr. Wolper?" she asked, ice in her voice, in the way she looked at him. He was sweating heavily; an ugly man, she thought then, sagging jowls, paunchy, eyes too small and too restless, with a gaze that never settled anywhere more than a second or two. "You expect me to back up a story about a heart condition? I won't. He didn't have a bad heart. His blood pressure was normal for his age. He was healthy, wasn't he?"

"He was eighty years old," he cried, nearly whining. "Of course, he could have had a heart attack just like that."

"Why did you go to my uncle that day, instead of coming to me? I am legally the next of kin."

"I . . . There wasn't any reason. You seemed very upset, and I knew Ralph and Michael, that's all."

"And when you learned of the autopsy, your first thought was to call Uncle Peter. Why?"

"Sarah," Uncle Peter said, his voice hard and sharp, "what the devil are you implying? Where is this leading? For God's sake, Freddie isn't on trial here!"

"I don't know where this might go. This smacks of the good old boy network, though, doesn't it? The three of you making decisions about what to put on the death certificate, keeping in touch."

"Sarah, be rational," Uncle Peter snapped. "We intend to stop this nonsense. We thought you would want it stopped, also, and you have the legal expertise to know how to put an end to it. Your father had an unfortunate heart attack and fell into the pool and drowned. What good can come of disturbing his grave? Of upsetting everyone all over again? If you're going to become silly over this, just say so, and I'll call Krueger."

She had forgotten that Krueger, her father's lawyer, was also Uncle Peter's attorney. She glanced at her watch. "You won't reach him. And Fernandez intends to do the exhumation very early in the morning. You can't stop it, Uncle Peter. The police not only have the right, they have the duty to investigate suspicious deaths. Krueger can't stop him."

"Oh, God," Wolper said with an agonized expression. He went to the table with the tray and poured himself half a glass of bourbon and drank it as if it were water.

"That's the point," Michael said. "No one had any reason to think it was a suspicious death. At his age a sudden death is not suspicious. He complained of dizziness a time or two, didn't he, Dad?"

"Yes. He was not well. Not sick, but not really well."

"Dr. Wolper, tell them," Sarah said harshly. "What will an autopsy reveal?"

"I don't know," he mumbled.

"Not a bad heart, not a stroke, not anything out of the ordinary? Won't it show a very ordinary, healthy man?" She looked from him to Michael, to her uncle. "Why are you doing this? Why are you fighting so hard?"

"It's the institute," Michael said after a moment. "We can't afford bad publicity at the institute now. We have a stockholders' meeting coming up next month, some important decisions to be made. You know, Jarlstadt's really out, but who's going to replace him? If Freddie gets bad press, and the Kellerman name gets dragged through shit, they'll go to someone from outside, and that would be a mistake."

"My father was on the board of directors," she said slowly. "He never made a cent from the institute, did he? I take it that's not true for you, any of you."

"He sold his shares when he moved out here," Uncle Peter said irritably, as if she should know this already. "He put the money in the gardens, the fool. Freddie had just come along, the institute was changing directions, climbing up out of a trough, not a good time to sell out. He got practically nothing. Then it turned the corner and it has been a good investment for the past fifteen or twenty years. We've always had a connection, the Kellerman family and the institute, you know that. We all thought it was time for a Kellerman to take over the directorship, but now, bad press, scandal, God knows what all. Jarlstadt's going senile, he's no help . . ."

"You should have thought of that before you conspired to sign a false death certificate," Sarah said coldly.

"Come on, Sarah, ease up," Michael said. "I told you. At the time there didn't seem any reason not to believe heart attack. There still isn't any reason to suspect anything else. If it turns out wrong, well, perfect hindsight is not one of the gifts we share."

She shrugged, watching Freddie Wolper, who had been following the conversation with a despairing look. He knew what he had done, she thought grimly, and he knew what it would do for his reputation if it turned out that he was wrong. If anyone wanted to cause trouble legally, he would be in deep trouble; falsifying a legal document was as serious a crime as any district attorney decided to make it; covering up a murder could cost him his license, put him in prison. Wolper was a large man in his forties; he had a long unhappy face with haunted eyes. Haunted by his own dreams, his own ambition cast aside in order to settle for the security of the institute position, by other wrong decisions? She knew nothing about him except that Winnie had been forced to warn him about his hands. That was to know enough, she decided. She watched him pour more bourbon and drink it down and then he put the glass on the table, and started toward the front door without looking at any of them.

"Funny, isn't it, how the institute keeps turning up?" Sarah said then. "Uncle Peter, did the lieutenant tell you yet that they traced calls the woman detective made, they think they know what she was investigating for my father? It was the disappearance of your students twenty-eight years ago. Isn't that strange?"

He looked uncomprehending. "What are you talking about now?"

"He didn't tell you yet? He will. She was looking into that affair for my father. I keep wondering why."

Uncle Peter shook his head. "There's nothing to investigate. It was all over the papers, the newscasts, everywhere."

"They came out here, to the institute that night," Sarah said slowly. "That's what I mean, it keeps turning up at crucial times. The boys visited the institute, they left, and vanished. Mother and Dad came down from Oregon; he left her here and came over to meet my plane and then you came home. I had forgotten all that until today. I've been going over Mother's diaries."

"Well, you might as well put it out of mind again," Uncle Peter said. "There was nothing to investigate. Your father knew as much about it when it happened as anyone else did. What could have turned up so many years later?"

"I don't know," she said. "That's the question, isn't it?"

"Sarah, I know law and science are about as far apart as any two disciplines can be, but didn't you have to learn that it's of absolutely no use to ask questions that can't be answered? Is there a god? Do we have a soul? When the only two people who knew something are both dead without leaving a record of what it was they knew or believed, there's no point in asking what it was. Next you'll propose we hire a channeler or a clairvoyant, a medium."

"Like Mrs. Betancort and her dowser," Sarah said, and shrugged. "If the normal routes don't work, go for the abnormal."

"It was that girl," Michael said then in a savage voice. "Damn her eyes! She had an accomplice around here, sneaking off to be with him, and when Uncle Ralph found out something about her, they had to get rid of his detective and him. And now God only knows where they are. This could all drag on for years!"

Uncle Peter was nodding soberly. "She just turned up, you know. Out of nowhere, talked her way into the gardens. I bet he didn't check on references or anything else. Just took her on."

"What are you both talking about?" Sarah demanded.

"Surely you're not going to make an accusation like that based on absolutely nothing!"

"It's not nothing," Michael said with a slight shrug. "I tried to talk to her once a few months back, and she as much as told me to back off because her friend had a violent temper. I wasn't even a threat, and she told me that. What would it have been if I had posed a real threat?"

Sarah studied him curiously. "How little we all know each other," she murmured. He met her gaze defiantly, then, flushed and angry, he turned away, went to the makeshift bar and poured wine for himself. She remembered Maria Florinda more clearly, how long and beautiful her hair was, how lovely her eyes were, the slender waist, beautifully tapered fingers on the handlebar of a bicycle ... A beautiful young woman. Michael probably had been mildly interested; his marriage was okay, he had said once with a shrug, about what you expect after a time. Bernice was okay, the kids were fine, his career was progressing exactly on course; life was okay, he had said that afternoon six or seven years ago. He would avoid jeopardizing any of it, she felt certain, but, on the other hand, he would not have objected to testing the waters with Maria, the way Freddie had tested the waters with Winnie. And now they would happily offer Maria on the altar of sacrifice.

And it might well work, she knew; if any serious checking was done, Maria's status as an illegal alien would not be hidden very long. If you can't pin it on a drug pusher, go for the alien, any minority, the most helpless ... And usually they were the guilty ones, she reminded herself, the lesson she had learned at Blaine's elbow.

"I think you've got it," Dr. Wolper said, returning from the doorway where he had stopped to listen. "She wouldn't let me examine her last fall, for the insurance policy. She said she would have it done down in Susanville, but I don't think she ever did. I think she has something—AIDS maybe, HIV positive, at least— and she didn't want it to show up on a physical. That would explain why a trained botanist who is also young and beautiful would waste herself on the gardens, wouldn't it?"

Michael nodded thoughtfully, and Uncle Peter drained his glass and set it down hard. "They'll never find her; I bet she's back in Mexico or wherever she came from, and that's the end of that. Let's go, Michael, Freddie."

He nodded curtly to Sarah and stalked out, followed closely by Michael, who shrugged and raised his hands as if to suggest utter helplessness in all this. Wolper did not even glance at her.

Sarah watched them cross the dry grass toward the driveway. They would convince themselves that it was all right to give Maria to Fernandez, with whatever suggestions, tidbits, facts and fancies they dreamed up to support their case, exactly the way they had convinced themselves it was all right to falsify a death certificate. Deny reality and make it go away, she thought at their backs, and, curiously, most of the time it seemed to work for them, while for her it never did. She lacked faith in the rightness of her denial, she thought to herself, and nodded. Exactly so.

The problem was, she understood, that she had no way of knowing if Maria was implicated in the murders or not. What Michael had proposed made a certain amount of sense if Maria was that desperate, and had a friend that desperate. What would it mean to have it discovered that she was an illegal alien, and probably involved in drug smuggling as well? What price had Maria paid for her entry into the United States? Was she still paying the price? Sarah shook her head over the useless speculations. Even Wolper could be right; she might be infected with AIDS or some other horror. Apparently Maria had given Michael the cold shoulder and she had not encouraged Virgil, and for that Sarah was grateful.

Then the thought came to her that if Maria was as innocent as she had appeared, coming back here would be the most dangerous thing she could do. If INS did not get her for illegal entry, or the police arrest her on suspicion of murder, then a killer might well try to get to her, frame her for the murders, fake an accident, a suicide, something.

FOURTEEN

AFTER DINNER UNCLE Peter called and asked if he could drop in. Sarah raised her eyebrows at Winnie and Virgil, and told him, of course.

"Well, I'm out of here," Winnie said firmly. "He's not going to exercise his vocal cords on me again today."

"Me too," Virgil said. "Hey, want to go shoot some pool?"

Winnie looked surprised, then nodded. "Sounds good to me. Let's walk to town."

They both had to put on shoes before they could leave. Virgil was wearing the thongs that he used in the dome, and Winnie was barefoot. Her feet were swelling, she had announced earlier, almost as if proud. "Protect yourself at all times," Winnie said to Sarah at the door. "Belt him one for me if he gets out of hand."

"Respect," Sarah said, rolling her eyes, "where's the respect in this family?"

Virgil and Winnie laughed and walked out.

Sarah went to the kitchen and made a pot of coffee; Uncle Peter probably would not want any, but she would, if only to give her hands something to do.

"Michael and Freddie are playing cards with a couple of the nurses and patients," Uncle Peter said when he arrived. "We had dinner at the institute, you know. They have an extremely gifted cook over there, a real master chef."

Sarah knew he ate over there frequently when he was in the area. She nodded and waited for him to get to the point. They were on the back veranda; the warm glow of the night lights on the paths was just beginning to show up well in the darkening evening.

"You've been reading your mother's papers?" he said finally. "You're going to come across an account of that night we were talking about. Maybe you already have?"

She shook her head. In fact, she had not gone back to the notebooks again, and had no idea when she would do so. It still felt like an intrusion.

"Sarah, I'd better tell you about it. You'll come across something and it's better to hear it firsthand, I guess. Just try to understand." If she did not look at him, did not pay any attention to the meaning of the words, just heard the cadences, the rhythms, he sounded uncannily like her father. She realized she was pressing her feet against the floor, grasping the arm of her chair hard, almost as if she were bracing herself for a roller-coaster ride.

"That day," he said, "back at Hayward, the boys came to the lab and said they were coming out here to see Jarlstadt, exactly as it was reported. They were feeling so good about the work; in another month or six weeks we were going to write our first big paper. In six months we would all be world-famous . . ." His voice sank lower and lower. She had to strain to hear him. "I was going through hell, plain hell, with Emma and the divorce, and working too hard. They said they were taking the weekend off, and were going to play, and on

Monday back to the grind without another pause until the first paper was done, the results made known. And all at once, I just wanted to play too. I hadn't planned on going with them, it was the last thing I had thought about. I had an all-night job running on the computer; it took all night for most things in those days, all night, days, weeks. Anyway, I had signed on for that night and all day Saturday. I thought your folks were at the house, Ralph would want to talk about his woods and rivers and fish, and your mother would bake bread, make cakes, pies, things she missed out in the woods living in a tent or whatever. That seemed like a wonderful way to spend a weekend. No work, no lab, no Emma, no lawyers, just talk about woods and rivers, play hearts, or chess, relax, have some decent home-cooked food. I could take the train back on Sunday, be rested for the next big push."

Sarah remembered how he had come into their house so many times, eating as if famished, praising everything her mother made. Her mother had been an excellent cook, and his appreciation had pleased her; Sarah's father always had taken food for granted and had not given it any thought except when he was hungry, and then he ate everything with what always had seemed the same enthusiasm.

"So I just left things in the lab and came with them," Uncle Peter went on, his voice firmer now. He glanced at her and drew himself up straighter in his chair. "I came with them," he repeated. "They let me out at the driveway and I walked on up to the house while they went to the institute to see Jarlstadt. And I found your mother here alone. Obviously I couldn't stay with her alone in the house. We talked for a few minutes, and I left, and met the boys on their way into town. They planned to go over to three-ninety-five and buy gas and head back to the coast. I think Jarlstadt's reception must have cooled them down; whatever happened, they wanted to be on their way, and I said we could take the gas from the house and skip the detour, just head on back, save an hour at least that way. That's what we did. We always kept two five-gallon cans of gas on hand, you remember? I borrowed it, and we drove back. That was one of the things the police concentrated on, where they got gas for the return trip, who saw them, at what time, and I didn't say a word." He sounded almost defiant now, almost as if lecturing to a class of reluctant students who doubted his methods, his data, or his conclusions. His face was in deep shadow, invisible.

"Anyway, they let me off at school. It was after two in the morning. I simply dropped onto a cot and fell asleep before my head got all the way down."

He became silent. Sarah got up and poured coffee for both of them. "And you didn't tell anyone," she said softly.

"No. God, I don't know why now. At the time I was in shock, afraid, I don't know what I felt. I drove out here late on Saturday and talked it over with Ralph and Rebecca, and we all agreed that I should not get involved. No one knew I had been with them earlier, and it really didn't matter that I had been. I mean their deaths, the accident, whatever happened had nothing to do with coming out here. And it would have destroyed me completely. Drinking with students, running around the countryside with students, abandoning them when they had been drinking. They weren't drunk, but they had been drinking beer; I had been drinking beer earlier, far as that goes. They might have had enough to drink to make them do something reckless, something dangerous, foolish, I don't know . . . But we knew, your father and I knew, how it would look, what I'd be accused of, what it would mean, the consequences for me, and I never told, and neither did Ralph or Rebecca."

Sarah lifted her coffee, thinking of the work he had not published in time for it to have meaning, the way he had dedicated his life to his students, how he had become an exemplary teacher, no longer deeply into research of his own, but encouraging, prodding, goading, whatever it had taken to get his students to be the best. He was right, she knew; his life would have been completely ruined if he had talked then.

"Uncle Peter," she said after a long silence, "I just don't understand why anyone would call my father about that. Even if someone had seen you that night and finally remembered, why call him; why not call you?"

"I don't know," he said heavily. "I believe Mrs. Betancort must have seen me that night. Rebecca said later that Mrs. Betancort hinted that she knew something that concerned me; we thought she assumed I had come out to be with your mother."

Sarah considered this. Someone could have seen him, could have known he was getting divorced in a messy, public way, could have known her mother was here alone, could have made that assumption, but would that someone have waited twenty-eight years to act? Fifteen years after her mother's death. Why? What kind of terrible hatred would fester unrevealed that long? Even if someone had called her father and made such an ugly claim, would he have acted on it? She shook her head. He would not have believed it in the first place, and even if he had been given reason to doubt, he would have known there was no way to prove or disprove any such assertion after so many years. It made no more sense than it had before Uncle Peter's revelations. But it cleared up one mystery, she realized; her father had raged over people taking the gas cans and not replacing them, leaving other people stranded. Gas, she thought then; it kept coming back to gasoline.

"Sarah," Uncle Peter said suddenly, "if the police think your father's death was not natural, and if they try to link his death with that woman's death, a lot of the past is going to be aired again. Ugliness doesn't die, it hides itself, and comes back when you least expect it. I wasn't aware that Rebecca even kept a diary, but there's no reason I should have known that. Your mother didn't really like me much, you know. I thought that if you came across a reference that seems to contradict what was made known at the time, it was only fair to warn you, to prepare you. Now you know."

Exactly what she had thought when she decided she had to tell him about Winnie: prepare him, not let the newspapers break the news to him, not let strangers ask him a lot of questions he was not ready for.

Sarah remembered how much her mother had hated coming to the house after he had been there with his family. She had called them pigs. She always had washed all the dishes, all the pots and pans before using them for her family. She had spent the first day in the Kellerman house cleaning on every trip Sarah could remember. She wondered if the house was filthy now; she had not been inside it in years, and her memories were of her mother sweeping, vacuuming, dusting, scrubbing, and the house needing it. When Uncle Peter was in East

Shasta for more than a few days, she knew, he had a woman come in and clean for him, cook, do laundry. But so often he came over, stayed one or two days, and drove back to his apartment near the college. Back and forth. She suspected he was here long enough to add to the general mess in the house, and rarely here long enough for anyone to do a thorough cleaning job.

She wondered, as she had frequently in the past, why he bothered to come over here at all. He did not seem to derive any great pleasure from the countryside; his tomatoes always died; he bemoaned the lack of restaurants. Michael had made it very clear that he would never set foot in East Shasta if it were not for his father, and, she supposed, the institute. For the first time she wondered which of them intended to take over the institute. Uncle Peter had said a Kellerman, and she had not asked, had not thought to ask then. She had assumed he meant himself. But maybe he had meant Michael. What a plum for him! Become a provost and chairman of the board at the institute in the same summer.

"Uncle Peter," she said, and realized that the silence had extended well past what good manners would have dictated. She had been wrapped in her own thoughts, as evidently he had also. "The morning my father was found, it was nearly nine before anyone had time to go over to your house, and by then you and Michael were both gone. But if Bernice's plane didn't get into Reno until four in the afternoon, why did he go so early?"

"You don't understand a man like Michael, the responsibility he has," Uncle Peter said after a lengthy pause. "He is under a public microscope most of the time. There's never any opportunity to play, to have a drink, to relax. Someone might notice, might talk, might raise doubts about his character, some damn fool nonsense like that. I know that pressure very well, I've lived with it all my life, but you've been saved. Ralph wouldn't have any part of it in his time. It's the price you pay for the security of academia. That day Michael saw an opportunity to play a little, and he took it. A few hours in Reno, who would know? Who would talk? He got up and made coffee and left before six. He was being quiet but I heard him, saw the time; living alone makes one hear every unusual sound in a house, I'm afraid. I don't care how suspicious it appears, it was that simple."

She felt rigid with the memory of walking into a tavern with the purpose of finding a man, any man, for an hour, and then of driving for hours, too fast, too hard, going nowhere and unable to stop. She was grateful that the shadows that concealed him also concealed her. "I understand," she said very quietly. "I think I understand perfectly."

"And the other, the night the boys vanished? You understand that, also, why no one talked about my role in it?"

"Yes," she said in an even lower voice. "I won't bring any of it up, no matter what I find in Mother's diaries."

Uncle Peter left soon after that, and then Winnie and Virgil returned, and Sarah sidestepped their questions about what Uncle Peter had wanted; talk about old times, she said noncommittally. She made a point of showing them how she intended to lock up every night as long as she stayed in the house. She had found a heavy stick that she used for the sliding door. Winnie nodded approval, and Virgil shrugged, not caring one way or the other.

Then, alone again in her room, Sarah got out her mother's notebooks and looked for the year 1963. Her mother had written very little about the incident itself, but she had taped in several newspaper items concerning the disappearance of the students. The youngest of the boys had been Wesley Leszno, who had had polio as a child, and who had talked the others into the weekend outing. He had been twenty-one. The picture showed him to be a thin-faced boy with black hair, dark eyes, walking with crutches. He looked no more than fourteen or fifteen. Mitchell Bookman had been twenty-three, a big-faced blond boy with owlish eyes magnified by thick glasses, and a dimple in his cheek. The paper said he played the cornet. The oldest of them had been Duane Barcleigh, twenty-four, newly married, with a bride twenty years old, Joan Harrison Barcleigh. She looked terrified, very thin, with long straight hair, blond the paper said; it was hard to tell from the picture. She had been visiting her mother in Santa Barbara at the time of the accident, and was staying there to wait for word from her missing husband. Duane Barcleigh had been skeletal, with black-rimmed glasses, heavy dark hair tumbled down nearly to his eyes, an intense stare. He looked like a very young Frank Sinatra.

The print account was the same story everyone already knew, the difference was that now the boys had names, a widow had been named. Suppose someone had seen Uncle Peter with the boys here in East Shasta, or someone had seen them back at the coast, proving he had stayed with them until they were swept out to sea, why call Sarah's father, why call now? Sarah could imagine an accident in which Uncle Peter had not acted, and had found himself trapped by the silence he would have felt forced to maintain.

More than that? No, she decided. His work had been lost with the students; some of it was missing, some indecipherable, some incomplete, and by the time he could have recruited a new team, trained new students, it would have been too late; the biggest prize of all already spoken for. Too many teams in too many laboratories had been searching for the same elusive thing—the structure of DNA. And, although his team had found it, second place was the best he could do after the disaster with the students. His life had been taken off one track, put on another with their deaths.

His lie about his part of the tragedy was understandable, but why someone had called her father about it was not. The question came back repeatedly—irritating, maddening, persistent, unanswerable.

All right, she told herself then, forget that part for now. The police would not care who the suspect was as long as they could prove opportunity. They seldom concerned themselves with motive; that was for the defense team, for the prosecutors, the grand jury, the judge, the probation officers, the tame shrinks hired by both sides. And as far as opportunity was concerned, it was wide open. Sarah might have been the only one in the immediate cast of suspicious characters who had not had an opportunity to get over to Sacramento and go through the office and apartment of Fran Donatio.

After opportunity, suspicious behavior would count heavily. And Maria Florinda had behaved suspiciously by leaving now. If they got seriously interested in her, she would lead them to Virgil. As far as the police were concerned, Virgil would make a classic suspect, better than most because as soon as they started digging, his past would be certain to come out, he would be tagged drug dealer, and the case would be closed right there. The wicking strip, the plastic bag, his prints on Fran's car, his knowledge that she was a detective before anyone had been told ... A very good suspect, Sarah had to admit.

Starting with the conclusion that Virgil didn't do it, then who did? If Carlos, Rosa was also involved. He could not have gone to Sacramento without her knowledge; he could not have come to the gardens early enough to kill Ralph Kellerman without her knowledge. He even had a motive; he had inherited ten percent of a growing business. If guilty, would Carlos have handed the hat over to her? She shook her head. And Carlos had never owned a gun in his life, Rosa had said once. Nor had Rosa. This was what defense attorneys did, she thought then, surprised at the role she had assumed, exactly as Fernandez had said.

Not Winnie. No reasons needed for the way Sarah was playing the game now, she thought almost derisively. She hesitated over Maria. She did not have a car, and to borrow a car to follow someone in order to kill her was ludicrous, and then borrow it again to go to Sacramento. But had Maria had a mysterious friend lurking around the area? Maybe, Sarah conceded, but no stranger had come on the grounds to steal the wicking material, or the plastic bag. Maria and an accomplice? She did not strike Maria's name from the list.

Wolper? She did not know if he owned a gun, if he had an alibi for any of the crucial times, and none of that seemed important. He had lied about her father's death. She realized that it would give her great satisfaction to see him being hauled away by the police. Bias, she warned herself, and nodded, absolutely right.

Michael? She knew he could shoot and hit a target; they had practiced at Ghost Lake many years ago, shooting cans off ruined buildings, pretending they were actors in a wild west extravaganza. He had had the opportunity, and he had a reputation to protect.

Uncle Peter. Although the disappearance of his students seemed to have been the only incident of interest in a life thereafter devoted to teaching, and there was no apparent reason for that incident to have been revived now, it seemed to have been the catalyst for whatever else had happened. What did he do all the time? she wondered suddenly. She supposed there might have been some women in his life, but if so he had been very discreet about them. Her father had commented on the celibate role the two of them had assumed, her father when he became a widower, Uncle Peter through divorce. All her father's excess passion had gone into the gardens when Rebecca died, but what about her uncle? Had his devotion to his students been enough? She did not know.

She realized she did not know how Michael or his sisters felt about their father now. As children, they had complained about his strictness, his temper. She had complained about her father's temper, too, she recalled, although he had not been strict, and she could not remember a time when his rage had been directed at her. She vaguely remembered Michael's mother, Emma, a plump dimply woman, with a hearty laugh, and a blind eye to dirty dishes, unmade beds, all the things that had bothered Sarah's mother so much. Michael had been very fond of her, but what he thought of his father she could not guess. A sense of duty, responsibility, but was there more than that? They shared such a need for propriety, she thought, and admitted that she did, also, and resented it more than she could say. If she admitted to Michael how much it disturbed her, would he admit to the same deep hatred for the hypocrisy they both had to maintain? At one time in their lives, many years ago, she felt she could have answered that question without hesitation; now she did not even attempt an answer. Michael was a stranger to her, as was his father.

She paced, found herself down in the living room pacing there, back up the stairs, her thoughts going in circles. If they had been tangible, she would have found herself tightly bound in a cocoon, she told herself irritably.

The gun, she thought then, in the kitchen, water pouring over the rim of a glass she held. Absently she turned off the water, and put the glass down, walked back upstairs and got ready for bed as she pondered: Where was the gun? Any of them had had ample opportunity to get rid of a weapon, but she didn't believe anyone would have got rid of a gun; it would still be somewhere nearby, handy to use again if necessary, or else to use to frame someone else. She lay in bed staring at the ceiling that was marginally paler than the walls.

Then she thought of Lieutenant Fernandez, and thinking of him, she found herself restless again. She had not had sexual arousal like that for many years; she and Blaine had settled into a relationship in which sexuality had been important, but not blatant, not forcing itself at unexpected times, unexpected places. Their rhythms

FIFTEEN

ALL MORNING SARAH wandered from room to room, picking up a book, putting it down, picking up the latest horticulture magazine, putting it down, arranging, rearranging water lilies in a crystal bowl, pacing out to the veranda, back inside. At ten Rosa came to tell her, "It's done. They're gone now."

Sarah sat down heavily and nodded. And soon they would know, she thought, but that wasn't right; she and Fernandez already knew. Soon they would have something to show the world, to let the world know. Winnie came to the living-room door, looking haunted, the way she did these days.

"I'm going to take the color film to the drugstore," Winnie said. "Rusty Curlow flies into Reno this evening. I want to get the color shots in to the processor."

Sarah jumped up. "I'll come with you. Walking?"

"Yes. It isn't very hot out yet. I need to walk every day, they tell me."

"So do we all," Sarah said. Walk, run, move, do something.

As long as they walked in the shade, the air was pleasantly cool, but the sun was brutal already, and they passed in and out of shade, in and out. They would both

233

burn, Sarah thought, and tried to banish the worry about diminished ozone layers, about the hole in the atmosphere growing larger day by day, about ultraviolet rays cooking her eyes, her brain cells, her skin. She could almost feel the freckles popping; sometimes she thought she could hear them as if they were popcorn exploding.

"I thought you had a darkroom in the upstairs bathroom," she said as they walked.

"That's just for black and white stuff. All the shots I took out at Ghost Lake, things like that. The garden shots are color for the catalog, and that gets into lab work." She went on moodily, "I don't know what to do about Maria and Virgil, how I'll finish the cassette for the franchise idea."

She walked briskly, faster than Sarah would have chosen, but Winnie was the one who felt the need for x hours of exercise daily, Sarah conceded, and kept up, getting hotter and hotter.

"I'll wrap it up this weekend," Winnie was going on, muttering to herself more than to her mother. "And later I'll try some fancy editing, move the image of Maria from here to there a few times. What a mess!"

"You can do that? I know you can with film, but I didn't realize you could with videos."

Winnie began to describe some of the equipment she and her partner Andi already had, and what they intended to buy in the coming years, all high tech and complicated-sounding—remote-control devices, programmable timers, editing machines. Most of it sounded like equipment for a space launch, as if it had nothing to do with art.

Then Sarah was thinking that there had been timers around for half a century or even more, of one sort or another. It wasn't that the ideas were new, it was the equipment that had become more powerful, more accessible. Suddenly she thought she knew how Ghost Lake had been haunted.

"Mother?"

"Hm? Sorry, honey. What?"

"Nothing. You do that a lot, you know? We're here, and I asked if you want something cold to drink."

It was not that she had been unaware of her surroundings; she knew perfectly well that they had passed the few blocks that were not "downtown" and had arrived at the two-square-blocks hub of East Shasta. The hardware store was here, and the grocery, the tiny K-Mart discount store, and before them the drugstore and department store combination. They had passed the Baptist Church, and the Church of Jesus Christ; they had stopped for the red light at the traffic signal, and today there had even been two cars at the intersection.

Sarah grinned at her daughter. "Sorry. Thinking, and about the drink, you bet. I wonder if Milton Flink is here."

They went inside the small building painted blue that housed the drugstore as well as a general merchandise department that had things like hammers and dish towels, nylon string for weed cutters, diapers and picture frames, all jumbled more or less together in no discernible order. There was a soda fountain, with iron tables and folding chairs with gray vinyl seat pads. Milton Flink was in the pharmacy section.

He was a balding man two or three years younger than Sarah, and one of the best dancers she had ever seen. They had danced together many times during her various visits home.

"Hi, Milton," she said.

He looked up, saw who it was and came around the counter to take her hand. "Sarah, I can't tell you how awful I feel about . . . you know. Everyone in town feels the same way. If there's anything I can do . . ."

She withdrew her hand gently. "Thanks, Milton. Thanks a lot. I'd really rather not talk about it. How are you?"

Winnie had nodded to him and moved on past to talk to a young woman behind a different counter, one marked *Post Office, UPS, Wrapping, Copies Made, Videos.*

Milton was telling Sarah how he was, not too bad considering, but the kids were coming down with something, he hoped not summer colds, you know how mean they can be, and Judy was not very well, pregnant again, you know . . .

She nodded from time to time. "Can we get a Coke? Want to join us for something to drink?"

He did. He went back around the counter and put drinks and glasses with ice on a tray, and came back out. "My treat," he said seriously.

"Thanks," she said, just as seriously. She took a drink, burned her tongue as she had known she would, and nodded. "That's better. Are you still at the institute most of the time?"

"Yes, three or four days a week there, a few hours here, all day Saturday and Sunday." She had forgotten how conscientious he was, how he always explained everything. "I'm working too hard, I guess. Workaholic, as they say, Type A, that's me. Things are pretty quiet at the institute these days, though, it comes and goes, busyness, I mean . . ."

He talked on and she did not interrupt him for several minutes until Winnie joined them and gulped her drink.

"Winnie's been taking pictures of local attractions," Sarah said. "Like the Ghost Lake area. I think she needs some history to go with the pictures. I mean, not many lakes get renamed within the memory of the local residents."

"It was Rabbit Lake when I was a boy," Milton said earnestly, right on cue, to Winnie, who looked bewildered. "No water, but a shoreline that's still there, and a lake bed with pockets of quicksand. Just plain old Rabbit Lake, without any rabbits by that time." He laughed. "Should have called it No-Rabbit Lake."

He laughed again, and Sarah was remembering why she had been willing to dance with him frequently: he was a great dancer, and he did not talk while he danced. She nodded encouragingly to him. "You were there when they renamed it, weren't you?"

"Sure was. Let's see, that would be along about nineteen sixty-eight or sixty-nine. Sixty-eight," he said almost triumphantly. "I still had braces on. Year Mrs. Betancort tried to start a commune out there. She had her scientist climbing all over the hillside looking for water, and he kept saying there wasn't any, but she'd send him up to look under another rock. She tried to make him hit the rocks with a willow stick, but he wouldn't do it. He didn't stay more than two or three days altogether, and he went away saying what he said when he got there, no water. The lake was still Rabbit Lake then."

He was gazing thoughtfully into space, considering, recalling the time. He nodded then. "Yes, it was still Rabbit Lake then. Wasn't until the Indian came in that

it turned to Ghost Lake. Mrs. Betancort got hold of this
Indian who could find water, dowse for it, and come up
with water every time, if there was any to find. He said
he was from Black Horse, Nevada. Never heard of it,
myself, but that's what he said. I think Mrs. Betancort
sort of overlooked part of what he said, if water was
there to find, he'd find it. I think she believed her Indian could make it happen no matter what. She was all
over town crowing about him, his successes everywhere
he went, and that she had hired him on. So there was a
good little audience when he went out there trying to
find water, and he used a stick, but I don't know what
kind. It could have been willow, but I never got close
enough to examine it. He brought it with him. And the
first day he was out there, the ghosts started, just as if
they thought he might find water and disturb their rest
or something. We hadn't heard anything like them before he turned up. He quit for the day, and the next
morning he started again, and in the afternoon so did
the ghosts. No one came out from town that day, as I
recall. I suppose they all thought the show was over already."

Winnie had been restless and fidgety at first, but she
had stopped moving and was listening with attention.
Milton grinned at Winnie, evidently pleased with her
fascination, and continued his story.

"Well, me and two others, we knew someone was
just playing a trick, and we laid low the next day up on
the road before you get to the lake, and we waited. He,
someone, would come along and make the noises, we
thought, and we'd grab him. We thought it would be
someone from town because all the commune folks
were real believers; they wouldn't have dared pull a

trick like that on Mrs. Betancort. Only no one came. The ghosts started just like they had done before, and they kept it up and kept it up, the voices floating out from the lake, but there wasn't anyone on the road, or in the scrub, or behind a rock. No one was out there but the commune folks and the Indian dowser, and he wasn't there much longer. I think he lasted three days. Maybe four. And the ghosts just went on and on for most of the summer. We headed back to town, me, my dad and mom, Johnny and Rae, we'd had enough of Mrs. Betancort, the ruins, the lake you not only couldn't drink or swim in, but couldn't even walk on, and now ghosts. It was enough. No one stayed after that. Within a week it was over, no more commune. No more Rabbit Lake, either. It was Ghost Lake from then on. Mrs. Betancort went back to her big house and waited for the end to come, the way she had predicted it would, and we've been waiting ever since. Reckon one of these days, it will happen." He laughed again.

"Was the Indian trying to find water on the hillside, the way the hydrologist had?" Sarah asked.

"Nope. He said if there was quicksand, there was water, and he went out on the lake to find it. He used a long pole, felt his way with a pole before he took a step. Like feeling for river bottom in a boat, like Mark Twain."

"And you thought someone was playing a dirty trick on you all?" Winnie asked then. "Do you still think so?"

"I don't know what to think. We looked for someone, we really did look, but there wasn't anyone out there. I tried to imagine how anyone could have pulled it off, and maybe someone could have, but it would be complicated, not just a prank, and what for? That's what stopped me, there just wasn't any reason for a complicated trick, one that took smarts and equipment and time to set up. I mean, if anyone wanted to get at Mrs. Betancort, all he had to do was wait until the commune was going and the end didn't come. Or just wait for the weather to change. Those folks wouldn't have lasted through the winter. First good freeze, they'd have scattered. Wasn't as if anyone wanted to drive them out to get at the hidden gold, or the lost silver mine, or because the train was coming through and this would make a stopping place. No movie gimmicks worked, is what I'm saying. The ghosts started, the commune left, the ghosts kept on for a month or so, and stopped. And that's it."

"You don't believe they were ghosts, do you?" Winnie demanded.

"I don't know what I believe," he said slowly. "I didn't, then I did, then I didn't. Problem is that I don't believe in ghosts, but we heard something, all right. Like a moaning, crying, soft voices rising and falling, sort of calling for help, stopping and then starting up again. We all heard it, the Indian heard it and left. What we heard, I don't know. That's what makes ghost stories so unsatisfactory, isn't it? You never really know what you've tangled with."

"You went back and heard the same noises?" Winnie asked, as intense as before, as demanding. Sarah felt an uneasiness stir in her at Winnie's intensity.

"A couple of times," Milton said contentedly. At first he apparently had assumed Sarah was the audience, his story had been directed at her, but gradually he had switched to Winnie and by now he was paying very little attention to Sarah. "Never alone, though. Three times to be exact. Same time of day, late in the afternoon, but before dark. It always started about three or four, and went on for a few hours, sometimes until well after dark. Spooky thing to hear if you believe in ghosts or don't."

"That's a terrific story," Winnie said, leaning back in her chair, satisfied at last. "I'll put it with the pictures, all right. I love it!"

"You like to dance?" Milton asked, surprising them both; he sounded almost mournful.

Sarah bit her tongue to keep from smiling, and Winnie nodded. "Sure. Why?"

"Well, I just thought that if you show up at Dacey's Saturday night, we might dance a little. Sarah dances like an angel, but probably this isn't a good time for her."

"Oh. I guess I'm not feeling much like dancing either right now, Mr. Flink," Winnie said carefully. "Mother, shouldn't we be on our way soon?"

"Yes indeed. Milton, it's good to see you again. Please give my best to Judy." He looked so sad that she was inclined to pat his head as they walked past him; she resisted, and by the time she and Winnie reached the door, he had gone behind the pharmacy counter and was busy again.

Back out in the sunlight, the heat, walking more slowly now than they had before, Winnie looked at Sarah suspiciously. "You dance like an angel? I never saw you dance at all."

"Oh well, Blaine didn't care for dancing, and it sort of fell out of my life. Except when I came here to visit. Mother and Dad and I used to dance out in the wilderness, in a cabin, a tent, whatever." Her voice was soft, remembering. "They taught me, but Milton is the best dancer I've ever seen. Hard to believe, isn't it?"

"Hard is not exactly the word I'd choose," Winnie said. "Who's Judy?"

"His wife," Sarah said airily. "Thought it was time to remind him of her."

Winnie laughed a low dirty laugh, and linked her arm through Sarah's. "He's a creepo, but that was a great story."

Sarah nodded, still remembering her childhood, her youth. "One time when I was little and we were up in the Blue Mountains in Oregon, it rained for a solid week, day after day after day. We were all going stir crazy, Mother, Dad, I. You know, I've told you, how they tutored me all the time. By the time I was ready to be enrolled in school, and should have been in the third or fourth grade, I was ready for junior high; that's how hard they worked me. Anyway, this rainy week Dad decided to give me some lessons in chemistry and in engineering, I think. He rigged up an experiment that used something like mercury, but not mercury, I'm sure. He put it in a tiny vial with a membrane cover that was pliable. I seem to remember it as leaf gold, but that's probably wrong. It's been a long time," she said with a soft sigh.

They had been in a cabin with two rooms and a small bath that had a shower in the center of the ceiling so that everything got wet when it was on. She remembered how shocked and furious she had been the first time she used it, and her pajamas and towel had been soaked.

In her mind's eye she could see the Rube Goldberg invention of her father's. The vial with something that was not mercury, the membrane cover, and a thin wire taped to it. The wire connected to a battery and that connected to a doorbell. Carefully they positioned the vial on the windowsill that rainy afternoon, and then they played hearts for the next few hours. Most likely they had danced after dinner; they often had done so. She had danced with her father, with her mother, the three of them together, her parents together and Sarah alone ... Days passed, but eventually the sun had come out again, and her mother had dropped a skillet when suddenly the doorbell began to ring; it played chimes, "How Dry I Am," over and over and over until they disconnected the wire.

"The sun heated the vial, expanded the contents and raised the membrane, and so on," Sarah said, walking with Winnie, thinking of her own childhood. "As long as it was hot enough to keep the membrane up, keep the connection, that silly doorbell would have kept playing. When it cooled off, it stopped. The next day it did it again, of course."

Winnie laughed. "You think one of the boys did something like that? Maybe your dancing angel himself?"

"Who knows who did it, or why? But I'd be willing to bet that it was something like that doorbell trick, maybe with a tape player, a tape loop. The sun hit a certain place in the rocks, a connection was made, and it started, and when it cooled off after dark, it stopped."

"Grandpa might have done it," Winnie said after a moment. "It's the sort of thing he might have done." She looked pleased with the idea of her grandfather playing this sort of prank.

"I know. He would have loved doing just that when

he was young; he hated fanatics of any stripe, especially religious, superstitious fanatics. However, he and Mother were up in Oregon by then, in Portland, where he had that office job he loathed, and he was not young anymore. We heard about Ghost Lake in the fall when we came here for Thanksgiving. Today is the first time I've heard the whole story told by someone who was actually there. Before, it was just that ghosts came out and drove people away. It's a good story."

"Boy, if I could get photographs of two or three more special places, like the lake, and great stories to go with them, and put it all together in a book . . ."

As Winnie talked on, Sarah felt her eyes burn. *Honey, she wanted to scream, stop this. You're going to be a single parent, remember?* Angrily she pushed the thoughts away; Winnie was smart, smarter than she had been at that age, and she, Sarah, was damned if she would play her own mother's role. Winnie would find her way, she told herself. Hers and her child's.

Several people came up to her as they walked, shook her hand, one woman patted her shoulder, and Winnie's, and walked away shaking her head. Mrs. Betancort appeared across the street, walking heavily with her cane; she began to hurry across the empty street, her gait very awkward.

"Who calls forth the spirits, who disturbs their rest is himself called from rest," Mrs. Betancort said, starting to speak while still in the middle of the street. Sarah and Winnie had come to a stop. "And when they shall say unto you, Seek unto them that have familiar spirits, and unto wizards that peep, and that mutter: should not a people seek unto their God? for the living to the dead?"

"Mrs. Betancort, I don't understand what you are trying to tell me," Sarah said.

"Hah! She speaks, the wicked Jezebel speaks. I saw three unclean spirits like frogs come out of the mouth of the dragon, and out of the mouth of the beast, and out of the mouth of the false prophet."

Sarah took Winnie by the hand. "Let's go," she said angrily.

"Go! Go! O daughter of Babylon, who art to be destroyed."

Sarah and Winnie were nearly running, leaving her on the sidewalk talking to them, her words mixed with loud laughter now.

"Flee, flee! Steal no more, o backsliding daughter. Leave me in peace, and my bed, and my chairs, and my water. Bring your pails to my well no more!"

"Why does she hate us so much?" Winnie whispered when they were halfway down the block.

"I believe she thinks my parents stole the water from Ghost Lake," Sarah said in a low voice.

"You're kidding."

"I wish."

"But Grandpa didn't even start the gardens until years after her stupid commune failed."

"I know. Rosa said she's lost in time, it's all now for her, no before and after. She just knows what she knows. She's pathetic."

"Yeah, like a witch is pathetic." She made a rude grunting sound. "If she offers you an apple, run."

There would be nothing for Fernandez to report today, Sarah told herself that afternoon. And probably nothing over the weekend, although that was less certain. She suspected that if Fernandez ordered the autopsy pronto, it would be done pronto; she suspected that he got his way more often than not. And that took them to Monday or Tuesday, she continued, leaving it open if anything would be done over the weekend. Even if it were, she probably wouldn't be told until next week. And Dirk Walters was due to call back on Monday or Tuesday.

"It's just too goddamned much," she muttered under her breath. She couldn't rid her mind of the image of her father standing at the edge of the pool, talking quietly to the fish he loved, and then the blow to the back of his head, the fall forward ... She sat on the veranda brooding over it, seeing it play through again and again until she was forced to her feet, to pace again, although she was exhausted from so much aimless walking.

She would tell Dirk no. If Virgil was arrested, charged with murder, she would have to be on his defense team; she did not trust anyone else to win his case, although she was uncertain that she had any chance of winning either. She was not at all certain there was an attorney in the country who could be any more sure than she was of winning: if they charged him with murder, they would convict him of smuggling both people and drugs. And the murderer would still be at large. Her nails dug into her palms and she forced her hands to open, to relax.

So, she went back to her practice conversation with Dirk, she would tell him no, no reason, of course, and then wait and see. How long? Until they charged Virgil or found the killer, she answered. Who could say how long either one would take?

What made it harder to bear was the fact that Virgil did not know the danger he was in. He was working long hours, doing his work, Maria's work; no doubt some of her father's work had landed on his shoulders also. He was tired every night, up early every morning, withdrawn and silent, preoccupied with worry about Maria, and oblivious to his own predicament. No more fun and games for him these days, no more monkeying around with skates, teasing his sister. It was as if her son, who had been a child only two weeks ago, was her adult son now with no transition period. One day, child, next day, mature adult.

Fernandez had not told her in so many words to keep his confidences quiet, but it was there by implication, and even if not, she would have kept quiet at this time simply because there was no reason to frighten Virgil until it was necessary. She was glad he did not see the danger yet. At least, he was sleeping well; she knew Winnie was not, and neither was she.

She sat and gazed at the ponds, and she thought, all her life she had been so used to her father's decisions to do this, to do that, go here, go there; she never had questioned any of them, any more than her mother had questioned. And how oblivious he had been; he had assumed that because he hated being stationed in Portland, his wife also had hated it, when actually she had rejoiced at a real house, a real roof, a real bathroom, all the things other women never had to think about. Sarah thought about his ignorance of what it was that her mother had wanted to do and never attempted. He had had no clue about what it was or, indeed, that there could have been anything she yearned for beyond the life he gave her.

And they had been a loving couple, both of them loving to their only child, solicitous, deeply concerned with her. Even at the time that she had thought with terrible guilt that she was tearing them apart with such an early marriage, they had shown nothing but love for her. She had had to stay in one place to finish up high school, and none of them had wanted her to go to a boarding school; her mother had opted to stay put for those four years, provide her a home, and a home for Ralph when he was free to come home. If that period had lasted any longer than four years, she was certain, they would have exploded, one, all of them. A boarding school would have been better, she knew now, but at the time the arrangement had seemed to work. She had been aware of the unhappiness of both her parents, the loneliness of her mother, while her father had spent most of those years tramping the mountains of eastern Oregon and northeast California alone. Her mother had worried so about him, afraid he would have an accident, afraid he was not eating properly, not dressing for the weather, not sleeping ... Then he would appear and they would have a joyous reunion, followed by recrimination and tears on her mother's part, and puzzlement on his. It was terribly obvious that he had not worried about her and Sarah for even one second during their separation. Missed them, of course, loved them, no doubt, but worry about them? What for? Never.

Her mother's existence had consisted of a lifetime of going where she didn't want to go, being where she didn't want to be, living in a way that most of the time was hateful to her, lonely, all because she was married to him, a man she had loved fiercely, but who was her destroyer.

Sarah hugged her arms hard about herself at the thought, and could not deny it because she had been in the same trap that had snared her mother. She had loved her father very much, and she had been dragged here and there from camp to cabin to trailer to tent for years because he had to have it that way. She had not questioned his need, or her own, or her mother's. That was how life was.

It was no good asking why her mother had put up with it, why she had not objected, struck out for herself. What she might have done was really beside the point, maybe nothing, maybe something wonderful, but she put aside ambition, talent, whatever it had been. Sarah doubted that her mother had ever considered a choice possible, the idea that she might have had a separate life never occurred to her. She had loved her husband, it was that simple.

Staring ahead, Sarah saw her life as walking from box to box, boxes placed before her by someone else, never examined, but merely accepted, no choice ever consciously made. Her father's box, the school box, Blaine's. Now her son was determining her future, shaping her decisions, and he was not even aware of it. But neither had Blaine been aware, nor had her father been aware. That was the position of real power, she thought bleakly; you never had to consider the other, but expected what was good for you couldn't be bad for her. What's good for GM is good for the country, she said to herself. That same bland easy assumption. If she went out to the greenhouse to find Virgil, to tell him the position he was placing her in, he would be as bewildered as her father had been the time she asked him what her mother had wanted to do with her life.

Virgil would insist that she didn't have to pass up anything on his account, she knew; she could almost hear the words in his voice. She had heard those words in Blaine's voice, and, earlier, in her father's voice. What he would mean was that in her place *he* would not have to pass up anything.

She knew she would not tell him, he would never suspect even. Now, in full awareness of the choice she was making, she still could not confront the other with it; it would be humiliating. She was acknowledging her position, her place in the scheme of things, her acceptance that her life, her future, was forfeit, that his needs came before hers. But his needs concern life and death, she argued with herself, and mockingly asked, *And your needs don't?*

Wearily she got up to go take an aspirin. A headache lived at the edge of her consciousness permanently, it seemed, and now and again, it surged forward demanding attention. She had not banished it altogether for the two weeks she had been here; the most she could hope for was to make it recede, go back to the boundary that separated awareness and non-awareness where it had taken up residence.

How wonderful it would be, she thought, to be able to will oneself into unawareness, into obliviousness, not unconsciousness, but rather ignorance of the others around. Blind to them for periods of hours, days the way children are, with no more malice than children harbor, the way her children regarded her most of the time, the way she had regarded her own mother most of the time. A string of women back through history, she went on, the mothers we don't know, don't dare know. The headache was a stabbing pain behind her eyes by then. She hurried for her aspirin.

SIXTEEN

SHE WAS MISSING something, Sarah thought later that day, watching Winnie's bright hair appear and vanish as she ducked her head over her camera, straightened up, ducked again. The sun on her hair was brilliant. Her own hair must have looked much like that a few years earlier, Sarah thought, and she recalled that her mother's hair had glowed like fire in the sunlight. It was no wonder that poor old Mrs. Betancort could not keep them straight. And, she mused, how strange it was that her thoughts came back again and again to Mrs. Betancort, who did not seem to differentiate between the generations of Kellerman women.

Apparently Mrs. Betancort had seen Uncle Peter with the gas cans, and Sarah's mother, but how? Where? And presumably she had mistaken Uncle Peter for Sarah's father, whom she accused of stealing her water. She couldn't keep the men straight, couldn't keep the women straight.

Slowly Sarah walked back inside and upstairs again, and began to read through her mother's account of that night once more. She was missing something, not only concerning the gas cans, but something else, she felt certain.

She skimmed through the newspaper stories, paused

at the photographs, tried to find the false note that she
knew was there. Slowly she went back to the start of
this section. As far as Sarah knew, her mother never had
mentioned that Uncle Peter had turned up that night,
and it seemed obvious that she had not put it in writing
either. There was no personal recollection of that night
in her notebook, what she had seen, said, done, and no
mention of the gas. Sarah reread Dr. Jarlstadt's interview, his grief, his regret at not having the boys wait inside the house, all there, immediate. Then she read part
of the interview again, slower: "Wesley said they would
go see the ghost town and come back in two hours. We
waited up for them, but they never returned."

The ghost town and the dry lake that had been called
Rabbit Lake at that time, again.

She sat on the side of the bed, staring at nothing, trying to work out the scenario for that night. Her father
had dropped off her mother at the house in the afternoon, and had driven over to Sacramento in order to
meet Sarah early the next morning. Uncle Peter had arrived in East Shasta at seven or a little later. That was
the time the boys had shown up at Jarlstadt's house.
Uncle Peter had left and met the boys on the road, and
they told him they were going back to the coast. On
foot, he would have gone the closest way to join the
boys again, out his driveway, past the property that later
became the gardens, and into the driveway of the institute, less than a quarter of a mile altogether, and there
was no way anyone in town could have seen him if he
had stayed at this end of East Shasta. But then when did
they get the gas, and had Mrs. Betancort seen them do
it? Her house was a mile from his, at the far end of
town, and there was no reason for him to have been

there, or for her to have been at this end. Maybe she had meant something else altogether, Sarah admitted, and the reference to Sarah's mother had nothing to do with gas and that night.

Suddenly Sarah knew what had been bothering her. Her father had not known that Uncle Peter had taken the gas; that accounted for his anger over being stranded. She remembered clearly how furious he had been because he did not have enough gas to get to Susanville one day that week, and not only had there been no gas, but the cans themselves had been taken. And she remembered her mother's silence during his rage. She had not told him Uncle Peter had been there, Sarah realized; Uncle Peter had shown up late on Saturday and told them about the missing students, and he and her mother had acted as if he had not been there on Friday night. He had stayed with them for several days, and the following week her father had borrowed enough gas from the institute to get to Susanville, where he had bought two new cans and filled them. She had gone with him to the institute to return the gas he had borrowed that afternoon and he still had been furious with the idiot who had taken cans and all.

Very slowly now she went back to the spiral notebook and examined it, read the entries through once more about the night Uncle Peter's students had vanished. Often her mother had written very little, let the events speak through the assortment of things she associated with them—newspaper items in this case. But she would have mentioned something about this, Sarah argued silently; this was too big for her not to write about it. Yet there was nothing in her fine script.

Sarah looked at the cover of the notebook, seventy-five pages, and then began to count. There were seventy-three pages. Proving what? she demanded of herself, and had no answer. Her mother, her father, someone else could have removed the pages at any time.

Uncle Peter had said Rebecca never did like him, Sarah remembered. She felt as if she had been blind for many years, and only now had been granted the gift of sight. Her mother had *hated* him, and all her ranting about the mess in the house had been displaced anger. She had not singled him out, but had lumped them all together, him, his wife, his children, and raged against them all; she had discharged her anger that way. And she never had told Ralph what had caused such anger; Sarah was certain that he had been as blind to her anger as Sarah had been. Her mother never had told anyone, not her husband, not her daughter. She had written nothing to indicate how angry she was or why.

Had Uncle Peter known she would be alone in the house that night? What had happened between them? Sarah found herself running her fingers gently over the notebook, asking, "Who were you? What were your secrets?" Had she never confided in anyone? Her anger with Uncle Peter reached back to the beginnings of memory; Sarah did not know a time that her mother had been easy with him, friendly with him, only polite. Always mercilessly polite, and angry.

And her father had never suspected, any more than Sarah had. Was that why Uncle Peter had come to East Shasta the next day, to make certain she had not told, would not tell that he had been there the previous night? Sarah remembered Fernandez's surprise that Uncle Peter had come here at that time, and her explanation that he had turned to his only family for comfort, and she knew now that she had been hasty. Maybe that had been the reason, maybe not.

Uncle Peter was ten years younger than her father, seven years younger than her mother. When Sarah was born in 1944, Uncle Peter had been twenty-three, her mother thirty. Those were the war years, she remembered, her father in Intelligence, Uncle Peter in the Air Corps, her mother a war bride stranded alone in Washington part of the time, in California part of the time working for a munitions plant. And whatever had happened between Uncle Peter and her mother must have happened then, before Sarah's memory started, possibly even before she had been born. Sarah shook her head then and stood up.

"All right," she said to the notebooks. "All right." She would take them with her, keep them with her, study them, and try to learn her mother. The picture in her mind of the tutor, the woman who had played games with her, who had danced with her, who had watched with her while a snake shed its skin, who had taught her to bake and to sew, who had wept at her marriage and pregnancy, that woman was no more than a shadow on the wall, Sarah had come to realize finally, and also that to get to know the woman who had cast the shadow was impossible now, but she would start, she would try.

And none of this had anything to do with her father's death, with Fran Donatio's death, she reminded herself.

Was this what grief was all about, she asked herself then, a replaying of the past with the omissions, the guilt, the bits of carelessness all on display to be examined over and over? The knowledge that now that your eyes had been opened you couldn't tell the one person to whom it was important what it was that you saw at last? The need to say "I'm sorry," and the awareness of the immensity of the vacuum in which to hurl and lose the words?

She had gone through this for Blaine, night after night of her own private picture shows of the past played over and over; and now fifteen years too late she was grieving for her mother.

Winnie came to fetch her down to dinner, and she was grateful for the outside imposition of order on her chaotic thoughts.

Winnie told Virgil the story Milton Flink had passed on about the ghost voices at Ghost Lake. "So," she concluded, "someone played a dirty trick, but why? Why would anyone go to that kind of trouble? Would teenagers?"

"Are you kidding?" Virgil asked. "You know they would. And someone who's crazy would do it. Someone who really hated old lady Betancort. Pick one."

"Teenagers here?" Winnie asked, frowning. "In a city probably, but out in a wasteland like this? Someone would snitch on them for sure, and then it's up-the-creek time."

Virgil considered this, and finally agreed. "Yeah, they always tell, sooner or later. Like the time we put Dutch Boylston's VW bug in the middle of the fountain. Remember? Before a week passed, Richie was blabbing about how we did it."

Sarah bit her cheek and concentrated on her roast pork, which was succulent, spicy, and excellent. She had not learned of that escapade for a month after it happened, and by then everyone knew all about it.

"So then someone who really hated Mrs. Betancort. Enough to go to that kind of trouble. And as Milton Flink said, why bother? Why not wait for weather, or no water, to drive them away?"

"Sometimes you can't wait," Virgil said. "You know, it's worth whatever it costs to do it right now."

Winnie nodded soberly. "Yeah."

For a time they all ate in silence. No one brought up the problem of a crazy trickster again, Sarah thought, watching her two beautiful children. What was the use? East Shasta had its share of eccentrics, including the number one candidate, Mrs. Betancort, but if there was anyone homicidally insane, that person had perfected a method of hiding it.

"I bet it's still there," Winnie said then, her eyes sparkling. "I bet we could find it."

"Find what?" Virgil asked.

"The tape player, tape loop, whatever it was and the contraption that triggered it. I bet it's in those rocks somewhere."

"Yeah?" Virgil asked, and helped himself to more rice, "then what?"

"Don't know. Just interesting, don't you think?" She tapped her fingers on the table, a typical gesture of Blaine's; he had not been able to think through deciding on dessert without that motion.

"Look," Winnie said then. "Let's go over there tomorrow or Sunday and look around a little. I want some more pictures in daylight now that I'm going to do a book, and we can just poke around a little. You want to come with me?"

That was it, Sarah thought then; Winnie was setting him up because she didn't want to go to Ghost Lake alone. She watched Virgil consider this, and finally nod. "Sure," he said. She wanted to congratulate Winnie, but held back, not at all certain her daughter and son understood what had just happened.

Probably they both would deny the manipulation, she told herself, and thought of the Maslow trinity that drove people: security, sex, and self-esteem. To say aloud that Winnie had just manipulated her brother without mercy would hit them both in their self-esteem; they both would have to deny it.

"Sunday," Virgil said then. "We've got fish breeding like crazy, and someone has to be at the tanks to take out the spawning mats and move them to the nursery tank. If the eggs hatch in the big tanks, the other fish eat them, mama and papa first in line for the treat. Tomorrow's my turn, and Carlos will be here on Sunday. Okay?"

"Sunday," Winnie said. "And tomorrow I'll finish up with the video. I think I see how to edit the tape I already have." Virgil's expression changed to one of unrelieved misery as Winnie started a long detailed explanation and Sarah stopped listening. They all knew they had to get that cassette finished and out to the stores or the whole venture of franchising garden ponds would fizzle before it was even launched.

While they talked, Sarah rearranged Maslow's three drives to fit the different patterns of life: youth demanded sex, self-esteem and then security. Middle age needed security, sex, and self-esteem in that order. And old age? She felt certain self-esteem came first, then security, and as a distant third, sex. She smiled to herself; eventually she would know enough to be certain, but not yet, and at her place in life, sex seemed terribly important, right up there with security.

Then she thought that was not right, either. In fact, the three shifted and danced around each other, and the one that appeared threatened became the one to fight for, to kill for if necessary.

Slowly she put down her fork and lifted her wine and sipped, thinking again that she was missing something. Virgil was toying with his food now; she watched the play of tendons on the back of his hand, the play of muscles in his arm, and suddenly she was seeing Maria Florinda's arm and hand as she entered the kitchen of Rosa's house. Maria had been carrying her suitcase, and set it down, then moved it out of the way. Tell Virgil good-bye, she had said, and Sarah remembered the look of satisfaction that had swiftly crossed Rosa's face, then vanished. But Maria's hand and arm had not shown any strain; the muscles had not bulged even a little. The suitcase had been light, so light it required no effort whatever to lift, to move. Empty, Sarah knew. That suitcase had been empty.

She carried coffee to the veranda after dinner, and sat staring at the water streaked with sunset colors, trying to make sense of Maria and Rosa and Carlos. Winnie was helping Rosa clean up the dishes; she had volunteered to help out every evening. Carlos and Virgil were in the office making plans for the franchise marketing strategy. Hire an expert, she had advised, and they had looked at her blankly and had gone back to discussing what they should do, the sequence, the timing. There was not enough money to hire anyone, Virgil had said patiently later. They were simply grateful to have a real artist work on the visual parts, and as for marketing, they would feel their way into it.

Carlos, Rosa, Maria, she thought over and over. They could have done it between them—to keep their illegal status secret? She was certain Carlos and Rosa had nothing to fear; they had been with her father for twenty years. Even if they had entered illegally, they would have been eligible for the amnesty declared a few years earlier. But not Maria. She was an illegal. Carlos and Rosa mixed up in murder for someone else? She shook her head. Maria alone, and now using them? Why would they go along with that?

Winnie came to the door. "I'm going on up, Mother. Not to bed yet, but to stretch out a while. I'm ready to fall."

"I'll look in after a while," Sarah said.

In the kitchen a minute or two later, she stood at the table cradling a cup of coffee in her hands. Rosa was at the table, a magazine pushed to one side now, her own coffee before her. Such a tiny woman, Sarah thought; not a mark on her face to indicate the passing of the years, and jet eyes that were totally foreign, unreadable.

"I was wondering," Sarah said, "when Maria first came, how she got here. She didn't have a car, did she?"

Rosa looked imperturbable and shook her head. "No car. She took the bus to Susanville, and I met her there and brought her the rest of the way. Happened she was there on my market day."

"Just happened," Sarah said. Now she drew out a chair and sat down. She kept her voice very low as she asked, "Rosa, had you known her before? A relative, maybe?"

Rosa shook her head. "No. I met her in Susanville. But we had mutual friends, acquaintances, people back in El Salvador that we both knew. Why are you asking these things, Sarah?"

"She hasn't gone anywhere, has she?" Sarah asked, nearly whispering.

For several seconds Rosa did not move, seemed not to breathe, then she said, "She has not gone. And now, with Mr. Ralph's death being questioned, we, Carlos and I, are afraid for her, afraid for us, ourselves."

"Will you tell me about it?" Sarah asked gently.

"Yes," Rosa said with a long exhalation, as if she had been saving her breath for this one word for a long time. "I met her at the market, just as I said. She said who she is, where she was from, and I asked if she knew someone, and she said yes, and did I know someone else, and we were both laughing and crying then. I took her home with me. And I called my brother in Brownsville, and he called people we knew in El Savador, and in the end we knew she was who she said, and she was in need of a job, and I said I would bring it up with Mr. Ralph. He hired her the next day. He knew that if Carlos and I said she was okay, that was enough. Then, when that lady detective was killed, Maria became very frightened that someone might want to see her green card, her papers, whatever it was that she did not have, and at first she said she would really leave, go far away. We talked her out of that. She had been sending her money to her family; she had nothing, and nowhere to go. We said it should appear that she had left, and then for her to stay indoors until they found the crazy who shot that poor lady, and then she could come out and go back to work."

"And then things got even more complicated," Sarah murmured. "Dear God, that poor girl. She can't come out yet, Rosa. Whatever she does, she has to stay hidden. She may be in grave danger if she surfaces now."

"Danger from the law? Arrest, all that?"

"That, too," Sarah said.

They heard Virgil's voice coming close, and they looked up. "Especially don't let him find out," Sarah said softly. "He could never hide it if he knew."

Rosa lifted her coffee as Virgil and Carlos entered the kitchen, talking about ads, about radio advertising because they couldn't afford television. Sarah shook her head. The ponds had to be seen, not just discussed. Carlos was shaking his head, too.

And her poor child, Sarah thought, looking at her son's face. He had taken a giant step from adolescence into maturity this past week or so, new lines on his face, new shadows in his eyes, a new strength? Possibly that too, she thought. He was not scouring the countryside, beating his brains out, tearing out his hair; he was doing exactly what he should be doing, patiently waiting for the return of the woman he loved. He could no more control the spasms of pain that showed when her name was mentioned than he could control his heartbeat, his breaths, and yet he was doing nothing, waiting. She wanted to take him into her arms and rock him, soothe and comfort him, make the pain go away, but she could only watch and wait with him.

She excused herself then and went upstairs to her room, where she could pace endlessly without drawing looks of concern, without anyone's suggesting that there was a show on television she might like, or that it was getting near bedtime or any other dumb thing. Blaine had always tapped his fingers when in deep thought; she paced.

They couldn't sneak the girl out now, not at this late date, she knew, but if Michael or Freddie or even Uncle Peter learned she was in the area, one of them would turn her in, or if she surfaced someone might even kill her and plant the missing gun on her. What a convenient end to such a messy matter, she thought bitterly. She considered the possibility that Maria and an accomplice had for some unknown reason killed Fran and then Ralph Kellerman, but Maria alone, never. Too difficult without a car, and if Maria was still hiding in the area, that meant there was no accomplice. But, she continued the line of thought, the girl was in terrible danger, and Sarah was not at all certain that Rosa had understood that she meant real physical personal danger, not merely the threat of being arrested.

She had to talk to Fernandez, she decided that night. Whom had Fran gone to see in Los Angeles? She had called the Leszno numbers in the Chicago area, and then the Bookman numbers in Utah, and the Barcleigh numbers in Los Angeles, and then had gone to see someone there. Duane Barcleigh's parents? His widow? And what had she learned?

Sarah did not have enough to trade with Fernandez, she knew. The false death certificate? He would come around to that without any help. Her uncle and cousin's sacrificial offering of Maria? Not without Maria herself, and she would not be the one to turn her in. An idea for a trap?

She stopped moving to consider this. As a defense attorney she had always treated entrapment as a bitter boomerang if she had had any suspicions that it had been used against her clients. The massive power of a modern state directed against one individual was an abomination, she had declared more than once. And the weight of a nation against an individual who had not been proven guilty of anything was nothing short of a sin. Her arguments against entrapment had been good, she knew, because she believed in them fervently. The state must not lie to, hoodwink, deceive its citizens; it must never exploit the weakness—inherent in humankind—of its citizenry. The state could not be allowed to steamroll its citizens into a puddle, period. She had argued with Blaine, who often had taken the opposite position, and especially as a district attorney had felt that frequently entrapment was the only means available to be certain of getting an individual off the streets and into prison. Entrapment was simply another weapon to be used against drug runners, against molesters, kidnappers . . . He had drawn out a long list and she had been forced to agree that almost any price was acceptable in order to get them off the streets, but she always came back to her original stance: not through entrapment, however.

Catch them at it, prove they did it with circumstantial evidence, get a confession, find eyewitnesses, perfect methods of proof through physical evidence, do whatever the law allowed; the law did not condone tempting anyone to commit a crime and then arresting that person for the ensuing crime that might never have been committed without enticement. Any other reading of the law was a misreading. It was that clear-cut.

As a defense attorney for a threatened client, she knew well her position, but as a judge, she asked herself, what position would she take? There was no answer. The problem had not yet arisen in her court. It

would, she knew; sooner or later it would, and then . . .
She shrugged, and put off trying to arrive at the decision a minute before she had to.

Meanwhile, she said to herself, she had no certain
plan through entrapment of pinpointing the killer. Fur-
thermore, she went on relentlessly, even if she did have
such a plan, she could not discuss it with Fernandez, because officially he was the state, while officially she
was simply another murder suspect. She could not ask
him to take part in what she thought of as an abomination, or to condone it through inaction if he became
aware of it. No, no state seine to drag in a killer, but a
single line, a single person casting the right bait . . .

She had to find out from Fernandez what Fran had
learned, and what the threat of the Damocles sword really was. Would that knowledge provide the clincher for
the shark she intended to land? But first, she had to be
sure that she landed her shark with enough evidence to
make her charges stick like a second skin, at least long
enough to convince Fernandez. The gun, for openers; a
confession? She shook her head. Deniability was an issue, also. As a judge she paid a lot of attention to how
a confession was obtained. A confession through coer-
cion or trickery was worthless; at least in her court it
was. But if she could prod the killer into producing the
right gun, hard physical evidence like that was undeni-
able.

All right, she said under her breath, all she had to do
was learn who the murderer was and then turn him over
to Fernandez, and hope that Fernandez applied what
they called the "realist" view in the judiciary, the one in
which the judge first had a notion of the outcome, and
then applied the legal principles that would make it hap-

pen. She would offer to give Fernandez the killer with enough hard evidence to be convincing, and let him earn his state salary and gather enough proof to take to the grand jury.

Such a deal, how could he resist? she mocked herself, but it was the best, indeed the only, thing she could think of to offer for a trade. He had what she needed; she had promises.

SEVENTEEN

THE NEXT MORNING when she tried to reach Fernandez by phone a woman with a New Jersey accent said she would pass on the message, and was it important, and did Sarah want someone else from the department? She sounded very bored. Just ask him to call, Sarah said and hung up. Before she had got out of reach, the phone rang, and this time it was Fran Donatio's sister, Patricia Lagorno.

"Yes," Sarah said, surprised at how hard her heart had started beating.

"Look, I said if anything else came up, I'd give you a call, and I don't know if this is something, or just nothing, but it's weird. And here I am."

"I appreciate it," Sarah said. "What came up?"

"Well, yesterday when I got home from work here was this notice from the library about some overdue books that Fran checked out a few weeks ago. We put a forward on her mail so it gets sent here, and this card came. I thought you might be interested because one of the books was written by your father."

Sarah could not follow any of this conversation. "The books are overdue? Didn't you find them in the apartment?"

"No. They aren't there. I guess the guy who messed up

everything took them, or they got lost somewhere else. I don't know."

"You say one of them was written by my father?" She knew he had never written a book.

"Yeah, *Genetics, Form and Patterns*."

Sarah frowned. Uncle Peter's book. "What are the other titles? Do you have the card there now?"

"Yes. Here, I'll read them for you."

She read three other titles on genetics or DNA, including the famous one, *The Double Helix*, and Uncle Peter's one and only book. Sarah wrote down the titles and then thanked Patricia.

"That's all right," she said. "I just hope it helps, but I can't see how. Anyway, if you hadn't come that day, I'd still be rooted in that messed-up room. You know what I mean?"

When Sarah hung up, she studied the titles for another moment, then slipped the paper into her pocket. All books on genetics, on DNA, the discovery, the early pioneers. Fran Donatio must have left them somewhere herself; it was insane for anyone to have stolen library books.

Then she stopped moving. Patricia Lagorno had said Sarah's father had written the book, not Peter Kellerman. She had assumed the only Kellerman she had heard of must be the author. Sarah sank down into a chair in the living room.

"Of course," she breathed. Whoever had called her father must have assumed the same thing, that he was the other Kellerman, the one connected to genetics, to the missing students, the university, Michael or his sisters, even the institute—the other Kellerman. The call had followed the item in the paper about her father's birthday, and that article had said only that he was retired, not what he had retired from. She felt for the first time that she finally understood why this whole ugly sequence of events had started. The caller had said something awful, but incomprehensible, to her father, something he couldn't accept, couldn't believe, and couldn't talk about without being sure, and he had hired a detective. And it was something that Uncle Peter would have understood, she finished, and stood up, returned to the telephone and stood there for a few seconds, thinking.

She didn't need Fernandez, after all, she realized. She felt so certain that the call to her father had been intended for Uncle Peter that it seemed transparently clear, and would be that clear to anyone else. And Uncle Peter's life was a vast unexplored plain to her, she could not imagine how anything except the most mundane message to him would be comprehensible. She knew the near-euphoria she was feeling was a mistake, that her certainty would not carry much weight in the corridors of officialdom, but the relief was there, the certainty was real; no one had called about Virgil, or Winnie, or her, Sarah, or Blaine. The relief was so great because it had been too hideous to live with, the idea that one of her children, or her dead husband, could have had a secret so terrible that it had required a detective to ferret it out, and had resulted in two deaths.

She had not believed that, she told herself, but she could not deny the relief she felt, because she knew how often a parent had been brought up short by the actions of a child; she had seen too many parents devastated by what their children had done, parents who had not believed, had denied, had defended, exactly like her. And Dirk Walters had shaken her through and through by saying Blaine had been their man. She felt so relieved that she felt buoyant, in danger of leaving the floor altogether, of drifting through the house. She had not quite realized how deep her fear had been, how heavy the dread.

All right, she thought then, all right. She had looked up the number for the institute earlier, and now pushed the numbers, and asked for Dr. Wolper.

"I wondered if you could prescribe a sleeping pill for me," she said to him when he came on the line.

"Oh, of course, Mrs. Drexler."

"I don't usually take anything," she rushed on before he could ask any questions. "And Saturday isn't a good time to get a doctor out of state, is it? I'm not even sure he could prescribe across a state line. But something not too strong, just enough to see me through the next few weeks. I know it's foolish to let the children upset me so, when they both are grown, but there it is."

"The children?" he asked cautiously. "Is there some trouble there?"

"No! Of course not! It's just that Winnie is determined to go back out to Ghost Lake for more pictures, and I know it's not safe. And Virgil has dropped out of school, and I'm afraid he's in touch with that girl. Anyway, I need something to help me sleep."

"Of course," Dr. Wolper said soothingly. "This has been a tough time for you. I'll call in a prescription to Milton right away. Or—Sarah, I'll drop by with something. That might be even better."

"Fine," she said. "I'm about to call Uncle Peter and Michael and invite them for drinks, cheese at five, really to bury the hatchet. We've all been pretty snappish with each other. Please, if you're free, you come, too."

"Five it is," he said. "Thanks. And I'll just bring something for you then. You're not allergic to any medications, I hope."

She assured him that she was not, and they hung up, and she immediately called her uncle and invited him and Michael for cocktails at five.

All day Virgil played midwife to the fish. Winnie finished taping the garden video, and then wandered out to the fish section to photograph the process of fertilization and separation. She came in to tell Sarah about it. "They get these knobs, protuberances, nuptial tubercles Virgil says, on their heads and gills, that's how you can tell they're ready to breed. Then the females lay their eggs on or above the spawning mat, and the male comes along and shoots the milt over them and it's done, except they do it more than once. Seems pretty Victorian to me."

Sarah laughed. "And they eat the babies as soon as they hatch; all the way back to Chronos, if you ask me."

Winnie and Virgil looked at her with dismay when she told them about the cocktail party. "You're kidding," Winnie breathed. "I can't believe this."

"Well, believe. It's time to put the past behind us."

"Hey, Winnie, want to go over to the Eagle Lake resort and catch the show? It's a dinner show on Saturdays."

"Sure," she said morosely. "What time?"

"We should probably leave before five," Virgil said, with a sidelong glance at Sarah. "We'll get together with Uncle Peter and Michael some other time."

"Fine," Sarah said. "How are you guys fixed for money? Let me get this evening. Okay?"

"Why don't you call off the party and come with us?" Virgil asked.

She shook her head. "Next time. But I really would like to pay for your night out."

They exchanged glances, both of them glad to let her pay, and both of them a bit ashamed for being poor, she knew.

She made a mental list of the things she had to do: call Rosa and tell her not to bother to come to prepare dinner. That was first. And have her call back to test the telephone, and tape the ring. That was second. Get the Winchester out and clean it, put the shells in her bag. Make some sandwiches, find and fill the thermos. Load her camera.

Methodically she went down the list and accomplished everything, and then Winnie and Virgil came in to get ready to go to the dinner show. Sarah prepared the cocktail snacks and a tray, and put a cloth on the table on the veranda. The phone rang as Virgil was running down the stairs ready to leave; he picked the telephone up and listened, then called her.

"The cop," he said, making a face.

She covered the mouthpiece, blew Virgil a kiss, and Winnie, who had appeared by then, and watched them depart, hand in hand, the way they had done in childhood.

"Hello, Lieutenant," she said then.

"Hello, Judge. You called?"

"It's nothing. Just a little antsy, I guess. I know you'll be in touch when you have information."

There was a pause. Then he said. "Are you all right?"

"Of course."

"Okay. Nothing yet. And I will be in touch."

A most unsatisfactory phone call, she thought a moment later after hanging up, but there was nothing to say to him, not now. It was nearly five by then.

"Oh, Michael," she said later. "Surely you remember when I told you about that experiment with the timer and the chemical and the chimes. I remember distinctly telling you about it."

He shrugged. "I give. So you told me. So what?"

"Winnie and Virgil think that's the kind of trick someone used to drive the people away from the lake. A sun-activated timer, a tape player, a tape loop of ghostly voices. And they think it might still be up there somewhere. They're going to look for it tomorrow."

"Why?" Dr. Wolper asked. "What's the point?"

She shrugged. "No point. I think they're both just getting bored. Next week Winnie will go back to San Francisco; I'll be on my way; things will gradually get to some kind of normalcy again, I guess. But right now, they're bored."

"They know about the quicksand out there?" Uncle Peter asked. "Were we all that foolish at that age? I don't think so."

He was drinking a tall vodka collins, nibbling on cheese and crackers, and he looked more relaxed than he had since Sarah's arrival, as if finally he had gotten some missed sleep, or stopped worrying a problem, or had a reprieve on owed income taxes or something.

"Sarah, don't you have any control over them, or not control, but authority they listen to?" he asked, but it was good-natured, as if his heavy weight had shifted, as hers had, and he was feeling comfortable with her, with the world.

She glanced at Michael, who was wearing shorts, a Hayward T-shirt and white Reeboks; he looked like a real jock, not an administrator. "How much authority did you have with your kids when they hit their twenties?" she asked Uncle Peter, as good-natured as he had been. "Michael, does he control you, or your sisters?" Instantly, she regretted the question.

Michael laughed. "Sure. All the way, all the time. I'm back here again, aren't I?" His laugh was forced-sounding, the words too clipped.

He was drinking a bloody mary, as was Dr. Wolper. Freddie Wolper had pressed a small container into her hand on arriving, and held her hand for just a moment too long, gazing at her soulfully, or sincerely; it was hard to read his expression. "I'm so sorry you're not feeling chipper," he had said. "This will help, I'm sure."

"What's this about Maria?" Michael asked then. "Freddie says she's been in touch with Virgil? Is she still hanging around?"

Sarah gave Freddie Wolper a look sharp enough to make him avert his face. "I'm afraid so," she said, looking at the wine in her glass. "You know, she's very pretty, and he's young and lonesome. He has no resistance, naturally. He's so young."

"Don't you think we should tell the police?" Dr. Wolper asked.

She shrugged. "Virgil would never forgive me."

"Well, not you then. One of us."

"Let's think about it," she said. "Excuse me, I'll get some more ice." She went inside and turned on the tape recorder as she passed the telephone table. In two minutes the tape would play five telephone rings. She returned to the veranda with ice cubes. "Uncle Peter, did your tomatoes recover?"

"Nope. Lost every damn one. They're those hybrids." He continued to talk about hybrid vegetables until the phone rang.

"Excuse me," Sarah said, and left again. "Hello," she said, as she reached into the drawer with the tape recorder and flicked the switch to off. "Hello," she repeated, louder. "Who is that? . . . No, Virgil isn't here. Where are you? What do you want? . . . I see. How much?" There was not a sound from the veranda. "No!" she exclaimed in an even louder voice that she lowered instantly. "Don't come here! I'll meet you. Where? . . . All right . . . Eight-thirty? Yes, I can make that. But if I'm late, wait for me, and if you're late, I'll wait for you. Yes, of course, I know where it is. There's only one dry lake in the area as far as I'm aware. Yes, I'll bring it! Don't call back!" She hung up and stood with her hand on the receiver, her head bowed for several seconds, waiting for her adrenaline to subside, her heart to subside.

"Sarah, are you all right?" Michael asked at her elbow then.

She nodded. "Fine. Fine. It's nothing."

"It was her, wasn't it? That girl, Maria?"

She looked up at him quickly, moistened her lips, and nodded. "Let's go finish our drinks," she said.

They were all watching her, she knew, waiting for her to make some reference to the call. Deliberately she began to talk about the drought, the danger of fires, the climatic warming that was so alarming. "But you know more about that than I do," she said to her uncle and waited for him to take the cue, which he did after an almost imperceptible pause.

"Not really my field," he said, "but as far as I can tell from the literature, it's serious, more so than the present administration realizes. People are worried about the farmlands, and the forests, but it's really the phyto-plankton, the diatoms, the algae in the seas that will change the face of the earth. As they die off in the sur-face waters, the entire food chain is thrown into disor-der, the gas exchange undergoes drastic alterations that we can't even predict, and no one knows today what all that will mean. They're doing computer models, but not fast enough, and no one pays any attention . . ."

At six-thirty she glanced at her watch and stood up. "I'm afraid I'll have to excuse myself," she said. "I have a headache and really would like to lie down for a bit. Please, help yourselves to whatever you want."

"Don't be ridiculous," Uncle Peter said, taking her hand. "Sarah, this has been so hard on all of us, but es-pecially you, and you've been a tower of strength for the children, for me, all of us. I just wanted to tell you, and now we'll be off and let you rest."

Michael put glasses and the cheese plate on the tray and carried it inside, and Dr. Wolper gulped down his drink and took the empty glass to the kitchen. Michael kissed her cheek, and Uncle Peter kissed her forehead, and Dr. Wolper would have kissed her if she had not drawn back, and then they all left.

As soon as they were out of sight, she retrieved the tape player and raced upstairs to change her clothes. She rewound the tape player and stuffed it into the day pack she had already prepared, and then after another mental check of her mental list, she nodded and went downstairs, out to her car, and started to drive.

EIGHTEEN

GOING INTO THE valley she passed a corral on the left, the remnants of a stable, a stone step, a broad leveled place where a hitching post had been, no doubt. Many pines had invaded the corral; her father would have known at a glance what kind of pines they were—piñons, jackpines, lodgepole ... Sage grew well in the valley, and many gray-green grasses. Desert colors, she thought, gray, faded green, gray-green, tan, ocher ... She had never spent much time on the desert with her parents; they had gone searching for the sources of the many mountain streams in the high Cascades, or the Blue Mountains, or the Ochocos, her father mapping his way through the state, her mother tagging along, keeping house in a tent, a cabin, the truck bed at times, and the daughter also tagging along, never realizing she might be lonely, or that life should include playmates and classes, happy with the frogs and rabbits, the birds, the lizards and snakes ... In the high mountains everything was green, everything dripped, snow lingered on the north side of the trees; the moss crept down the trunk, the snow edged up to meet it.

Here, in the dead town, the silvered remains gleamed; a tumbleweed danced in front of her car; the lake had taken on a reddish hue in the lowering sunlight, and the breeze flowed through the valley, whispering in the sand. The second she turned off her motor, she heard the whispers. She parked at a spot where the road was no more than ten feet from the encroaching desert-lake. A building had fallen backward here when the desert claimed footage at some time in the past. She could imagine the scene, the building groaning, struggling to stay upright, then the collapse, and a cloud of dusty sand swirling for a few minutes, and again the murmurous whispers.

She did not hurry, but neither did she dally. She took out the backpack, a day pack actually, jammed full, and another bag that had the rifle sticking out the top, and she walked away from the car, not bothering to lock it, although she took the keys, through the ruins, out the other side, and toward the hillside strewn with boulders. It was seven-fifteen, time to be positioned, to make certain everything she would need was at hand, and then wait.

She knew exactly the spot she wanted, a place twenty feet or a little more up the hill where the land leveled out a bit, and three boulders formed an arc. If they had not rolled on down the hill, if there was no rattlesnake in residence, if there were no scorpions or black widows or brown recluse spiders, that was the place. She found it and it was perfect.

She fixed her camera in one of the angles where the boulders met, and decided it would work okay, not as well as she had hoped, but okay. The lens was a telephoto, instantly adjustable according to the ad she had succumbed to, and she could read her license plate numbers looking through it. Then she rested the rifle in the other notch and it was equally satisfactory. She left the camera and the rifle in place and descended to the valley floor to study the hillside carefully. Nothing showed. She returned to her post and sat down to eat a sandwich and drink coffee. It was twenty minutes before eight.

It was two minutes before eight when a black car appeared on the road coming down into the valley, a Lincoln. The car looked like a mammoth predatory beetle, shiny carapace, black eyes, pausing to smell the air before advancing farther. Then it eased down the road, vanished behind some ruins, reappeared at the side of her car. She could not see into the Lincoln; the windows were tinted and looked black from this distance.

It stopped next to her car, then began to inch forward, as if the driver was scanning the surrounding ruins for her. It stopped again, and backed up even with her car once more. Nothing happened for what seemed a long time, but then she saw that the hood of her car had been raised; again the body of the other car hid the person completely; he must have got out the passenger side, or there were two of them. She doubted that. Disabling her car, she decided. She snapped the camera several times, but these were not the pictures she was after. He didn't want her to make a dash for it when he went on down the road to see if Maria was parked there around the bend. She nodded. That was what she would have done, too.

The Lincoln left after another second or two; the hood of her car was down again. She watched the black car roll out of sight, around the bend, and eased her position to get more comfortable. He would come back, and now for the first time, she began to doubt what she was doing. She had not recognized the car. Michael had

driven a station wagon before, and her uncle had a
green Buick. Wolper's car? She had never seen him in
a car, only on foot, and she did not know.

The car returned within a few minutes, moving even
more slowly than it had before. What would he be
thinking? she wondered, trying to put herself in his
head. That she was among the ruins somewhere, or that
she was taking a walk, hiking, or that Maria had come
and they had gone off in her car together. She could
think of no reason for him to suspect that she might be
hiding. No one knew she knew about the wicking material, about the trick with the gas, about her father's hat.
No one knew she had pieced together the clues about
the phone call that had sent her father to the detective
in the first place. She nodded to herself. Either he
would drive on and keep going and this whole thing
would be a bust, a non-event to be put out of mind, or
he would—

The car stopped and the door opened and her uncle
stepped out, carrying what looked like a plastic grocery
bag. She let out a long breath and took pictures of him
as he approached her car. He looked inside, and then
turned to scan the ruins again slowly. Next he walked to
the edge of the lake and stood for several seconds
studying it, regarding it, facing it, at any rate. Finally he
started to walk out on the sand. Sarah caught her breath
in surprise; the story about the ghost noises, the tape recorder and tape player was paying off, she thought, as-
tonished. Uncle Peter moved with caution, but as if he
was safe. He seemed to be following a line of rocks to
a group of boulders about a third of the way across the
expanse of sand. She kept snapping his picture as he
moved, and when he got to the boulders, his profile was

perfect when he knelt on the ground and began to dig around the base of the biggest boulder with a trowel he had taken from his bag. With her unaided eyes she could not make out what he was doing, but through the lens she could see very well that there was a small rock cairn, covered with sand, and that he had dug through to the rocks; he reached into a cavity and pulled out an old-fashioned tape player, about three times bigger than the one she used. There were a couple of other objects that were not clear to her, the apparatus to make the tape start, she assumed. He put everything in the plastic bag, turned, and retraced his steps across the lake. The shadows had grown long and dark by then; the lighting was fine, just fine, she thought absently. Winnie would be jealous.

And this made no sense at all, she realized. Uncle Peter haunted Ghost Lake? What on earth for? She watched him get back to the roadway and head once more for the two cars. He scanned the town again, and finally walked back to the Lincoln and opened the trunk. He put the bag inside, and removed some other objects; one of them looked very much like a gallon milk jug, another looked like a golf bag. Sarah moistened her lips and continued to watch as he set everything on the ground, then got behind the wheel and started the Lincoln. He drove a hundred yards away and parked.

She had to wipe her hands on her jeans; they were too sweaty to handle the camera. Hardly breathing, she watched him take a rifle from the golf bag, and her breath came out hard when she realized it was an assault rifle. Fernandez never had said what kind of gun had been used, she remembered. Then she recalled his words: it stopped being a game when someone's head got blown away. Fran's head had been blown away, she knew now. Her own Winchester .22 looked like a toy in comparison to the rifle her uncle had. She snapped five or six good shots with the camera as he loaded the rifle and then crossed the road with it, and vanished into one of the ruined buildings. He emerged a few seconds later empty-handed and returned to the jug and proceeded to make a booby-trap for her car. She watched in icy fury now, periodically taking pictures. She finished one roll and reloaded the camera. She put the first film in a small tightly-closed plastic container and dug a hole in the ground a few feet from her hiding place and put the container in it, covered it carefully, scattered dust and gravel on it, and was content. If he got the camera, she thought grimly, she still had the real evidence she had come for. The sight of the assault rifle had unnerved her, she admitted, and she considered changing her plans completely, not revealing herself at all. But then he would eventually retrieve the rifle, dismantle the trap, and leave again, and have plenty of time to get rid of everything. She shook her head slightly.

He had loosened the top of the jug, gasoline, she guessed, and had uncoiled a length of twine, twenty feet long, thirty feet, and recoiled it more loosely. A wick, she thought. Gasoline and a wick. She was supposed to reappear with Maria, she thought, and they would part; she would get in her car, start it, and he would light the wick and the car would explode into flames. And then? He must have planned to get rid of Maria, and leave the rifle in her car? Perfect solution to the problem. Let the chicana take the blame. In a day or two someone would come by and find the dead women, one burned to a crisp in her car, the other on the road in a different car, equally dead, with her prints on the rifle that had killed Fran Donatio. Enough for any sane person.

"All right," she muttered then. "All bloody right." She moved from the camera to the rifle and carefully sighted and aimed it at his car, at the back wheel, and fired. She missed. Uncle Peter threw himself to the ground at the shockingly loud report from her rifle; the noise echoed and re-echoed through the valley, racing from rock to rock, from wall to wall, quieting the whispering lake. Before the echoes died all the way, she fired again. She knew Uncle Peter would not be able to guess where the shots came from, not with the strange acoustics the valley provided. She had target practiced here years ago, and she knew how the echoes of the shots would distort the source. This time when she looked through the camera lens to see if her second shot had missed, she saw with satisfaction that although she had not shot out a tire, as she had intended, she had punctured the gas tank. Gas again, she thought, nodding. That would do.

The silence after the two explosions was profound. No bird flew, no mouse scurried, no lizard ran. Only the lake whispered, whispered.

For a long time Uncle Peter did not show himself, did not move into sight from around the side of her car. Then he dashed across the roadway and into the same building he had entered before with the rifle. She had been waiting for this, and now, the rifle already aimed and ready, she fired once more, this time at her own car. The windshield shattered; she fired a second shot, and the front wheel exploded. She leaned back, out of breath, almost light-headed. No doubt he knew how to hot-wire a car, she thought, and, no doubt he had thought he could do that later, possibly after dark. They were both stranded out here now, twenty-three miles from East Shasta.

Then there was a burst of gunfire that sounded like a bomb going off, and she closed her eyes in relief. He was shooting at one of the buildings in the ruined town. The noise eclipsed the shots she had fired, made them sound more like firecrackers than a deadly weapon. The echoes of the assault rifle in the enclosed valley were deafening.

"How do you plead, Uncle?" she said in the deep silence that followed. "Are you ready to plead?" She spoke in a voice that was not raised particularly, and she dirécted her words at the hillside at the east side of the town, not down into the buildings. The effect was what she expected it would be: an answering burst of gunfire aimed at the easternmost section of the rising hillside. She nodded. A scattering of rocks raced down the hill, dislodged by the fusillade. He fired again.

Arresting officer, prosecutor, judge, jury. He would have to be his own defense attorney, she decided. It was asking too much for her to play that role also.

"You have the right to remain silent, Uncle," she said, this time directing her voice to the western end of the valley. It echoed hollowly. This time he did not shoot.

He was on to the trick, she assumed, trying to think of some way to make her reveal her location.

"Sarah, let's talk," he called from within the building. "There's no Maria, is there? That was a ploy?"

She nodded silently. Yes, Uncle.

"Does anyone know you're here? Will anyone come looking for you? I didn't tell anyone I was coming. Sarah, we could both die out here, do you understand that?"

Not me, she thought at him, watching the building closely. She had brought water, coffee, sandwiches, a space blanket, a flashlight, a sweater for later, and she had on hiking boots. She could walk twenty-three miles tomorrow.

The sky had turned a deep cerulean blue without a trace of clouds; a quiet uneventful sunset was happening. The sun was slipping down the horizon as if on a greased sliding board. An hour of light, she thought, and wondered if he knew that. She suspected that when it became very dark, he would feel panicked, and she would be as comfortable as she was now. All those years as her father's daughter living in the wilderness would serve her well finally. It would be a very dark night, the dark of the moon, a few days from the new moon, new starts, new cycles.

"Sarah, you're sick. My dear Sarah, you know that? You're very ill. You need help. Let me help you, Sarah. I've always been as fond of you as of my own children. Come on down and let's talk about it, decide what we can do."

She smiled at the thought. Sick? Probably. *I intend to kill you, Uncle,* she thought at him. He would never make it back to East Shasta, not dressed the way he was, shiny dress shoes, silk socks. If he started now, he might get a mile or two away before he collapsed, and then he would be out in the open with no shelter, and the nights were very cold here in the mountains. He probably had forgotten how cold the nights could get because it was not important for him to remember. She knew very well that exposure, hypothermia could happen any month of the year in the mountains. A man his age, not in very good physical shape, not conditioned for a long hike ... She expected this night to kill him.

"The jury has found you guilty, Uncle," she said, speaking to the east wall again. The gunfire was instant, focused at the middle of the wall of surrounding hill now. He was learning.

"Sarah, you can't do this! This is murder! You can't judge me and condemn me all on your own!"

"Yes, I can," she whispered. No more dialogue with him, no leading him to try to find her with his murderous weapon. She waited.

His voice came after another moment, "Sarah, why are you doing this? I had to kill that woman, you know that. She would have brought ruination to all of us, including you. Your reputation is important, too, Sarah. Is that what you're after? My confession?"

No, Uncle. Your confession means nothing. I have what I came after, real evidence, hard physical evidence.

"Damn you, Sarah, answer me!"

Then he fired again, this time spraying the town with lethal gunfire. One of the shacks that had been on the verge of falling for years, succumbed and caved in, releasing a cloud of dust that swirled crazily. Another building seemed to sway, but did not fall.

"You're like your mother, Sarah, did you know that? Just like her. She was a hard woman, hard. We were lovers, Sarah. You could even be my own daughter for all I know."

She laughed. He shot again, closer, but still blindly.

"You're right. It's laughable. I was too young, too green, and she sent me away, and from then on she never forgave me. Isn't that a strange way to act, Sarah? One little mistake and a lifetime to pay for it. That's what I meant by hard. She was here that weekend, and I thought for just a minute that maybe we could put the past aside, be friends. And she laughed at me and sent me away a second time."

Dusk had descended; the town was in deep shadows, the buildings ghostly shapes without definition. She had not known if he would decide to spend the night in the shelter of the ruins or start walking out, but he was showing more sense than she had credited him with. She stretched one leg, then the other, and rearranged her belongings. No more pictures. She put the camera in the day pack, but kept the rifle at hand, and put the flashlight next to it, within reach. She uncapped one of the thermoses and poured half a cup of coffee and sipped it.

"Sarah, I'm not going to shoot at you any more. Isn't that a funny thing for a man to say to his niece? You know, it's much harder to hit something shooting uphill than down? I suppose you knew that already."

"Why did you do it, Uncle?"

She listened to the whispering lake for several seconds, and then he said, "Ralph told me a man called him, mistook him for me, and accused him of killing his father, Duane Barcleigh. Duane's son, like a specter from the other side, walking into our lives out of nowhere, destroying us." He stopped for a long time, then said, "I told Ralph I didn't know what the boy was talking about, and he hired the detective. He didn't tell me about her for a long time, not until she had found out some things. I followed her out here that night, down farther than this, and I shot her through the car window. It was as easy as they make it appear in the movies. I was surprised at how easy it was."

The silence extended longer this time. Sarah sipped her coffee and did not otherwise move.

"I went back and at six the next morning I was at the house waiting for Ralph. He was very angry with me, making threats, I was going to lose the chair they had named for me. I hit him. We fought when we were boys, really fought sometimes, and this was like that, only he fell into the water, and I stood there, and then ran away. I went to Reno and took the first plane to Sacramento, found all the papers the detective had gathered, everything, and flew back to Reno, then drove to Susanville and bought tomatoes. Everything was so easy, Sarah. It was remarkable how easy it all was, except for fatigue. I was terribly tired, of course."

She shivered and wrapped herself in the space blanket, but her chill was not from the weather; the blanket did not help.

"Sarah, can you hear me?"

"I can hear you."

"I want to tell you about that night, Sarah. I've never told anyone, and sometimes I've felt as if I might die if I can't explain. I didn't want anything bad to happen to them, Sarah. You have to believe that. I honestly did not want anything to happen."

"I believe that," she said.

"Yes. We came out here. Your mother would not let me stay at the house, not without Ralph there, and I went back to the road and found Duane and Wesley and Mitchell, just as I told you before. But they wanted to come out here. Wesley never had seen a ghost town; it really was to satisfy him that we all came out here. We had been drinking a little and hadn't eaten yet. We were planning to go on over to three-ninety-five, to a diner over there, after we inspected the ghost town, and then come back to East Shasta to see Dr. Jarlstadt. We got out here."

Suddenly she saw him; he left the ruined building and walked to the roadway and stood in the center of it looking out over the lake. He was not carrying the rifle.

"We got out here," he said again. His voice carried as if he were on a stage designed by an expert acoustical engineer. "Wesley and Mitchell went out on the lake. I told them there was quicksand and they didn't really believe it. Why didn't someone do something about it, if there was, Wesley demanded, as if quicksand was something fixable, drainable. He was on crutches, you know. He had polio as a child, and he had to use crutches much of the time. Not all the time. Brilliant, he was truly gifted, more than the others, more than I was. On crutches. They went out there and they were dancing in the moonlight. Wesley and Mitchell dancing, happy. Wesley was waving one crutch around, hopping. They were going to get the Nobel, you know. And they would have. The three of them would have earned it. Dancing out on the lake, singing, howling really. And then Wesley was yelling and Mitchell was yelling, and they were both going down. Duane came running in to me. I hadn't gone on the lake at all; I knew there was quicksand, you see, and I refused to go out on it. Duane had gone only ten feet or so, and he came running, yelling to get a board, or a rope. A board he said, get a board from one of the buildings, and I pulled a board loose and came back with it, but Wesley and Mitchell were gone. And Duane was running back and forth, toward them, back to me, and I swung the board and hit him. I couldn't face knowing the two boys were out there dead, and Duane would have told all of it. I hit him. I covered him enough that night, and I drove back to town to put gas in the car and then drove back to the coast and left the car at the cliffs and went to the lab and dropped into bed and fell asleep."

"That's why you had to come back the next day," Sarah said after a long pause. "You had to bury Duane Barcleigh."

"Yes."

"And you frightened the commune people away so they wouldn't dig up bodies," she said faintly.

"Yes. Mrs. Betancort knows something, but I never could tell how much, or how much she knows and how much she guesses. It doesn't matter."

"No. No one pays any attention to her ravings." Past his shape that was almost featureless now, the lake was a long pale expanse, ghostly against the dark hill on the far side. Soon nothing would be visible, the long night would begin.

"I've been thinking, Sarah. I have Alzheimer's, you know."

"You don't!"

"I'm telling you I do, Sarah, and since you're relatively honest, you will repeat that to others. That I said I have it, that I feared it more than anything. That explains all my current activities, don't you see? And there's no need to bring the past into the picture, is there?"

"What are you suggesting, Uncle?"

"I'm going to shoot myself, Sarah. You know that.

Isn't that how you planned this evening to end? Wasn't that your scenario from the start? Judge, jury, prosecutor. You've taken all the roles for yourself. But I'll be the executioner."

"Uncle, if you'll put the gun where I can get it, and leave the keys to the Lincoln where I can get them, I'll take the tape recorder and the rifle and start walking back to East Shasta. You can stay here and rest. Tomorrow someone will come for you with a car."

"Don't be ridiculous!" he snapped. "Do you want a note, an explanation? Will your word be sufficient? Will you agree not to bring up the past, and let us be done with this?"

This time the silence was so long that she hesitated finally to break it. The whispers seemed to be nearly coherent.

"I can't make such a promise," she said. "Those boys will be buried, their families notified."

He turned and reentered the tumbling-down building. Sarah crouched lower behind the massive boulder and waited.

The noise of the shot was deafening. She did not move until all the echoes had died and the whispers were the only sound, and finally the sounds of dusk resumed—a rustling in the dry grass, a twittering in a nearby pine tree ... She got to her feet and started down the hillside, using her flashlight, picking her way cautiously. She carried her day pack, the other bag that again held her rifle, and the food she had brought with her. Then she heard a new noise, the creaking of a floorboard, a cracking sound, and she threw the flashlight, dropped to the ground and rolled, as the assault rifle sprayed the spot where she had been. While there was still the noise of stones clattering down the hillside, and of the echoing shots, she rolled once more, until she was behind a low rock. He fired again, this time at the place where she had thrown the flashlight.

"You bitch," he yelled. "You think I'll let you have anything? You won't walk anywhere, bitch! You'll die here in this goddamn valley just like me. And we'll all dance in the quicksand together, you, me, the boys, Wesley with his goddamn crutches." He fired again. He was moving through the ghost town, shooting as he walked, screaming at her.

He couldn't see any more than she could, she knew, and she did not move, tried not to breathe. He lurched over a timber or a rock, and fired a round, and moved on. She could not see him, could only gauge his distance by the noises he made, the curses he was flinging at her.

"Bitch, just like your goddamn mother! Selfish bitch! I'll go down, Sarah, but you will, too. First you! And we'll all dance out on the lake in the moonlight. Wesley was laughing, singing, yowling, swinging one of the crutches over his head, pretending it was a lasso. Laughing, and then yelling. God, yelling!"

He was crying, his voice was choked and thick. "Laughing, dancing, yelling. I yelled, don't struggle! Lie down flat, that's what they always tell you, isn't it? That's what I yelled to them, but they were fighting it, and his crutches were pulling him down."

She heard him fall, a heavy thump and a low-voiced moan and a curse, then the sound of wood breaking and another moan.

"I'm going to light a match, Sarah. If you have your rifle, now's your chance. I don't know where I am, my leg's caught." The match flared; she kept her head down and did not look at him, and in fact she was not at all certain she could have seen him from where she was. Part of a shack loomed almost directly in front of her, and the other buildings were beyond that; he was back among them somewhere.

"I'm tired, Sarah. Just tired. I think I might have fractured my leg. It's not broken, but a hairline fracture, isn't that what they call . . ." He groaned. "You're winning by default, Sarah. You just hold your tongue and you win. Who would have thought any woman could ever win that way." He groaned again. "I'm going to sit down and rest a minute. I guess I knew you wouldn't promise anything. It wouldn't hurt you, or cost you a thing, but you won't do it. You'll bury them. Who's that for, Sarah? Not the boys. They couldn't care less. Dead, gone, never been. That's how that goes. Their families? What difference can it make for them? It's for you, Sarah, isn't it? You're scared of death, of dying. Decent burial, isn't that the phrase? Say a few words over them, shovel in the dirt, what difference does it make? I said a few words, and I shoveled dirt." He laughed. "Oh, my, the words I said. I cursed Wesley and Mitchell and I cursed Duane. And they're out there whispering and waiting. They always knew I'd come back. Christ, my leg hurts! Maybe it's really broken."

"Are you bleeding?"

She kept very low, half expecting a new round of gunfire; it didn't come.

"No. Worse luck. They say bleeding to death is peaceful." He laughed. "They say that about drowning, and I never believed that, either. Never. Sarah, they drowned in sand and mud and filth. Filling their eyes, their mouths. God, they screamed and yelled." He was weeping softly.

She did not move for a long time; she was stretched out on the ground on her stomach, her face cushioned by her arm, but stones were digging into her thighs, and her arms, and she was afraid her legs would go to sleep.

At last her uncle spoke again. "Sarah, I'm hurting, but I can walk. I'm going back to the cars. If you can see me, Sarah, you'd better shoot now, because I'm going to burn you out and shoot the first thing that moves."

"I won't be your executioner, Uncle," she said. "You claimed that job for yourself."

"I lied," he said. "I won't do it. You will, or I'll kill you. All these years no one's suspected anything, or if they suspected, they had to keep it to themselves. They're going to honor me, Sarah. I intend to claim that honor. No one can connect me to that woman detective, or to Ralph's death, except you. So I'll kill you, and while I'm waiting for someone to come for me, I'll have time to think up a good story. Maybe not as good as the one you've already thought up, but sufficient, sufficient. I'm going to the cars, Sarah. This is probably your last chance."

She listened intently, and heard the low groans he could not suppress when he moved. She picked up a rock and threw it as far and hard as she could, and there was a spray of deafening gunfire almost instantly, followed by a hail of tumbling rocks and stones on the hill to her left. She ducked her face back down to her arm and listened, waited.

If she had the rifle, she thought, she would use it. She denied the thought vehemently, but it was there, and she admitted to herself that she would kill him if she had the gun. She tried to replay the moment she had hurled the light away from her, dropped everything, fallen to the ground and rolled. Then a second roll to this location. Back up there, she thought, trying to locate herself, locate the spot where she might have dropped the bag with the rifle. Up there, ten, fifteen, twenty feet away. Not more than that.

He groaned and there was a thump; he had fallen, or had sat down heavily, dropped the rifle. She held her breath; he moved again, groaning aloud, and there was a harsh dragging sound, his foot on a wooden floor. He would be using the walls for support, she thought, and one of the walls would give under his weight, he would fall again ... She flexed her legs and pulled them in under her, ready to stand and run if she heard another falling noise.

If he started a fire, it would escape, she thought clearly. It would race up the hillsides, wildfire, the worst nightmare of all. And she had not thought of that. She bit her lip hard, and worked her way up to her feet, crouching low, and then began to inch her way up the hill, the way she hoped she had come down. There was a crashing sound, much farther away than he had been only moments ago. Was he lying about his leg? Was he running through the ruins to the cars? She stopped and listened, and he screamed hoarsely.

"Sarah! Jesus God, Sarah, help me!"

It was a cry of agony, of desperation. She did not move yet, but waited, listening, and then heard him whimpering, his breath ragged and harsh. She started to move carefully in that direction, around the first ruined building, using the side of it to direct her, feeling the ground with her foot before she took each step. She remembered the half basement in one of the buildings, the holes in the ground left by some of them. She stopped again; he was talking, jabbering, whimpering and sobbing and talking all at once.

"They would have got the prize, the three of them. They would have got it ... A white-tie affair, the governor, the legislators, all of them rising, a real standing ovation, don't you know? ... Ladies and gentlemen, thank you. This is an honor that few of us ever dream of achieving ... Lie down flat, don't fight, damn you! Goddamn you all! Don't fight! ... It couldn't be Duane Barcleigh, it couldn't. Duane is dead, you see. I know because I hit him with the board and I buried him. So it couldn't be Duane ..."

She homed in on his rambling voice, and realized that he was moving, dragging himself through the sandy spaces between the ruins, over rocks, over whatever lay in front of him, going where? Why?

"What I'll do is burn up her car, you see, and if she tries to get out, then I'll shoot her, and they'll think the girl did it, the foreigner. And I'll leave the gun in her car. Remember to put her hands on it, fingerprints. Mustn't forget fingerprints. White tie and a formal dinner. A speech. Yes, speech. Ladies and gentlemen, thank you. Thank you. This is an honor that few of us ever dream of achieving ..."

Sarah reached the roadway midway between the two cars, and she saw a match flare near her car, and his form huddled down near the ground. Another match flared, and the twine wick he had fashioned began to blaze. He stood up, leaning against the rear fender of her car, and now she saw that he carried no rifle.

"Uncle, get away from the car!" she yelled at him. The twine must have been dipped in something very flammable, she realized, and it was still coiled loosely. The whole mass was burning brightly now. He did not appear to have heard her. She cried out to him again, running toward him now, and suddenly the milk jug of gasoline erupted with a dull explosion. She fell to the ground, stunned by the sound, by the shock wave, a blast of heat.

NINETEEN

SHE FOUND HERSELF sitting against the Lincoln watching the fire burn itself out. Soon, she told herself, she would go find her day pack, find a sweater, find her flashlight, and coffee. Coffee, she thought, shivering hard. Sweater and coffee. Soon. Although the fire had blazed furiously for a short time, it was taking a long time to burn out. The smoke was acrid, bitter, foul. Twice she had moved when the capricious wind had changed and brought the smoke into her face; now it was blowing toward the east, away from her. Soon she would go find her day pack, find a sweater . . .

She should make her own fire, she thought then, gather some of the dry wood and stack it, and make a fire in the middle of the roadway where it could do no harm. She was so cold.

She was still sitting there when the fire was no more than a pile of embers smoldering, and headlights came down the hill from the direction of East Shasta. At first she thought it was dawn lighting the valley after an impossibly long night; then she realized dawn was rising in the west, and she jumped to her feet to watch the approaching automobile. It tore down the road at a dangerous speed, and skidded to a stop next to the Lincoln. A door slammed and

Fernandez appeared in the headlights racing toward her.

"Sarah! Are you all right? I saw your car burning . . ."

"I'm all right," she said. "My uncle . . . He's by the Toyota."

Fernandez was at her side, it seemed almost magical to her that he had been in the car, in front of the car, and now was at her side. He felt her forehead, and took her hands and led her to the car he had been driving, seated her in the passenger side and tucked a blanket around her.

"Here, sip this," he said, holding a flask to her lips. Brandy? Whiskey? It burned and then felt warming. "A little more," he said.

"I have things scattered all over the hillside," she said, "and he dropped an assault rifle in the ruins somewhere. He burned up my car."

"Shh. Later. Tell me about it later. Getting warm yet?"

Although he had turned on the ignition, and the heater was blasting hot air at her, she continued to shiver. But less than before.

She heard him talking and thought for a second he was speaking to her, but he was on his car radio. "They're sending someone," he said. "Meanwhile we'll sit here and wait. Okay? It'll be a while, they're coming in from Susanville." He looked at her, then away, at the ghost town. "You have some explaining to do, Judge."

"There's a thermos of coffee up on the hill somewhere, if it isn't broken, and a sweater," she said in a low voice, finally warm enough not to shiver. "I'd really like some of the coffee. There's enough for two."

He took a powerful flashlight and began searching the hillside; she watched the light that was like a will o' the wisp, here, there, gone. He returned at last with her day pack and the bag that had the Winchester. The thermos was intact, but her camera had sprung open and was broken. She told him about the film she had buried for safekeeping, and he said, tomorrow. It would keep until tomorrow. They shared the coffee in silence.

And then, holding her thermos cup in both hands, watching it, she told him about that night.

"You expected your uncle?"

"Yes. I kept hoping it would be Dr. Wolper, but that was just wishful thinking. It had to be someone Dad talked to about the call, and that meant Uncle Peter. He wouldn't have talked to Michael about it, or Dr. Wolper. They had nothing to do with the students. And whoever killed Fran Donatio had to know ahead of time, had to plan, prepare."

"And you got the pictures." He sighed.

"Why did you come out here?" she asked after another moment of silence. "Whose car did Uncle Peter use? I never saw it before."

"Your call bothered me. I was pretty busy, but when I had a couple of minutes to think about it, I knew you were up to something. I decided to spend the night in Susanville, be out and around first thing in the morning, but when I couldn't get an answer at your place, I drove on into East Shasta, and talked to your one and only policeman. He knew you'd headed out for Ghost Lake a couple of hours earlier. He saw your uncle drive out this way later." He finished in a flat voice, "It was Michael's car."

"You knew it was Uncle Peter?"

"Pretty sure. Those students, who else could it have been? I thought the wrong Kellerman got the call."

She nodded. "Me too."

"The person who called your father back in April was Duane Barcleigh's son, born eight months after his father's death. I talked to Joan Harrison Barcleigh-Hazlett, one of the numbers on Fran's list, Duane Barcleigh's widow, junior's mother. She remarried, her husband adopted the child and changed his name to Hazlett. Sometime last winter she gave her son all his father's papers, and sent him packing. That was the first time he'd heard anything about his real father, she says. We haven't found him yet, but we've put out a bulletin. He's been in and out of school, in and out of trouble for the past ten years or more. Clean at the moment, though. He'll check in sooner or later, and we'll nail it down. His mother said he called her in early spring, full of questions about the work, what his father did at the university, about Kellerman. As far as he knew, there was only one Kellerman, I guess."

"He couldn't have known any more about his father's death than anyone else did at the time," Sarah said after a moment. "It was something in his father's papers, then, something about the work."

"We think so," Fernandez said. "You know about the library books?"

"Yes."

He sighed again, deeper this time. "There's something about the work they were doing, something wrong about it. I found a tame biochemist to go over those books, see if he can find a link, anything. We'll know in a week or so, sooner if we find Duane, Junior."

She was hearing again her uncle's voice, ragged, incoherent words, but words with meaning, nevertheless: They would have got the Nobel. Not *we* would have, *they*, the students. "I think he didn't have anything to do with their work," she said dully. "He stole their work and published it as if it were his own, as if they had assisted him, that's what he couldn't face having revealed. Duane's papers must have information, notes, something to prove that the students were working without Uncle Peter. All these years, pretending he came that close to the Nobel Prize, pretending he missed out because of a stupid accident ..." She felt Fernandez's hand on her arm and stiffened. "Lieutenant, I wanted him to die out here. You know that, don't you?"

"I know that, Judge."

"He would have hired a team of good lawyers, it would have dragged through the courts for years, ruining all our lives in the process—Winnie, Virgil, me, Michael, all of us, in an insane effort to keep his self-esteem, keep his reputation. Crazy, Alzheimer's, that was all right; he would have accepted that, but he had to keep the pretense of the great man alive. A great man finally brought down by fate, that was his role. He would have fought forever to maintain that illusion. I wanted him to die instead."

"He tried to kill you, Sarah. Remember that."

"I knew he would. He had to. I set him up so that he saw no other choice. I thought I could stay hidden, and then walk out and leave him dead, or dying. Justice, my style."

"Sarah, listen to me. In just a few minutes a whole team will be here, swarming all around us. Tonight you've been shot at, you've had a couple of nasty falls, you're bruised and battered and cut, you were nearly blown up and burned up, you're in a state of shock. Period. I intend to send you home with a young woman, Sergeant Pulaski, and she will help you get to bed, if you need help, and she'll see to it that no one bothers you tonight. And tomorrow I'll come around for a statement. Until then you make no statements to anyone. Understand? You clam up totally."

"Justice, my style. Justice, your style."

"That's exactly right," he said sharply. "Listen. I told them to come by way of three ninety-five. I think they're here."

There were car sounds now, and lights came into view, shining directly into his car, blinding Sarah. She closed her eyes and leaned her head back, waiting for them to tell her what to do, as if his words, that she was in a state of shock, were enough to induce a state in which she no longer had to act, no longer had to think of what next. Now she could close her eyes and wait, knowing things would get done without her.

When she woke up the next morning, she felt as if she had emerged from a dream that had gone on for many nights, on and on eerily, with disjointed bits of reality intermixed with great gobs of pure fantasy. Sergeant Pulaski had cleaned her cuts, as gentle as any nurse, and she had put Sarah to bed as firmly as a nanny. Sarah had heard her talking to Winnie and Virgil, but the words had been too difficult to follow, too far into the fantasy realm that she slipped in and out of all night. When she moved that morning, she yearned to escape again into the fantasy that had permitted her to watch this wretched woman from a safe distance, and say *tsk, tsk*. Instead she was forced to be the wretched woman who ached from top to toe, who was a mass of bruises, one on her cheek that glared red with purple and yellow already shading into it. A scrape on her arm, another on her leg, and everywhere an ache or a pain or a burning sensation, and every muscle hurting . . .

She dragged herself into the bathroom and stood under the shower for a long time, and then began to think of coffee. Winnie met her in the hallway outside her bedroom door.

"Mother! Oh, Mother! Maybe you should stay in bed today. I'll bring whatever you want . . ." She was crying.

"Hush," Sarah said, and put her arm about Winnie's shoulder. "Let's go down, but I'm in no hurry, you understand."

Virgil came bounding up the stairs and started to reach for her, to hug her, she thought, but drew back as if afraid to touch her. She held out her arms for him, and he embraced her tenderly, gently.

They went down to the kitchen and she had her coffee. "The lieutenant's been here for a couple of hours," Winnie said. "He's over at Uncle Peter's house, but he'll be right back. Uncle Peter . . . He's dead, isn't he?"

Sarah nodded. "What did the lieutenant tell you?"

"Only that he's dead, that he killed the detective and Grandpa, and killed himself out at Ghost Lake." Winnie blew her nose. "We promised him not to ask you anything until he's had a chance to talk to you." She picked up the coffee carafe, which shook dangerously in her hands; Virgil took it and set it down. "Mother, did Uncle Peter try to kill you, too?"

"I . . . I'm not sure, honey. I think he was quite mad at the end."

"Mother, I'm not going to march. You know, the solstice march. I kept thinking of the baby, and how there are only three of us left. Michael and his sisters don't really count, do they? I mean, I hardly even know them. There's just you and Virgil and me, and now the baby. And I have to take such good care of her."

At last she had acknowledged mortality, Sarah knew. When Blaine died, she had thought how little the children cared, how little it meant to them. They had been separated by a thousand miles, by many years broken by short visits during which everyone had been painfully polite. Alienated, Sarah had come to realize. Her children had grown apart, had accepted their shortcomings, the fact that they had not measured up in some mysterious way; his death had changed nothing for them really. But Winnie had kissed her grandfather goodnight, and had seen his body the next morning. She had avoided her uncle in the evening only to learn of his death hours later. She had realized how very near death her mother had been. Mortality had come home to her; she had glimpsed close up the fragility of the tie that bound them to life. Now she stood with both hands protectively over her stomach, tears in her eyes.

"You remind me of myself when I was pregnant," Sarah said softly. "I cried for three months, and I had no idea why. I was happy, healthy, no problems, no complications, and I kept crying. Then it stopped. Some women have morning sickness, I had the weeps, like you."

Winnie laughed and wept and laughed harder.

Virgil was looking embarrassed when Sarah turned to

him. "After the lieutenant comes and leaves again, we have to talk, you and I."

He looked at her intently, and she saw her father in the gaze; then he was gone and it was only Virgil again. "Will you try me, Mother? Sentence me?"

She nodded. "Later. Yes, I will."

"Good," he said softly. "I'll be ready. I tried to sentence myself, but that doesn't work, does it?"

"No. I don't think it ever does." She drew in a breath and added, "You have to tell me every detail about the smuggling ring, how they approached you, who they were, the exact procedures. Before some other young man or woman is hurt." She had an image of the fresh-faced boys from Iowa, or Sacramento, or anywhere, out for a lark, being used, beaten, discarded, betrayed, sacrificed, turned in to the law, living in terror, dying in terror, while the masters counted the profits. "I'll find the right way to inform the authorities," she said. "We have to stop them if we can." Virgil hesitated briefly, then nodded. She tilted her head, listening, and heard footsteps on the front porch. "Later," she said softly to Virgil.

He stood up, paused at her side to kiss her forehead, and then went to the front door to admit Lieutenant Fernandez.

"You look like hell, Judge," the lieutenant said cheerfully, seating himself at the kitchen table. Winnie made an indignant sound, and he raised his eyebrows at her. "Well, she does."

"You'll want us to go where we can make the statement," Sarah said, and started to get up.

"Sit still. We'll go on out to the hatchery," Virgil said, glaring at the lieutenant. Winnie gave Fernandez a disdainful look, kissed Sarah's cheek, and left with Virgil.

"You feel as bad as you look?" the lieutenant asked, still cheerful. "Mind if I have coffee?"

"Help yourself. And yes, I do. All over."

"Sorry about that. I, uh, with a little help from Pulaski, I made up a statement for you, Judge. You don't have to sign it, of course. You might want to make an altogether different one, but here it is." He drew a piece of folded paper from his pocket and placed it on the table before her, and then began to look for a cup in the cabinets across the kitchen.

"Left of the sink," she said, picking up the statement. It was factual, she had to admit. Factual in an antiseptic, Dick and Jane sort of way. She had gone out to Ghost Lake, her uncle had followed, had recovered his tape recorder, and then started shooting at her. He had set fire to her car, had been caught in the flames and died. Nothing about the murders, nothing about the students. Well, of course, she thought; none of that had anything to do with her, with last night. Just the facts, ma'am. Just the facts.

While she was reading Fernandez had helped himself to the coffee and sat down now watching her.

"You left out my gun, the fact that I disabled both cars. The fact that I lured him out there to begin with."

He shrugged. "You know as well as I do that things get stripped in a statement like this, some things just seem to get left out along the way." He raised his cup, watching her over the rim. "I mean if you really insist on adding that he thought he might find Maria Florinda out there, I can't stop you, that's for sure. But what for? That's a whole other can of worms, isn't it?"

She regarded him for a moment; his gaze was level, knowing. She turned back to the paper. No reasons were given explicitly or implicitly in the brief statement for anyone's actions. She had gone out there. He had gone out. He had started to shoot at her. Period. And it would do, she understood. No one would question her statement, not after Fernandez began exhibiting proof that Uncle Peter had killed his student, a detective, and his own brother. Sarah's name would be forgotten overnight as an actor in the little melodrama. "Are they searching for the bodies yet?" she asked.

"Not yet. We're bringing in some dogs and handlers this afternoon. The dogs find people trapped after earthquakes, that kind of thing. We think they'll work out for this. If it doesn't, we'll get a dowser or something."

She felt her lips twitch at his gallows humor, but she did not respond.

"When are you leaving here, Judge?" he asked, watching her as she signed the statement.

"Tuesday or Wednesday. I'm not sure yet."

"I'll drive you over to the coast, if you'd like," he said, paying scrupulous attention to the paper he refolded and returned to his pocket, and then to the pen which he recapped and replaced in his pocket. "You don't have to decide right now," he said, standing up. "I'll be around. We have to go through that old house, inch by inch, and then the search for the bodies will take some time. I'll be hanging around for the next couple of days."

After Fernandez left she wandered to the living room and sat down in a deep chair, aching and tired, depressed.

"Sarah, can I come in?" Michael's voice floated through the screen door.

"I'm in the living room," she said. "Come on in." She stood up to greet him. "Michael, I'm so sorry."

He nodded. "They're over there tearing up the house, literally tearing up the house. God knows what they're looking for. That lieutenant said they put a padlock on Dad's apartment in Hayward; he plans to go over there later in the week and tear up the apartment, too." Michael looked haggard and old. "I had to get out of the house, they're going through drawers, searching under the beds, bookshelves. What on earth can they be looking for?"

"I don't know," she said. "Michael, sit down. How much did they tell you?"

"Plenty," he said bitterly. He sat down but jumped up again instantly, and paced through the room to the front windows, back. "Plenty. He wasn't himself, Sarah. You must realize that. He wasn't normal last night. He was very fond of you. He wouldn't have tried to hurt you normally."

She shrugged. She had not told Fernandez about her uncle's saying he had Alzheimer's, she remembered suddenly. It had been so patently untrue that she had forgotten, but it would comfort Michael and his sisters to think that. She started to speak but Michael swung around and walked across the room, his hands jammed deep in his pockets, his shoulders hunched.

"Sarah, that morning, after he argued with your father, I saw him. He was ill, very ill, he looked gray. I thought he might be having a heart attack, but he drank a cup of coffee and rushed off. That's why I left so early. I thought he was too ill to be out driving, but I never caught up with him. Sarah, he was a sick man!" He looked at her then, his face haggard, haunted.

"You knew," she whispered. "You knew."

"Your father had an accident that nearly did my father in, too, and that woman . . . He was driven to do it. He couldn't see any choice. You know he was sick."

"You knew all the time," she said again, and stood up, walked to the window where she stared out at the limp poplar leaves, gray-green, dusty. "Did you know about the students, too?" she asked in a whisper.

"No! My God, Sarah, no one suspected anything like that."

"It wasn't just their deaths," she went on, hardly audible even to her own ears. "It was the work. He stole their work. That's what the call was about."

"He paid for that!" Michael yelled, reacting so swiftly she felt certain that he had known. "He devoted a lifetime to teaching, that's how he paid."

She shook her head. "It was a lifetime of being afraid someone would guess he was not a very good researcher, guess that he never did that original work, but that the three missing students had done it. A lifetime of fear."

"You're not going to leave us anything, are you?" Michael asked tiredly. "Even this, even this, his professional reputation has to be sacrificed."

"What about Duane Barcleigh's son?" she asked. "What does he have from the father he never knew? You think he should go on paying for the sins of *your* father? That's not the way the Bible says it works, Michael. Ask Mrs. Betancort." She faced him finally, her back to the window, and saw again the fierce hatred that she had glimpsed one other time, the day she told Uncle Peter that Winnie might be arrested.

For a time they regarded each other across the room, then he turned away and left. She watched him walk across the dry grass to the driveway and vanish finally among the trees.

"If Uncle Peter had lived to face trial," Sarah said to Virgil later that day, "and if he had been found guilty of murder, his sentence probably would have been ten years to life, and he would have been back out in about seven years. But chances are good that he would have found a medical or psychiatric reason to avoid prison altogether. If you, Virgil, had faced trial over drug smuggling and if you had been found guilty, as no doubt you would have been, your sentence would have been life without parole on each count, to run consecutively. Those are the guidelines, the sentences the federal courts are imposing." She spread her hands in a wide helpless gesture, and added, "There's not much any judge can do about the federal guidelines, crazy as they are. You might have been asked to plea bargain, in which case the sentence would have been lighter, but you would have turned state's evidence, and after the trial, after your part became known, you would have been a protected witness, maybe forever. In hiding, an assumed name, never certain if you would be in the same house for a day or a month or a decade. They often move protected witnesses in the middle of the night, the families are not allowed to communicate. No contact is possible with anyone from the past. Life in prison, life in prison without walls, those would have been your choices."

Virgil had turned very pale. At the opposite side of the table where they were all sitting, Winnie was as pale as death, her freckles almost garish against her white face.

Sarah paused to let them both consider her words, and then went on, "Your sentence, Virgil, is, of course, community service. One full day on Saturday or Sunday every week for forty-eight weeks a year for the next five years. I understand there is a youth center in Susanville; that's where you will volunteer your services."

Virgil stared at her, and then nodded. "And what else?"

"That's all. You'll be living in this big house, it may be that you will consider housing one or two boys at a time, train them in plant and fish care, in maintenance, or something else. I won't impose that on you, however."

Again he was nodding. "I will," he said in a low voice. "Thank you, Mother, Your Honor."

She nodded and then continued, "We, the four of us who now own the gardens, will prepare a statement to sponsor Maria Florinda, and to affirm that she is the only person we know who is qualified to do the work she does here at the gardens, as an aquatic plant botanist, for the money we can afford to pay her. That, and her willingness to abide by the rules imposed by the immigration service may be enough to get her a green card, and start the process for her to become a legal citizen, even if she chooses never to marry an American man."

Virgil had jumped up, his hands clenched hard.

"What if it doesn't work, what if they won't accept that?"

"I don't know," Sarah said slowly. "First things first, however. This is step number one. If we need step number two, we'll discover it when we reach it."

Alone again on the veranda, she closed her eyes and thought about tomorrow, all the tomorrows. Dirk would call and she would tell him yes, and she would actively campaign, seek the office of state judge. She doubted that Dirk would suggest her for the federal judgeship when it came up. But he might; she did not really understand what he was planning, and she did not really care. She had not told Winnie yet, but she would soon; she had decided to take her place in the solstice day march. And that was why Dirk might not support her. She could almost hear him in her head trying to persuade her to be reasonable. She smiled slightly. But she knew she didn't really need his support, not for the state judge position. As he had said so assuredly, an incumbent was a shoo-in, maybe even an incumbent who marched for civil rights, for the rights of others. She would find out. Okay, she said to herself. That took care of a whole bunch of tomorrows, but not all. Not all.

She heard a soft splash and opened her eyes to watch spreading ripples vanish among the bronze-colored leaves of water lilies, undulating them gently. How many evenings her mother and father had sat here, watching the fish, watching the sky, watching each other. And the mystery of her mother; that was for another whole bunch of tomorrows. So much to do, so many tomorrows already reserved.

How light Virgil's steps had become following her

sentencing. Confession, expiation, forgiveness, redemption, how important they were. Not just important, she amended: necessary. With the thought she became rigid, and when she shifted to ease her stiffness, she groaned. Later, she told herself. Later she would think about what she had done, what it meant, seek redemption if that was possible. Later. She closed her eyes hard.

Fernandez, she thought then. They would drive back to the coast where he would go on to Hayward to search her uncle's apartment, and she would go to San Francisco to do a little shopping ... She had to buy a car, and then ...

Fernandez. *Arthur.* She would call the proprietor of the cabin on the Oregon coast, make sure her reservation for next week was for a double. She nodded to herself. Yes.

Available now in bookstores everywhere ...

THE BEST DEFENSE
by Kate Wilhelm.

Published in hardcover by St. Martin's Press.
Read on for the compelling opening pages of
THE BEST DEFENSE ...

PROLOGUE

PAULA KENNERMAN IS lost, confused. Thursdays are her best days, she keeps thinking. She is off work on Thursdays; there is time to play with Lori, take her to the park, or shopping, or the library. Thursdays are good days.

Packing, she was packing their things, hers and Lori's. Yes, that was Thursday. Packing. And now she is here, someplace with a curtain around her bed, needles in her arms. Thursday, she reminds herself.

"What the fuck are you doing?" Jack demands, standing in the doorway.

"Packing. Leaving. I told you."

"You're not going anywhere! Don't give me this shit."

"Leaving."

She closes her eyes and drifts away. Leaving. He took the money out of the bank. She sees herself on the floor, stunned, clutching the door frame because the floor tilts crazily. There was no pain, she realizes, puzzled, because now there is so much pain. She watches herself watching him as if from a terrible distance. He pickes up Lori and throws her down on the bed. "Next time, out the window," he says.

Her eyes jerk open. In her head Lori screams and screams.

There was a fire, she remembers, seeing it again through a window, a kitchen blazing, flames licking against the door. Running. She took a taxi, but not to that house, another house. No suitcase. She could not lift the suitcase because something was broken, and she had to hold Lori's hand. She drifts again.

She is on the edge of a woods waiting for Lori. Another little girl comes running out. "She's sleeping," she says, and from somewhere else a second child calls, "Annie, come here. Look what I'm making." Annie darts away.

Sleeping, she thinks, standing against a tree, using it for support. She is so tired; and she hurts so much. Sleeping. What if Lori wakes up alone? What if she screams, in there alone?

"If she wakes up alone, she'll be afraid. I'd better go back." There is someone by her, she remembers, walking away from her, a woman.

"Whatever you want."

The woman is heading toward the children playing under a big bouquet. Paula moves slowly; every step brings a stabbing pain through her side, across her shoulder, down her arm. Two cracked ribs, they said. "I won't go to the hospital," she remembers crying. "I won't leave Lori. Let her come with me." The other side hurts as much as the side with the cracked ribs. From being slammed against the door frame, she recalls, thinking how crazily the floor kept tilting.

At the kitchen door. Flames. The kitchen blazing. She is running, running, like nightmare running: all that effort and so little gain. In the front door, up the stairs, screaming, "Lori! Lori!" The bed is empty. She plummets into oblivion again.

"Mrs. Kennerman, can you hear me?"

Against her will her eyes come open. Her tongue is

thick and dry. "Take a sip of water," a voice says, and a straw is placed in her mouth. The water helps.

"I can hear you," she whispers hoarsely.

"Can you tell us what happened back at the Canby house? Do you remember?"

"I couldn't find Lori," she whispers. "I looked in every room, under the beds, in the closets, and I couldn't find her." She pulls against restraints on her arms. "Where is she? Where is Lori?" She is crying, her voice wild and out of control. "Where is she?"

"Mrs. Kennerman, here, a little more water." A washcloth is against her eyes, gently wiping her cheeks. It is removed and she opens her eyes.

Now she can see them, a man and a woman. She is very broad, with a broad, almost flat face; he is tall and heavy, thick through the shoulders, with thick gray hair.

"Who are you?" she whispers. "Tell me where my child is, please."

"Don't you remember the rest of it?" the man asks.

Now she does. "I kept yelling for her to come out, not to hide, because the house was on fire. I went down the stairs, and then . . . I don't know what happened. I was outside on the ground and people were all around and the house was burning, all the windows, the door, everywhere. Lori!" It was not a question this time. *Lori!*

Later the same man came back with the same woman.

"Why would she hide from you? Was she afraid of you?"

"Did you see anyone?"

"What did she say to you? Did she want to go home again? Did she want to go back to her father?"

"Why do you say you went upstairs? She fell asleep watching television, and the TV is in the living room downstairs."

"Mrs. Kennerman, you'll feel better if you just tell us exactly what happened. Believe me, you'll feel better then."

In her mind Lori is screaming, screaming. Dreamlike

slow motion: Jack picks her up and throws her onto the bed. *Next time, out the window.* Lori whimpering in her sleep in a strange house, a strange bed; her every movement brings jabs of pain to Paula. Lori waking up, crying out, screaming in her sleep.

"Just tell us what happened, Mrs. Kennerman."

She told them and told them, and then she stopped telling them, and in her head Lori screamed.

ONE

FRANK HOLLOWAY FELT out of place here in the Whiteaker neighborhood; his car was too big and expensive and shiny clean, his suit, a very nice blend of silk and wool, was too well tailored. He drove slowly past the small houses, most of them well-kept and neat enough, he had to admit, past the mural wall he had read about—not exactly pretty but impressive, he also had to admit: a jungle with unlikely creatures and more unlikely variously colored people who all seemed happy. Continuing, he passed a black beauty shop, a small appliance repair shop, a Mexican grocery store with a sale advertised in big letters on the window: JICA-MAS, TOMATILLOS, PLANTAINS, SIXTY-NINE CENTS A POUND.

He spotted *Martin's Fine Food* stenciled in white letters on a picture window out of the fifties and drove past, parked with misgivings at the curb, and sat for a moment rethinking his plan. Finally he left the car and approached the small restaurant housed in one of the old buildings. . . .

White half curtains hid the bottom of the glass panes, hid the diners from the public, but at the moment three people were standing in a tight group clearly visible, obviously yelling—a tall black man, a tall brown man, and his daughter, Barbara.

Frank drew in a breath and opened the door, entered. The trio did not glance his way, and it seemed that a squad car with siren blaring could have gone through without their noticing. Frank shook his head at another black man leaning against a door frame; he was wearing an apron and was very large and very black. There was an amused expression on his face. Frank passed him to take a seat in a booth near the rear of the dining room. There were only three tables and four booths altogether. Barbara and her two companions were by the front window, all standing up, holding down the table, as if it might float away without their intense effort.

"What's the matter, you can't walk?"

"My mother can't walk that late. I told you!"

"Don't give me that shit, man!"

"I said that's enough!" Barbara yelled, leaning closer to the tall black man.

He was yelling loudest. He was skinny, over six feet, dressed in stained chino pants and a white T-shirt. "What you mean, that's enough? He stole! He's a robber! That ain't enough!"

"You don't just want your money back, you want revenge, and I told you what the court would do. Roberto, what are you studying at LCC?"

"I'm going to be a dental technician. You know, false teeth, caps, bridges, braces, stuff like that." Roberto was also thin; he was brown, with long hair caught up in a ponytail. Barbara looked small and vulnerable between the two angry men. "I told you, I pay you back! I already paid some back!"

Abruptly the black man sat down. "You going to make false teeth? No shit?"

"Yeah. You got a problem with that?"

"Man, take it easy, okay? False teeth? Bridges?"

Barbara put her hand on Roberto's arm, and they both sat down again, and their voices faded, became too faint for Frank to catch the words. The aproned man vanished behind the swinging door to the kitchen and quickly reappeared with a tray that had two Cokes and a cup of coffee. He took it to Barbara's table, patted the other black man on the shoulder, and then approached Frank's booth.

"Just coffee," Frank said.

The waiter went to the next booth. Frank had passed it without noticing anyone sitting there. "You sure you don't want something to drink, miss? A Coke or juice or something? No charge if you're waiting for Barbara."

"No, no. I'm fine. Thank you." Her voice was very nearly inaudible.

By the time Frank's coffee came, Barbara and her clients were standing up again, but this time peaceably. She reached over the table to shake hands with the black man, and then shook hands with Roberto, and the two men walked out together. The black man was saying, "You gonna make false teeth! That's a hoot and a half!"

Frank stood up and watched Barbara without moving toward her. She looked tired, he thought with regret. It was often a shock to see her when she didn't know he was there; how like her mother she was in appearance, although not at all like her in any other way.... She had lost weight in the last few months and her jeans were a touch baggy; she looked fragile, too young to be thirty-seven, thirty-eight, whatever it was. Fragile, he repeated in self-derision. She was about as fragile as a six-foot length of rebar. Actually, he didn't want to think about her age any more than he wanted to think of her hair turning gray.

She had faced the door during his swift scrutiny; now she turned toward him, her face brightening as she took a quick step in his direction. "Dad! How long have you been here?"

"Not long."

The woman in the next booth stood up and started to walk toward the door.

"Did you want to see me?" Barbara asked.

"Yes, but not if you're too busy. I mean, I'll come back some other time."

"That's just my father," Barbara said easily. "He'll wait. Won't you, Dad?"

"Yep. No problem." He sat down again and watched the woman approaching Barbara. Plump, in black stirrup pants and a red top, sandals. Not the way people dressed when they came to his office, he thought grumpily, and Barbara, in jeans and a ridiculous T-shirt, was not dressed the way anyone expected an attorney in a prestigious office to dress either, he added, and picked up his coffee. Just the father. He could wait. The coffee was very good.

Barbara had been surprised to see her father, but not terribly. She had known curiosity would bring him to her "office" sooner or later. When he sank back down into the booth, she turned her attention to the young woman, who had been crying recently. Automatically Barbara examined her arms for bruises, marks of any kind, and found only nice pink boneless limbs. She motioned to the table where Martin already had cleared away the Coke cans and glasses and her cup. Even as she was resuming her own chair, Martin came back with a tray and two cups of coffee and put them on the table wordlessly.

She mouthed her thanks to him and said to the other woman, "What can I do for you?"

"It's not me, not really. It's for my sister, I mean." She stopped, and began adding sugar to her coffee. Her hands were trembling.

"Okay. But who are you? What do I call you?"

"Oh. Lucille. Lucille Reiner." She started to tear open a third packet of sugar and Barbara reached across the table and took it from her hands, which were icy. Lucille ducked her head and groped in her bag for a tissue.

"Just tell me about it," Barbara said after a moment.

"I was in the jail, visiting her, and it's like she's turned to stone or something. She won't talk or cry or anything, she just stares off somewhere else. They gave her a lawyer, the court did, I mean, but he thinks she did it and he says she should plead guilty. And the psychiatrist they sent her to, in the hospital, I mean, he thinks she did it, too, and he says she isn't crazy or sick or anything, she can be tried and go to prison. Or maybe even worse. But if she did it, she had to be so sick, and she's sick now, not talking, not crying, not eating, I don't think. And one of the women visitors told me to just talk to you about it. I mean, if she has a public defender, doesn't he have to work for her?"

Barbara nodded. "He does. All that means is that when a defendant can't afford to hire an attorney, under the law the court has to appoint one. And that attorney is required to treat this client exactly the way he would any other client. He'll do the best he can for her. The court will be watching to see that he does."

"But he wants her to plead guilty. I talked to him this morning, and that's what he said. . . .

"Who is he, the attorney? Maybe I know him and can reassure you about him."

"Spassero. William, I think. He's young, real young."

Barbara shook her head. "New to me. But I can find out something about him. Do you live here in town? Can you come back in a few days, Friday? I'll find out what I can."

"We live down at Cottage Grove. I come up to see her three, four times a week, but it's hard, I've got two kids, I mean, seven and eight, and I work four days a week, but I'll come on Friday. I promise."

"Fine. About this same time?"

"Yeah, that's good for me, late afternoon, I mean."

Late afternoon, four forty-five. Time for a glass of wine, time to relax, time to see what her father was after. . . . Barbara felt herself make the few internal preliminary adjustments that meant she would stand up now and finish this last bit of business, get on with relaxing.

Lucille Reiner leaned forward and said, "If he's no good, this other lawyer, I mean, he might be okay, but not for her. Would you take the case for us? I have a little money, eight hundred dollars. I mean, I know you don't charge people here, that's what the lady in jail said, but this would be different. I mean, you'd have to go on trial and everything."

Barbara shook her head slightly. "Mrs. Reiner, I don't even know what case you're talking about."

"Oh, I thought I told you." She ducked her head again. "It's my sister, Paula Kennerman."

The words *baby killer* leaped into Barbara's mind. "Let me find out what I can about Mr. Spassero," she said, feeling a new tightness in her throat, "and talk to you again on Friday."

Barbara watched Lucille leave and then consciously put a smile on her face and turned to the back of the restaurant. "You can come out now." She picked up her briefcase and laptop computer and put them on the table, and then stretched as far as she could reach.

"Done for the day?" Frank asked as he drew near.

"Yep. One-thirty to about this time, Tuesdays and Fridays. I want you to meet Martin Owens, the best cook in the city, and the best secretary. He keeps the coffee coming."

She introduced the two and then said, "See you on Friday, Martin. Thanks. . . ."

"Where are you parked?" Frank asked.

"I usually walk over," she said. "It's only three blocks."

He knew that, and he knew that two blocks beyond her house the railroad switch yards started, lined with warehouses, lumber yards, industrial buildings of various sorts. This strip north of Sixth to the river had been built early when people still clung to the railroad and the river; those with enough money left, others moved in and stayed until they made enough money to leave, and the cycle continued. Now it had become the only real ethnically mixed neighborhood in the city, and the only reason anyone stayed on was that the cheapest housing was here. Every drug bust seemed to happen here, every knifing, street brawls—

He banished the ugly thoughts and said, "Well, let

me drive you. A couple of things I want to talk about, if you're not busy."

"Free as the air," she said, getting into the car.

Frank stashed her things on the back seat, got in behind the wheel. "Mind a little detour first?"

"Nope."

He drove in silence until she asked, "You said things to talk about? Today?"

"Martin Owens. He's the football player, isn't he? Or was. He lets you use his restaurant as an office?"

"He's the one. I did him a little favor a few months ago. A legal matter. He's barely making it in the restaurant, but he seems to think he owes me. Good guy."

"Storefront lawyer," Frank muttered, and she turned to look out the window.

She did not ask again what was on his mind. She knew he would get around to it in his own way, first bring it up obliquely, then change the subject, refer to it again later with more details, talk about the weather or something, and so on until it was all out. She was content to wait. When he finally got to it in detail he would pretend to assume that she was in agreement, that since they already had discussed the matter, and he had responded in advance to every possible objection she might raise, the whole issue was already settled. She doubted very much that such would be the case, but meanwhile it was a beautiful June day and she was tired. Her two days a week as a storefront lawyer were wearing.

"God, I hate condos," he said suddenly.

She looked at him in surprise. "So do I, but what's that supposed to mean?"

"And apartments, too," he added. "I've been looking at condos and apartments."

She nodded. "An investment?"

"My accountant says I'm paying too much in taxes."

"Aren't we all?"

He was driving slowly now, watching for house numbers over the top of his half-glasses. Then he stopped. They were on Twenty-first, typical of Eugene in every respect, with tall trees, low buildings, lots of greenery, lots of flowers. "What do you think?" he asked, nodding toward the house he had located.

"I think it's green." Apple green, in fact, with rust-red trim.

"Well, it could be painted. Blue or something."

"That house will always be green no matter how hard you try to cover it up."

He sighed. "I'm afraid you're right." He began to drive again. "There's another one."

"You're going to buy a house," she said. "Is that it?"

"Might as well, seeing as how much I hate condos. I've looked at a few. You buy a condo, what do you own? A piece of someone else's building. Want a place I can walk to the office from."

"You're leaving the house at Turner's Point?" Too late she realized she had played right into his hands again.

"Not exactly. See, how it's working out is that some of those old fogies get so set in their ways, they've got roots clear down to bedrock and nothing's going to change them. . . . It's too damn far to drive three days a week," he added glumly.

"Three days? I thought you were easing yourself out of the office, getting ready to retire."

"I am, I am. It's just more complicated than I thought it would be." He had driven through the downtown section, where traffic had thickened into what Eugeneans thought was real congestion. Five cars at a red light meant gridlock here.

At Fifth, instead of turning left toward her house, he made a right turn, and a block later he turned left on Pearl Street, where three of the four corners housed dozens of small shops selling everything from gourmet coffee and some of the best bread to be found to handmade wooden toys, books, natural-fiber clothes— Yuppie Heaven, they called it. He was heading for Skinner Butte Park, she thought then as he drove on. She had walked hours, miles along the river here, walking off trial tension, thinking, scheming. But he turned again, and she suddenly caught her breath. Once, years ago, he had driven up here with her and her mother, just looking. "This is where I want to live," Barbara had said, and Frank had laughed. "The only way you can get a house in this neighborhood is by waiting for the owner to die, and all the heirs, too. Then if the real-estate agent doesn't grab it, you might have a chance."

This was a tiny area, a few square blocks, but she thought of it as an oasis of sanity, serenity, stability. The houses were spacious, old-fashioned, with porches and gabled windows, lots of leaded glass, even stained-glass windows, detached garages. No two houses were similar, but they were all of a piece, well constructed with individual detail work, well maintained, beautifully landscaped, without a hint of pretentiousness.

He stopped before a two-story house that was dove gray, with white trim. An old hemlock tree, top bowed as if in thought, shaded the front; tall rhododendrons lined a driveway, screened the yard on one side; the other side had deep bushes, some in bloom, all mature and lovely.

"Not a bad location," Frank said. "Park and the trail two blocks away, six blocks to the courthouse, seven to the office. Not bad. Walk to the post office, the performing arts center, even the jail. Not bad." He glanced at her. "Well?"

"Not much yard," she said in a low voice.

"Big backyard, even garden space. And a rose arbor. Let's look inside."

"You just happen to have the key?"

He didn't answer, but pulled into the driveway and got out on his side. Slowly Barbara got out and they went inside the house that he obviously intended to buy. It was everything she knew it would be—white-oak floors, a modernized kitchen, bright living room, dining room ... There were stained-glass panels in the living room windows. Upstairs were three rooms, one of them small, a child's room perhaps, and a bath. Another bedroom and den were downstairs.

"It's very nice," she said after they had looked it over. "But pretty big."

"Oh, well, I get claustrophobic in those little boxes they call houses. Come on, let's go. You up for dinner?"

"You bet. But first a shower and a glass of wine or something. Take me home."

He had put down earnest money, she knew as well as she knew what the rest of his little chat would be. And her answer? That she didn't know yet.

Over dinner he gossiped about the office, about what was going on in court, about a client or two. He did not mention Turner's Point. She asked him about William Spassero.

"Bill Spassero," he said, thinking. "Young, too young maybe. In the public defender's office, couple of years now. About thirty, if that much, but he seems more like twenty. A whiz kid at law school. Hot-shot attitude. Ambitious. Why?"

"His name came up. I wondered. I feel about whiz kids the way you feel about condos."

He grinned, and she thought how well they understood each other. They both understood that it was time to get back to the subject at hand.

"Let's have some dessert," he said, "and some of that pressed coffee they make here. It's a real production number."

They watched in appreciative silence as their waiter performed, he ground the coffee at their table, brought water to a boil over a burner, measured the coffee into the glass pot, poured the not-quite-boiling water over it, and tightened the top in place carefully. Then he set a timer. Barbara laughed, and he grinned at her. . . .

Frank said, "I thought maybe it would work out for me to get a house, like I said. I really did look at condos, and apartments, and even a hotel apartment, but hated the idea of all of them. A real house, that's what I need. I'd come in on Tuesday and go to the office, like I've been doing, and stay over until Friday morning and head back out. Or maybe Thursday afternoon. Depends on how busy I am."

She nodded. "When do you sign the papers?"

Without hesitation he said, "Monday. But it wasn't that cut-and-dried from the start. That other house, the first one, that's the kind of stuff they showed me when I finally said no to apartments, condos, and such. Thought you should see it first, as I did." There wasn't a trace of shame in his expression. "What I thought might be a good idea, Bobby, is for you to move in, too. I mean, you'd be alone most of the time, but the house wouldn't be empty, ripe for the barbarians to sack."

"I'll have to think about it, Dad."

"Of course." He looked past her then and said in a low voice, "Going out there was the best thing I did after your mother died. I needed the solitude, I guess. It was good for me for a long time. Then, after you left, it was different. I kept listening for your steps, kept listening for the car to drive in. I knew you couldn't stay, but Bobby, God, I've missed you."

"I'm sorry," she said.

"No, no. I didn't mean to lay it on you, honey. It's my problem, I know that. And I think I've solved it. You want a brandy?"

What had she said at the time, just six months ago? A lifetime ago. What she had said was that she couldn't stay, she had to move, and he had said simply, I know. And he had known, had understood. No arguments, no trying to persuade her to remain. He had understood. What she had not said was that she couldn't look at the river; she was afraid she would see Mike's body being tumbled in the current; she was afraid she would see his body washed up on shore, tangled in the undergrowth.

No brandy, she said firmly, and he said none for him either, and soon they left the restaurant and he drove her home.

"Almost forgot," he said. "We had a conference down at the office today. You're still a member of the firm, you know."

"And will be as long as you're second on the list of partners," she said lightly.

"Damn right. But there's an interesting case at hand. Young playwright in town here claims one of the big studios stole his material. Maybe they did. Someone's going to be doing some fancy traveling on this one. New York, Hollywood. Meet some pretty interesting people along the way." He stopped at her house. "Should be an exciting case, probably won't go to trial, but you never know."

She laughed. "Good night, Dad. Thanks for dinner."

"They pay you anything, those folks who drop in at the restaurant?"

"Some do, some don't. I'm okay, Dad. Don't worry. You want to stay over?"

"And sleep on the floor?" He didn't hide his incredulity. "I'm at the Hilton tonight, tomorrow night." He walked to the door with her and then left.

Actually it was a futon, and she had grown rather fond of it. And yes, her clients paid her, when they could. Fifty dollars here, twenty there, free dinners, all the coffee she could drink. She stood in the doorway to her bedroom and surveyed it critically. . . .

She was a pig, she had to admit, but on the other hand this house had no room to put anything. Four rooms and a bath. One closet. Period.

She went into the small living room that held only a couch, one chair, two lamps, more shelves, more books, a CD player, and a special rack for cassettes. More than she needed, she told herself. She could sit in one chair at a time, read one book at a time, hear one cassette at a time. She sank down into the chair.

He was lonely. Of course. But he had brought it all back, and she had been so sure that her grief had passed over into acceptance finally. Wrong, Barbara, she told herself mockingly. Abruptly she jerked up out of the chair and crossed the room to check the door, knowing as she did that it was locked, that this was a meaningless motion. . . . She had been afraid to give up her grief. If she didn't feel that, what would she feel, she had wondered, and the answer had come: nothing.

At the sink, holding a glass of water she did not want, she surveyed the kitchen: ancient electric stove that had two working burners, a table that wobbled, two straight chairs, two and a half feet of counter space, a small refrigerator that dated back to the sixties. And by the back door was the ever-growing stack of newspapers destined for recycling when she remembered to take them out. The house was dingy with age and neglect and she despised it.

Spassero, she thought then almost in desperation. Maybe he had made the news in the last month or so. She picked up a stack of newspapers and put it on the table, prepared for a long night. She had found that if she worked, the grief receded; lately she had believed it had changed to something else, but it was there, it was there. She started to go through the papers.